FATHER OF THE MAN

FATHER OF THE MAN

A NOVEL

ANTHONY ROBINSON

A BLUESTONE BOOK

Contact: tonytherob@gmail.com

ISBN-13: 978-1718856820
ISBN-10: 1718856822

For Tania, who shares my history, then and now.

The Child is father of the Man;
And I could wish my days to be
Bound each to each by natural piety.

William Wordsworth

Chapter One

Mr. Marr stepped onto the porch of the one-room schoolhouse in West Hurley and looked around at his students lazing in the sun, seesawing, playing baseball on School Field. He took in a breath of fresh upstate air, gave his son serving in the Pacific a loving thought, then rang his bell ending noon recess.

The kids began walking in; they stomped up the steps and went into the boxy old classroom. When they were settled at their desks, in rows according to grade, the teacher announced his afternoon classes, starting with eighth-grade science...to fifth-grade reading. Tall and skinny, in a dark-blue suit that had a metallic sheen to it, he instructed his students to open their books. "Study your lessons, no talking or passing of notes." Then he moved to the side of the room with windows and spoke, in a quieter tone, to the class of four boys and a girl.

"We are continuing our study of the Scientific Revolution when great changes were taking place, like the Industrial Revolution of our own time," Mr. Marr said. "People were asking questions, learning about the physical world and the world of stars and planets they couldn't see. Our topic today is gravity. Let's start with Galileo and the experiment he conducted in 1620. Picture him standing on the top of the Leaning Tower of Pisa in Italy."

Billy Darden, trying to get the difference between a transitive and intransitive verb into his head—seventh-grade English was next—sensed his attention drifting. Mr. Marr was on one of his teaching narratives.

"Galileo is holding two cannonballs, one weighing two pounds, the other seven," he said, his arms extended. "He lets the cannonballs go, watches them fall. *Bam!* They land at precisely the same moment. Question: What did Galileo's experiment prove?"

He called on Frank, Henrietta, and Jimmy, got plenty of words, excuses, but no answer, at least not the one he was after. "Clarence?"

"It proved that gravity existed."

"No. People knew it existed." He looked at the heavyset boy in the middle of the row. "Serge?"

"It proved that objects, regardless of weight, fall at the same speed—"

"Thank you."

"—of thirty-two point two feet per second per second. But that's in theory only," Serge went on. "If you drop a stone and a flower from a high place—say from a ladder or a tree—the stone will hit the ground first. A flower offers more resistance to the air than a stone, so it doesn't fall as fast. In a perfect vacuum, a flower and a stone would hit the ground at the same time."

"Nicely stated," Mr. Marr said. "As for thirty-two point two feet per second per second, enlighten us on that, please."

Which Serge commenced to do. Frank, Jimmy, and Clarence sat at their desks, jaws stiffly set; and Billy Darden's mind drifted again—going to the day late last summer when he'd met a chunky kid with a lot of dark-red hair on Bluestone Road. His name was Serge Rustovsky, his father was an artist, and the family had arrived in the Maverick Art Colony three days earlier.

"I'm Billy Darden. We're neighbors," Billy had said.

"Great. There's an old steam-driven crane in the woods near our house," the new boy said.

"I know, I grew up playing on it."

"I'd like to get it up and running again."

Who is this kid? Billy thought. "That's crazy. It's a rusty piece of junk."

"I'm looking for someone to come in with me," Serge Rustovsky said.

****

Classes over for the day, Frank Santarelli, Jimmy McMullan and Clarence Bumgardner were standing on Schoolhouse Corner, where Hammond Street and Bonesteel Road intersected. Why they were waiting there, Billy wasn't sure, but he had an idea. He was standing slightly apart from the eighth graders and was waiting for Serge himself. Every day they walked to school in the morning, then back to the art colony once school was out.

The door to the schoolhouse opened. It was Freddie Longo. He had taken down the flag and delivered it to Mr. Marr. The kid had long, scuzzy hair and green teeth, not the whole tooth, just in between.

Billy was getting restless. Where the hell was Serge? He liked the kids in West Hurley except for Clarence Bumgardner, a string bean of a boy whose father was a big shot in local politics. Jimmy McMullan was the best all-around ballplayer and was king of infield chatter. It had a cadence, a music-like sound. Sometimes at home Billy would practice chattering, seeing himself at shortstop with the bases loaded, but it always came out sounding like a serious case of the stutters. Frank Santarelli had launched a mammoth drive over Hammond Street into old Mrs. Schmulke's front yard in today's game. With their only ball suddenly gone, Frank went over to retrieve it. Woman was scrappy, but finally he got it away and came back a hero.

Jill Santarelli came down the steps in a purple dress and little black shoes with silver buckles. Girls didn't come any prettier than li'l Jill with her soft brown eyes and dark hair. Mr. Marr's '41 Plymouth was parked beneath a shade tree. He'd bought it new two years ago in Kingston and still babied it. Two hundred yards farther along Bonesteel Road, you could see the new schoolhouse, almost completed. Ready by next year, was the word. Then Dom, another member of the Santarelli clan—he and Billy had started first grade together here in West Hurley—was saying, "Here he is now."

Serge trudged across the schoolyard with a couple of books. As he drew near the boys, he veered toward Billy, and they started walking.

"Wait a minute!" Jimmy McMullan yelled.

Billy turned. "What is it?"

"Not you, Billy. *Him!*"

Serge looked at Jimmy McMullan.

"Your sport is running, right?" Jimmy said to Serge. "Ain't that what you've been telling us, you run the *distances*? In my opinion the only distance you ever run is the distance to the outhouse! So, come on, let's settle this. We'll go around Bonesteel, then back to the school on Hammond."

Bonesteel Road was in the shape of a giant horseshoe. It went by the schools, old and new, then curved through the township. Looking across School Field, you could see where Bonesteel reappeared, passed in front of the West Hurley Fire Department and finally hit Hammond Street 200 yards from schoolhouse corner.

Looking at Clarence Bumgardner, Jimmy said, "That's about a mile, right?"

"Closer to one and a half," Clarence said, always the big shot.

Jimmy said to Serge, "Let's go." Then to Frank, "Start us."

Frank Santarelli drew a line with a stick on Hammond twenty feet from the corner and Jimmy went out and stood at it. Serge didn't move.

"Well?" Jimmy said.

"In two weeks," Serge came back.

"What do you mean, two weeks?"

"Two weeks until we run, and twice around."

Clarence said, "He's yanking your chain, Jimmy. The people over there in the Maverick Art Colony? They're a bunch of dirty Reds, my father calls them Bolsheviks. You can't trust a Bolshevik, that's a proven fact. Tell Serge to cram it!"

Billy thought Jimmy would go along with Clarence. He was surprised when Jimmy said to Serge, "OK. Saturday in two weeks, twice around. Nine o'clock sharp."

They shook hands, and Billy and Serge began walking up Hammond Street. Shy of where Bonesteel Road came in, they took a narrow path that cut left and hit Rt. 375. Directly across 375, a wide driveway slanted down to Rowe's Lumber. The smell of fresh-cut wood floated in the air. Not far beyond, the West Hurley woods began; thick and dark, they stretched for thirteen miles north to Marion Corners. Via the main roads, the Maverick Art Colony was three miles away. Going through the woods it was three-quarters of a mile and took you fifteen minutes, if you knew the trail.

They followed it along a ridge of white pines, then circled a swampy area where dead trees stood like skeletons. Maybe fifty crows were perched in the brittle branches of the tallest tree, cawing away. Serge said they were holding a caucus. A what? A political discussion to choose a candidate. Farther on, in a damp, shaded patch, pink flowers were growing. Earlier this spring, Serge had wanted to pick one and bring it to his mother, but Billy told him they were wild orchids, called lady's slippers, and were protected by law. Up ahead, a limb on a maple tree dipped and snapped back. Squirrel, Billy told himself. Sure enough, a big gray scurried up the trunk of a neighboring pine.

Serge hadn't noticed. His mind was elsewhere, possibly the war. Last fall he'd told Billy that Hitler had Europe under his heel. The dictator had plans to invade England. After that, who knew? America? Billy thought about the war also, the one with Japan—Pearl Harbor, Guadalcanal, kamikaze dive bombers—but not to the point where he wouldn't notice a squirrel in a tree.

Up ahead a fallen oak lay across the trail. The boys stopped and sat on the trunk. Serge's feet touched the ground; Billy's had a couple of inches to go. In a nearby grove of evergreens, a large birch tree grew, alone, isolated. On first seeing it on any day, Billy always thought someone, all in white, was looking after him and Serge.

"Serge," he said, "what did Clarence mean calling people in the Maverick dirty reds? Then another word, started with a B."

"Bolsheviks," Serge said. "It's a Russian word. Like a football team has its colors, the Bolsheviks wore red—sweaters, vests, hats. After the Russian Revolution in 1917, they took control and became the Communist Party. Bolshevik, Red, Communist—one and the same."

"Is is true what Clarence said about the Maverick?"

"It's a reputation it has. His father is in the Ulster County Legislature and thinks everyone in the art colony is a threat to the

American way. Clarence is a parrot."

"He gave us both a look."

"I noticed."

"Is my father a Bolshevik?"

Serge came out with a short, amused laugh. "According to my dad, your father had the reputation of being a good lefty. *Had* the reputation. Then he took a job with Reader's Digest, 'America's Magazine.' Conservative to the core." Serge slapped the fallen tree. "Let's go."

They started walking again. The only "good lefty" Billy knew was Lefty Gomez, star pitcher for the Yankees.

Chapter Two

The trail came out on tar-patched Bluestone Road that ran along the base of Ohayo Mountain. At 1007 feet, Ohayo just made the height to qualify as "mountain" in New York State, old-timer Sherman Marshall had once told Billy. Bluestone Road ran down the middle of the Maverick Art Colony: to the west, the mountain half; to the east, the plateau half. On both sides of the road, houses—two rooms, screened-in porches, sidings of rough-hewn timber—began appearing, over half still unoccupied in early May; but soon musicians and artists and actors would start coming in, including Harlan Gray. In the last three years, he had taken to spending winters in south Georgia. At first Billy couldn't understand how that could be. If the founder of the Maverick Art Colony couldn't handle a Maverick winter, who could? Then it came to him. Harlan was getting on.

As Serge and Billy continued walking on Bluestone Road, a single-lane dirt road veered slightly off to the right and more or less paralleled Bluestone Road. Some called it "old Bluestone Road," others "the spur." It was a segment of the original road into an area once known for its quarries. A ten-yard-wide strip of rocky, brush-heavy land—commonly referred to as "no man's land"—was revered by artists for the privacy it supposedly gave them, though Bluestone traffic was very light. A car might go by every twenty minutes, Billy had once judged, and now and again a team of horses.

The boys came to Intelligentsia, a restaurant where artists got together to socialize after a day's work to have a cup of coffee, a glass of wine, home-prepared food. Benches on both sides of a long table, rough chairs scattered about. A rotating menu of meatloaf, Italian spaghetti with meatballs, and Hungarian goulash. Christine, who ran Intelligentsia, made a little extra money for herself posing for artists. Sometimes Billy would rake the yard for her or sweep the floor, and once she gave him a meatloaf sandwich on crunchy bread and a can of Royal Crown Cola. Billy's father would occasionally stop in for a wine. He'd once told Billy that Christine was a mulatto and had then licked his lips, as if a mulatto was a rich caramel dessert he especially liked.

Cayuga Quarry, the largest of the dozen or so quarries in the Bluestone area, lay between Intelligentsia and Serge's house. Through the trees, you could see the huge excavation, the rubble circling the top like a jagged collar. They came to Serge's driveway, thick with pine needles; parked in it was the family's Model A Ford. The house, Quarryman, had siding of different sizes and shapes of bluestone, the pieces fitting together like a not-too-precise jigsaw puzzle. Serge almost stumbled over two empty pails sitting at the start of the driveway. But that was the idea: to remind him to get water.

"See you, Billy," he said, putting down his books.

"I'll give you a hand."

"Forget it. You have chores at home."

But Billy picked up a pail and they followed a path across no man's land to Bluestone Road, then across it to Ohayo Road, which ran straight back into the western half of the colony on an upward slant until Ohayo Mountain raised a big hand and said stop. At that point a weather-beaten hand-pump, once red, stood on a stone base. Instead of a standard, curved handle, it had a round iron bar seven feet long. With a well 525 feet deep, it was no easy task getting water to rise. One of the pails wasn't completely empty and Serge poured what little was in it down the throat of the pump. Then they both grabbed the bar and pressed down on it again and again, ten times in all. Finally cold water tumbled from the spout.

When both pails were filled, Serge set his eyeglasses aside and told Billy to keep the handle going. He did the best he could but, at five-foot-two and 87 pounds, it wasn't easy. The flow slowed but Serge, cupping his hands, got plenty of water to drink and splash on his face. Then it was his turn at the handle and Billy's at the tap.

In the fast-dropping sun, they sat with their legs outstretched. A long yellow meadow hugged the base of Ohayo Mountain. Off to their right, several hundred yards away, stood a pair of rustic, barn-sized buildings, the Maverick Theater and Maverick Concert Hall.

"I've been wanting to tell you," Serge was saying. "I've news on William D. My dad was in Kingston yesterday browsing around in Stan's, a secondhand shop he likes. He found an old book called *The Principles of Steam Locomotion* and picked it up for fifteen cents."

"Great." William D. was the name Billy had given the crane three years ago, after the weathered initials and numbers on the chassis.

So far they had cleared away huge amounts of leaves, branches, debris, and had done a good bit of scraping and painting. Chips Doolin, a man of all trades in the art colony, had made and installed a new roof over the cab.

"No excuses now," Serge said.

A hawk was gliding with the wind over Ohayo. A breeze, sliding off the mountain, rippled the yellow grass. "I better get home," Billy said.

"There's something else."

With Serge there always was. Billy didn't say anything and his friend said, "I don't think I can run three miles."

"Serge, you're the one who said 'twice around,' not Jimmy."

"It was a bluff."

"No one bluffs Jimmy McMullan." Billy asked his friend the question he'd wanted to ask him since last fall. "Did you *ever* run the distances, Serge?"

"At first I ran because I had to, when we lived in Illinois," Serge said. "School kids waiting for me — I'd have to hightail it two miles down a back road to get home, or get beat up. The next year we

9

moved to Indiana. My school had a track team. I went out for it, finished second in a tri-county run over hill and dale—what later became 'cross-country.' I was a good runner, not fast on a straightaway but I had good endurance. Then we moved again, this time to Chicago. I started hitting the books, gained weight, and haven't run since."

"So, start again," Billy said.

"I'll never do it on my own."

"Then you'll end up in a ditch on Bonesteel Road."

"I want you to be my trainer, Billy."

"Your trainer? I'm not a distance runner!"

"You can pace me on your bike and keep me to a schedule."

Billy thought about it for a moment. The kids Billy went to school with, had known for years, would call him a traitor. "I don't know, Serge."

"What's the problem?"

"I don't feel right about it."

"Billy, it's OK. I've eaten crow before," Serge said.

Each taking a pail, they started back down Ohayo Road. Billy shifted his pail from one hand to the other, then again, and water sloshed around, some spilling over. Finally he set his pail down outside Quarryman's door.

"Whew!" Billy flexed both arms. Then he said, "Meet me at my mailbox in twenty minutes."

"What's up?"

"I changed my mind. I'll do it, best I can."

Serge looked into his face. "Thanks."

"See you," Billy said.

He went down the Rustovsky driveway, turned right on the spur. Across from him, on the west side of Bluestone, a black man was tilling a good-sized vegetable garden. Catching sight of the boy, he lifted his hoe in the salute he always gave Billy, who raised his hand. "Hey, Buford!" he cried out. He stayed on the spur, soon coming to the intersection where Maverick Road, which embraced the colony like a great arm, hit Bluestone Road. At that meeting point, at that corner, an abstract sculpture of a wild horse, as if on a mountain crag, rose fifteen feet into the air. Carved by a Maverick sculptor from a single chestnut log years earlier, it became the Maverick Horse. Billy's eyes rose to it now. The only way he could describe the feeling that always came to him was like those first minutes after receiving Communion, when you felt blessed, strengthened. Billy stayed on old Bluestone Road.

A hundred yards ahead sat his family garage; and well back, beneath three mast-tall pines on a broad lawn, stood the house. Billy stepped off the road onto a parcel of open, grassy land. A brown and black dog with yellow front legs, of no known breed—no one would even guess the mix—came running to greet the boy.

Chapter Three

Jacob Darden was working on his favorite outdoor project, burning out a stump; actually it was the last of the seven stumps that had once scarred his property. He hadn't cut the trees down—he was unskilled in such matters—but he knew of nothing that provided an opportunity, an environment, to think, to ponder one's life, like the tending of a burning stump.

With a stout stick, Jacob poked the smoldering fire, sending up a spray of sparks. He had long envisioned sitting on the terrace in front of his house and viewing Mount Overlook, prince of the Catskill Mountains; but a magnificent oak had made that impossible. After considerable discussion—Holly, his younger daughter, had recited "Trees" in an attempt to save the oak—it fell victim to the saw. Jacob looked at Mount Overlook now, a regal shade of purple, and the grand, ghostly Mountain House Hotel on its summit, begun in the easy-money Twenties, only to die, unfinished, in the Depression.

A breeze coming off Ohayo, the neighborhood mountain, fanned Jacob's pale, cleanly shaven face. He was pleased that he had provided his family with a handsome, comfortable place to live. When he and Hedwig had first bought the house, thirteen years ago, the main thing it had, that their house in the Maverick Art Colony didn't have, was a well. At the time unpainted, their new house had vertical wood siding with a couple of dormer windows on the second floor and a quaint front hall that jutted out like a sentry box. Plus an unfinished upstairs and, of special interest to Jacob, a one-room studio a small distance away. Nothing representing a lawn had existed at the time, just dirt and rocks and trees.

Now the siding on the house was conventionally horizontal, painted white, with light-green trim on the windows and doors; it had a bluestone front terrace and a fine lawn that Jacob hoped would one day surpass his father's at the family compound in Green Harbor, Massachusetts, say in the next five years.

A dog was barking. Glancing up, Jacob saw Buck, his son's dog, running to meet Billy on Harlan's Field. The two romped about, then continued to the house. When he spotted the man at the smoking stump, Buck broke away and headed for the backyard. Disliking dogs and inordinately fearful of them, Jacob remembered the day Buck had growled at him and, blazing stick in hand, he'd gone after the mutt to establish indisputably who had authority in the family. Jacob called to his son and waved him over.

"Lovely day like this, I had to get out of the city," he said, observing the boy as he crossed the lawn—no heft to him, close to scrawny. Not how he wanted his son to look. "How are you, Billy?"

"I'm OK."

"How was school?"

"It was OK."

"You can do better than that," Jacob said, hating the boy's dependency on slang. "Start over."

"At the end of the game today," Billy said, "I yelled at Clarence Bumgardner."

"What happened?"

"I was up and Donny Osterhoudt was on third with the tying run," Billy said. "Clarence sees Mr. Marr on the porch with his bell. The game ends when he rings it, not before. Clarence holds the ball like he's trying to get a good grip. He's not throwing. Finally Mr. Marr rings his bell, game over. I could've brung Donny in but never had the chance."

"Could have *brought* Donny in," Jacob said. "'Brung' is

13

substandard."

"OK."

"Then say it."

"I could have brought Donny in."

Jacob poked with his stick sending up sparks. He was bald, had a good-sized girth, certainly not tall at five feet seven but no one had ever called him short. He had a full, sensuous mouth; chin and forehead of a similar mold, nicely rounded. Expressive brown eyes that didn't see so much as talk.

"What else happened?"

"Jimmy McMullan challenged Serge to a race."

"What kind of race?"

"A foot race."

"There are many categories of foot races, Billy."

"To a distance run. Twice around the Bonesteel Road/Hammond Street loop, ending at the school."

Jacob fanned away another smoky breeze. "Did he accept?"

"Yes, but he gave himself two weeks."

A blue '37 Plymouth with a high polish (even its tires shone) pulled into the driveway, and Billy's sister leaned toward the driver, and the driver toward her. Whenever Billy saw Rachel and Andy together, they were always kissing. She started up the stone path in her saddle shoes and pleated navy skirt and buttercup-yellow sweater, giving her father and brother a wave. Jacob lifted his hand in response, following her with his eyes, giving his tongue a little swipe on his lower lip.

To his son, "In two weeks Serge is going to be ready to run three miles, is that what you're saying?"

"We hope."

"Who's we?"

"Me and Serge. I'm his trainer."

"Wrong case."

"Sorry, Serge and I."

"You're Serge Rustovsky's trainer," Jacob said. It wasn't a question but called for an answer.

"I am. He's out of shape."

"Can you get him *in* shape in two weeks?"

"That's what we'll be working on."

"Billy, Serge Rustovsky is a dreamer. It's not going to happen."

"He was a good runner when he lived in Indiana."

Jacob paused thoughtfully. Serge was an eighth grader, a year older than Billy, and Jacob had doubts as to Serge's intentions. "What kind of things do you and he talk about walking back and forth to school every day?"

"Nothing special."

"Tell me one thing you've talked about in recent days."

"Sometimes we don't say anything."

"Does he ever suggest having a little fun?"

"Dad, we have fun every day. As to what we talk about, today we talked about the Bolsheviks."

Jacob's arms, shoulders, momentarily stiffened. "How did that come up?"

"After school we were standing around and Clarence Bumgardner said his father called the writers and artists in the Maverick Art Colony dirty Reds," Billy said, "Bolsheviks. On the walk home I asked Serge what it meant."

"What did he say?"

"He told me who the Bolsheviks were, how they wore red in the Russian Revolution in 1791. Sweaters, hats, scarves. So, if you call someone a Red, or a Bolshevik, you're calling them a Communist."

"The Russian Revolution was in 1917. Did Clarence mention any names—as to who his father said was a Red or a Bolshevik?"

"No. Serge said you used to be a 'good lefty.'"

"What else did this paragon of knowledge have to say?"

"I asked him if you were a Bolshevik and he kind of laughed."

Jacob thrust his stick into the fire, like a matador for the kill. "Billy, how could you ask such a stupid question?"

Billy took a precautionary half-step back. "You're a writer, we live in the Maverick Art Colony."

"We haven't lived in the Maverick Art Colony for thirteen years!" Jacob said.

"Maybe not *in* the colony, but we're right next to it. Like Harlan's Field. To me it's one and the same."

A yell for Billy came from the mailbox on Bluestone Road.

15

Jacob tossed his hand, as if waving away a bug. "Go train."

****

Billy's bike was in the tool room, a small structure attached to the garage. Unlike the garage, which opened to old Bluestone Road, the tool room faced the house. He grabbed his bike, circled about with it, and met Serge at the mailbox. He pedaled while Serge ran, though it wasn't so much a run as a kind of fall-and-catch. The pace was slow; pedaling wasn't really necessary; in fact, Billy had to brake to keep from getting too far ahead.

Head lowered, eyes fixed on the road, Serge puffed away. Bluestone Road, from one end to the other, was three miles long, intersecting at one end with Route 375 and, in the other direction, with Route 28. The Darden mailbox was approximately in the middle; out and back in either direction, as Billy figured, would equal Serge's run with Jimmy.

"How you doing?" the trainer asked.

"Not dead—yet."

"Good."

About 100 yards from Route 375, at a big old barn, Billy told Serge to stop running. No argument from Serge whose face had taken on the color, if not the look, of a large, ripe tomato. Billy got off his bicycle and let it drop by the sliding door of the barn. His schoolmate Donny Osterhoudt lived across the road in a small gray house with window boxes that gave an otherwise cheerless home a friendly, come-in look. Behind the house, at the end of a long dusty road, squatted a large, windowless, cinderblock building. You would have no idea what went on inside unless you happened to hear blood-curdling squeals or saw a truck rolling down the dusty road carrying cattle. Just then Donny's father, Rolf Osterhoudt, stepped out of the house and gave the boys a wave. Serge paid no attention but Billy raised an arm. The man had a good-sized stomach like his own father but was taller and had a full head of hair.

Serge had his hands linked behind his head as they walked to the intersection with Route 375. On the corner stood a large brown building with ornate molding, Blatz's Bavarian Inn, a favorite local restaurant and bar. From here, Mount Overlook seemed higher, larger, its bluish-purple hue now a brownish-green. A station wagon went by on Route 375 going toward Woodstock.

Serge's breathing was settling down and his face had lost some of the red. He was pleased, he said, how his heart beat was easing. It made him feel he wasn't totally out of shape. They walked back to the old barn. Before picking up his bike, Billy looked into the gloomy space hoping to catch a glimpse of Donny Osterhoudt's Welsh pony, Champ. Other animals in the barn, no pony. Champ was probably in the Osterhoudt mountain pasture where he stayed a good part of the year, untended. Billy picked up his bike and Serge told him to yell "kick" fifty yards from the finish—in this instance, Billy's mailbox.

"You're joking, right?" Billy said.

"I won't have a kick but I want the word in my mind," Serge said, "hanging there, ready. Say you yelled 'kick' for the first time on the day of the run. What impact would it have? It's Santayana's 'Concept of Association' I'm talking about."

"OK."

They began the second half of the run. Not far from the Osterhoudt barn they passed the brown-timbered gate to the mountain pasture. A car was coming along Bluestone Road. It was Zachery Denver in his '35 Studebaker. Zach beeped his squeaky horn and Billy waved and Serge slogged on. Thud thud thud. Opposite Mr. Bagovitch's yellow house, below road level, was the doomed enterprise the Russian had undertaken years earlier to lure families and kids to a sandy beach, a spring-fed pond, and a platform with diving boards, a whole day of sun and swimming for 50¢.

Billy waited another half-minute, then shouted "Kick!" It had no effect whatsoever. Serge stumbled to the mailbox and stopped, unsteady. Billy ditched his bike and hurried over, ready to break his fall if necessary. Instead of clasping his hands behind his head, Serge dropped an arm on Billy's shoulder—it landed like the limb of an oak—and they both nearly went sprawling. Billy felt like a soldier escorting a wounded infantryman to safety, buckling under the load.

Once around the bend in Bluestone Road, Serge was pretty

17

much on his own, scraping rather than lifting his feet. When they reached Quarryman, Billy thought to head on home and make himself a snack but Serge said there was fresh lemonade in the icebox and they walked in, pine needles soft underfoot. The Model A was parked in the driveway. Serge said the car was "moody"—for no apparent reason it would refuse to start. But his father was smart in matters mechanical and so was Serge, so by hook or by crook they kept it running.

Once inside, Serge went to change his shirt and Billy peered through an open doorway into Mr. Rustovsky's studio. It took up half of the house. The north side of it had a large window and the light coming in was like clear, pure water. You could almost hold up a glass and drink it. A painting Mr. Rustovsky was working on took up most of one wall. Billy had seen it once before in an early stage, a kind of sketch; now it had come to life. It showed a scene on the Hudson River—a huge brick-making factory in the background, smoke pouring from the chimneys, men driving trucks and loading bricks onto a great barge, a man on the deck of a tugboat throwing a line, another man in a black cap in the pilothouse gripping the wheel. You knew what Mr. Rustovsky was painting—a tugboat was a tugboat—but everything to Billy's eye had a unique angular look. Elsewhere in the studio, on a plain wooden table, lay books, magazines, newspapers: Daily Worker, New Masses, Le Monde —

"Here you go," Serge said, handing Billy a glass of lemonade and an oatmeal cookie.

They walked out and sat on a sagging 8-inch plank supported at either end by cinder blocks, their backs to the stone siding. Straight out from the house, maybe 100 yards, Mr. and Mrs. Rustovsky were sitting on rustic chairs at the lip of the quarry, a small table between them; on it was a bottle of wine.

Billy had a quick bite of the cookie and a swallow of lemonade. "I like your dad's painting," he said. "Everybody's busy, pitching in. It makes you feel like you're right there. But whose house is big enough for it?"

"It's not meant for a house," Serge said. "It's for the Federal Office Building in Kingston."

"Why there?"

"It's where the WPA wants it."

"Serge, the WPA repairs roads and bridges." It felt good setting Serge straight; he didn't have the chance very often. "The Santarelli boys' uncle is doing flood-control work on Esopus Creek—"

"You're missing something," Serge came back. "There's a branch of the WPA for artists. One project is called 'American Rivers.' The Hudson was chosen for mid-Atlantic states and my father got the nod. Thank you, President Roosevelt."

"What did he do?"

"It's a federal program, Billy." Serge set down his glass. "Let's go take a look at William D."

"My father's on the warpath," Billy said. "I have to get back. See you tomorrow at ten."

"We're training on weekends?"

"Saturdays, yes. Sundays, I'll give you a break."

Billy walked down the pine-needle strewn driveway to old Bluestone Road, then broke into a run.

Chapter Four

Dom Santarelli, sitting across the main aisle in St. Joan of Arc's Church in Woodstock, was trying to communicate with Billy, not by whispering but by mouthing words. One word started with a "b" and finally Billy made it out—"boat." Hedi saw her son was drifting and gave his arm a yank. At the altar, Father Riordan was reading the day's Gospel. From what Billy was getting from it, Jesus was on a mountain talking to a bunch of people. Church wasn't important to Billy; his view of it—except for taking Communion—was like Dom's view of school. It was required. Sunday morning Billy and sisters would put on "church clothes." Hedi would hustle them into the car, and after church they would always have a big family breakfast, which Jacob happily sat down to. He was Catholic, but the only time he ever went with his wife and kids to St. Joan of Arc's was midnight Mass at Christmas.

Seated with Dom were his twin sister li'l Jill, brother Frank, and Mrs. Santarelli, an ample, easy-going woman. Father Riordan started his sermon, losing Billy from the start. Clearly Dom had his eye on a boat at the Ashokan Reservoir. There was no end to the number of rowboats pulled up on its shores, all chained to trees. The idea was to choose the right boat, one you could "borrow" from time to time to go fishing in and not have the owner or the sheriff come running after you.

Holy Communion was next and Mrs. Santarelli and her children walked to the altar. They knelt to receive the sacrament. Father Riordan placed the sacred wafer on each communicant's tongue. Once Dom had his, he shuffled back to his pew, an altar boy look on his face. Li'l had on a peach dress with a white curlicue collar; a lace veil lay on her dark hair like snowflakes. Just before sliding next to her brother, she raised her eyes, catching Billy, then lowered them again.

Father Riordan rambled on, offered a final blessing, and the congregation filed out to the churchyard. Joan of Arc's was virtually at the foot of Mount Overlook in Woodstock and people stood about and talked with each other under its quiet shadow. Dom singled Billy out and began his rap. After three days of scouting, he'd come upon the "perfect boat" in a grove of hemlocks. Big brass numbers on it, 3133. It had everything they wanted, including a set of oars tucked underneath. Billy asked about the boat they'd used last year. Dom said it was still there, but in case he'd forgotten, the damn thing leaked and they were always bailing; and to return it they had to drag it a good ways. This boat was closer to the water.

"Is it chained?"

"It is, but—"

"Dom, we're not breaking any chain. That's the rule," Billy reminded him. "Last year all we had to do was untie a rope. But when you break a chain— "

"Listen to me. Jeez, I'm trying to learn you something," Dom said.

Father Riordan came out of the church to chat with parishioners. Seeing the priest, Dom said to Billy in a lower voice, "The boat I'm talking about, no one owns it."

"Of course someone owns it," Billy said.

"Someone *did* own it. Gus Wilbraham, who lived in Marion Corners, kicked last week."

"What about his family?"

"No wife, no kids."

"But it's chained," Billy said.

Dom shielded his lips as he spoke. "It has a chain but don't worry. I'm talking padlock. It looks closed but it's not. Old guy probably lost the key so that was how he done it. He closed the U-bolt but not all the way, didn't snap it shut. Do you know what I'm saying? There's a hairline space, if you look real close—"

His sister came over. Dom told Billy they'd go over details in school and sauntered away.

"How are you, li'l Jill?"

"I'm fine, Billy. How about yourself?"

"I'm OK."

"Have you decided?"

"No, not yet. I'm thinking on it."

In truth, he hadn't thought about it at all. Every so often, maybe twice a year, he would spend the night with the Santarellis. The main floor of their home on Route 28 was the West Hurley Inn, a popular local hangout. Just a couple of weeks ago he and Dom were running around in the rambling old building, and Billy found himself on the sofa in the Santarelli parlor...with li'l Jill. She sat close and asked him if he wanted to kiss. He had never kissed a girl, so he said OK. The next day in school she'd written him a note.

"Let's go steady. How about it?"

His mother and sisters were leaving the churchyard. Li'l Jill put her hand on his. "See you, Billy."

Soon Hedi and her children were in the car, heading home.

Chapter Five

The shift was mounted on the steering column, not on the floor—an "engineering advance" on the Ford that Jacob had bought last fall at Len Willet's Garage in Woodstock; and Hedi still hadn't mastered it. In the beginning, almost every time she had to shift, the car would buck, sometimes stall. She was getting better but leaving church just now, she and another driver arrived at the exit simultaneously. Hedi braked, forgot to depress the clutch, and the car jerked; engine sputtered, conked. She got it going again but trying to get into low gear was giving her problems. Especially because she was smoking a cigarette and smoke was getting into her eyes. Sitting beside her in the front seat, Billy did what he hadn't done in church, pray. In the back, Holly waited patiently, as at a traffic light, and Rachel groaned, then muttered something under her breath when her mother finally managed to get the car under control.

"What did you say?" Hedi asked her daughter.

"Nothing," Rachel said.

"You said something, I heard you."

"I was frustrated, OK?"

"Keep your frustrations to yourself, Rachel."

They had already had a spat and here they were at it again. Earlier, Rachel had said that Andy wanted to take her out for breakfast in Big Bear, a village thirty-five miles to the northwest where he had his own log cabin. Hedi had answered her daughter's request by saying there could possibly be a reason for missing Mass, but having breakfast with Andy Sickler wasn't one of them. Breakfast after church was a family ritual, Jacob put great importance on it, and it certainly took precedence over her boyfriend's wish.

They drove through the center of Woodstock. It was a busy little town, with a village green and an Honor Roll—already three names were on it with gold stars—a couple of restaurants, two art galleries, a movie house, three bars, a grocery store, a barber shop, a hotel, a liquor store, and a shoe maker. For many reasons Hedi would drive into Woodstock, but for everyday marketing she preferred Happy's General Store in West Hurley. It was quieter; easier parking; and she liked Fred Happy...had good reason to. When she and Jacob were first married and living in Bird's Eye, he had let them buy on credit, at one time close to $200.

When they came to Blatz's, Hedi slowed and turned onto Bluestone Road, shifting gears to second to keep the car moving, then back to third as they passed the Osterhoudt barn. Rachel sat with her eyes closed shaking her head. Her mother was so behind the times, and Hedi's German accent was embarrassing, what with Germany under Hitler running roughshod over Europe. Rachel saw the way her father sometimes looked at Hedi...at the unflattering clothes she had on or the hasty way she had applied lipstick, the only makeup she wore. She had perfumes and powders but almost never used them. Rachel resented how her mother had made her wear dark, heavy bloomers to school in West Hurley when everyone else wore snowsuits. Rachel knew she was conceived in the Maverick Art Colony and in her first years slept in a rickety old crib that artist Millicent Yeager had left behind in Canal Boat and that Harlan had then delivered to Bird's Eye. Nobody had anything in those days. She didn't feel abused but God Almighty her mother got under her skin and her father's also. Rachel knew he looked around and wasn't sure he didn't see women in New York and even in Woodstock. She tried her hardest to believe he was faithful but couldn't help thinking—

The car came to a reasonable stop in their driveway.

They all got out and walked up the curving stone path to the terrace. On one side of the front hall was a narrow table with a lamp; on the other side were two shelves, filled with sports equipment, mostly Billy's: two baseball gloves, a couple of tennis racquets, a regulation football. A Dutch door opened to the living room. Big stone fireplace, a sofa, and a couple of easy chairs and lamps. Jacob believed every chair should have its own lamp. Paintings by local artists, oils and water colors, on the walls. A painting of Billy in football togs, at eight, hung to the right of the fireplace.

Instead of changing into everyday clothes, the children and Hedi stayed dressed for Mass. Jacob took great pleasure in having his family well turned out at Sunday breakfast. Hedi issued a reminder to her children to wash up, and took bacon, eggs, butter from the icebox. It was a new Kelvinator with a freezer unit but to her it was still, and always would be, an icebox. Rachel cut slices of her mother's bread, and Billy and Holly set the table. No one-two-three task. It took care and thought. Their father had to have his own salt and pepper, bread, butter, jam, glass of water, and handy ash tray and matchbook for his after-dinner cigarette. He did not like to ask for anything, let alone reach for it.

He was late coming in from his studio, the kids drifted away, and Hedi sat at the kitchen table and found herself staring at space, thinking back, remembering....knocking on the door of a Mrs. Jacob Darden in Green Harbor, Massachusetts, two weeks after stepping off the S.S. Waindok from Bremen, Germany. A buxom woman with a round, smiling face and strawberry-blond hair came to the door. Hedi presented the letter of introduction written by her mother's aunt, who knew Mrs. Darden was looking for a mother's helper. With eleven children, she needed one. Was Hedi a Christian? Mrs. Darden asked almost immediately. Yes, she was a Catholic. Mrs. Darden was pleased. The young woman looked strong, had clear brown eyes, seemed to have no outward quirks or habits; a language problem, yes, but Mrs. Darden didn't see it lasting long or getting in the way. She would pay Hedwig twenty dollars a week. "My dear," Mrs. Darden had said with false intimacy to the German girl, "let me say what I'll be expecting."

It was plenty. Hedi had come close to backing away at Mrs. Darden's expectations. Truth was, she hadn't come to America to work but the first thing her aunt had said to her when she arrived was she had to have a job. She found one, and then some. The Dardens lived in a huge beachside house with a veranda. Hedi would start at six, have a half-hour for lunch, and didn't finish for the day until the dishes were washed after dinner. There was a little church on Beasley Street and Mrs. Darden would give Hedi an hour to attend eight o'clock Mass. Hedi should note, Mrs. Darden said with great seriousness, that church matters were never to be discussed or brought up with Mr. Darden in the room or anywhere around. The reason wasn't given. He was a polite, a formal man, she soon discovered, always saying "Good morning, Hedwig. Thank you, Hedwig," when she brought him his morning coffee punctually at six-thirty unless, as frequently happened, he left the house as early as four. On such occasions he always turned his coffee cup upside down in the kitchen on his way out. She wouldn't dare ask any of the Darden girls about their father. Where he was from, his background, clearly it wasn't information to be divulged. Mrs. Darden (born Flynn) was Catholic, ardently Catholic. Her husband? Don't ask. Everyone in the Darden household was Catholic.

The three oldest sons would visit the Green Harbor compound now and again. The eldest, Jacob Jr., was the author of a book-length poem about Columbia College in New York, written while an undergrad, and was currently doing graduate work in English poetry. John, the second son, was just below Jacob Sr. in the family wholesale florist business. Twin brother Nathan was also in the business but without John's professional bearing. He had entered the priesthood but it hadn't gone well and he hadn't stayed. Nigel, the youngest son, was Hedi's favorite, just starting college when Hedi had come to work for the family. They became good friends, real pals. In a sense Nigel had made her employ with the Darden family, under the mother, bearable.

But what of the third son, Charles, in Harvard Medical School? The sisters were always saying to Hedi how tall and handsome he was. Hedwig would smile and agree, but it was Jacob Jr. whom she had reserved a place for in her heart. In the manner of Jacob Sr., he was cordial but indifferent. She was the German girl learning English and generally helping Mrs. Darden around the house. All Mrs. Darden did was give instructions, often harshly, to Hedi, whom she watched, observed, with a narrow, unswerving eye. As for Jacob Jr., whenever he came home from the university he dated Rose McBride. On several occasions Rose visited Jacob Jr. in Green Harbor. Stunning redhead, lovely bearing, fabulous clothes. Hedi had no right to be jealous but she was, as if she were in the running for Jacob's affection! There was talk of a betrothal in the fall, marriage in the spring. Mrs. Darden was ecstatic, the proudest woman in Boston. Rose's father, Patrick X. McBride, was the sole importer of Irish whiskey in New England and was a powerful spokesman for the Boston archdiocese under Francis Cardinal O'Connor. When the betrothal was announced, Hedi told Jacob Jr. she was happy for him and Rose and wished them well, all the best. He smiled, thanked her—he was the only member of the Darden family, except for the father, who called her Hedwig—and went on his way. Hedi, herself, was engaged to a twenty-year-old coal miner in Biskupitz, Heini Schnitzler. He wrote her every week, saying his life was on hold until she returned. One year in America became two, then two and a half, and she kept assuring Heini she would come back to him. What else could she do? It was her destiny to marry a man she didn't love and live in a depressed coal-mining town in Lower Silesia...

Billy wandered into the kitchen. "Mom, I'm starving."

"Your father will be in soon."

"He keeps *us* waiting— "

Hedi said, "Sit down with me, Billy."

He pulled out a chair.

"Jacob told me about the talk he had with you on Friday," Hedi said.

"He called it a talk?"

"What did you say to him?"

"I told him about my day in school, walking home with Serge. When I said we lived in the Maverick Art Colony, he blew up—he

27

yanked the stick, the one he uses when he burns out a stump—I didn't know what he was going to do with it."

"Billy, listen to me to me," Hedi said in a calming voice. "Thirteen years ago, we were in our new house, meaning right here." Her index finger tapped the cloth. "We'd just moved in. You weren't even born. Your father and I decided to attend the Maverick Festival, held each year. It was called 'the Party in the Mountain,' and it was wild. Everyone in crazy costumes, games, music, dancing—stage shows—plenty of food grilled on open fires, bootlegged liquor. Artists from all over, and not just artists, stage personalities. Jacob had a new job with Reader's Digest and we were celebrating. About ten-thirty, state troopers raided the Festival. A local politician named Wolfgang Bumgardner— Clarence's father, no less—had set it up. The Maverick Festival, he claimed, benefited the Communist Party, and he would see to it that the revelry was shut down. Arrests were made, artists questioned. Your father said, 'Hedwig, we have to get out of here.' He'd had a shot of applejack and would have resisted—and that would have been his job. Wallis Dupree would've fired him, if for nothing else, for breaking the law. Prohibition ruled. We left the festival and ran to our house here on old Bluestone Road. In an article that appeared in the Woodstock Record, Bumgardner took credit for shutting down Harlan's annual festival—there was never another. Since then, your father has kept a distance between himself and the Maverick Art Colony. It's isn't a judgment, Billy. It's his job, it's politics."

Just then the front door opened. "Here he is now," Hedi said, and got to her feet.

****

"Can you imagine any family having a finer Sunday breakfast than we're having right now?" Jacob said to his wife and children seated at the long apple-wood table in the sunroom. Warm light was coming through the windows, good food on the table, children well-dressed.

Jacob looked with pleasure at his family and everyone started in. Happy in his captain's chair, he picked up his personal saltshaker, sprinkled his scrambled eggs and brought a forkful to his mouth, followed by a bite of bacon. Crisp. A small piece fell on his lap; instead of retrieving it and putting it on his plate, he flicked it to the floor. He helped himself to his private source of butter, dabbed a corner of toast, then added Hedwig's homemade strawberry jam. Jacob didn't eat a whole lot but each bite was special, his alone, like a shirt with monogrammed cuffs. Conducting from the chair, Jacob gave Hedwig a minuscule hand gesture. She got up, took his cup into the kitchen, and in a moment placed a fresh cup at his hand.

"Just now, while you were in church," Jacob said, "I had this idea. Three or four years ago I started a one-act play in my New York office, pretty much to clear my brain. Editing other writers' work was wearing me down. It's light, humorous; it carries a message but most of all it's fun. I think we should stage it this summer on our terrace. By then the lawn will be done and our guests will sit in comfort watching our production. It will be a great end-of-season party."

Rachel wanted to know what the play was about. Before answering, Jacob had a bite of his toast, first spreading on a little jam. "It's about a king in a make-believe land who craves pork chops and each year he sends an envoy into the country to locate a perfect pig to produce the most succulent of pork shops. If he isn't satisfied, the king will cause the whole nation to fall under a severe famine."

"What happens?"

"The pig chosen belongs to a farm family miles and miles and miles from the palace. Trouble is," Jacob went on, "the children have raised the pig from her earliest days and love her like a member of the family. No way will they give in to the evil king's demand."

"Oh my goodness," Holly said.

"I'm leaving behind copies of the play," Jacob said. "Right now I just want to put this out as a plan for our summer."

Jacob took in his children, his wife. "As to a more immediate issue. After talking it over with Hedwig, I've decided to leave Reader's Digest. I'd come to the Maverick Art Colony, with your mother, as a poet and writer. The country was in a great depression and writing jobs were hard to come by. I wrote articles and reviews when and where I could. My first novel, *If Winter Comes,* made us fifty dollars on an advance. I wrote a nonfiction book on Hernando Cortez and his conquest of Mexico. It paid a few bills, kept us going. Then Rachel appeared on the scene, and Holly wasn't far away. Our two-room cabin couldn't handle a family of four. With three, it was crowded. We moved to a house a stone's throw from the Colony, right here, where we are today. We weren't going broke, we *were* broke. Fortuitously, Reader's Digest, in the name of senior editor Rod Holloway and his wife Beth, knocked on our door on a cold winter's day. Rod said that he and Wallis Dupree liked my work, my articles and books. After we'd talked for an hour in front of our fireplace—what a perfect fire we had going, remember, Hedwig?— Rod offered me a job at a salary of four thousand five hundred dollars. Hedwig and I looked at each other. Was this for real?"

Jacob picked a bit of bacon from his plate, savored it. "That day, excited as we were, I promised myself, and Hedwig, I wouldn't spend more than ten years with the Digest. Editing other writers' work wasn't how I saw myself, wasn't how I wanted to spend the rest of my life. Ten years is now thirteen. The job has paid me well. Whatever we have, Reader's Digest made possible, put within our reach. Additions to our house, this summer we're having a basement put in, central heating installed, a new car last year, our own telephone. But now it's time to break away, to be my own boss. First and foremost, I want to spend more time with you, my family—no more back and forth to the city to make a living. I plan to finish the novel I started years ago, catching an hour in my New York office whenever I could but writing most of it here on weekends. I'm roughly halfway through. I've waited for this day, prayed for it to come, when I could work on my novel fulltime in my Bluestone studio."

"Called *The Red Hat,* right?" Rachel said. "About the priest, Stephen Rossel."

"Yes," Jacob said.

"I like the title but what does it mean?" Holly asked.

"A cardinal's hat is one of the world's great identifying symbols," Jacob said. "Who, but a cardinal, wears a red hat?"

Billy raised his hand. "A Bolshevik."

The girls laughed and Hedi couldn't keep from smiling. Jacob fixed his son in a stare. "Humor is wonderful, if appropriate. If inappropriate, it's disrespectful. You owe me an apology."

"OK."

"OK is not an apology!"

"Sorry."

Jacob fished a pack of Old Gold cigarettes from his shirt pocket, tore a match from a handy book, and lighted up. A crystal ashtray was close but he put the burnt-out match on his breakfast plate. He had a puff, took smoke in but didn't inhale, then blew it out in a refined fashion. Every so often at Sunday breakfast he would ask his children to relate what had transpired at Mass, the relevant issues. Looking around, he focused on Holly. "In church this morning," he said, "what was the sermon about?"

"The topic," she said, "was turning the other cheek. Instead of fighting and retaliating, Father Riordan said people should behave in peaceful ways."

"What word could take the place of 'peaceful?' in your opinion?"

"Christian."

"Rachel, any other word?"

"Loving."

"'Love thy neighbor as thyself.' Good. Billy?"

"Going steady."

The girls laughed again. Jacob sat there, restraining himself. The spike horn making a thrust at the aging stag, one day to force him off the hill. Well, not yet. He turned to his lovely seventeen-year-old daughter. "Rachel, what was the Gospel about?"

"It was from St. Matthew where Jesus said the meek shall inherit the earth."

"Excellent." He had another mild, almost a delicate, puff. "Billy, what did Jesus mean when he said the meek shall inherit the earth?"

"That's a good question."

"Thank you. Who are the meek, Billy?"

"It's hard to say."

"Do you know the meaning of the word?"

31

"Not really."

"The Sermon on the Mount is the heart and soul of Christianity," Jacob instructed. "Is there *anything* you remember about today's Gospel?"

All that came to Billy about church this morning was Dom Santarelli trying to say "boat" without saying it. Then, miraculously, a word popped into his head. "Peacemakers."

"Good. Who were they? What was their function?"

"They protected Jesus."

"How? Give me an example."

"They stopped those who were opposed to His views," Billy said.

Growing impatient, "Stopped them how?"

"With their peacemakers."

"Explain that, please"

"With their guns."

"They had guns in Jesus' day?"

"The New Testament says they did."

"Where, in what chapter?"

"I'm not sure what chapter but it's there."

"Define the word 'peacemaker,'" Jacob said.

"It's the Colt 44-40 revolver."

Jacob cupped his hands firmly in front of his chest. "I won't call your comment blasphemous but it comes close. I want to see you in my studio with a definition of 'meek' in thirty minutes." Jacob drowned his cigarette in the spilled coffee in his saucer. He thanked Hedwig for a wonderful breakfast and left the sunroom.

The children had set the table; now they began clearing it. Hedi swept under Jacob's chair. Billy held the dustpan and emptied it into the garbage.

****

The stairs going to the second floor of the house were steep and narrow, opening to a small hall at the top with two doors. The one on the left opened to Holly's room, the door straight ahead to Billy's. He lifted the latch and went in. A fieldstone chimney hugged the far wall. A dormer, with two windows, ran along the west wall of his room, each with a cushioned seat. The room had a maple desk, a small easy chair, and a painted, handmade bookcase.

A gray squirrel mounted on a piece of driftwood sat on top of it. On the lowest shelf were back issues of Outdoor Life and Field and Stream; on the middle shelves books on hunting, fishing, trapping, animal tracks, guns, a book called *Trees of North America* and another *Wild Animals of North America* and another *Birds of the North East*; also the novel *Smoky the Cowhorse* by Will James and *The Call of the Wild* by Jack London; and three novels by Joseph Altsheler, *The Young Trailers, The Forest Runners,* and *The Eyes of The Woods.* Also a Webster's dictionary.

Billy pulled it out and went to a window seat, leafing through the m's for "meak" —not here. Now what? Tell his father the word wasn't in the dictionary? But then he saw it just down the page— **meek**. Adj. *Quiet, gentle; submissive.*

How the meek, or the gentle, could inherit the earth, Billy didn't know, but at least he had the definition. He looked across Bluestone Road, his eyes rising to an opening near the top of Ohayo Mountain, an opening so small you'd never notice it. But one day— he was nine at the time—he had noticed it; and, looking hard, realized it wasn't merely an opening; in the opening was a cabin. He had asked Harlan what he knew about it, and Harlan said he'd seen a man on two or three occasions coming out of the woods at the sharp turn on Maverick Road, near the concert hall. Went by the name Adam. Man was a trapper—bobcat, red fox, mink, muskrat, raccoon, all indigenous to the upper reaches of Ohayo. He lived in a cabin near the top of the mountain. But Harlan hadn't seen him since they'd spoken, years ago.

Chapter Six

Jacob sat at his studio desk looking at the sheet of paper in his typewriter, ostensibly page 190 of his novel: a scene showing newly ordained Stephen Rossel searching the streets of Malden for his 17-year-old sister who had lost her way in life. Jacob banged out another two sentences. Fingers feeling stiff, unresponsive. So many typos, page almost unreadable. He worked his way through a page: Tina's voice, crying out from a bleak, dimly lighted room in a rundown section of Medford. Stephen, a priest, holding his sister in his arms. She was pregnant, in labor, near death. Telling her to hold on, running out to the street to get help, hail an ambulance—

A knock on the studio door and Billy came in, stood at the desk waiting for his father to speak.

"Well, what did you find out?"

"Meek is an adjective that means gentle or submissive," Billy said.

"What does an adjective do in a sentence?"

"It tells you about a noun."

"It modifies a noun, right," Jacob said. "In the sentence, 'The meek shall inherit the earth,' 'meek' modifies what noun?"

"Earth."

"No. It isn't the 'meek' earth." Jacob rubbed the fingers of his left hand; pain, stiffness, kept getting worse. "Let's start from the beginning. What is the subject of our sentence, 'The meek shall...?'"

"Meek."

"That makes it a noun. You told me meek was an adjective."

"The dictionary said it was."

"How is 'meek' used in the sentence, as a noun or adjective?"

Billy was getting rattled; guessing, he said, "A noun."

"How do you know?"

"It's the name of something."

"Good. So here's what we've learned," Jacob said. "First, you're right. Meek is an adjective. But any part of speech may be used as a noun; then it becomes 'noun-like.' When a word becomes noun-like it's called a substantive. In the sentence, for example, 'The race goes to the swift,' swift, an adjective, is used as a noun. That makes swift noun-like, or a—?"

"Substitute."

"*Substantive*," Jacob said. "But defining 'peacemakers' as the gun that won the west. You knew there were no firearms in Jesus' day. You knew that, right?"

"Yes."

"Then coming in with a comment about *The Red Hat* and Bolsheviks," Jacob said. "Billy, leave cuteness and silliness to girls. Boys should answer questions seriously and directly. Sit down."

His son pulled out the chair at the corner of the desk.

"I've decided to put you on a new regimen," Jacob said.

Billy said nothing; it sounded awful.

"Everything at Mass this morning went right through your head, if you even listened." Jacob gave the soft part of his chest, near the armpit, a squeeze; had a flash thought of his mother. Woman had glorious breasts. No wonder her husband banged her all those years, horny old Jew. "Assuming Dom Santarelli stays out of jail," he said to Billy, "where will he be in five years?"

"I don't know."

"Has he ever had an original thought?"

"He's smart," Billy said.

"What do you base that on?"

"He can think like an animal."

"Is that a quality to be admired?"

"If you're fishing or hunting or trapping, definitely. He outthinks what he's after; it pays."

Jacob nodded quietly. "How many deer did Dom shoot last year?"

"Three."

"You're allowed one, am I right?"

"Yes."

"Do you look up to him for that?"

He didn't have an answer. His father said, "It's called breaking the law, Billy. Breaking the law gets you into jail. Does that concern you about Dom?"

"Some. It's who he is."

"What do you like about trapping?"

"It's hard to explain it," Billy said.

"Well, try."

"When it's cold and dark and your hands are freezing and you're looking at a trapped muskrat that hates you, that would kill you if it could; and you have to kill it. You can yell and scream for help, no one's going to come. You could walk away, but then you'd never live it down."

After a pause, Jacob said, "I want to be clear with you, Billy. I'm not taking a moral stance. If I thought you were trapping or hunting irresponsibly, I'd tell you. I'm not asking you to alter your ways. I think you're falling behind—" he tapped his forehead, "— here. I'm putting you on a regimen: reading, writing, appreciation of the arts."

Billy blinked a couple of times; his eyes were stinging. "Dad, it's why I go to school!"

"Mr. Marr is a fine teacher," Jacob said. "When you take his pupils into account—they aren't the brightest pennies in the jar— he's remarkable. But the intellectual atmosphere in West Hurley is dead. Mr. Marr is painfully overworked. Jimmy McMullan, Donny Osterhoudt, Frank Santarelli, Henrietta Joy—will they finish high school? Name one boy or girl in West Hurley who'll be going to college."

"Serge Rustovsky."

"He's a different breed altogether; more on him later," Jacob said. He picked up a thin volume on his cluttered desk. "This book contains Abraham Lincoln's greatest speeches. I want you to have the Gettysburg Address ready to deliver next weekend."

"Deliver?"

"Recite from memory," Jacob said, "to me, seated at my desk. In a similar vein, boys your age should be well along in the classics. Will James tells a good cowboy story, Joseph Altsheler writes about the early American frontier. They're both genre authors. It's time you expand your reading: *David Copperfield, Robinson Crusoe, The Odyssey, The Scarlet Letter, Julius Caesar, Huckleberry Finn, Billy Budd,* as examples. First we'll have a discussion on the book you've read; the following week you'll write a critique, roughly five-hundred words on what you consider the key points. But to start the regimen we'll do exercises in memory and recitation."

Billy felt his face drop. "This—this regiment, how long will we be on it?"

"'*Regimen*'" his father corrected. "You can't put a time limit on intellectual growth and development, Billy. My hope is you'll be on it for the rest of your life."

Jacob passed his son Lincoln's Greatest Speeches.

****

Five minutes after leaving his father's studio, Billy spun into the Rustovskys' driveway on his bicycle, pedaled to the house and leaned it against the jigsaw-puzzle siding. Mrs. Rustovsky was hanging laundry. She was a big woman, big all around, with a haystack of hair interwoven with straws both dark and gray. She had on a loose, full-length, multi-colored smock and tired brown sandals. For someone carrying a lot of extra pounds, she moved with surprising lightness in pinning a pair of coveralls to a clothesline.

"Hello, Mrs. Rustovsky," he said.

"Billy, ciao." From the bushel basket she pulled a faded denim shirt with a dark-blue patch on both sleeves. "Serge is at the quarry with his new book. Have you seen it?"

"I have. It's complicated stuff."

Bea Rustovsky pinned a pair of pinkish-gray bloomers to the line. "Keep at it. How's your mother, Billy?"

"She's fine.

"Give her my regards. Tell her to come by for tea."

"I will." A breeze, catching the bloomers, made them flutter like a low-lying cumulous cloud. "Excuse me, Mrs. Rustovsky."

Billy started off at a run. Just before getting to the table and chairs where Serge's parents often sat, he cut left, doing an end-around on Cayuga Quarry, then followed a path bordering the side of it—and there, in a clearing, on big steel wheels with knobby treads, black smokestack sticking through the roof, stood the crane. Why the departing quarrymen had left the jib elevated, instead of lowered, "at rest," no one had a definitive answer. Serge, in the cab, gave Billy a wave.

A big pine log served as a step-up. Still, Serge reached down and offered his friend a hand. No sooner was Billy in the cab than Serge handed him *Principles*. "There's something I want you to see, right off. I came upon it last night. Turn to the marker."

They sat with their legs hanging over the side of the cab. Opening to the marked page, Billy found himself looking at a photo of a small boxy crane. The longer he looked, the sharper his focus became. Then, finally, he saw it. "It's William D.!"

"His brother, anyway."

The manufacture's number was WMD77G-64x. Billy began laughing. "Serge, this is crazy!"

"Read on, you'll see that the William Delafield Company in Rome, New York, made the first 77G on or about 1885," Serge said. "It was called the 'Grappler,' the only compact crane on the market made for 'smaller environments'—like the Cayuga Quarry. The author, Abraham Raditz, didn't give it as an example, I'm just filling in. Listen to this." Serge leaned over and read a paragraph. "'The Grappler has the greatest lift capability of any crane its size, with tremendous 'equalizing distribution.' In other words, this model was exceptionally stable under heavy loads."

"Of course it was," Billy said, proudly.

Buck came running down the path, lay down at the big pine log. "My father is putting me on a new regiment, I mean *regimen,*" Billy told Serge. "He says I'm falling behind."

"Falling behind what?"

"He didn't say. I have to learn Lincoln's Gettysburg Address and recite it by next weekend."

"Where, on a great battlefield?"

"In his studio."

"Same thing," Serge said.

They took two steps to the back of William D. Except for the boiler, lying horizontally, the steam engine had no resemblance to a bear, but Billy thought of it as one, a burly fellow that had gone into hibernation long ago. And now a couple of kids were trying to stir the old bear out of his slumber.

"Here's what I've learned so far," Serge said. "William D. is a double-acting stationary steam engine. A head of steam pushes against a piston to create the power stroke." He pointed to the piston, then extended his arm with his hand in a fist. "Steam under pressure is released, hits the head of the piston, and drives it—this is the power stroke." Serge pulled his arm in, cocking it, then delivered a punch. "To repeat the power stroke, the piston has to return to its starting point, but with the flow of steam still coming in, how can it? Say a big wind is pushing at your door, can you open it?"

"Not easily."

"If you don't block the steam, the piston will never get back for a new stroke," Serge said. "Here's how it's done."

Serge grabbed hold of a rusting metal wheel, the size of a small bicycle tire, on one side of the steam engine. "This is the flywheel," he said. "The circular disk attached to the center of it? That's the eccentric. Last night I went over and over this, Billy, until I had it. In a nutshell, the eccentric—it means off center, like a person who's 'eccentric' is off center—cuts the flow of steam just long enough, a millisecond, allowing the piston to get into position for a new power stroke." Serge rammed his fist forward, pulled it back, then rammed it again. "Over and over and over in the blink of an eye, and the eccentric is never late in doing what it does. The fly wheel, by nature of its spinning—a body in motion stays in motion— Newton's first law—uses kinetic energy to complete the cycle. That's what's happening when the 20th Century Limited roars across the Great Plains at 85 MPH. Somewhere in the heart of that crack express, an eccentric works to shut off the flow of steam, enabling the piston to get into position for a new hit. Is it any wonder that Freud compared the human brain to a steam engine?"

"None whatsoever."

Serge paused for two or three seconds. "What I just gave you is theory, the textbook explanation of a steam engine," he said. "Now we shift from the theoretical to the practical."

A wire brush, several pads of steel wool, a paint scraper, a can of 3-in-1 household oil, and a couple of ragged towels lay in a cardboard box. "You do the flywheel," Serge said. "Every so often give the axle a shot of oil. We can't get anywhere until we free it up. I'll work on the boiler."

They started in. The smallest bit of red started showing as Billy scraped and sanded the wheel. The crane was pointing due west; in front of it, a wide, level path led to the quarry a hundred feet away. Billy remembered thinking, when he had first started playing on William D., how bare the path was. Grass and weeds grew on it but no trees. He gave the axle a shot of oil.

Serge, working on the underside of the boiler, mentioned that his father had just learned he was a finalist in a major government-sponsored competition.

"To do what?"

"To paint a mural in a San Francisco post office."

"How long will you be gone?"

"Billy, he hasn't won it. We may not go at all. If he wins, it's a huge payout, the largest ever: Twenty-five thousand five-hundred dollars."

"For one painting?"

"Billy, it's twenty or more paintings," Serge said. "But it's considered one painting when it's finished. A mural can take years to do. Sometimes the painter has to stand on a ladder."

"Is that a requirement?"

Serge chuckled. "If brush strokes are made directly on the walls, in a technique called fresco, the painter needs a ladder. The walls of public buildings are high, how else could it get done? Or they could rig a scaffold. When Michelangelo painted the Sistine Chapel, he lay on his back seventy feet off the floor."

"What was he painting?"

"Angels."

"Sounds right."

"Let's try to get the flywheel to turn," Serge said.

They grabbed hold of it, tugged and pulled—nothing doing. With *Principles* open, they spent the next hour tracing the steam line between the boiler and engine. "— and this is the safety valve," Serge said, pointing to a valve atop the boiler. "If there's too much buildup of steam, too much pressure in the boiler, it blows."

"So that's a good thing," Billy said.

"I guess! If it doesn't blow, we're dead."

Chapter Seven

Almost at the garage pedaling home from Serge's, Billy spotted a convertible, top lowered, coming down Bluestone Road. As it drew near, it slowed, came to a stop. A woman in sunglasses, wearing an orange dress, its hem pulled above her knees, was driving; sitting next to her was a girl about twelve.

"Excuse me," the woman said. "I'm looking for the Maverick Art Colony."

"You've found it," Billy said.

She looked around as for a sign, a landmark; seeing nothing, she said, "Would you happen to know where Canal Boat is?"

"Stay on Bluestone about a half-mile. When you get to Rocky Hill Road—" He took a closer look at the car, a low-slung touring vehicle. "Forget Rocky Hill. I don't know why I even mentioned it. I'll take you to Canal Boat."

"Wonderful! I'm Mia Littlebird and this is my daughter, Bzy."

"I'm Billy."

"Hi," the girl said. She had blond hair done in pigtails that fell forward and clear blue eyes. "Do you live here?"

"I do." He ditched his bike. "I'll stand on the running board."

"No, please get in," Mia said. "Bzy, make room."

She moved closer to her mother, and Billy slid in. "Take Maverick Road," he said, "here on the right. It's a lot better than

Rocky Hill, but easy does it."

Mia made the turn and braked immediately to look up at the tall sculpture of a horse. "This is amazing," she said. "Who did it?"

"James Flannery, a Maverick sculptor. It's called the Maverick Horse. He carved it using an ax and finished it in three days."

"What a wonderful way to enter the Maverick Art Colony," Mia said. "Is Flannery still here?"

"The last time I saw him was four years ago. Do you know Harlan?"

"Not personally," Mia said.

"That's his house." Billy pointed to a structure roughly six feet by eight, mountain laurel hemming it in. Siding of pine slabs, bark intact. A roof, a window, a door.

"My goodness," Mia said.

"He used to live in a bigger house, Bearcamp, where he had a printing press," Billy said, "but for the last three or so years he's lived here in Morning Star."

Mia let out her clutch and they moved on. Maverick Road tended upward, car bumping along. Billy and the girl, their legs touching, bounced along with it. The engine sounded like someone unable to get his breath. Mia asked him how long he'd lived in the Maverick. He said the house was just over the colony line but he'd always considered it the Maverick. All his life.

When they got to the base of Ohayo Mountain, Maverick Road bore sharply left and leveled off. Just ahead was the Maverick Concert Hall. It had no windows in the side walls but upward of a hundred in the north and south, higher up, all frames tilted a quarter turn. To Billy's eye, each frame resembled a baseball diamond. A six-foot roof overhang, where concert goers bought tickets and had coffee during rainy intermissions, was built around the trunk of a great maple. Chips Doolin was making repairs to outside benches as the car went slowly by.

The ex-ship's carpenter waved and Mia waved back. Then he saw who else was in the car. "Billy, keeping company with beautiful women, I see!"

"They're kidnapping me, Chips."

"I don't see ye fighting it, lad."

43

Mia and Bzy laughed.

At the Maverick Theater, Mia slowed, put the gearshift in neutral and gave the building a long look. She was an actress, she said, here for the summer with a regional group called Bunker Hill Players. Most of the troupe would be arriving in another week or two. She put the car back in gear. They went by the yellow meadow and the laurel-trimmed base of Ohayo, drove by the red pump with the long straight handle and a small quarry. Maverick houses started appearing. Billy named a few as they passed: Wagon Wheel, Hickory Nut, Raccoon. Outside Raccoon, a woman was holding an infant, and a man was working on a window, as if to loosen it. There on the hemlock ridge, Billy said, was the house where his mother and father had first lived in the Maverick, Bird's Eye. Between Foxtail and the next house, Salamander, was colony pump #2. This one had a standard handle. They continued on, going by Wild Apple. A moment later a steeply pitched, badly washed-out road came up from Bluestone Road.

"That's Rocky Hill," Billy said.

"Does anyone actually use it?" Mia asked.

"Mostly as a ski slope in winter. The driveway straight ahead? That's Canal Boat."

It wasn't a driveway so much as a deep, wide parcel of land. Mia parked her car near the front door. The house was stone-sided like Quarryman but had a bigger look, probably because the screened-in porch was on one side of the house instead of behind it. It sat in a yellow meadow and two white birches framed the front door. They got out and Billy decided to help unload the car.

They started in, carrying boxes and suitcases and baskets of food into the house. The girl—Billy had forgotten her name—had her own room, big enough for a narrow bed and a chest of drawers. It had a good-sized window with a view of the yard and the mountain. He laid a duffel bag on the bed and a red, junior-sized rucksack.

When everything was inside, Mia suggested they should all have a glass of lemonade. With the water pail empty, she was going to use what was left in her canteen, but Billy said Maverick water was cold and fresh and the area art-colony pump wasn't far. He'd fill the pail.

"Thank you, Billy."

"I'll go with you," the girl said.

They went out to Maverick Road. She had a lively nature and he seemed to take joy in what they were doing. He had the urge to grab hold of a pigtail. As for her name, he said he wasn't sure he had it.

"It's Bzy. B-Z-Y. Think 'bee,' then add a 'z.' Without the 'y' people would think 'Bzzzz.'"

"It's a great name. How did you get it?"

"As a child, I was always busy, in and out of everything. My father started calling me Bzy when I was three. The name on my birth certificate is Brigid."

Just past Wild Apple, they came to the pump. Billy hooked the pail over the spout and began working the handle, way easier to use than the pump with the extra-long handle. He pumped eight times, water started flowing. When the pail was full, he set it to one side; if Bzy cupped her hands under the spout he'd pump and she could have a drink. Bzy leaned over, hands cupped; her loosely buttoned shirt fell partly open, sufficiently open for Billy to—look elsewhere.

The water came in something of a rush, flooding her hands and splashing her chin. She brought her hands to her mouth, drinking freely. Did he want a drink? He said sure. Bzy dried her hands on her shirt and worked the handle. Billy got splashed also and they both laughed.

Instead of heading back to Canal Boat, they sat on a wooden bench. After a short while he asked her if her father would be coming to Bluestone later this summer.

"That would be very nice if he could. He died in a car crash."

"That's terrible. I'm sorry," Billy said.

"I thought I'd be over it by now, but I'm not."

He tried to imagine how he'd feel if his father were to suddenly die. Part of him would be sad; part of him...wouldn't really care. He never missed his father when he went to New York each week. "Where were you at the time?"

"In Colorado, on a hiking vacation," Bzy said. "My father was an actor. He was in a few plays, a couple of movies, but he didn't like being tied down. He was a great hiker and sports-car driver. We had so much planned, Billy, so many great hikes. Then one night he had to go into town from our campsite. His car skidded on a mountain turn and went over the edge. That was it."

She was pressing her lips together, eyes tightly shut. Billy raised his arm and rested it on her shoulder. They sat there for a minute; then she was drying her cheeks, trying to smile. "We should get back."

A man walked up to the pump carrying a pail; he positioned it and took hold of the handle. "Hi kids, how are you?"

"We're doing OK," Billy said.

He had dark hair and wore frameless eyeglasses low on a sharp nose. "We just moved into Raccoon."

"We just moved into Canal Boat," Bzy said.

"Jack and Jill fetching a pail of water," the man said in a friendly tone.

"Are you an artist?" Bzy asked.

"Writer. I'm Roland Schiff. Stop by and meet my wife and our baby daughter."

Bzy said she would. They gave their names and started back. She offered to help carry the pail; clearly she'd be doing it a lot. Just then, the sound of a bugle reverberated through the woods, the dips and quarries of the Maverick Art Colony.

"Damn!" Billy said. "I'm late for dinner. That's my father calling me."

"How do you know?"

"Because it's what he does."

"With a horn?"

"Well, a bugle."

Billy set the pail of water on the floor in the kitchen and explained to Mia why he couldn't stay.

She thanked him profusely and Bzy went with him to the door, telling him to come back. He said he would, then was off at a run, past Wild Apple, the hand pump, Salamander, Raccoon. Waves from the man and woman sitting in front of it with their child. Billy's run had slowed to a jog as he went by the theater and concert hall. Chips had finished work on the benches and was clearing the land in the immediate area of the outdoor seats.

"Billy, whoever blew that rendition of 'Retreat' is an embarrassment to any bugler worth his salt; but it sure gets a boy home."

"I'm in for it, Chips."

"Fine looking ladies you were with. It's the price ye pay, lad."

Billy made the sharp turn at the bend in Maverick Road, ran downhill past Harlan's house and the Maverick Horse, crossed Bluestone Road to the spur and, on Harlan's Field, continued to the front terrace. He stopped for a second, took a deep breath, and went in. They were all but finishing Sunday afternoon dinner: roast beef, roast potatoes, string beans, salad.

Rachel gave him a look that said trouble ahead, Billy.

Without turning around his father said, "You know we have Sunday dinner at four."

"I was on my way home from the quarry and a car stopped. They wanted directions to Canal Boat."

Jacob twisted about in his chair; his son's unkempt appearance added to his displeasure. "Who did? Be specific."

"A woman and her daughter."

"You gave them directions. Fine. That doesn't explain why you're late."

"They'd come a long way, they were tired," Billy said,. "I helped them unload their car. They were friendly, the girl was very nice and pretty too. I filled a pail with water—"

"So a pretty girl influenced your thinking."

"Her and her mother, not just the girl."

"*Her* did not influence your thinking. Get your cases straight. In the *Odyssey,* the Sirens are very lovely," Jacob said. "Their song seduces sailors to steer their ships close, the better to hear and see the beautiful women—and they crash against the rocky shoreline and die."

"That's too bad."

"It's a lesson to be learned! Go to your room."

Rachel gave the floor an angry stomp. "Daddy! That's unfair!"

"I think so too," Holly said. "He was helping people, new arrivals to the Maverick."

Jacob gave Billy a sharp look. "Did you hear what I said?"

Billy left the table. A moment afterward, his sisters got up abruptly and left the room.

Jacob sat there taking his time finishing his coffee. "It was a lovely dinner, Hedwig."

He walked out and she sat there looking at the four plates, the empty chairs, having to tell herself—not the first time—that she had made the right decision seventeen years ago in Green Harbor.

She had bought the return ticket home. Heini, her fiancé, would take her in his arms when her ship pulled in. She would get used to the coal dust under his fingernails, in the lines in his face and neck, to the drab surroundings of Biskupitz. As she was washing up lunch dishes before saying goodbye to the Darden family in Green Harbor, Jacob Jr. came into the kitchen to say a private farewell. Why else would he come by? He asked Hedwig to take a walk with him on the beach.

It was the last thing she would ever expect to hear and she didn't know what to make of it. But was she going to say no? At two o'clock they met on the veranda of the big, rambling house and walked on the sandy path toward the ocean. The tide was just coming in and Jacob talked about his job as they walked along the beach. Teaching at Columbia and becoming involved in course development and committees wasn't what he wanted to do, wasn't a career he wanted to have. His plan was to leave the academic life and live in an art colony in upstate New York. At heart he was a writer, a poet. Jacob Jr. suggested that they sit on a dune; they sat on a dune. A cool ocean breeze was coming in.

"Hedwig," he said, taking her hands, holding them at his chest, "I want you to marry me. I'm asking you to be my wife."

She was so stunned she couldn't speak.

"Come with me to the Maverick Art Colony, Hedwig."

What was he saying? Was she hearing things?

"Will you, Hedwig?"

She said the word that was going to change her life forever. "Yes."

Jacob Jr. took her in his arms. They kissed, and then again.

Hedi was certain she would wake up in her maid's room and make her final preparations for leaving America. But the moment on the dunes was a reality. Jacob Jr. told his mother the news. Crushed, devastated by her eldest son's decision to take the help as his wife, Mrs. Darden sat stonily in the first row of St. Bonaventure's two months later as they exchanged vows. The reception was in Nathan's colorless apartment in South Boston with five family members present; ginger ale and Fig Newtons were served. Mrs. Darden, the *elder* Mrs. Darden, kissed the bride, cheeks hardly touching—so beneath her brilliant, handsome son. How had it happened? How had Hedwig managed to land Jacob Jr.?

Hedi took the Sunday dinner dishes into the kitchen, covering her daughters' plates with waxed paper should they want to continue...once Jacob left for New York.

****

At six sharp, Woodstock taxi driver Luther Ryan tapped his horn outside the Darden house, and Jacob—showered, shaved, dressed for New York—was saying goodbye to his wife and children. As far as Hedi knew, he had nothing planned when he got to the city except to go to his office/apartment on East 63rd Street, but he always dressed as if for an occasion. She never questioned her husband on his life in New York. Most things, in time, came out in casual conversation. She had picked up bits of knowledge: Gloria Smith, his secretary for five years, had moved to Savannah, Georgia, following her husband who had landed a job at a pier reconstruction site in connection with the navy. Enter Elizabeth Trill. Hedi had the feeling that Jacob was pleased with her appearance and her work. She "typed rings around" Gloria, kept her work station spotless, and lived with her mother in New Jersey.

"She lives with her mother?"

"She says they're very close," Jacob said.

"Was she ever married?"

"She was. It ended in a highly contested divorce. Elizabeth—she goes by Betty— told me it soured her on men."

"How old is she?"

"I'd say my age, maybe a year or two older."

Now, Jacob gave his kids their weekly allowance of twenty-five cents. Rachel had no problem planting a kiss on her father's

49

smooth, pink cheek. For Holly, it was a Sunday evening obligation: have a good week, Daddy. Billy felt uncomfortable kissing his father; plus he disliked his smell. The closest Billy could come to identifying it was of sliced cucumbers on a plate left out too long in the summer. Jacob hugged and kissed Hedwig, then, briefcase in hand, left the house.

****

Wanting to get housework behind her before starting a new week, Hedi went into the master-bedroom, an addition made to the house three years ago. Jacob liked afternoon naps and the bed looked as if a walrus had flopped around on it. Hedi smoothed the sheets, tucked in the blankets, fluffed the pillows and pulled over the rose-colored spread. Then she picked up the clothing he had tossed about, socks, undershorts, a shirt, and put them together for laundering. Next she went into the bathroom. It was the place she dreaded most. Wet towels on the floor, cluttered counters, urine in the bowl; but what to Hedi seemed the ultimate in selfishness, disregard, insensitivity, was the mess of whiskers, soap and shaving cream in the sink. She stood looking down at the ungainly sight. It always made her wonder how long Jacob would have stayed married to Rose McBride. No way would she have put up with his ill behavior, his sense of entitlement. Her mind went back to the dunes on the Green Harbor beach and Jacob Jr. holding her hands and saying, *Will you marry me?*

Would she have been happier living with a coal miner in gloomy Biskupitz for the rest of her life? The rigors of the Maverick Art Colony were as nothing by comparison; and she had to admit, with a small sense of satisfaction, that she had bested Rose McBride.

Through the bathroom window in the dimming light, Hedi viewed Mount Overlook. Then she stopped reflecting and wondering, ran the hot water, sprinkled on a cleanser, and washed the sink.

Chapter Eight

After a training run the next day—Serge was getting stronger; soon he'd have a kick—Billy grabbed the mower from the shed, oiled the bearings, and started in, going around the oak stump his father would finish burning over the weekend. The lawn was his father's pet project, just as it was his grandfather's in Green Harbor. Billy remembering how Jacob Sr. would water the lawn on an evening and tend to the flower garden. He had once asked Billy which flower he liked best and, without really thinking, Billy had said the rose, then had asked his grandfather which flower he liked best and his answer was, "I love all flowers." During the years Billy had come to love his grandfather. His grandmother tended to be bossy, snippy, a scold—you didn't want to take an extra tablespoon of blueberries at breakfast. After flowers and his lawn, Grandfather Darden's favorite pastime was fishing. On every visit he would take Billy to reedy Massachusetts ponds to fish for pickerel. One day, wandering around the house, Billy found himself in his grandfather's upstairs room. It had a unique, unforgettable smell, a mix of cigar smoke, fishing gear, and whiskey. A bottle of Old Overholt sat on his bureau with a crystal glass. At the head of the table, at a festive, family gathering when Billy was eight or nine, Jacob Sr. liked talking to his grandchildren, kidding with them. Once, when Billy wasn't looking, he took his grandson's milk glass, concealing it behind his elbow, and when Billy asked him where his milk had gone, Jacob Sr. said, "Why, you drank it."

"I drank my glass too, didn't I?" his grandson came back. No one laughed louder than Jacob Sr.

Stopping for a rest before pushing his mower into Harlan's Field—each week he cut a portion of it— Billy had another flashback. Four years ago his father had asked Harlan to give him permission to clear a piece of harsh, scrubby, but nonetheless level land overrun with anthills, sumac, and wild grasses. There was no place in the art colony where kids could play sports. Harlan liked the idea; he just didn't want anyone thinking that the land had suddenly become the property of Jacob Darden and family. On weekends, for the better part of the summer, Jacob and Billy worked on clearing the land. Billy would continue during the week, but on weekends the best gains were made. The tiny red ants were a menace, occasionally getting in their socks...oh, they made you dance! When the work was finished, the land playable, Jacob took a flat piece of wood—4" x 16"—and with a fine brush painted in two words, then nailed the sign to a locust tree on the side of old Bluestone Road. HARLAN'S FIELD.

Billy looked at it now, wondering where the connection, the love he'd felt so strongly for his father then, had gone. Would it ever come back? Gathering his strength and will, he pushed his mower into the field.

As he was putting it away in the tool room, Billy heard Sherman Marshall's team clomping down the road, and he ran out. Sherman's farm was on Bluestone Road, a short distance from the Rt. 28 intersection, and at times through the years Billy would stop by to see the horses and other animals in the big red barn. To his surprise, Sherman and his buckboard weren't continuing on by; they were turning onto the broad path connecting Bluestone Road with the spur and were coming onto the property between Harlan's Field and the garage.

"Whoa Betsy, whoa Molly!"

In flannel shirt and overalls, Sherman Marshall jumped down from his seat, a big man with weathered, deep-toned skin and a thick, drooping, dark-red mustache. "Billy," he said, "good seeing you."

"Hey, Sherman." He was patting Molly's face.

"I've stopped by to see your mother."

"I'll get her. Can I bring the horses a carrot?"

"Remembering their last time here, they almost turned in on their own."

He went inside, telling his mother Sherman was here, then grabbing a carrot from the refrigerator, cutting it into sections and putting the pieces into his pockets. Hedi went out the kitchen door and greeted Sherman as he ambled over. They started talking and Billy continued to the team. They saw him coming, eyes alert, their long ears bending forward. First Molly got a carrot, then Betsy; then again. He patted them, scratched their ears, and went back to the house. Hedi and Sherman were standing behind it looking at the cinder blocks on which the foundation rested.

Sherman was saying, "How high a basement do you want, Mrs. Darden?"

"Between six and seven feet," Hedi said. "As for size, match the sunroom floor."

"The rubble. Do you have a plan for it?"

"Dump it over the cliff but scatter it evenly."

"All right then," he said.

"When can you start, Sherman?" Hedi asked.

"Next month. I'll be with my brother, Ben."

"Can you give me an estimate?"

Sherman said, "We'll work for a dollar an hour, combined—both men fifty cents. Plus material. Lumber, cement, shoring. Sometimes the city will call—emergency repair. If and when that happens, we'll do your basement for forty cents an hour. If we're gone for two days, we'll work for eighty cents an hour for two days."

"That's reasonable. Thank you, Sherman."

"What do you do for the city?" Billy wanted to know.

"Between the portal, the weir, the dikes and aeration plant, the Ashokan Reservoir needs upkeep, repairs," Sherman Marshall said. "Me and Ben helped build it—thirty-three years ago. What a day that was when the order come to open the gates and 'let her run!'" Then to Hedi, "I'll be stopping by now and then with Ben to make sketches, take measurement, plan out the job. You'll have your basement by Labor Day, Mrs. Darden."

****

By the tone of his first words, when Hedi answered the phone in the kitchen of her house, she knew the meeting had gone well. "The 21 Club," Jacob was saying, "is always a delight. The lunch with Wally couldn't have been finer."

"That's wonderful, darling."

"He tried to keep me on. He offered me a five-hundred dollar bonus. I could hear my old man shouting, 'Take the money!' The Digest offers two pension plans," Jacob explained, "one at fifteen years, one at twenty. But because my contributions to the magazine were 'outstanding,' his word, and because I wasn't jumping to another publication, he considered me an exception. Wally wouldn't call it a pension but it was only marginally smaller than the one they offer at fifteen years. Then he said he'd give me an 'open-door option.' If I were to have a change of heart before June 30, he'd take me back at my current salary and give me the bonus he'd promised earlier."

"How pleased you must be!"

"I am. Now onward to a new adventure, Hedwig," Jacob said.

****

Billy picked up *Lincoln's Greatest Speeches* in his room and went outside, following Serge's advice to take it away from the house. No way would he ever memorize the Address in an environment that was "repressive and arbitrary." He should try a place that was conducive to learning. Like the Maverick Concert Hall. If that doesn't work for you, Serge said, before going to sleep at night, lay the book on your head open to the right page. While you're sleeping a process called osmosis will take place and you'll wake up with the speech fully in your brain. Billy thought it sounded farfetched. But he'd try anything to nail the Gettysburg Address. His father was coming home the day after tomorrow.

Carrying the book, Billy crossed Bluestone Road and started walking on Maverick Road. A dark-green pickup was parked on the side of it.

"How are ye, my lad?"

"I'm OK, Chips. What are you doing?"

"Harlan's place took a beating during the winter. Door won't open or shut."

"When is he coming back?"

"Next week. A lot of places need work," Chips said. "Wagon Wheel had to have a new roof. Now what book is that you're reading?"

"Lincoln's Greatest Speeches."

"The Gettysburg Address saved my life," Chips said.

"Really?"

"We were rounding the tip of South America, in the Drake passage, with a load of gunpowder," Chips said. "God-awful storm broke out. You could hear the kegs straining to break loose. Blown us to the heavens, they would've. Our brave skipper quoting the Bible, and I to him, what passage is that, sir? It's a line from the Gettysburg Address, he says— 'shall not perish from the earth. Be it so, Chips,' he says, 'be it so today!' And glory be to God—or perhaps Abe Lincoln — we pull through, and our powder dry."

"My father wants me to learn it."

"Now a lad could do a lot worse. I have some new charts I want you to see of the South Pacific."

"I'll stop by."

Maverick Road made a sharp turn at the base of Ohayo and continued to the Concert Hall. A cellist and a pianist were on the stage, practicing, and Billy went on by. Maybe the benches in the theater would be a good place, but people were milling about the entrance and he decided to give up on the idea. If he was going to learn the speech, he just had to sit down in his room and do it. He walked down Stage Door Road. Thinking to see if Bzy was about, he climbed the outside stairs and looked in. Mia Littlebird was on her knees nailing together two pieces of framing, as for a set. Working with her was a thin, bearded man; the girl standing nearby saw Billy and cried out his name.

"Hey, Bzy," he said.

"I'm so happy to see you," she said, coming over.

"Are you liking your house?"

"Very much. All kinds of birds and animals are living with us."

55

"Inside?"

"No, just around. What are you reading?"

"The Gettysburg Address. I have to memorize it."

"How come?"

"It's an assignment my father gave me, to learn and recite when he gets home. I'm not getting it."

"I can help you," Bzy said.

"That's nice. How?"

"Billy, I've helped my mother with lines for years. It's how she prepares. Have you read it through?"

"Many times. I know it but can't say it."

"Come on," she said.

They went down the stage-door stairs, walked up to Maverick Road, and soon were sitting in the deep yellow grass at the base of Ohayo Mountain. "This is what I do with Mia," Bzy said. "When she stumbles, I give her a word, maybe two. And she takes it from there. Give me the book."

"Page twenty-one," Billy said.

"Go as far as you can," Bzy instructed. "When you stop, I'll feed you a prompt."

"What's a prompt?"

"A line or a part of a line—to jar your memory."

Billy went along, but after saying, "'Now we are engaged in a great Civil War,'" he drew a blank.

"'—testing whether—'" Bzy put in.

"'—that nation or any nation can long endure.'" He went on for a couple of more lines. His next stumble came at, "'The world will little note—'"

Prompt: "'—nor long remember—'"

"'—what we say here but it can never forget what they did here.'"

"Terrific, Billy!" Bzy said.

And so it went...right through to the end. And only seven prompts!

"One more rehearsal," she said, "you'll knock your father's socks off!"

They sat for a while in the tall grass. Billy nabbed a grasshopper and sent it flying. Now that the prompt session was over, he

56

couldn't think of anything to say. Then something jumped into his head. "I couldn't help notice your rucksack when you moved in."

"My father bought it for me."

"Are you still into hiking?"

"I'm always ready for a hike," she said.

"Me and my pal Serge take a trail to school every day through the woods. It's not really a hike, it's a walk, a special walk. There's a patch of lady's slippers on it."

"It sounds nice."

A small yellow butterfly was interested in one of Bzy's pigtails. "Stop to think of it, I know of a hike," Billy said, "probably more like the ones you're used to."

"Tell me about it."`

"It's a trail that only one person knows."

She sat across from him, a teasing look in her clear blue eyes. "Could that be you?"

"Definitely not me. It's an old trapper. He lived in a cabin on top of Ohayo Mountain," Billy said. "I can see it from my window. Harlan saw the man step out of the woods a couple of times, five or six years ago. His name is Adam."

"Is he still there?"

"I'd like to find out."

"Now that's a hike we have to take," Bzy said.

Chapter Nine

In his father's studio to deliver the Gettysburg Address, Billy could hear Bzy telling him "break a leg" at the end of their 'dress rehearsal.' He passed the book to his father who said, "Fourscore and seven years ago, etc., etc. Go ahead."

He was going along at a good clip, words coming to him easily. No stumbling, pausing. But as Billy said the line: "—far above our poor power to add or detract," Jacob cut in.

"You're swallowing your words." He was sitting back in his chair, fingers tucked comfortably under the waistband of his trousers. "Project your words, let your words fly. Go ahead, 'the world will little note—'"

"The world will little note, nor long remember, what we say here—"

After three more sentences his father stopped him again. "Yelling isn't projecting, Billy. Speak from your diaphragm—" he patted himself just about his belly, "—from a deep place."

"OK."

He gave his son a signal to go on. "'—to the great task—'"

"—to the great task remaining before us, that from these honored dead we take increased devotion to that cause for which they gave—"

As he was coming near the end, his father interrupted yet again. "Billy, you're running your words together, slurring. Pretend each word is a piece of celery." Jacob clamped his teeth together. "Give your words *bite*. Demosthenes, the greatest orator of all time, spoke into the roaring Aegean Sea with pebbles in his mouth to perfect his enunciation."

Between celery and pebbles, Billy somehow carried on, finally saying the last six words: "—shall not perish from the earth."

Jacob said, "All right, you learned it. Good." He reached for a book roughly the size of Life magazine but with a hard cover. "Next, the 'Star Spangled Banner'—also called the National Anthem. Most people think it's one stanza. *'Oh, say can you see—?'* It's four." Jacob handed his son *Famous American Documents*. "I want you to learn all four. You'll be the only boy in America to know our national song in its entirety."

Jacob smiled, made happy by the thought. He made a little gesture. "Sit down. Hedwig said she told you what Reader's Digest offered me in retirement."

Pulling out a chair, Billy said, "She mentioned it."

"Wally came through with a bona-fide pension; it will only amount to half of my salary so we're counting on you to sell more muskrat pelts this winter."

Billy couldn't remember the last time he'd laughed in his father's company.

"How's it going with you and Serge?" Jacob asked.

"You mean with the crane?"

"I mean with training for the run in West Hurley."

"We're doing OK. He still doesn't have a kick but we're working on it."

"Are you keeping it to yourselves?"

Billy frowned. "What to ourselves?"

"The training. Outside of you and him, who knows?"

"No one."

"Good. Keep it that way. On Saturday, pretend you don't know him."

"That isn't fair. I'm his trainer!"

"On race day, trainers sit back. They've done what they could,"

Jacob said.

"Dad!"

"Stay detached, Billy. Do you understand?"

"OK."

"Not *OK!*"

"All right, then."

Later that afternoon Billy found Bzy at her house and told her about his audition. He hadn't stumbled once but his father criticized him on delivery. It wasn't sharp enough; he should bite off words like each was a piece of celery. Bzy laughed. That would be a lot of celery. A light rain was falling with early-season thunder and they sat on her bed cross-legged, talking. She had a pack of cards and taught him how to play gin rummy. He got the hang of it but she beat him three straight games. The rain stopped; saying goodbye outside Canal Boat, Bzy asked him when he thought they could go hiking to find the old trapper's cabin.

"The run between Serge and Jimmy is Saturday. After that, any time."

Chapter Ten

Donny Osterhoudt had bad news on Wednesday—they were selling Champ. Man and his boy came by in a van to take the pony. Champ was nowhere in the upper pasture.

"Where was he?"

"It's the size of a mountain, Billy. Who knows? But they're coming back," Donny said. "My father says I have to find him and bring him in. Champ has become a liability, he says."

Billy wasn't sure what that meant but he became nervous, worried. Last year in the mountain pasture with Donny he'd caught a glimpse of Champ. When they had tried to get near him, he ran. Oh, did he run! Black mane and long black tail flying, red-tinted bay coat shining in the October sun. Billy had never seen anything so awe-inspiring. Why wasn't Donny riding Champ? he'd once asked his friend. When he'd had Geraldine, Donny had ridden all the time; on any day, he and Billy would take turns riding the black and white Shetland pony. But Donny said Champ was too much pony for him; it wasn't his size. Just under fourteen hands, Champ was like a small horse; as it turned out, a temperamental small horse. When Donny and his father had bought Champ across the river in Dutchess County, the woman who ran the farm had mentioned that he was a rig. He was such a handsome pony, it didn't make any difference to Mr. Osterhoudt. His son needed the challenge. Geraldine had a spunky nature but was too much like a pet.

"What's a rig?" Billy had asked, standing with Donny that day in the rocky, forested pasture with pockets of rich green grass everywhere you looked.

"When they go to geld a horse," Donny said, "now and then one of his balls don't drop. It happened with Champ. That explains why he's so ornery—stallions tend to be ornery."

"Champ is a stallion?"

"Well, half-stallion," Donny said. "But he still has the traits. Like his attitude. I also think he was beaten."

"Beaten?"

"My father took a two-by-four to him one day. I'm talking earlier. Do you know what's really behind this, Billy? My dad wants to get his money back, what he paid for him. A hundred bucks."

At recess later that week Dom Santarelli told Billy he'd taken out the new boat. What with the good oars and rounded bottom, she moves along like a dream. "Got me two yellow perch, two bullheads and a fifteen-inch smallmouth. Jeez, Billy, when you coming out with me?"

"Soon."

"It's yours as much as mine, we're in it together."

The next day Billy struck out two times facing Clarence Bumgardner. Pimply-chinned gawk threw heat. After the game Jimmy McMullan asked Billy if Serge had a plan for their run. Walking back and forth, does he ever say anything about strategy? Billy said no. All he talks about is the old crane he's working on. Does he train, do roadwork? Jimmy asked. Not that I know of, Billy said.

Li'l Jill sidled up to him. Could they sit together on the bus when they went on the school roller-skating party in May? Billy thought of Bzy but no one was going steady with anyone. "Sure," he said.

After school he and Serge had their final session. The day before a meet, a runner never trained, Serge said. Tomorrow, he'd lie around lazy and read *Ulysses*. Billy was more interested in today. They'd been at it for two weeks and, finally, Serge was mustering something of a kick. He was running well, head lowered, pounding out the distance. Standing roadside by his yellow house with a whistle around his neck was Mr. Bagovitch. Who were these ruffians, this runner/cyclist reconnaissance team sizing up the landowner's property day after day? Young Bolsheviks! Billy thought the émigré might blow his whistle as a warning. The finish line, Billy's mailbox, was just ahead. A car was coming down Bluestone Road and Billy decided to let it go by before shouting "Kick!" Sticking his head out the passenger window, ratty hair, green teeth and all, was Freddie Longo. His big brother was driving.

"Well, look at this, will you?" Freddie sneered.

The car went by, too close. Billy turned his wheel, bicycle slipped on loose gravel, he went sprawling. Serge came over. "You...all right?" he said, heaving, his shirt soaked.

Billy grimaced, jaw tightening. "Don't know."

"What...happened?"

"Car sideswiped...me."

"Who...yelled?"

"Freddie."

Serge gave him a hand and picked up the bicycle. Billy pushed it along, limping, thinking the worst. At his mailbox he told Serge he was going in.

Serge glanced at the blood coming through his pal's pants at the knee. "That's your Red Badge of Courage, Billy, right there," he said.

****

His mother cleaned the scrape, put on an antiseptic, applied a bandage. Billy hobbled upstairs, looked through back issues of Field and Stream, read an article on the difference between a bullhead and a catfish. "Catfish" was a major grouping; "bullhead" was a subgroup, smaller, usually one to two pounds. Billy leafed through a four-page spread in the back of a Sears catalog. The Rules and Regulations for entering the Best Muskrat Pelt Annual Competition in last year's trapping season. He'd gone through it so many times that the pages were wrinkled. First Prize: $500. The judges examine each pelt submitted in three specific categories: Skinning, Scraping, Stretching. The pelt itself, its size, color, texture, has a lot to do with it. You aren't going to win with a small or even medium-sized pelt. To win, you have to have an exceptional pelt and it has to be perfectly presented. Billy gave himself a moment to dream about the announcement: *Billy Darden, 13, is the youngest-ever winner of the competition.* Then he picked up one of his favorite Joseph Altsheler novels, *The Eyes of The Woods;* read for twenty minutes and fell asleep.

In the morning he woke early. His knee was sore, stiff, but not bad enough to interfere, to get in the way. What bothered Billy was what had always bothered him. That the West Hurley kids would find out he was coaching Serge; and now they had found out.

His mother was just coming into the kitchen when he went downstairs. He said his leg was hurting and she said he should go back to his room and rest. What he did was spend a good deal of time reading and rereading the National Anthem. Unless you had a good idea of the lines, prompting didn't work, Bzy had told him. He hadn't seen her for a while. The trees were turning green atop Ohayo but he could still see, if barely, the trapper's cabin.

Shortly after his sisters left for school, Billy went downstairs. His mother was peeling and washing potatoes in the sink, except they were too round for potatoes. "Go freshen up, Billy," she said. "I'll make you breakfast."

He washed and dried his face and hands and sat down at the kitchen table. When he looked at his mother, who was scrambling eggs in an iron frying pan, she had the look he often saw in her eyes, a kind of faraway gaze. She put the plate before Billy and sat down with him with a cup of coffee.

"Thanks, Mom."

"After breakfast I'll change your bandage."

"OK."

"Don't eat so fast."

He laid down his fork. "Are those turnips?" he asked, glancing at the sink.

"They are. We're having them for dinner tonight. Mashed turnips are one of your father's favorite dishes."

"I like mashed potatoes more," Billy said.

"So did we," his mother said. "But then the war came, the first war, all the good food went to the soldiers. To make matters worse, one winter we had an early freeze and it killed the potato crop. We had nothing but turnips. They saved our lives."

"How did they save your lives?"

"Billy, we were starving, there was nothing else," Hedi said. "Everything was the war effort. Farmers planted turnips. Little shriveled ones came up. Oh, we ate them. My mother cooked turnips all winter. It was called the 'turnips winter' of 1916. My brother Joseph, eighth years old, made box traps and occasionally caught a rabbit. The fur made a little money and the rabbits, not much meat on them but it was something. It all helped. One day I was walking home from school and a truck was rolling down the street and a chunk of lard fell off the back of it, the size of a grapefruit. I grabbed it and ran home. Billy, you can't imagine the joy on my mother's face. How delighted she was, my father too. I was kissed, I was hugged—"

"For a chunk of lard?"

"Melted down, we had oil for cooking. Just what we needed and how sparingly we used it. Then the war ended," Hedi said, "and the boys came home, those who came home. I was nine when it started. They had marched away proudly to music on the street, and the few who came back were crippled, beaten—how old they looked! Heini's older brother was killed in the Battle of the Somme. You're supposed to celebrate when a war ends. We were glad it was over but there was no celebration. We were a badly beaten country and now we're in a new war led by a Nazi dictator." Hedi pressed her hands together, held them to her lips. "My mother and father, our family, everyday people all over Germany, facing deprivation again, defeat. It's like we're a cursed nation."

****

Serge, stopping by after school, talked to Billy upstairs in his room. He said his father had brought home an old block and tackle from a surplus depot in downtown Kingston for fifty cents, plus a can of super-penetrating oil. Each block has two sheaves, Serge said; that means you get four times the power. His father had given them advice: use penetrating oil on the flywheel every day for a week before trying to free it using the block and tackle. Under

65

pressure, a frozen mechanism can break.

"How are you doing?" Serge asked his friend.

"Not great," Billy said.

His mother had doctored up his knee but it was hurting. You're *hors de combat*, Serge said, wounded, out of action. The kids kept sneaking looks at me at school today, Serge said. Billy wanted to know if Fred Longo had said anything. He had, and then some. Don't sweat it, Billy, we have a race to run, Serge said. On a happy note, Li'l Jill Santarelli was asking after him.

"Little dark-eyed honey has you two walking down the aisle," Serge said.

****

Jacob had spent his entire Thursday session with his therapist going over his decision to leave Reader's Digest. He had outlived the allotted time he'd given himself to serve as an editor, to put his family on a secure financial footing, and now wanted to reclaim the creative Jacob Darden, to give the writer in him another chance. Why was it, then, that he was having misgivings, feelings of deprivation, even before he left? Where was the courage he'd had to leave Columbia, a promising career as a university professor, to establish himself as a poet, a novelist?

Now in Luther Ryan's car heading home for the weekend, Jacob was replaying his session. Why don't you say what is really going on? the psychiatrist Smiley Blandon had put to him. What do you remember most deeply, Jacob, about growing up, the early years, your first years? Jacob reflected, then mentioned how, after his father left the house before dawn to receive the day's shipment of flowers, he, a two-year old, would crawl into bed with his mother. She would draw him in, hold him against her breasts. She was lactating at one such occasion and directed her swollen nipples into his mouth. As a child, Jacob could only think, as his mother cooed and stroked his hair, that he never wanted it to end.

"And you wonder why you're having misgivings about leaving Reader's Digest?" Smiley Blandon said. "It's a tough world out there, Jacob. Writing a novel. Failure. The threat of poverty. Who wouldn't like staying in his mother's nourishing bosom forever?"

****

Billy Darden awoke on Saturday morning feeling uneasy, badly pressured. He pulled on clothes, went downstairs, checked the kitchen clock. Unless he left now, he wouldn't make it in time. His leg was bothering him, was still healing. Doctor's orders were a perfect excuse. You don't need me there anyway, Serge. Run your race. That's the import thing. Billy went out. Truth was, his leg was only an excuse if he wanted to make it one, and that was his plan. Going to bed last night he'd thought of it. He didn't want to face the crowd, the jeering, the hostility. West Hurley was his school, and who was Serge Rustovsky anyway? A know-it-all from Chicago everyone had come to hate.

Billy walked out to Harlan's Field, wanting to speed up the clock. To get it all behind him. He would play up the doctor's orders, and that would be it. No one would say anything. Not even Serge.

The sun was rising; it threw warm light on Ohayo Mountain and, closer to where he was walking, on a wild horse standing proudly on a crag. Billy looked at it for a long second, then started for school.

****

Tired, breathing hard, his knee aching, he stumbled up the slanted driveway at Rowe's Lumber and crossed Rt. 375 to Hammond Street, his eyes darting toward schoolhouse corner. He had expected to see ten kids, a few grownups. Gathered there were sixty or more people, most of them adults. Serge and Jimmy were standing on a white line short of the intersection with Bonesteel Road. Frank Santarelli was giving them instructions. Billy moved closer.

The white line was the start and the finish, Frank said. The run was twice around. If one runner dropped out, the other had to finish to win. If both dropped out but at different times, it was a tie. Any questions? People crowding in were giving Jimmy encouragement. He was a colt at the gate, lean, quick, his mop of straw-colored hair a forelock. Serge, in his old corduroys and black, ankle-high sneakers, kept his eyes lowered.

Frank said, "All right, take your marks. Get set." He hesitated, then shouted, "Go!"

The runners made quick turns at the corner and Jimmy opened an immediate lead on Bonesteel Road. They ran past the construction site of the new school, then disappeared at the bend. For the next several minutes everyone was looking across School Field waiting for the boys to come into view. Billy spotted Clarence Bumgardner standing diagonally across from him on the opposite side of Hammond Street. Clarence caught Billy's eye, then said something to the large, thick-faced man beside him, who looked over at Billy. Suddenly a big cheer went up. Jimmy appeared across the field with the same springy step. Fifty yards back, plodded Serge. Billy could almost hear his feet hitting the road. The firehouse blocked one runner, then another. Jimmy made the turn onto Hammond Street and was halfway to schoolhouse corner when Serge made the turn. People were clapping and yelling support as Jimmy crossed the white line and started the second lap. Head lowered, Serge thudded on. Behind Billy a woman was saying, "They're a Communist family, their boy comes to school here."

"No."

"There should be a law."

"Where do they live?"

"In the art colony on Bluestone Road."

Everyone was again staring across School Field, waiting. When the boys came into view, Jimmy was still ahead but Serge was gaining. First Jimmy, then Serge, disappeared behind the firehouse; they were closer when they reappeared. They turned onto Hammond separated by ten steps, both gasping for air, faces twisted. Everyone screaming, urging Jimmy to hold on.

"Win it for America, Jimmy!" yelled Wolfgang Bumgardner.

On impulse, against his father's order, Billy shouted at the top of his lungs, "Kick, Serge! KICK!"

Serge closed the gap to three feet, then two—it was how they finished. Both boys dropped immediately to the grass on either side of Hammond Street—Jimmy flat on his face breathing raggedly, Serge slumped over, coughing.

Frank announced: "Winner is Jimmy McMullan!"

Sustained cheering. As the two women behind Billy were

leaving, one of them said to his face, "You should be ashamed of yourself."

An older man kneeled beside Jimmy, held his wrist; a heavy-set woman draped a purple cardigan over the his back and shoulders. Billy went over to Serge, sat with him, then helped him to his feet. "Come on, Serge, you have to keep moving."

Mr. Bumgardner singled Billy out as they passed. And he wasn't the only one to comment, to say something mean, spiteful, calling Billy "un-American." He was immensely relieved when they reached the cutoff on Hammond, then crossed Rt. 375 to Rowe's Lumber.

They shuffled along, passing the truck-parking area and entering the West Hurley woods. Serge's breathing was beginning to even out but he was wobbly, unsteady, and at one point he became dizzy and Billy kept him from falling into, of all places, the patch of lady slippers. At the oak lying across the trail, they stopped and rested.

"Who suggested...three miles anyway?" Serge said.

"You did."

"Once around...would've been...enough. I wasn't running...to win."

"By going twice around you almost did," Billy said.

"I heard you shout 'kick.' I didn't have anything left—"

"No, you made a move. I saw it."

They began walking again. Serge said, "Now we can...finish our important work, Billy. Of resuscitating...William D."

Chapter Eleven

Hedi put a fresh cup of coffee on the kitchen table for Jacob, who had just come in from his studio, serving it with a piece of her own freshly made strudel. Buck was sprawled on the roof of the coal-shed in the sun; you could see him through the window facing east, and Jacob had taken a chair facing west, away from the snoozing animal. He had already had a slice of strudel at breakfast; now it was time to have another piece as a late-morning snack. Hedi sat down with him, also with a coffee; she asked him how it was going.

"I'm having mixed feelings," he said.

"About?" She'd never known him not to have mixed feelings.

"I had an excellent session with Smiley last week—we get used to things. Familiarity is addictive, and breaking away isn't easy."

"You're talking about Reader's Digest," Hedi said.

"I am."

"Are you considering taking Wally up on his 'open door?'"

"Hedwig, there's no turning back. It's just difficult. I'm not doing well."

The kitchen door opened and Billy came in, limping, disheveled. "Oh, hi," he said, surprised to see his parents at the table.

"Hello, Billy," Hedi said. "How are you?"

"My knee is hurting, otherwise OK. It was a great run."

"Go wash up, I'll make you breakfast."

"You haven't had breakfast?" his father inquired.

"I was at school."

"Right, the big track event of the season," Jacob said.

Billy left the kitchen and Jacob said, "I hate when he walks in all scattered and frayed."

"The run was very important to Billy. He gave himself to it."

"West Hurley, by definition, is bad news."

"You keep saying that," Hedi said. "Rachel and Holly both got through and are doing well, and Mr. Marr is a good teacher."

"That's because they're both bright girls. It's not an environment conducive to intellectual growth."

"Be more grateful to Serge then," Hedi said. "Look at him as a balance—"

"Serge is an entirely different problem. I think he's 'that way,'" Jacob said quietly, "and all the time they spend together—"

Billy crossed to the table and pulled out a chair; before he sat down, Jacob said, "Who won?"

"Jimmy."

"Did Serge drop out?"

"No. Two feet was between them at the finish."

"Serge is heavy in the ass. That's hard to believe."

"He had a good trainer," Hedi put in.

"How many people showed up?" Jacob asked.

"I wasn't paying attention. Maybe ten."

"Was anyone for Serge?"

"No."

"Just you, right? Pull up your pant leg."

"Dad, I'm OK."

"Pull it up."

Billy tugged his pant leg up and Jacob had a close look. "Hedwig, this isn't good. It has to be thoroughly cleaned and bandaged. My brother Donald almost died from sepsis."

Jacob excused himself to Hedi and went out.

She brought a plate of French toast to the table with butter and maple syrup, then poured a glass of milk and set it down. "Eat slowly," she said.

****

He stayed off his leg the rest of the day and on Sunday went to church with his mother and sisters and made himself remember what the Gospel and sermon were about— in case his father decided to have another church quiz at breakfast. After Mass, Dom Santarelli came up to Billy and said the kids were calling him a turncoat.

"Fred Longo seen yez on Bluestone Road—Serge running, you on your bike. You told Jimmy that Serge wasn't training, you lied to his face."

"OK," Billy said.

"I can't trust you no longer," Dom said. "You'd rat on me if the city got to poking around as to who was borrowing Gus Wilbraham's boat."

"I wouldn't."

"You bullshitted Jimmy. Right now you're bullshitting me. If we're a team, you have to have confidence in each other! After what you went and did, my confidence in you is shot."

"Then go fishing by yourself," Billy said.

"It's a goddamn good thing Jimmy won, that's what I'm saying."

As a precaution, Hedi kept him home on Monday. A fight she and Rachel were having woke him; it was always over Andy. Wanting to see him more. Not wanting to come home so early. Hedi was strict, and she didn't like when Rachel talked back. Billy read the National Anthem over and over, all four stanzas. He loved how Bzy gave him a few words in a prompt sitting there in the field and how the line then came to him. He was beginning to like the memorization part of the regimen. After a while he went downstairs. The house had an empty feel. His mother was likely sorting through clothing for the Library Fair later in the summer. Billy cut a piece of bread and sat at the table with a glass of milk and a jar of strawberry jam. Holly was the only one who routinely went with their mother to pick strawberries in a special meadow on Bagovitch's property. Rachel had never done it and he'd gone along a couple of times. Hedi had scolded him for his method of saving one strawberry and eating one; his new method became saving two, eating one. How red your fingers got! There wasn't anything better than his mother's wild strawberry jam. Billy was already thinking of a second go-around when he noticed the message. He reached across the table; when he picked it up, a quarter lay there.

"Billy, get a bunch of rhubarb from Buford, also a head of lettuce. Home by noon. Mother."

It wasn't an emergency but with National Anthem stanzas clattering around in his head he was glad having something to do. Billy finished his snack, rinsed his hands at the sink, and went out. Buck was lying on the rickety back terrace. Dog tagging along, Billy crossed Harlan's Field diagonally and cut over to Bluestone Road, soon turning onto Stage Door. Buford was working his garden at the far end, near his house.

Billy had a wonderful feeling in his heart, and also a sadness, for Buford. As to how he had happened to come to the Maverick. Billy knew the story, or at least the part of it that most people knew— Stuart Farr and his wife Lucille, a writer and a painter, driving north on a lonely stretch of road in Virginia in bright daylight. A negro, about 40, walking along, an all but empty pack on his back. Stuart looking at Lucille, who was driving. She braked and Stuart asked the man where he was going.

"Jus goin'."

"How long you been walking?"

"Cupla days."

"We're going to an art colony in upstate New York. Hop in."

His name was Buford Williams and he'd ridden with Stuart and Lucile all the way to the colony and Bearcamp, Harlan's house. Harlan asked Buford what his interests were, and he said gardening and Harlan said he could stay in the colony if he made and cultivated a vegetable garden for the artists who lived there. He could sell produce to the artists and keep whatever money he took in. There was a piece of land at the foot of Stage Door Road. Fresh cold water at the pump. As for a place to stay, he would leave that up to Buford. The houses in the colony were spoken for. Did he understand?

Yes, sir.

You don't have to say 'sir,' Buford. We're all one and the same

73

in the Maverick. Do you have any questions?

He had asked if there was a shovel he could use until he could get one.

There was, and other tools also; and the next day Buford started clearing the land on the south side of Stage Door Road ...thirteen years ago.

"Mr. Billy," he was saying, bone and gristle, not an ounce of fat on him. Graying hair, crudely cut.

"Buford, how are you?"

"I's doin' jus fine, not gettin' any younger."

"Do you have any rhubarb?"

"Jus comin' in."

"Good, and a head of lettuce."

Buford went to get the produce and Billy took a look at the house. It was small, about the size of Harlan's, but where Harlan's house was open, little more than a shelter, Buford's was a box tightly sealed. Billy's father didn't like how it squatted there for people to see when they came to the colony for a play or a concert or to visit a friend. A tarpapered hovel gave the wrong message to anyone coming to the Maverick Art Colony. Billy had to admit it was hard to praise Buford's place but there was a mystery to it that kept him guessing, wondering. How could a man who lived so crudely create a garden brimming with color and health and goodness and make a fence from felled trees and cut branches linked wondrously together, strong, no nails, and could salute you in the morning with a hoe raised high?

"At's fifteen cents. Tell your mama strawberries 'nuther week."

"What's better than rhubarb and strawberry pie, Buford?"

"Dat's easy, Mr. Billy. A second slice uv it."

Billy put the dime in his pocket and Buford went back to work.

He continued on Stage Door to the theater but Bzy wasn't around and he continued on Maverick past the concert hall, stopping at the sharp turn. Right here was where the old trapper had come out of the woods, Harlan had said. There had to be some mark, some indication, that this was the start of his trail—or the end of it. Billy started down Maverick Road. In an oak a gray squirrel scurried on a branch and jumped to a hickory, and soon after another followed. He took interest; if you hunted it was important to size up where game was moving before a season began; then file it away. Good advice from Dom. Long before a season began, you had to start noticing, watching; it paid off.

Billy caught a glimpse of the Maverick Horse, then saw a faint column of smoke rising nearby. Billy drew closer; it was Harlan, kneeling at a small fire.

"Harlan!"

Getting stiffly to his feet, "Billy."

"You're back for the summer."

"More or less," Harlan said.

"I saw Chips doing some work on your house," Billy said.

"It's a wonder it stays up at all." Harlan added a few sticks to the fire. "Billy, I'm going to brew up a pot of coffee. Will you stay?"

"Next time. You just got back," Billy said, sensing his old friend was tired.

****

On Tuesday morning he walked to school with Serge. It was almost as if nothing had happened, but Billy knew no one would ever again tell Serge that the only distance he'd ever run was the distance to the outhouse. For all the shouting and names and frenzy, no one much cared who'd won or who'd lost; likely, Billy thought, because Jimmy had won. At recess he'd even seen the two talking together. Clarence Bumgardner wasn't coming around. On more than one occasion he'd caught Billy's eye with looks of out-and-out contempt.

Donny Osterhoudt brought a new baseball to school on Wednesday, shiny leather with handsome red stitching. The school district did nothing by way of supplying sports equipment. Billy had brought in the last ball and they'd played with it until the cover fell off. Frank Santarelli took the ball home and black-taped it but after a week it was no longer round. And now Billy, on the final day on the disabled list, sitting on a bench near the swing set, was trying not to think about the joy of playing with a crisp new ball. Who should come wandering up but li'l Jill in a jonquil yellow dress and shoes with silver buckles wanting to know why he was sitting all by his lonely. He was looking awfully sad, did he want company?

Sure, why not? How's the knee? she asked, sitting next to him. Getting better, he said, his mind on the game. Donny had got on base on a throwing error and Frank Santarelli was coming up. Li'l Jill said she'd had a dream about Billy last night, did he want to hear it? OK.

"You were on School Field," she said, "playing baseball, and I was telling you I could put magic in your bat."

"How?"

Clarence made a pitch and Frank Santarelli hit a grass-burner to Norman Wheat at second base. Donny was running in from third base and Norman's throw—

"I was so disappointed," li'l Jill said.

—was high. Donny scored.

"About what?"

"You wouldn't let me hold your bat," li'l Jill said.

"Well, I'm sorry," Billy said.

Mr. Marr rang his bell and Donny Osterhoudt came over, telling Billy that the father and son had come back but Champ was unruly as all hell, in other words, being himself. Man and boy drove off in a huff.

"What's next?" Billy said.

"Another man is coming."

"Just a man, no kids?"

"It's worrisome," Donny said.

****

The block and tackle, lying on the ground outside Quarryman, had two saucer-sized sheaves inside two hardwood housings and yards and yards of tangled rope. Mr. Rustovsky helped untangle the tackle, then threaded it over and around each sheave. He'd come out of his studio to lend a hand and, with Buck looking on— not a problem—set the apparatus up. With four strands of rope in play the user had a 4-1 mechanical advantage. He had on white pants spattered with paint, and a dark-green loose-fitting smock; he smelled of linseed oil and turpentine. He was a big man, solidly built, with a thick beard, and what Billy noticed in him particularly was an overall calm. Mr. Rustovsky, on his knees as he set the block and tackle up, twice reached out to pat Buck, as if it were important to him that Billy's dog feel included in the endeavor.

"Now the thing is," he said, in something of a huddle with the two boys, in an accent that wasn't German or Italian but, if Billy had to guess, was Russian, "the thing is to transport this to William D. as a unit, that is, not to mess it up. Sergei, you take the front block, I'll take the back, and Billy, you tackle the middle."

It wasn't an easy job. Billy found himself hefting a good bit of rope on his shoulders. It was smelly and harsh, scraping his neck and his arms. They trudged as a team toward the quarry, then detoured to the left. Mr. Rustovsky asked Billy how he was doing.

"OK."

"Sergei?"

"I'd rather run three miles."

"Not far now," Mr. Rustovsky said.

The last effort was getting the block and tackle into the cab. Once it was in, but not hooked up to perform a task, Mr. Rustovsky told the boys they were on their own. He clambered down from the crane and took the path back to the house.

"So, let's do it," Serge said.

Each block had a steel hook on it. They fastened one hook to the flywheel, the other hook to a solid section of the jib some ten feet away. Serge gave the flywheel bearings an extra squirt of penetrating oil for good measure. "Now we pull," he said.

They picked up the loose end of the tackle and drew it taut; the sheaves responded. "Are you ready, Billy?"

"I'm ready."

"Okay, pull!"

They pulled, and tugged, and heaved.

"Pull, Billy!"

"Jesus Christ, I'm pulling!"

"Pull harder!"

"You pull harder!"

Then something seemed to give, not all at once but slowly, as if the rope was rubber and they were stretching it. They took a step back, still holding on—except now the tackle was slack.

"We did it!" Serge sang out.

At the start, the block was hooked to the top of the flywheel. Still hooked, it was now two-thirds of the way down. Excited by the results, Billy suggested they give it another go. They re-latched the housing, Serge gave the bearing a new squirt, and they tugged again. This time the flywheel gave way readily and they could even move it, not easily, by arm-power alone.

They sat on the cab floor, legs over the side. "You know, if my dad wins the contract, we'll be moving to San Francisco," Serge said.

"You told me."

"We're not under the gun yet, but we have to make progress fast."

"Can't he paint the mural here?"

"Doing a mural is like building a bridge. You have to be on site."

"I want your father to win but I don't want you moving."

"You'd have to take over the William D. project."

"Serge, you're joking, right?"

"It's called stepping up, Billy," Serge said.

****

They were in the meadow at the base of Ohayo, facing each other sitting cross-legged, and Billy was trying to get through the third stanza of the National Anthem. Prompting him as needed, Bzy had *Famous American Documents* open across her knees and thighs.

"OK, take it from: 'No refuge could save— '" she said.

"'No refuge could save the hireling and slave/From the terror of flight or the—'" Billy hesitated, pushed his fingers against his forehead.

"'—gloom of—'" Bzy put in.

"'—gloom of the grave. And the star-spangled banner in triumph doth wave/O'er the land of the free and the home of the brave.'"

Bzy said with a happy clap of her hand, "Now the fourth stanza."

"I only know a little bit of it."

"Say what you can."

Billy spent a few seconds bringing the lines into his mind. Then he said, "'Oh thus be it ever, when freemen shall stand/Between their—'"

"'—loved home and the —'"

"'—war's desolation!/Blessed with victory and peace— '"

Bzy was right there. "—may the heaven-rescued land/Praise the power—'"

"'—that hath made and preserved us a nation!' That's as far as I got," Billy said.

"One day you'll tread the boards, your name in lights, Billy." Bzy closed the book. "Tomorrow we'll have the entire National Anthem in the can."

"What kind of can?"

"It's production talk. When a film's ready to roll, it's 'in the can.'"

"Starring Bzy Littlebird and Billy Darden," Billy said.

"In a new movie called 'Oh Say Can You See?'"

"I was thinking, 'Dawn's Early Light,'" Billy said.

"l like it. It has intrigue to it, mystery." She asked him what was next on his "regimen."

"Reading. Books my father calls classics; and a written report on each one."

She gave her head a sympathetic shake. "He never lets up, does he?"

"It doesn't seem that way."

They sat in the meadow in the quiet of a Maverick afternoon. Both pigtails were falling forward over Bzy's shoulders. She brought up what he'd said earlier about a certain trail that only one man had ever walked. "We've talked enough about it," she said. "Let's just do it. Billy."

"Your mother would have something to say."

"Mia lets me do anything," Bzy said. "Almost."

A cloud passed over the sun; the shadow fell over her face like the thinnest of veils. He reached out and took hold of a pigtail.

Chapter Twelve

Tired of resuscitating the work of lazy, self-satisfied writers, Jacob set aside an article he was editing in his Bluestone studio. If he knew anything about writing, and he knew a great deal, it was that too many writers were so caught up in the importance of their work that they refused to edit it in any way. Editing destroyed the freshness, the truth of a book, they argued. How words sprang from a writer's pen was the heart speaking, and editing the heart verged on blasphemy. Harlan Gray didn't believe in editing. Once you've written a page, leave it alone. Jacob had read Harlan's four novels, all published under the aegis of the Maverick Press. His best-known, *Ebbtide,* cried out for an editor's hand. Jacob had struggled to get through it and, in places, had actually skipped.

But enough. Harlan was a pure, generous spirit, and Jacob felt guilty about judging him, or his work. The man was beyond criticism, and he had brought Jacob to the Maverick. Jacob pushed back his chair and went out. As was his custom on Saturday morning, he drove into Woodstock to pick up a copy of the Times. He remembered how, not that many years ago, he would swing by the house of Anita Hairston, a bosomy potter who lived on lower Byrdcliffe Road, to have a cup of coffee, admire her latest efforts, then do a little creative molding of his own.

As Jacob motored along, thoughts continued to crowd his mind on leaving Reader's Digest and the option Wally had given him if he were to change his mind. Jacob had no intentions of taking him up on the "open door" but was grateful nonetheless to have it. On his own, he had made the decision to leave Reader's Digest just as he had walked out on Columbia as an instructor of literature and had settled, instead, with his new wife in the Maverick Art Colony. Thomas Wolfe's novel, *You Can't Go Home Again,* had expressed the impossibility of going back to an earlier time; and now—it really wasn't so but the feelings were similar—he and Hedwig were going home again, starting life anew after years with the Digest; anew in the sense that he was giving up his day job with full intention of finishing his novel on the Catholic Church. He'd written over a hundred pages of *The Red Hat,* here and in New York, but to take it on fulltime with no backup money? He wasn't brimming with confidence.

At Blatz's, Jacob turned onto Rt. 375, passed the nine-hole Woodstock Golf Course, then crossed Sawkill Creek on his way into the village. He was looking forward to spending more time with his family, especially with Billy, whom he had simply ignored as a child. It wasn't until one wintry day four years ago that Jacob had suddenly become aware of him as a living, breathing individual, a boy—seeing him with his sisters and another girl playing with paper dolls in front of the fireplace. Jacob called him over, telling him that girls played with paper dolls, boys went out and split logs. That spring Jacob tossed a baseball with his son for the first time, then set to work with Billy's help transforming a ragged, adjacent parcel of Maverick land into an athletic field. Occasionally Billy would have a friend over, and now and then the two, father and son, would throw a ball on Harlan's Field; but to Jacob it was always an attempt to make up for lost time. The important childhood years had passed. He had never had time for Billy.

Jacob drove up Mill Hill Street to the village green. Woodstock had become, through the years, an important, well-known art center. It had galleries, a couple of good restaurants and bars—his favorite, the Irvington Inn, was the choice watering hole of Woodstock artists and writers. But Woodstock didn't become an art colony on its own. It was a sleepy Dutch village of farmers, tanners, and quarriers; it was Byrdcliffe, a crafts and arts colony in the hills above the village, founded by Richard Whiteley, a wealthy Englishman, in 1901, that lighted an artistic fire in Woodstock and the Maverick. Once caught, it had never stopped burning...

Jacob parked his car and got out. The Roll of Honor stood on the village green and, by the names of two local boy, Oscar Stanhope and Thomas Bell, gold stars shone. The News Shop was just across the street. To its left was the Woodstock Post Office; to the right, Mower's Grocery.

Entering the News Shop, Jacob picked up the New York Times and a copy of the Woodstock Record. Jacob also bought a pack of Old Gold cigarettes. Back in the car he headed out of the village, slowing as a woman ran across the street from Pepper's Garage, her thumb out. Jacob's side window was down and, braking, he asked her where she was going.

"Maverick Art Colony."

"Hop in." He tossed the newspapers onto the back seat.

"Thanks." She had soft-falling light-brown hair, had on tan pants, a loose-fitting navy shirt, and a pair of black-rimmed sun glasses.

"Car problems?"

"Problems on top of problems," she said. "I'm afraid it's on its last legs."

"Chris Piper's a good mechanic," he said, continuing down Mill Hill. "And reasonable. What are you doing in the Maverick Art Colony?"

"I'm with the Bunker Hill Players, here for the summer."

"What with the war and all, talk had it that the Maverick Theater wouldn't open this year," Jacob said. "The country has gone on a different footing, a war mentality is setting in. And here you are. I'm delighted."

"It was big talk with us too," she said, "but in times like these, theater is more important than ever."

"Very true, "Jacob said. "What plays will you be doing?"

"We're starting with 'Boy Meets Girl.' It was on Broadway in 1935—"

"I saw it with Joyce Arling."

"As 'Susie.' I'm rehearsing for the part now. Are you in the colony?"

"I was, twelve years ago. When we started having children, we had to move."

"You're an artist," she said.

"Writer. But for the past dozen years I've worked for Reader's Digest. Right now I'm in the process of leaving."

"Then what will you be doing?"

"Finishing a novel I started some years ago."

"Do you have a name for it?"

"*The Red Hat.*"

"In a nutshell, what's it about?"

"The rise of a parish priest in the Catholic Church to the rank of cardinal."

"Sounds intriguing. I'll look for it."

"It's going very slowly but thank you."

"What's your name?" she asked.

"Jacob Darden. And you are—?"

"Mia Littlebird."

"Where are you staying in the Maverick?"

"In Canal Boat."

They were passing Mr. Bagovitch's house and she asked him what he knew about the diving platform and murky, sand-fringed pond. She loved swimming and wondered if it was open for business.

"Yes—for turtles, frogs and muskrats," Jacob said.

"How about back then?"

"He was asking a fifty-cent entrance fee per person. At the end of the second season—in the midst of the Depression—the Maverick Beach went under."

Just before turning onto Maverick Road, planning to take Mia to Canal Boat, he pointed to a white house with a terrace and a lawn. "That's my place."

"It's lovely." Then, after a moment, "Is your son's name Billy?"

"Yes."

"He was the first person we met," Mia said. "He directed us to Canal Boat, then helped us unload the car. Bzy, my daughter, was worried about spending the summer here. No longer."

"I'm delighted to hear it."

Jacob shifted to low gear on the upgrade on Maverick, gave the car gas, rear wheels shooting back stones and dirt. Mia Littlebird was a superbly attractive woman. Summers were long. They jounced past the Concert Hall.

"Where can I let you off, Mia? Theater or Canal Boat?"

"Theater. Please."

Jacob braked to a stop just shy of the stage door, saying he was looking forward to her performance.

"I hope you'll be able to make it," she said. She took off her shades. Her eyes were the deep blue of a mountain lake. "Thanks for the lift."

"It was my pleasure, Mia."

She mounted the stairs; he felt a stirring in his body, a heat-rush, then tapped his horn and drove on.

****

Jacob glanced at the lead story in the Times—Soviet Forces Launch Counter-Offensive, Stop a Powerful Nazi Thrust. It was amazing to Jacob how Germany had signed a treaty with Russia and then both had invaded Poland to start the war. The two nations were as one in Hitler's battle against the West. And now, a year and a half after America had entered the war, Russia was dealing Germany crippling blows. As if Russia and America were suddenly the best of friends. For now, Jacob was trying to perceive how it would all settle down. He couldn't envision Stalin and Roosevelt seeing eye-to-eye when it came to treaty or resolution.

A knock on his door. "Come in!"

Billy had *Famous American Documents* in his hand; he set it on his father's desk. "Go ahead," Jacob said, opening the book.

His son began; halfway through the third stanza he needed a prompt. Jacob got him going again, and Billy skipped along surprisingly well.

"Sit, down," his father said. "Well done, you got your teeth into it."

He pulled out the chair. "Bzy's been helping me."

"She lives in Canal Boat, you said?"

84

"Yes, with her mother."

"Is her father around?"

"He was killed in a car crash in Colorado."

"How long ago?"

"Last year. I have to run," Billy said. "We're going on a hike."

"Anywhere special?"

"There's a trail on Ohayo Mountain I'm looking for."

Billy went out. His son fresh in his mind, Jacob reflected on his session with Smiley Blandon Thursday. He surprised himself by admitting—out loud—that for the first ten years of Billy's life he had hardly known the boy existed. The child might have lived elsewhere for all Jacob knew or cared.

The therapist said, "What was a skinny five-year-old kid going to do for your image?"

"I'm afraid to say, not very much."

"Wouldn't a father want to hug his son on occasion or nibble his ear, out of simple love?"

"You would think so."

Smiley Blandon kept on. "Take Hedwig. At the Breakers in Palm Beach, did she shine for you, reflect on you so as to enhance your persona?"

"Not really."

"Jacob, how she dressed, how she entered a room without causing a single head to turn, rankled you in no small way. Do you see a pattern here?"

"I'm a difficult man to please."

The therapist pushed on. "Let's talk about the hang-up you have with your 'half-Jewish' side."

"Smiley, what can I say? Who doesn't have idiosyncrasies?"

"I don't think it's idiosyncratic. Does your 'Jewish side' interfere with your daily life?"

"It's there. I don't like it."

"So you look at yourself the way you look at Hedwig and Billy."

"When I see a deformed person in an Automat, I either walk out or sit at a distant table."

"Is a deformed person going to hurt you in some way?"

"Yes, by making me feel uneasy."

"How old was Billy when your brother Charles sent him a football outfit?"

They had talked about it once before, on an earlier visit, and Jacob didn't want to rehash the incident; it was too fraught with misgivings. "Dr. Blandon, we've been through that—"

"Fine. We'll go over it again. How old was Billy at the time?"

"Eight or nine."

"Your artist neighbor said he'd like to paint Billy in his new togs, as I recall."

"Yes."

"What happened?"

"He painted Billy."

"Jacob, what happened?"

"The football pants were too long. The protection panels, meant to cover the thighs, covered Billy's knees and part of his shins. There was something cartoonish about the painting."

"Keep on," Dr. Blandon said.

"I talked to Wes Jamison about it," Jacob said. "He argued in defense of the work. It's who Billy is; it's the charm and honesty of the painting. He's a young boy! True, but I wanted the painting to give Billy a little stature, at least." Jacob paused; his left eye was twitching. "We were in Wes's Maverick studio," he went on. "I held a handy sketch pad against the portrait, blocking out everything from the bottom of the thigh panels to the floor. With that part gone, a viewer would picture the boy as having longer legs. I told the artist I wanted him to cut the painting. He didn't say it was ethically wrong but deep down he didn't want to do it. I just wanted my son to look like a normal kid, not a shrimp in a football suit. I added fifty dollars to the established four hundred. Everyone in the Maverick Art Colony was living hand-to-mouth. Wes hesitated a second, then traced a line straight across, picked up a scissors, and cut off the lower part of the canvas."

"Which contained—?" Smiley queried.

"It improved the painting!"

"Answer the question, Jacob."

"The boy's legs."

"The *boy's* legs?"

"My son's legs."

"That does it for today, Jacob," Smiley Blandon said.

Chapter Thirteen

In loose-fitting tan pants rolled two or three times at the cuff, a long-sleeved blue shirt, calf-height stockings and sneakers, Bzy was ready to go—her rucksack packed with sandwiches and other necessary items—when Billy arrived at Canal Boat. As prearranged, he would carry it up the mountain; she on the way back down. He slipped the rucksack on, gave his shoulders a twist to settle it, and they began walking, Buck tagging along. Whether they would see him again, Billy couldn't say; the dog had a way of running off on his own and showing up eventually, who knew when?

Bzy gave him an affectionate pat. Then to Billy, "How did the National Anthem go?"

"My father only had to give me two prompts."

"Wonderful!"

They walked on Maverick Road the full breadth of the art colony, passing the theater and concert hall; where it turned and sloped downward, they stopped. "This is where Harlan saw the trapper coming out of the woods," Billy said. "If there's a trail, we'll find it up here."

"Let's go," Bzy said. "Come on, Buck."

They pushed into the thick underbrush that lined the road. Once through, they sized up the land before them—steep, rocky, uneven, thick with trees and bushes—and began climbing, clambering over rocks, grabbing hold of a branch or sapling and pulling themselves up. Billy all the while searching for a trail, a small pile of stones, a slash in the bark of a tree. He was in the lead but she wasn't simply stepping in his tracks. She was a great scrambler, for all he knew a more accomplished hiker than he was. Billy held a branch for her and she passed through before he let it go.

"How you doing, Bzy?"

"So far, so good. How about you?"

"It's a tough climb."

She was standing close; he smoothed away little beads of sweat above her eyebrows with his sleeve. They moved on, at various times having to lean into the mountain using their hands. Ahead of them loomed a ridge, a huge rock outcropping. Because there was no way they could scale it, they circled it. When they reached the top of the ridge, they stopped and looked back. A great body of water, the Ashokan Reservoir, glimmered in the sun. The slope seemed to be getting sharper, and almost at every step they had to grab hold of a tree or a branch and pull themselves up. It was slow going, they'd been at it for two hours, and Billy began thinking his direction was off. He checked his compass and said they should veer slightly north. Otherwise they'd get to the top only to realize they'd missed the cabin. It also came to Billy that it was unlikely the old trapper used the face of Ohayo in leaving and returning to his cabin except in rare instance; it was too unfriendly a trek.

They continued the hike. At one point Bzy slipped and fell and he had the scare that she might slide and tumble a good way down the mountain. She got right up, rubbed her knee, and kept on. At the base of a rocky ledge Billy noticed a spring hidden in a small grove of laurel. Time for a break. Billy shed the rucksack and they sat, bracing their feet against a boulder. Billy asked her if her knee was hurting.

"No, it's nothing. Let's have a cookie."

They munched on a chocolate chip, taking turns drinking water from the spring. A hawk swooping in low, "Kree! Kree!"

"He's telling us something," Billy said.

"What?"

"'Keep going.'"

Billy checked his compass, estimating they should veer a bit more to the north. He shouldered the pack and they started in. He began seriously to consider that their hike was really more of a climb, an ascent. At the three-hour mark Billy seemed to think they were at a place that had the look, the feel of a trail. He didn't know why; the going was still steep and rocky but you didn't feel you were working your way along, step by step. Someone had walked here. Before them was another cliff, larger than any they had already faced; perhaps fifty feet above it, instead of more rocky mountainside, was bright air. Sky. The sky! A kind of natural ramp ran along the face of the cliff. They were both weary, and the ramp was probably a mirage; half-expecting it to vanish, they went toward it.

It wasn't a mirage at all but good solid ground . They followed it to the top and then were standing on a plateau covered with deep yellow grass. A large oak tree grew on it, and on the far side of the tree...stood the log cabin.

"Billy, we made it!" She gave him a big congratulatory hug.

They walked through the grass. The cabin, worn, weathered, didn't give the appearance of a rundown, abandoned place. It had a narrow front porch with a rustic bench on it and a gabled roof with an overhang. Single window, oak door, heavy strap hinges, a wrought-iron latch but no lock.

"Is anyone here, do you think?" Bzy said.

"We'll find out."

Billy looked in the window. Individual panes were coated with grime, and the glare of the sun didn't help; he only saw a vague interior. He knocked on the door, waited, then pressed the thumb latch. The door swung easily and they went in. The room had a stone fireplace, a table not much larger than a checkerboard, and two chairs; also a window in the far wall and a loft with a ladder leading up to it.

"Billy, it's wonderful!" Bzy said.

"Luck was on our side getting here."

"No way luck! My father used to say hiking a trail is one thing, forging one is something else. We forged a trail, Billy."

"Your dad would be proud of you, Bzy."

"He'd be proud of us."

They had lunch, peanut butter and jelly sandwiches and a small thermos of milk, on the porch bench. Then they went out to the long grass and sat in it, talked for a minute or two, then lay down and soon nodded off; when they awoke the sun was falling, almost behind Ohayo and the plateau lay in early shadow. Time to go. But first Billy said they should circle the cabin. You always saw a lot of stuff behind houses. Ten feet separated the back wall from the last, final rise of the mountain. Looking up, Billy spotted an animal on the branch of a pine, size of a small cat, with a long brown tail, rich fur, sharp little ears. He had never seen a marten, except in books. He gave Bzy a tug on her sleeve, pointed it out. Startled, the marten scurried away. A slanted roof attached to the back wall protected a worktable with cedar legs. A half-dozen old steel traps hung from rusty nails. He wanted to take one down and examine it, an Oneida long-spring 1½ — fox, raccoon, beaver.

They rounded the cabin and came out on the grassy plateau. Billy wasn't looking forward to the rough, downhill trek to Maverick Road; you were more likely to fall going down than trudging up. Bzy shouldered the rucksack and, on the porch, Billy pushed the door tightly shut. He looked at both ends of the plateau—the end where they had first set foot, then the north end somewhat closer to the cabin. Something about it—the woods weren't as closed in, for one; and he recognized what had the appearance of a trail, comparable to the trail he and Serge took to West Hurley.

"Bzy," he said, "we're going to try a different way off the mountain.

"Good."

They began walking, taking the new route, soon coming to an open area roughly the size of a tennis court. It had no trees on it, no growth of any kind. It was an expanse of whitish-gray stone with gentle dips in it, as if scooped by a giant spoon, and the hollows contained pools of water. Billy took Bzy's hand and they walked onto the hard surface. He kneeled and dipped his hand into one of the pools. The water, soft to the touch, had no taste to it and was oddly warm.

91

"This is very weird," he said to Bzy.

"What would you call it?"

"A warm, underground spring—I'm guessing."

She kneeled beside him and put her hand in the water. "This is a beautiful place, so mysterious."

They continued walking. The wood trail ran along the top of Ohayo and seemed to have a small downhill slant or pitch, and Billy thought they should follow it. The mountain paralleled Bluestone Road, so they were never going to be totally lost, no matter what. Still, Billy hoped they were on a good path. Soon they came to another plateau thick with yellow grass, a meadow, much like the meadow at the cabin. They were walking along in a kind of magical, ethereal place, so opposite to their climb. A stand of pines bordered the trail to the west, so dense it seemed a fortress; inside it would be like night, Billy was thinking. Just then he stopped. Something was moving inside; by the sound of it, a large, heavy, restless animal

"Oh, boy," Billy said, his heart pounding.

"What is it?" Bzy asked, moving closer to him.

"Don't know."

The only animal Billy could think of was a bear. A big black bear was in the woods fifty feet away. You didn't want to run from a bear; it would chase you and catch you and then you'd be in serious trouble. Bzy was grabbing hold of his arm.

"Billy, I'm frightened."

"Me too."

"Let's run."

He put his arms around her just as an animal burst from the thick pines and came into the open, snorting loudly. To Billy's great relief and excitement, it was a pony, Donny Osterhoudt's bay pony. He stood there, eyeing the two kids, snorting. Billy thought he'd run and then he ran—oh God did he ever!—long black tail flying.

"Billy, he's beautiful!" Bzy cried out.

"That's my friend's pony, Champ."

"What's he doing way up here in the mountain?"

"He runs free. Donny's father wants to sell him."

"Why?"

"Champ isn't manageable, and he wants his money back."

As they continued walking, Billy came to realize that the land was all part of the Osterhoudt upper pasture and, sooner or later, they would come to the gate on Bluestone Road. Until then, they still had to make decisions; there was no direct path. They wandered into a mountain pasture, rich in grass, then through a stand of hardwoods that came out to a surprisingly level section of land. Lying in it were crisscrossed piles of old timber. Someone, Billy found himself thinking, had once entertained the idea of building something here.

"I think we're getting close," Billy said.

Sure enough, 200 yards ahead was the fence to the mountain pasture; on the far side of it was Bluestone Road.

Chapter Fourteen

A breeze smelling of the lilac bushes in the backyard rippled through the open kitchen windows. Hedi ran her iron over Holly's daffodil dress, then a pair of Billy's pants, then one of Jacob's country shirts — a country shirt was a city shirt he no longer wore in the city. It was very pleasant ironing in an open window. She could hardly imagine what Biskupitz was like now with Germany engaged in a life and death struggle...and her family once again going through hell. It had been weeks and weeks since she had heard anything and what was there to hear in any case? A young American poet and university instructor had sat her on a sand dune and said he wanted to marry her. To this day, it came across as a dream. Hedi ironed her husband's undershirt and set it, with other items, on the countertop.

Buck got up from his morning nap on the back terrace and gave a bark. Looking out the window, Hedi saw Raphael Hagar, the sculptor, striding across Harlan's Field—big shoulders, powerful arms, with dark, tangled hair and a mat of hair on his chest. He always came to the house via the back door, not because he was servile; he didn't want anyone to know his business, though his business with Hedi was always the same. What might she give him by way of food and clothing? A tired pair of Jacob's socks perhaps. He was wearing the brown cotton sweater she'd given him two years ago, now with a hole in the left elbow. Hedi turned off her iron and put a kettle on the range.

At the knock, "Come in."

"Hedi," he said, opening the door, "good morning. My pot sprang a leak. I was hoping you might have an extra one somewhere."

He spoke with a middle-European accent and Hedi found him charming, if something of a pest. His real name was Aznavour Harjinian. Born in Armenia, he had served in the cavalry and had won medals defending the Armenian border against marauding Cossacks. But he had no plans or desire to remain a soldier. He followed his family to Istanbul where he began sculpting. How he got to America and found himself living, first in the Midwest and then in the Maverick Art Colony—always scraping by—Hedi had never fully comprehended. The only man Hedi knew who was more idiosyncratic than Raphael Hagar was her husband.

"Is it a pot you want or a sauce pan?"

He shrugged his shoulders. "Don't know."

"How many handles does it have?"

"Two. One on each side."

"That's a pot. I think I have one," Hedi said.

She rummaged through a cupboard next to the refrigerator, came out with an enamel ten-quart item she hadn't used in years. In good shape, hated giving it up. "How's this?"

"It pleases my eye, Hedi. Very nice." He sniffed the air. "Do I smell...bread?"

"Raphael, you know very well it is." She had just baked it.

"Might a poor sculptor have a slice?"

She took a loaf from the breadbox, cut two modest slices, wrapped them in waxed paper and put them in the pot. Raphael Hagar was smiling. "Thank you, Hedi. Jacob doesn't know what a good woman he has."

"I believe he does," she said; but, her thought went on, he takes her for granted. "How's your work coming along, Raph?"

"I've just started a new piece of black walnut. The grain on it is the nicest I've ever seen."

"Then you're set for the summer."

"Partly set."

"Everyone knows your work is your life, Raphael."

"It's a long day, Hedi." He paused for a moment, then, moving closer, kissed her cheek as was his custom. His lips seemed ever closer to hers each time; then he went out.

She watched him go across Harlan's Field clutching his pot. He may have simplified his life but not out of ignorance. She remembered in the early days how diligently Jacob sat at his old Corona working on an article, a short story, so absorbed in his work as to block out the real world—her view of the real world. He was determined to make a success of *his* world and, by it, support his family. It wasn't easy. Once, when they were down to their last ten dollars, a check for $50 came in the mail from Century Magazine for an article he'd written. Hedi sat there thinking he would rejoice...and he had cried. Her husband had cried. Maybe she could help, in some way lessen the burden. She could write a book about growing up in a coal-mining town during the Great War in Germany and coming to America and meeting Jacob Darden Jr. His proposal on the Green Harbor beach two years later, her absolute shock, the embarrassment of their wedding, the sickening patronization of her mother-in-law. First night with Jacob, en route to the Maverick Art Colony, in a Springfield, Massachusetts, hotel. On waking the following morning, going down to breakfast and, entering the crowded dining room, walking proudly to their table as if to let people know she was now a woman.

It could make a good story, Hedi thought, and bring in some money too; and, determined to write it, with Jacob seeing an editor in New York and Rachel asleep in her crib, Hedi had sat down at her kitchen table in Bird's Eye with lined paper and pencil and started writing slowly in English; choosing words, getting the right ones, was an effort. She wrote that on her third day in America, Aunt Agnes took her around looking for a job. A job? But she was in America to learn English! True, but she would have to work. In a factory that made galoshes, Aunt Agnes spoke to the manager in English. Later Hedi asked her aunt what she had said to the man when they had first walked in, and she answered in the language her niece understood. "I told him 'this is a German girl' so he wouldn't think you were ill-mannered for not talking."

Hedi went on writing the story of her life, all her memories, recollections. Jacob Darden Jr., how she was secretly in love with him. Mrs. Darden worked Hedi so hard that she got sick and had to rest in bed and, on payday at the end of the month, Mrs. Darden docked her for her down time: four days and a small part of a fifth— Mrs. Darden called it five. The proposal on the beach, the Maverick Art Colony, Bird's Eye, her first house, the birth of Rachel. That was as far as Hedi could go. She saw herself in four or five years writing a sequel, and then another one after that, maybe three volumes altogether.

Hedi put down the pencil. Done. Her life up to the moment. She even wrote "The End" at the bottom of the last page, then went to the beginning and printed in the title, "German Girl." But something wasn't adding up. After all the writing and all those years, she only had... four pages? Four pages wasn't a book!

She laughed, now, at her naiveté back then, though Hedi knew she was far from worldly or sophisticated today. People took with them through life what they were as kids, and what Hedi was in her "Biskupitz days" wasn't that much. Seven years of school. She was smart, she knew that; quick with numbers, with language, always one of the brightest in her classes. But with a "Great War" going on, that was as far as she got. The whole point of life, back then, was to stay alive. She trusted she'd grown in her years as Jacob's wife; she knew she had; but deep down she wasn't so sure. The braided rugs she made were an avocation learned from her mother. Throwing away a piece of clothing was verboten in Germany, and she felt the same way living here. She was working on a rug now on the sunroom table, making inch-wide strips of material from an old pair of gray flannel trousers that Jacob hadn't worn in years. The gray would go nicely with the sections of red from a coat—

The phone rang. Hedi set down her needle and thread on the braided rug lying on the sunroom table and went into the kitchen, unhooking the wall phone by the refrigerator. It was Jacob, calling midweek to see how she was doing. She always wished she had something exciting to tell him but apart from the children and the house, that was about it. He was working on his last piece for

Reader's Digest, he said, and he could hardly wait to get it all behind him so he could get down to the serious business of working on his novel fulltime, and finishing it.

"That's wonderful."

"The pages are rough. My typing is abominable."

"You'll be pushing right along with it in no time," she said.

"Something makes me think I jumped ship too soon."

"Jacob, it's something you had to do, and you did it."

"True. But I'm glad Wally kept the door open—"

"Don't talk like that, Jacob."

Later that afternoon she heard an easy-sounding knock at the front door. Hedi set down the material and went out to see who was stopping by. To her delight it was Julia Jamison, a Maverick artist in her own right and now pregnant, asking if she could use the phone. Something important had come up and she wanted to call her family in Carlisle

"By all means, Julia."

"I'll only be a minute."

"Please, don't rush."

While Julia spoke on the phone, Hedi went into the living room. Earlier she had noticed that the painting of Billy was slightly tilted. She righted it, remembering when the package had arrived from Uncle Chick in Boston. Inside was a complete junior-sized outfit— helmet, pants with thigh protection, shoulder pads, a red jersey with striped sleeves. Billy, nine at the time, was eager to put it on. There was, however, a problem. The shoulder pads. Did they go under the jersey or on top of it? Hedi didn't know. Billy seemed to think *under* but he wasn't sure. His father wasn't home. Who else was there? That was easy—Maverick artist Wes Jamison, a former halfback at Dartmouth.

"They go under, Billy," Jamison said when Billy came over that same afternoon. He helped the boy with the pads, then with the jersey. "Destined for gridiron fame," the painter said. Then he told Billy to come back in the next couple of days in the whole outfit. "Tell your mom and dad that I want to do a painting of you."

Julia came in from the kitchen with fifty cents in her hand but Hedi wouldn't think of taking it. She made tea and they sat at the glass-topped table on the terrace. Julia had a way of dressing and carrying herself that Hedi admired, casual but sophisticated—a look Hedi could only wish she had. As if one could learn, or buy, class. Julia had a sip of tea and came out with the news: the twenty-three sketches Wes had made for the Rincon post office mural were chosen. "He's one of the finalists."

Hedi was so happy for Julia and Wesley that tears came to her eyes. "How wonderful!"

"We have no right to celebrate at this stage," Julia said, "but I couldn't keep it in."

"When will you know?"

"Two of the three judges are Woodstock artists. The third is in California. It could be anytime."

"Who's the other finalist?"

"We're hearing it's Leo Rustovsky."

Hedi saw an impending fight, the taking of sides. Too close to home. "Julia, how can this be? The judges, and now the artists. It's a national competition, right?"

"Sponsored by the U.S. Treasury Department," Julia said.

"Then why is it all coming down to Woodstock and the Maverick? Like competition for a local show. It doesn't make sense."

"Do you know what the answer is? Wes and I have talked about it," Julia said. "Woodstock and the Maverick are the center of art in the country. It's not surprising at all."

Hedi smiled, her eyes going to her friend's middle. Julia was beginning to show. About this same time last year, she'd been pregnant but had had a miscarriage. Possibly from lugging around and setting up a cumbersome easel at the Cayuga Quarry, where she'd done a series of plein air paintings. This time, doctor's orders, Julia Jamison wasn't lifting anything heavier than a quart of milk.

"We're with you all the way," Hedi said. "Would you move?"

"If Wes wins, we'd have to."

After a moment, Hedi said, "Changes are coming for us also. Jacob is leaving Reader's Digest."

"Really?"

"He didn't come to the Maverick Art Colony to spend his life editing in New York," Hedi said.

"It's hard walking away from a good job," Julia said. "What will he be doing?"

"Working on a novel he'd started years ago in Bird's Eye."

"On the parish priest?"

"Yes."

Julia stayed for another fifteen minutes, then left, and Hedi took the tray inside, remembering how, unlike others in the Maverick Art Colony and in Woodstock, Wes and Julia had never judged Jacob, had never cast aspersions on him for taking a job with the Reader's Digest, unlike so many others who were quick to say that Jacob Darden had sold out to a conservative magazine. Harlan had stayed above it. With two sons of his own, now full-grown men living in the south and mid-west, he understood that art took a backseat to survival. Many artists Hedi had known through the years had chosen not to have children. Why? They were costly; also, they took up time.

Hedi removed the tea leaf holder but didn't empty the pot. Often she would talk with Holly when she came in from school and could warm the tea in a saucepan. Recently Holly had told her mother that boys weren't paying attention to her. And she didn't think it was just because of her braces. Wait and see what happens when they're removed, Hedi had said. But she knew the feeling; she'd lived it as a girl in Germany. What boys were in Biskupitz to start with? Then, lo and behold, a coal-miner's son began looking at Hedwig. Heini Schnitzler wasn't someone she would choose, given the privilege of choosing, which she didn't have living in Biskupitz. Better to settle than live the life of an old maid. She and Heini had kissed and that was the extent of it. No matter how hard he scrubbed his hands and face, he could never completely wash away the coal. They became engaged. About that time, her aunt, Agnes Danzinger, sent Hedi a letter from Boston where she lived, inviting Hedwig to visit—and to learn English while at it. Agnes knew the invitation alone wasn't going to make it happen. Stowed in the same envelope as the letter was an actual ticket, paid for, sailing date and all. Who could say no? Big sendoff in Bremerhaven. Waving, hugs—come back soon. Heini on the pier, shouting as the ship pulled away, "Ich liebe dich, Hedwig!" Tears streaming down his coal-scarred face.

Hedi heard the sound of young footstep in the backyard; then the backdoor opened and her son walked in. "Hi, Mom."

"Billy, how was your day?"

"We were given a tour of the new school."

"Do you like it?"

"It has two classrooms, two honest-to-goodness bathrooms, one for boys, one for girls, new desks, and a music room/lunch room. Do you know what's different about the rooms?"

"Tell me." Hedi poured a glass of milk for her son, cut him a slice of bread.

"They don't have inkwells." He gave his hands a quick wash, dried them and sat at the table.

"That tells you how old the schoolhouse is," Hedi said.

"We don't even have that kind of pen anymore, do we?"

"Holly has a few, plus different points. And a bottle of India ink for drawing and printing," Hedi said. "As for the new school, your father saw the need for one several years ago when you were all going to West Hurley at the same time. He went to a school board meeting—"

"Dad went to a school board meeting?"

"It was the only one he ever attended," Hedi said. "He broached the topic of a new school and got into a heated debate, a fight, with the board chairman, Wolfgang Bumgardner. Some people who remembered the occasion were on the board when a new vote came up and passed years later—Mr. Bumgardner was no longer chairman—and your father was mentioned."

"I never knew that," Billy said. "Dom's dropping out. I mentioned the new school and said we'd be the first kids to graduate from it. He said he had better things to do."

Hedi smiled. "He was the cutest kid I ever saw when you were both in third grade. Remember your birthday party here?"

He knew the story; it was a good one. "Tell it to me again, Mom."

"I was in the kitchen and he came in. It was a rainy day and you and the other kids were in the living room playing Pin The Tail on The Donkey. Dom, I said, what can I do for you? He wanted to know when the party was going to start. Why Dom, I said, the party has already started. He said, then where's the ice cream and cake?"

Mother and son laughed. "Julia Jamison was here earlier," Hedi said. "She wanted to use the phone—big news to tell her mother. It reminded me of the time she'd called home to say she was pregnant, the same excitement on her face. After making the call, she told me Wes was a finalist in a government competition, biggest award ever offered an artist."

"I hope he wins."

"I'm praying he wins," Hedi said. "Julia's having a baby, and the recognition after all these years for Wes. Plus the money."

"Who's the other artist?"

"It could be anyone who paints murals."

Murals? "Where would it be?"

"In a San Francisco post office," Hedi said.

He sat there staring at his mother.

"Are you all right, Billy?"

"Sure. Why?"

"You're looking at me as if—"

"No, I'm OK," he said.

Chapter Fifteen

In his Bluestone studio, Jacob was working on his novel, typing; trying to type. Fingers not only stiff, they were starting to ache. More x-outs on the page than words. He pushed on. Faulty key stroke, then another. "Son-of-a-bitch!"

What the hell was going on? Recalcitrant fingers could be bringing to an unceremonious halt his new drive to establish himself as a serious American novelist. Did anyone care? Besides him, besides Hedwig? No one was panting for a Jacob Darden novel after his first, *If Winter Comes,* took a few meager breaths and died. His father, of all people, might be disappointed. They spoke on the telephone maybe twice a year and Jacob Sr. always asked his eldest son how *The Red Hat* was coming along—when books and reading were not among his favorite interests. Jacob Jr. closed his eyes, recalling the lunch he'd had with his father a week before moving to the Maverick Art Colony with his 20-year-old bride. The two Jacobs walked into Cavanaugh's Bar & Grill, a popular businessman's restaurant on Tremont Street in Boston. Once they had settled down and ordered, Jacob Jr. told his father what was on his mind. He was leaving his teaching job at Columbia.

"Is that smart?"

"Probably not."

"Then why are you doing it, my son?"

"Because we're moving to an art colony in upstate New York."

Jacob Sr. wasn't impressed. "A teaching job at one of the great universities in the world, you're giving it up to go to an art colony?"

"I am, yes."

"What's behind it?"

"I'll be writing a book. I want the time."

"Is there any money in it?"

"There could be, down the road."

"What's it about?"

Jacob had never said "Catholic" in a talk with his father and had never envisioned himself doing it, but here he was doing it. "It's about a young priest in Boston who climbs through the ranks of the Catholic Church and becomes a cardinal."

As if his son had just nicked him, drawn blood, Jacob Sr. got to his feet ready to walk. "Is this why we're having lunch?"

"It's part of what I want to say, Father," Jacob replied. "Please, sit down."

Jacob Sr. waited a second before retaking his chair. Then he said, "All right. What is it?"

"I was twelve at the time," Jacob Jr. said, "you wrote me a letter asking me to worship with you in the synagogue. Do you remember that?"

"Yes. You wrote me back saying you had talked with your mother and she'd said absolutely not."

"You never mentioned it again but I had hurt you," Jacob Jr. went on. "More recently you asked me, your oldest son, to take over the family business once I'd finished college. I wasn't cut out to run a business, I told you. I had ambitions to be a writer. Again I let you down. Now I'm about to start a new life and I want to make amends. I'm offering you an apology."

"You want my blessing," Jacob Sr. said.

In truth, he hadn't thought of it, but he would like his father's blessing. "Yes."

Jacob Sr. gave his son a slow, unwavering look. "Convince me."

"Excuse me?"

"That you want my blessing,"

"I've apologized."

"Apologies are cheap, Jacob."

Jacob Jr. couldn't think of anything to offer, and Jacob Sr. started talking about the line of women's cosmetics his company had recently taken on, in addition to the ever-growing floral business. "Lillian's Non-Smear Lipsticks are outselling Revlon in Boston," he said. "Our Petal Smooth Face Powder is flying off the shelf in Filene's."

Jacob Jr. said he was glad to hear it; he had hardly heard a word.

"Well, this has been very nice," Jacob Sr. said, pushing aside his coffee cup. "I wish you luck in this...this art colony you're going to."

"Thank you, Father." It wasn't a blessing, pointedly made clear.

"And how is my dear Hedwig?"

"She's fine. She's a good wife and a good mother."

"A man can't ask for much more, can he? And that fine son of yours, oh how he loves to fish!"

"He got it from you, father."

The older Darden smiled. Jacob Jr. signaled for a check, sat quietly with his father before it came. In one of his favorite lines in the *Odyssey*: "Few sons are like their fathers. Generally they are worse, but just a few are better," Jacob Jr., by dint of his education, scholarship, intellect, choice of career, had always put himself among the few who were better. His father was a Russian immigrant with five years of grade school, a Jewish merchant in the floral business in Boston. But always in the back of Junior's mind was doubt; he might very well belong with the majority of sons *worse* than their fathers. Ralph Waldo Emerson said it better than anyone when he wrote that *character is higher than intellect.* Jacob didn't want his father's blessing... he needed it.

A thought flashed across his mind as Jr. and Sr. were ending their lunch. Before the thought slipped away, Jacob Jr. said, "When I first got the idea for the novel I was telling you about, I thought of making Stephen's father—Stephen is the priest, the future cardinal—I planned on making his father a good-natured trolley-car operator, loves his pub, loves Ireland, Catholic through and through, family name Cavanaugh, like our restaurant. Now I see Stephen in a way that will make it a better story, a more truthful story— mother and children on one side, father on the other side.

105

It was how we lived as a family, father. I see Stephen's father as a Jewish businessman, a dealer in dry goods, definitely not Cavanaugh. One of his sons becomes a priest. He rises in the church to the rank of cardinal, one step from pope. Think of your son John, my brother John, as a cardinal and you're his father. You're not boastful but you're proud."

"Stephen's father is a Jew, is that what you're saying?"

"Yes, his father is a Jew."

"His wife, is she religious?"

"She's a devout Catholic."

"You'll put that in your book?"

"I will. That's my pledge to you, Father."

Jacob Sr.'s deep brown eyes brightened; his smile had a thin, vindictive edge to it. Then he said, "The agent at Ellis Island threw 'Darden' at me. It's what he got out of Dardonavitz. Maybe he thought to make me a Christian!"

Outside on the street Jacob Sr. said, "I hope your book makes a lot of money, Jacob. You have my blessing." Reaching up, he put his hand gently on his son's head and kissed his face.

****

Jacob pulled a page of *The Red Hat* from his typewriter; riddled as it was with typos and x-outs, it was hardly worth keeping, but he decided to keep it on the hope that somewhere on it was one good sentence at least. But the ordeal was enough to make him contemplate calling Wally at Reader's Digest and asking if the door was still open. The security of having a commercial enterprise behind you, of taking care of you when you took ill—if, say, an arthritic malady was rendering you impotent in your chosen endeavor—was difficult to deny.

Jacob clutched his black Royal typewriter as if to take it up in his arm and bash it against the wall of his studio. This was destiny's way of saying he was facing failure as a writer; and the notion, the idea of it, was unbearable.

To get his mind off so rueful a thought, Jacob picked up the copy of the Woodstock Record he'd bought that morning. He breezed through a story on improvements made to the Art Students League building on Rt. 211; on the year-in, year-out fight to create a sewage system in the village; on a local boy, Robert Blackman, KHS graduate, killed in the battle of the Solomon Island; on a KKK attack on the Bearsville Flats that had horrified the community, the second attack in recent years. Then Jacob came to the article on the national mural competition he especially wanted to see. Two local artists named as finalists in a government program, Leonid Rustovsky and Wesley Jamison. He didn't know Rustovsky's work, only that he was a serious artist and politically leaned far left, if he wasn't an actual member of the Communist Party. As for Wes, Jacob knew of no finer painter in the Maverick and in Woodstock. No one was more dedicated to his work than his dear friend, Wesley Jamison.

Today's entry in Barbara Ann's column "In & Around" was called "West Hurley." Why she should write a column on the town, Jacob couldn't imagine. In his opinion, the Reservoir Commission of New York City should have paid off residents and shop keepers of the original town and then opened the floodgates. Goodbye West Hurley. But no. City workers around 1910 had picked up the town, house by house, brick by brick, and replanted it on the east side of Rt. 28. Since then, what other newsworthy event had ever happened in West Hurley? Aside from the fact that a new schoolhouse was opening in the fall. Jacob was proud of the part he had played in bringing the stingy, archly conservative local government to the realization that, moan as it might, a new school was absolutely necessary.

Jacob began reading Barbara Ann's piece. On West Hurley yet. He smiled inwardly; this had to be good.

"On Saturday morning, April 24, two eighth-grade schoolboys toed a chalk line on Hammond Street in West Hurley. Jimmy McMullan had challenged Serge Rustovsky to a 'distance run' of approximately three miles—"

Jacob resettled himself in his chair, picked the paper up, read quickly. Some 75 people, adults outnumbering kids. Serge's father, artist, born in Russia. Rustovsky family lives in Maverick Art Colony. Cries of "Commie!" and "Go back to Russia!" directed at Serge in the run. Seventh-grader Billy Darden comes to Serge's defense, shouts "Kick!" Billy's father, an editor at Reader's Digest—

Jacob snatched up the newspaper, strode across the lawn, pushed through the sentry-box hall into the house. He tossed the paper onto the coffee table, snatched bugle off brass hook, and went outside to the terrace. Feet planted firmly, he pressed the chromed mouthpiece to his lips—

"What are you doing,?" Hedi had come out of the house and was staring at her husband.

"I'm calling Billy in."

"Why?"

"Read Barbara Ann."

"Tell me what he did, Jacob."

"He lied to us last week, saying ten people were at the run in West Hurley. Barbara Ann puts the number at seventy-five." He lifted the bugle. "But that's the least of it. Read her piece!"

"Come inside."

"Goddammit, Hedwig. Let me handle this!"

"You're hurting the boy, Jacob."

"I'm teaching him there's a cost to irresponsible behavior!"

"Please, put the horn down. I'll read the story."

Swearing under his breath, he went into the house. Hedi sat on the sofa, taking her time getting through "West Hurley." Jacob paced in front of the fireplace. Finally she finished. "She commends Billy for standing up to the crowd. That should make you proud of him."

"It's not why I want to see him, Hedwig."

"I see nothing here to take offence at."

Jacob had high respect for Hedwig's intelligence, but when she crossed him on certain issues, he saw her as unsophisticated, unworldly. "Anything in print form that mentions the 'Reader's Digest' gets sent to Pleasantville," he replied. "I remember when the policy first started. Wally doesn't see all scans; pertinent ones go directly to his desk. This one—"

"And he'll call to say how happy he was reading about Billy."

"Hedwig," Jacob said, "I can guarantee you it's not what he'll say. An art colony forever linked with the left is the core of Barbara Ann's column. Russian-born painter Leonid Rustovsky is mentioned in it. A Communist. It's what comes across. His son is best friends with Billy Darden, the son of a Reader's Digest editor. What's Wally going to think when he sees this or hears about it? His whole career is based on American exceptionalism, on defeating Communism. He might re-think the special pension he gave his former editor—"

"I disagree. And you're too quick to blame Billy," Hedi said.

"Yelling at Serge to kick was wrong. I told him to his face, don't do it!"

"He's still a kid, Jacob. You expect too much."

"What, to obey his father?"

Glancing up, Jacob glimpsed activity on the lawn where it abutted with Harlan's Field. His son was coming home. Running from the backyard to greet him was the much-maligned Buck. To Hedi: "Billy is here."

"You can put the bugle away," she said.

"He's still going to hear from me."

"Just not now, Jacob. Please."

****

Rachel was spending the afternoon and evening with her boyfriend in Big Bear, much to Jacob's displeasure. He liked the notion of men going off to war, carrying a special memory with them; it was customary in every land, in every age. He just didn't want it happening with his daughter and her boyfriend. He had seen her running out to Andy's shiny blue car at three o'clock; that they were going to go to bed together, that she would give herself to Andy Sickler, stabbed at Jacob's heart; and, as he sat down to Sunday afternoon dinner with his family *minus Rachel*, he was uncomfortably preoccupied.

They were having roasted chicken with gravy, sweet potatoes and spinach. Jacob, separated from wife and children by a Maginot Line of butter, salt, pepper, cruets, wine glass, was talking about the disappointment and tension Julia and Wesley Jamison were going through waiting to hear who had won the San Francisco award. Jacob had stopped into the Irvington Inn yesterday afternoon to get the drift of the competition. Patrons were talking as much about the oddity of two painters in the same obscure art colony as finalists in a winner-take-all government prize...as they were about the painters themselves. Jacob seemed to gather that Wes had a larger number of supporters, and Ed Harrigan, blustery blowhard with the big droopy mustache, was solidly for Wes. What it comes down to, Harrigan said, is the judges. Two of the three are local artists! Who are *they* for?

"This morning when I went for the papers," Jacob said to his family, whose lovely daughter *will not give herself to Andy Sickler,* "people were talking in the News Shop on the same topic: Jamison vs. Rustovsky. Holly, anything to say?"

She had no idea what Mr. Rustovsky's paintings were like; she could only go by what she thought of Wes, and she thought he was wonderful.

"Billy, any comments?" Jacob said, his part in Barbara Ann's column still unmentioned; but the day wasn't over.

"I know one of Mr. Rustovsky's paintings. It's about making bricks on the Hudson. It's great."

"That's your opinion. What do you base that on?"

"It was my impression."

"Fine, but specifically what did you like in the painting?"

"It has a lot of life in it."

"Workers, common people, is a big theme in Russia," Jacob said, "all pulling together for the common good."

"OK."

Jacob objected to his son's "OK" but wasn't going to call him on it. "Who are you for?"

"I want Wes to win," Billy said.

"Just like you wanted Serge to win the race in West Hurley."

"I was his trainer. Of course I wanted him to win."

"Didn't I tell you not to mention—?"

Peach upside down cake, coffee, an Old Gold; after three puffs nicely drowned in his saucer. "Billy," Jacob said, "I've thought of a book I want you to read instead of *Robinson Crusoe* for next week. Put Defoe's novel aside for now. Meet me in the library in ten minutes."

****

The library in the house was next to the living room. Two ceiling-high shelves on either side of a large window through which you had a straight-on view of Mount Overlook. An upright Baldwin piano stood against one wall, two easy chairs with accompanying lamps guarded the bookcases, and a narrow sleigh bed with a navy blue spread hugged the east wall. The room had a quiet, private feel to it. Jacob sat in one of the chairs and Billy in the other. The door leading to the living room was closed. Jacob had a newspaper in his hand and he told Billy that he wanted him to read an article by Barbara Ann Bullock.

Billy breezed through it.

"Why did you tell your mother and me that maybe ten kids and a few grownups were at the run, when Barbara Ann puts the number at closer to seventy."

"Maybe I miscounted."

"Don't be snide with me, Billy! You didn't miscount. You lied."

"I wasn't thinking."

"Were people saying mean things to Serge?"

"They were."

"Now, the main point. Did you shout at Serge to kick?"

"I did."

Jacob said, "I told you to keep your relationship as Serge's trainer to yourself. Do you remember that?"

"Sort of."

"Sort of, kind of— it's what I said! And you acknowledged. Then you go and shout it to the world."

"I shouted at Serge."

"And everyone heard."

"Everyone who was there heard," Billy came back. "Is that important?"

"Yes. It's very important," Jacob said. "There's a larger picture here than meets the eye."

"Dad, I wanted Serge to win! He didn't win but I wanted him to. We didn't miss a day of training—"

"Billy, let's stay focused," Jacob said. "Because of your ill-delivered outburst, my pension from Reader's Digest, uniquely crafted for me, might be thrown out."

"I don't see why."

"Then listen, and I'll tell why," Jacob said. "Yelling at Serge to kick put me in a terrible light, politically. Serge's father is a Communist. Whether he's a card-carrying member of the Party, I don't know. But for all intents and purposes he's a Communist. In the next issue of Reader's Digest there's a story of a match between an American soldier and a Japanese jujitsu champion. I was instrumental in bringing it to Wally's attention and edited the piece for publication. If the jujitsu champion had won, would Reader's Digest be running the story?"

"I don't see why not."

"You do see, you just don't want to say," Jacob said. "In microcosm it's what we just had in West Hurley. The good guy and the bad guy. Of those two, who won the race—say in Mr. Dupree's opinion?"

"In his opinion, the good guy."

"And Jacob Darden's son is rooting for the jujitsu champion," Jacob said. "Reader's Digest has a clipping service. Whatever is written about the magazine is picked up and goes to Pleasantville, and certain clips go straight to Wally's desk. Like this one. He hates Communism so strongly that he supports Hitler—privately—because the Fuhrer is doing what Wally would like to do: wipe Communism off the map. And here Jacob Darden's son is backing a young Bolshevik against an All-American boy. Do you see the ramifications of that?"

Jacob pressed his hands together. "Billy," he said, "enlightenment always seems to hover over you, as if finally to settle in, but then passes on. I'm your father and you went over my head. I told you not to broadcast your relationship with Serge but you went ahead and broadcasted it...at my expense! Perhaps I should say, the Darden family's expense. My retirement plan might be sitting in Wally's wastepaper basket as we speak!"

He paused, winded, as from a run of his own. "I'm assigning you a novel that speaks to the issue of duty, responsibility and punishment, and the price a young man pays for problematic, irresponsible, if not blockheaded behavior. His name happens to be Billy, the main character in Herman Melville's novel, *Billy Budd*. We'll discuss it next week. Do you have anything to say?"

Billy's eyes were stinging. "Serge hadn't missed a single day in training. He cared, he worked, how could I not cheer for him as his trainer? I did nothing wrong!"

"Billy Budd didn't think he'd done anything wrong either," Jacob Darden said, "but Captain Veer thought differently and punished him." He pulled a small volume from his bookshelf. "Read this. We'll have a good discussion on whether the punishment was just or unjust."

****

Rachel and Andy got out of his pickup and sat on a rustic bench looking at and listening to the brook that ran behind his cabin. Rachel loved the sound a brook made running over rocks. As a girl of seven, eight, and nine, she was always looking for streamlets in the Maverick Art Colony to sit at and, if the water wasn't flowing freely, to clear away impeding twigs and leaves. She imagined herself an Indian maiden with acorn-colored skin and dark hair whose job was to keep streams gurgling.

Andy kissed her lips quietly. They had never gone past second base and here they were at his log cabin free to go all the way. They weren't married, weren't engaged even. Rachel didn't want him coming on too strong, too fast, and at the same time she wanted to get it over with so they could relax for the rest of the evening. Going to bed with Andy was definitely preoccupying her. They had gone together for almost a year and a half and she felt obliged to come across before he went off to war, to give him something he could take with him. It was the least a girl could do. They had talked about it and the absolute need for him to take precautions. Rachel didn't pay that close attention but she was probably in the "dangerous" part of the month. It was the least a girl could do.

They kept sitting by the brook and he asked her if she'd like a beer. She didn't like beer but she said sure; he went to his truck and came back with two bottles of Schlitz. They clinked bottles and he started talking about the future, which Rachel interpreted to mean *their* future. He owned twenty-three acres of land with the headwaters of Esopus Creek on it, prime fly-fishing water. When the war was over, he was planning on building a central meeting place for sportsmen and women with cabins to stay in and the finest equipment—rods, rifles, ammo, camping gear, outdoor clothing—to rent or sell. He was planning to build a house for himself and Rachel with a big fireplace and a cast-iron wood-burning furnace. They had enough firewood to last them a lifetime.

By then Rachel would likely be halfway through college. It was the only part of her life with Andy that they had never really talked about—her desire to continue her education. Now the country was at war and he was going away to punish the Japanese for their sneak attack on Pearl Harbor. Everything was on hold, and Rachel, in a way, was glad of it. Glad she didn't have to commit herself. She loved Andy. He was kind, responsible, loving, and good-looking too. But as to the life he wanted to lead, centered around hunting, fishing, and the hamlet of Big Bear (pop. 191), she couldn't resign herself to it. She wanted to go on to college and that really didn't fit in with how he saw life when he returned from the war. Marriage, family, Saturday night in the Borealis sitting at the bar. Rachel didn't know and she wasn't going to dwell on it at this stage of her life. He kissed her again, longer...and she participated, she wasn't doing him any favors. On the next kiss, his hand went to her waist and moved up a little, stopping as it hit the side of her breast, then slowly up and over.

"Let's go inside," Rachel said.

He used the bathroom first. When Rachel finished washing up, Andy was already in bed, lying on his side, a smile of adoration on his face as she came in. She took off her clothes, left them on a chair, and slid in beside him. They kissed, caressed each other, spoke endearingly. Then it was time, and what Rachel saw, what she glimpsed as he drew closer, caused her body to stiffen, her eyes to open wide in disbelief.

"Andy, stop."

"Why?"

"You have no protection!"

"Rachel, we love each other. What difference—?"

"You gave me your word!"

He didn't listen; he moved in. She was crying now, screaming. "No, stop!"

"I love you, Rachel."

Her right leg was relatively free, and, bringing it back, thrust out violently, catching him, where she didn't know. He cried out, lurched off the bed, disappeared into the bathroom. Still frantic, Rachel pulled on her clothes, didn't know whether to run out into the night, or sit and wait. She waited. The bathroom door opened and Andy came out, fully dressed.

"I'll drive you home."

"Thank you," Rachel said.

Chapter Sixteen

Trekking through the West Hurley Woods to school Monday morning, Serge was saying that spring had finally arrived. "The procreative urge is in high gear, Billy."

"The *what* urge?"

"It's means to renew, to give birth, to create life."

"Right."

"Guess what we have on the quarry pond?"

"Baby ducks."

"Seven of them, the size of tennis balls!" Serge said.

A doe and white-spotted fawn were moving quietly through the woods; at almost every step the newborn did a gleeful leap or jump. "Did you ever see anyone so delighted with himself as that little fellow?" Serge said.

"No."

"We should all learn to gambol," Serge said. "You're a good teacher, Billy. Say we were going to open a school for gamboling. How could we start?"

"What makes you think I'm a good teacher?"

"You've taught me stuff."

"What did I ever teach you, Serge?"

"Lady's slippers are wild orchids. All the different trees we have. Then all about muskrats."

"It's really important to know about muskrats," Billy said.

"Then perseverance," Serge said.

"How do you teach perseverance?"

"By example," Serge said. "You had me out there every day."

"I sat on a bicycle and you ran."

"I would've died if I hadn't run up and down Bluestone Road," Serge said.

They came to the fallen oak, negotiated it—first backing into it, then lifting legs and spinning around.

"Serge?" Billy said, when they were walking again.

"What?"

"Did you ever read a novel called *Billy Budd?*"

"I have. Why?"

"It's a reading assignment my father gave me."

"It's a damn good book."

"What's it's about?"

"An English sailor gets into trouble for insubordination."

"What's insubordination?"

"It means disrespect for authority."

"What happens to him?"

"Read the book and find out." Then, on a new topic, Serge said, "The judges are taking forever. It's painful waiting around."

It took Billy a second to zero in. Then he said, "It's a big decision they have to make."

"Whatever happens, let's make a pact, Billy," Serge said. "Whether it's my dad or Wes Jamison, we should congratulate each other and never say anything else."

"Fine. Break a leg."

"I see a Bzy influence there," Serge said. "Speaking of another pretty girl we know, what's with you and li'l Jill?"

"How do you mean?"

"What's she into?"

"Kissing."

"With the tongue?"

"*Kissing*, Serge. I didn't say licking!"

Up ahead two men were loading lumber onto a big orange truck.

****

At ten-minute morning recess that day, Billy saw Donny Osterhoudt standing at the bank of windows, and he went up to him. Two workers were building a stone platform about fifty feet from the main door of the new school. To Billy, it looked like the base for a flagpole. Donny clearly wasn't giving the new school much thought.

"What are you looking at, Donny?"

"Nothing."

"Any news on Champ?"

"It's making me sick, Billy."

"What's going on?"

"A man came by," Donny said.

"What did he say?"

"He didn't say anything. Champ wasn't there."

"Donny, what's going on?"

"My dad wants his money back," Donny said. "Pony's too ornery for kids."

"We know that," Billy said. "What did he pay for him?"

"A hundred bucks. But there are other people."

"What do you mean?"

"Who want the pony."

"Like who?"

"Don't make me spell it out, Billy."

"Just tell me!"

"Think of the business my father is in," Donny said.

"I am, but—"

"Ever hear of canned dog food?"

"Shut up, Donny! OK? Jesus Christ!"

"My father wants his money back, he don't care how he gets it. It's why I didn't bring Champ in," Donny said. "But there's more to it. Last year he kicked my father in the balls, damn near wrecked his sex life. Then he beat the shit out of Champ with a two by four, and Champ bit his ear, took a piece right out of it. You have to be ready."

"For what?"

"To rescue Champ."

"Me, rescue Champ?"

Donny looked at his pal, hand spread wide. "Who else is there, Billy?"

****

Putting aside obligations and chores when he got home—suddenly everything in his life was secondary to saving Champ—Billy went inside his house in the middle of a Hedi-Rachel fight, grabbed a carrot from the refrigerator, shoved it into his pocket and went back out; pedaled down Bluestone Road and parked his bike to one side of the weathered gate. Sliding a heavy timber from a slotted post allowed the gate to open; once inside, Billy slid the timber back, then walked into the Osterhoudt mountain pasture. It was hard, rocky terrain interspersed with areas of grass richly green and other areas of longer, softer grass. He moved along at a steady upward slant, here for the first time since his hike with Bzy. He didn't think Donny was playing him along, why would he, on something so serious? It was probably just how Donny's father saw it. Champ was too feisty for any responsible father to buy for his son or daughter, so what was left for Mr. Osterhoudt? Ponies made good horse meat.

Billy kept looking, alert to movement, sound. He may have been on a hunt; he was, for a bay pony. Come on, Champ. If you don't know what a carrot is, I'll introduce you to one. Come on now, show yourself. Where are you, Champ? The grade was getting sharper, pockets of grass smaller, woodland thicker. He pushed through a stand of hemlocks and came out onto a rocky, grassy patch the size of a baseball infield...and there he was. Billy stopped short and stood there, perfectly still, watching, wild horses stampeding in his chest.

In time—all living creatures know when they're being watched—Champ lifted his head and looked over. The pony didn't move and Billy didn't. He stood there looking at the pony and the pony at him. Billy took a step closer, then another, reaching out with the carrot. Champ snorted, tossed his head. Possibly he no longer saw the boy as a threat, was even getting to like him. He always seemed to have something in his hand good to eat...

"I have two friends," Billy said, "Betsy and Molly. Whenever Sherman visits, they turn on their own and come right in, knowing

119

they'll get a treat."

He took another easy step toward Champ. Pony gave his head a wild shake, a snort—then, at once, took off like a lightning streak. As for the carrot, Billy bit off a chunk and chewed on it. Very tasty.

****

He had a lawn to cut but now, with daylight lasting longer, he could put it off, even do it after supper. What he wanted to do was visit Harlan. They had chatted a few times but so far hadn't really talked. The Maverick founder was sitting in a chair outside his house engrossed in a book.

"Hello, Billy."

"You're reading. I'll come back."

"I'm leafing through a book I've read twenty times. Sit down."

"What is it?"

"Life in The Woods."

"I like the title," Billy said.

"Here, take a look."

Billy sat on a roughly assembled bench of sapling-sized branches. On the cover of the book: *Walden*; beneath it, *Life in The Woods*; beneath that, Henry David Thoreau; then the picture of a log cabin.

"This is really nice," Billy said, passing it back. "When did you buy this?"

"In an old bookstore in Cambridge when I was at Harvard." Harlan's chair was similarly made. He set the book down in a little table next to it. "What's going on?" he said.

"Serge and I are still working on the old crane. Mr. Rustovsky bought us a book on steam locomotion. It really helps."

"When I left last fall, I was wondering how far you'd get."

"We're getting ready to build up a head of steam," Billy said. "Not enough to get the crane running—more as a test."

"Best to do it on a rainy day," Harlan said.

"Chips said the same thing. He suggested we have a pail of water with us all the time."

"He's a smart man."

"Harlan, what's the difference between a suggestion and a demand?"

120

Harlan sat back a little, a smile coming to his lips. The boy liked baseball and hunting and tools but he was curious about ideas and liked words. "There's a world of difference between the two," Harlan said. "A demand has the feeling of an order. If an officer in the military gives an order, it's a demand and you'd better do it. Likely there's punishment involved if you refuse and do it halfheartedly. My father always suggested, but underneath you knew he meant what he was saying. It wasn't casual talk to ignore. It has to do with character. When Chips said don't light a fire in William D. unless it's raining, you know absolutely that he means it. People don't listen to demanding individuals, don't follow them. They scare others away. Demands aren't necessary; just believe in yourself and talk quietly."

"My father demands," Billy said.

"Jacob is a poet," Harlan said. "He gave up twelve years of his life to work for a magazine that has a view of life, politics, government, diametrically opposed to his view. Does he still have faith in himself? Those of us who remember the early Jacob Darden, hope so."

Harlan made to start a fire in the outside cooking place. When he got a little blaze going, he said to Billy, "But tell me about you. What's going on?"

He thought for a second, then said, "The other day Bzy and I went hiking on Ohayo Mountain. We started at the bend in Maverick where you saw the trapper come out. We went straight up. I was searching for a trail but didn't find one. Rocks and cliffs. Steep. It wasn't a hike, it was a training ground. Two and a half hours. Bzy is tough. She slipped once, I thought she might go rolling down the mountain. We were looking for the old trapper's cabin. By sheer luck we found it. We knocked, the door wasn't locked, and we went in."

Harlan Gray gave his hands a clap. "Billy, that is an adventure!"

"We looked around, saw some rusty old traps behind the cabin," Billy said. "I'd never seen a marten in the wild before. Then we spooked a big animal in a stand of pines. We were both terrified."

"I would think so," Harlan said, taken in. "What was it?"

"It was Donny Osterhoudt's Welsh pony."

121

****

Billy was finally getting around to finishing *Billy Budd, Sailor*. All in all, it was a pretty good story, confusing in places, as to why the master-at-arms of the British warship turns against the sailor, Billy, when everyone on the *HMS Belipotent* sang Billy's praises. Maybe it would become clear, Billy thought; he still had 23 pages to go. Trouble was, people were talking in the living room, it was almost ten o'clock, his eyes were getting heavy, and what made concentrating all the more difficult was he cared about what they were saying, a lot.

Every once in a while his father would speak up making another point for Wes. No one downstairs was against Wes but you knew a fight was on between the Maverick and Woodstock as to who would win the "Battle for San Francisco." Even now, as Billy lay in bed in his attic room, someone said "mortal combat." Whatever the outcome, lives would change; careers would either soar or sink. Billy marked the page in *Billy Budd* and closed the book.

Someone came back and said art and disappointment were inextricably linked. He didn't think either Wes or Leon would flounder if one or the other lost. A woman agreed; then a man said it all came down to politics anyway. If left to art and presentation Wes would win in a minute. Unfortunately Angus Beck, one of the judges, would likely be a swing vote, and Angus had strong leftist views...like Rustovsky. Paul Gerrard, as a judge, seems like a sure vote for Wes. For one they're close friends, and both are humanists, realists in the manner of Edward Hopper and Winslow Homer.

A new voice came in: That Beck is left-leaning doesn't necessarily put him in Rustovsky's corner. He doesn't paint at all like Rustovsky, whose work is more intellectual. Plus what in hell does Angus Beck know about murals? He doesn't have the faintest idea of what makes a mural, how a muralist thinks. How can he even be a judge? Art is art, whatever school! Beck is a good painter, highly regarded as head of the Art Students League in Woodstock. Politics gets in the way. Rustovsky doesn't come out and say he's a Communist; he doesn't have to. There's a third judge, don't forget, Virgil Armatov, a distinguished muralist, studied under Diego Rivera, and holds an important chair at Stanford. Here we go with politics again. Armatov is a Communist. There's no way he isn't going to vote for Rustovsky. Our only hope is Angus. Both he and Wes came to the Maverick at the same time. They started their professional careers in the Maverick. Had houses in the Colony. Wes is a solid liberal. Angus leans farther left but they speak the same language. What is Rustovsky to Angus? A fellow artist, all right. But what are the real ties? Don't tell me it's politics.

A new speaker: Beck has always been known as a social realist. Wes is a humanist, no one brings regional subjects to life like he does. They have a lot in common. We can cross off Virgil Armatov, a lost cause. A woman's voice: No problem with Paul Gerrard. I personally think Angus Beck will come over to Wes. How could he cast a vote for Rustovsky?

It went on for a good while; then voices quieted and pretty soon the Dutch door to the house opened; guests were leaving. Billy went back to reading, unsure, when he awoke, if he had finished. Facts and fiction were a huge jumble in his brain. The novel lay on the floor; he seemed to remember how it had slipped from his hands. Billy sat up, swung out his feet. He had a terrible crick in his neck.

****

In church the next morning Billy paid careful attention to the Gospel and the sermon, readying himself for the Sunday Breakfast Quiz. He was pretty sure he could handle any question his father might ask on the one or the other. After Mass, in the churchyard, li'l Jill reminded him of the roller skating party on Thursday. He had a date to sit with her on the bus. What with prepping William D. for the big day and going into the mountain pasture to see Champ and the homework his father had given him, his date with li'l Jill had slipped his mind.

"Right," he said. "Sure."

"I don't roller skate so well."

"Neither do I."

"Will you catch me if I take a spill?"

"I'll try."

Dom Santarelli ambled over. He told Billy he wanted to let bygones be bygones. It was a damn good race, he said. Serge showed he had a lot more spunk in him than people thought, and

Dom wasn't holding it against Billy for telling him to kick.

"OK."

"Bass are hitting like crazy," Dom said. "How's about later today?"

"Can't make it."

"Billy, you gotta break loose. Come on."

"Later this week sometime."

The congregation was splitting up; his mother and sisters were leaving. Li'l Jill said she'd see Billy tomorrow.

What was tomorrow? Then it came to him. School. "See you, li'l Jill."

****

Champ still hadn't let him get close enough to take a carrot from his hand; always at the last moment the pony would shy away; the carrot looked and smelled good but he wanted no part of Billy. Almost every day in school Donny Osterhoudt would mention Champ. At any hour the slaughterhouse crew might head into the mountain pasture with instructions to bring the pony in, dead or alive. Either way, he would be horsemeat soon enough. Three years ago Billy remembered playing with Donny in the pasture; one of the Osterhoudt cows had fallen and broken a front leg. Two men in a dirty red pickup came along. One of them was a hired hand with a sunken chest and bony fingers and the other, as Donny explained, was his mother's cousin, general handyman on the property and cleanup man in the slaughterhouse, Wilbur Quick. Basically, Donny said, his father kept Wilbur on the payroll as a "charity." He was a hopeless dimwit, kept referring to himself as "Wilbur he." They tied a rope to the cow's hind leg and dragged it out of the pasture and down Bluestone Road onto the long dusty road to the cinderblock building, and Donny said to Billy he had to come and watch. Billy didn't really want to but he found himself lassoed in. The men dragged the cow onto the wet concrete floor. The boys stood on the edge of the high-ceiling concrete room that smelled of blood and entrails and death. Billy felt sick to his stomach. Fastened to the ceiling was a winch with a thin cable hanging down. The second man fastened the cable to the cow's unbroken leg and got the winch going. It raised the cow with its head three feet from the floor and holding a knife with a glistening twelve-inch blade, the slaughterhouse hand sauntered up to the thrashing animal.

"Wilbur he cut the cow's throat, hanh?"

Chapter Seventeen

The phone in Jacob's 63rd Street New York office rang and Betty Trill, at her typing table, reached for the receiver on the main desk. "Good morning. Roving Editor, Reader's Digest."

She listened, scribbled a few words, then said, "Dr. Seymour, Mr. Darden is out of the office at the moment. Send your piece along, he'll give it a close and careful read...Two to three weeks... Yes... That is correct...Thank you for calling."

Betty made a detailed note of the talk and went back to her typewriter. Looking up from editing an article in the interviewing/socializing area of his office, Jacob gave her an appreciative look, smiling inwardly. Earlier that day she had come in at 8:50 with coffee and sweet rolls from a street-corner merchant. They had sat at the mosaic-topped coffee table. She had on a navy skirt and white blouse with sky-blue stitching at the collar and cuffs. Easy talk. How was the drive coming in from Morristown? Amazingly trouble-free. One fender-bender and a small tie-up at the tunnel. War news: Big Gains at Guadalcanal. Betty had an uncle, a Marine captain, who was in the thick of the war. But she and Jacob didn't linger over breakfast. The deadline for the next issue of the magazine was fast approaching.

Jacob returned to his edit of Prof. Stanley Davenport's article, How To Read a Book. Initially, Wally hadn't thought readers would be interested in the topic—too fussy, too academic; but when Jacob put a draft of it into his boss's hands, Wally found it interesting and enlightening. And humorous! Jacob should run with it. He had, and was all but finished rounding it into shape.

His telephone rang. He watched Betty swivel about to take the call....and found himself thinking back to her initial interview with him about a year ago, each in a club chair, sitting where he was now sitting. Elizabeth Trill was a smartly put together woman in her mid-forties. His former secretary, Gloria Smith, with a pear-shaped body, sometimes came to work with her hair in a net, which depressed him. The woman now sitting with him clearly cared for her appearance. She had dark-caramel hair in a pageboy cut, was wearing a sea-green dress loosely cinched, and had—by anyone who wasn't judging a woman's figure with the eyes of a model-agency manager—a lovely body. Just a guess: he seemed to feel she had just lost weight and was determined to keep it off. As for her education, she had gone to Morristown High, then to Bryn Mawr, graduated with a major in English and a minor in 'Piano Arts'—formal lessons, six hours of practice a week and year-end performances. In summer she'd worked at the library in Morristown and in her final year in high school at the library in Trenton. She loved books. After her marriage fell apart, she'd started a graduate course at NYU in Art History but dropped out halfway through, tired, emotionally exhausted: the horrors of the divorce were catching up with her. As for secretarial skills, she'd just finished a 12-week course at Gibbs, top of her class in short hand, typing, and dictation.

"I'm impressed," Jacob had said that day.

Her face had broken into an easy smile. He had asked her if she had any questions. She did. Was he married, where did he live, and did he have a family?

"I live in Woodstock, New York. I'm married and have three children, two girls and a boy."

"One more question," she said.

"Fire."

"Are you the author of a book on the conquistador, Hernando Cortez?"

Jacob sat back in his chair. "I am. How would you know of it?"

"My father, Michael Benitez, loved Spain; both his parents were from Barcelona. Sad to say, he died two years ago. He thought the world of your book, Mr. Darden. He kept it in his office bookshelf next to Hemingway's *Death In The Afternoon.*"

"That's nice company," Jacob said with a laugh.

"I can almost remember the title. It's from a poem—"

"A sonnet by John Keats," Jacob said, "'On First Looking Into Chapman's Homer.'"

Her eyes, an evocative greenish-gray, brightened. "*Stout Cortez!*"

"Now I'm doubly impressed, Elizabeth," he said.

She had asked him if he had written other books

"An early novel, *If Winter Comes.* Two books of poetry. Four years ago I did a monograph on James Joyce's *Finnegans Wake,* a novel no one reads, or reads through for its complexity of language. I'd done a master's degree thesis at Columbia on his earlier novel, *Ulysses:* a thesis much admired and often quoted to this day. So when the *Wake* came on the literary scene a few years ago, I immediately picked it up. I feel at home with Joyce's language. Most people are lost on the first page of *Finnegans Wake.* I can read it, not the way you'd read *Lord Jim* or *Grapes of Wrath,* but I understand it. Critics call Joyce's language gobbledygook. It's not. My monograph, called *Unlocking Finnegans Wake,* sold just over 300 copies. The reason was simple enough. People had limited or no interest in the novel. Why would they have interest in a book that was going to help them understand it?"

"They wouldn't."

"Right now I'm working on a novel," Jacob said.

"What you just said about Joyce is amazing," Elizabeth said. "As for *Ulysses,* it took me three starts before I finally finished it. What's your novel about?"

"It's the story of a priest who becomes a cardinal. Working title *The Red Hat.*"

"How's it going?"

"Not well. I'm determined to finish it, but at the rate I'm going, who knows when?" Jacob said, liking this woman, who seemed to have a fine literary sense, an appreciation of writing, of books. "If I ever have a free hour here in the office, I might pop into the bedroom, a.k.a. my studio; but mostly I write at home in upstate New York. You're from Morristown, New Jersey, I see."

"I was raised there," Elizabeth said. "After college I got a job with a major gallery and auction house in Manhattan and started going with an art dealer named Jonathan Hewett Trill III." She closed her eyes, holding them shut momentarily as if unhappy with an image, a time in her life, or just the name. "Jonathan didn't own the New York art world but he had played an important part in it. I was taken by the glitter, the lifestyle, the penthouse living on Central Park South. Jon got caught up in a nasty scandal over a Modigliani nude. I would have stood by him if there was something there to stand by. The superficiality of his life, of the man. I filed for divorce, wanting to make it short and sweet; it dragged on for almost three years. I was angry and disillusioned.

"I went home to stay with my mother. My father had died in a stupid ladder accident. Trying to free a branch from a power line at the house, he was dead before he hit the ground. My mother was devastated. I was there for her, she was there for me. It's now been another two years and I want to get out into the world again. Looking for a job is a way to start."

"I'm hoping your search has ended," Jacob said.

"I haven't had an offer yet."

"The roving editor of Reader's Digest will then make one," he said. "He would like you to work for him, Elizabeth."

She smiled generously. "Thank you. I accept."

"Terrific." Jacob put out his hand. She had a good firm grip.

"I have an immediate request," she said.

"Ask."

"Please call me 'Betty.' It's what I go by."

"Of course," he said. "I go by Jacob."

He came back to the present, cutting ten extraneous lines on Dr. Davenport's article in Modern Psychology, but again his mind returned to Betty...to her first weeks in the office. The copy from the Roving Editor's office got glowing reviews in Pleasantville. Rod Holloway called it "beautifully crisp" and a "delight to the eye," comments pleasing to Jacob's new secretary and Jacob too; but what had pleased him especially was the interest Betty continued having in his novel. He never wrote more than two or three pages during his week in New York. Betty typed them superbly, also any pages he gave her after a weekend at home. Wanting to have a fuller grasp of the story, she had asked if she could take the pages Gloria Smith had typed to Morristown for the weekend.

Of course she could.

She came in Monday morning saying that his novel-in-progress had knocked her off her feet.

"I hope you didn't get hurt."

"I'm recovering, not fully."

He remembered offering her a cup of coffee and some crumb cake. Betty was sitting in the maroon club chair when he went in. Breaking off bits of cake, sipping coffee, she brought up aspects of his novel she particularly liked, starting with the Rossel home life. Stephen Rossel is the oldest of eleven children. The mother's life revolves around her kids *and* the Catholic Church, not necessarily in that order. Milton Rossel is an immigrant from Russia, a dealer in imported fabrics.

"You do those scenes so well," Betty said. "I couldn't help thinking you took them from your own life."

"I did."

"In so 'Catholic' a novel, it was interesting to learn that Stephen Rossel's father is a Jewish immigrant," Betty said. "You don't come right out and say it but it's implied. He certainly isn't Irish Catholic. That makes Stephen, the young priest and future cardinal, half Jewish."

"Yes."

"What a new dimension that gives the story."

"I like to think so," Jacob said.

"But I wanted more," Betty said. "With all due respect, Jacob, I don't think the Jewish father theme is fully enough developed."

"I saw no need to hammer it home," Jacob said. "A careful reader will pick it up."

Betty had a last taste of coffee and went on talking about *The Red Hat* in positive terms. "So many beautiful scenes—like the poor, rundown parish near the Canadian border where newly ordained Stephen is sent to get it back on its feet, financially and spiritually. How well it's done. Stephen leaves a strong mark wherever he goes. The part about his unmanageable teen-aged sister who gets pregnant and runs away in shame and how her brother, a young priest, has to decide whom to save, the baby or his sister. Right there is the essence of Catholicism—how you handled it, Jacob, made me cry. Then the official trip to the Vatican. God, you have an eye! I spent ten days in Rome as a student. You know it like you know New York!"

"That's encouraging. I was never there."

"Jacob, of course you were. How else—?"

"By spending long afternoons in the New York Public Library," he said. "I have forty pages of notes on the Vatican, the ceremony of bestowing the red hat, the protocol of selecting a pope. Some places lend themselves to research, like the Vatican; other places you have to visit. Some years ago Wallace Dupree wanted a short piece on Harvard Square. What made it so special, so unique? An hour's research would suffice, right? No. I had to see for myself."

"But you didn't have to see the Vatican?"

"It wasn't necessary. You can fake the Vatican but you can't fake Harvard Square."

Betty laughed. The phone rang and she got to her feet, hurried over to take the call.

He sat there, thinking, reflecting. Maybe because Betty had just commented on a scene in his book where Catholic and Jew merge in the character of Stephen Rossel, a memory flickered through Jacob's mind. About three years ago he had applied for membership to the NYAC, well aware of its discriminatory policy. In an interview with three club members in charge of membership, Jacob answered their questions with pride. Birthplace, *Boston;* religion, *Roman Catholic;* mother's maiden name, *Flynn;* profession, *magazine editor at Reader's Digest;* references, *founder and editor of Reader's Digest, Wallis Dupree; the District Attorney of Manhattan, Franklin O'Hearn.* The membership committee, Messrs. Kelly, Martin, and McLaughlin nodded, shook Jacob's hand. He would be hearing shortly as to his application.

Club president Alexander D. Ryan—as a younger man, Ryan had run the mile in four minutes eleven seconds at Villanova and was the personification of the club's Winged Foot emblem—wrote Jacob a letter congratulating him on his acceptance with full privileges: solid citizen, strong sense of good American values. Code: no Jew in Jacob Darden. Since then, of an early evening, Jacob would walk into the club on Central Park South thinking to shoot a little pool, have a swim, sit down to a draft beer and a medium-rare porterhouse in the men's grill: a man at ease, comfortable in the environment. What wasn't there to like about the NYAC?

****

On average three times a week, usually in mid-afternoon, Jacob would say to Betty that he was going into the bedroom to work. At first she thought it was a euphemism, a way of saying "to take a nap," but then she would hear the clicking of his Smith-Corona portable. In time he would hand her a scruffy page, which she would then type (correcting typos in the process) and add to the pages his former secretary had already typed. Jacob wasn't setting any time record for writing a novel, that was becoming painfully clear to Betty. *The Red Hat* was obviously a very good book and should be out. Part of the problem was that Jacob was a professional editor and met deadlines religiously; his job took precedence over his own writing. But something else was holding him back as well. Clearly his heart was in the novel, not Reader's Digest.

Betty was at her table, working on Jacob's latest edit of an article; she realized that he was in the bedroom trying to get in a little writing time but the sounds coming from it weren't indicative of anyone at work. Unless cursing was part of the job. She had come to see that sitting at his typewriter had become a losing fight for him; she was yet to receive a single page of his novel this week. It was his fingers, he was saying. He had gone to two specialists, one a neurologist, the other a well-known orthopedist. Much discussion. Their one point of agreement: stay clear of your typewriter, Mr. Darden. It's killing you. Hire a secretary.

And who, good doctor, will create the pages for her to type?

From the bedroom came a string of words, ardently expressed: *"Shit! Son-of-a-bitch! Goddamn!"*

Startled, Betty hit a wrong key: a typo on the last line. She uttered a swear of her own. Her favorite, a clear, succinct "Fuck!" Under her breath, of course.

She pulled the page and sat back in her chair seeing the whole thing symbolically collapse, fall by the wayside. She remembered the day she'd met Jacob here in his office, knowing the job as his secretary was going to be exciting, emotional, depressing, difficult, wonderful...unlike her life with Jon Trill. Jacob was an artist, sidelined because he had a family to support, but an artist first. Jonathan was first a stuffed shirt, a man of pretense, a sycophant who dabbled in art to give himself a look of importance—

Another swear from the bedroom.

Betty pressed hands against her face, thinking to leave Jacob a note, saying she had left early to get away from his obsessive cursing. She would see him tomorrow at nine. As she was getting ready to leave, the bedroom door opened and he came out.

"Betty," he said, "sit with me for a while. Wrap up whatever you're doing."

He looked ruffled, knocked around, as if the muses had ganged up on him in a back room. In the kitchen he fixed himself a rye and ginger ale. "Can I make you anything, Betty?"

"No, I'm fine. Thank you."

He came out with a drink and sat with Betty at the low, round table in the interview room. "I was on my way out the door," she said. "Your swearing was getting tiresome."

"It won't happen again. I'm putting the novel aside."

"All you need is a rest."

"Just now my fingers stiffened so badly I almost cried out in pain." Jacob had a swallow of his drink. "Where is it getting me? Wally said he'd keep a door open for me through June."

"I can't believe you're talking like this," Betty said.

"I have family to support, a house to uphold. It takes money," Jacob said. "I can't make any money on a book I can't write."

"And your fingers are what's stopping you?"

"Betty, if an artist can't hold a brush, can he paint? If a sculptor's

133

hands fail him, he can't sculpt."

"Beethoven lost his hearing and composed some of his greatest works," Betty said. "When Milton went blind, did the muse abandon him?"

"The muse hasn't abandoned me," Jacob said. "I'm physically unable to write."

"When did this start happening?"

"Think back to when I began handing you shaggy pages," Jacob said, "last winter sometime. It's always surprised me that you've never said anything."

"Like scold the author for his strikeovers?"

"Say what you want, *The Red Hat* is dead in the water."

"I won't buy that, Jacob. There are alternative ways to write a novel. What did Homer use to write *The Odyssey*?"

Jacob had to laugh at the comparison. "He stood on a hilltop and shouted it."

"Who else is there, a bit closer to the modern era?"

"Betty, I'm an old dog. Stuck in his ways."

"What do you think of Henry James as a writer?"

"Rather too precious, too calm; but a great stylist and a major literary figure. Why do you ask?"

"He dictated his novels."

"I didn't know that," Jacob said.

"We were reading *What Daisy Knew* in college and my professor mentioned it. His secretary sat at a typewriter and Henry James 'spoke' the novel. Other novels after that as well. *The Ambassadors* and *The Wings of the Dove*."

He sat there mulling it over; it was certainly a way to skirt a problem.

"Jacob, you have a dramatic side to you," Betty said. "You'll be great at it."

Chapter Eighteen

In his Bluestone studio the following Saturday, Jacob was examining the nine new pages he had added to *The Red Hat* since he had started "speaking" the novel. He was looking at them to determine if there were any edits he might want to make, but all he saw were crisp, flawless pages. Nary a typo. And they read beautifully; there was a new freedom in his prose. In short, Jacob was delighted. His therapist, whom he'd seen on Thursday, congratulated him; to be resourceful under pressure, to come up with a new way of doing business when all seemed lost, was to his great credit. But Smiley Blandon was still concerned about the arthritic attack that had come to affect his fingers quite suddenly, several months ago. His fingers no less. It was a classic psychosomatic development in the therapist's opinion, and he thought they should talk about it. Jacob wasn't interested. He had a great new regimen with his secretary and he didn't want to second-guess himself; he wanted to keep going with it. He was concerned that the technique he and Betty were using might, overnight, implode; it seemed too good to last.

A knock on his studio door. "Come in, Billy."

The boy walked in and Jacob told him to sit. For a recitation you stand; in a literary discussion you sit. "I liked your comment on Father Riordan's sermon at breakfast," Jacob said.

"I decided to pay attention."

"Often that's all it takes," Jacob said. "*Billy Budd*—well, what do you think?"

"It's a sad story."

Jacob nodded. "That's a good general statement, a declarative sentence. How is it sad?"

"Billy is a good person. He gets into trouble and pays for it and it doesn't seem fair."

"He hit the master-at-arms," Jacob said. "That's a serious offence."

"Claggart was accusing him of something he didn't do!"

"Fill me in on that, Billy."

"He told the captain that Billy was part of a conspiracy."

"Was that true?"

"I didn't see it."

"Why would the master-at-arms lie to the captain?"

"I don't think that's clear," Billy said.

"Does the reader have an idea of Billy's appearance?"

"Young, very handsome."

"How would you describe the relationship of Claggart and Billy?"

"He seems to like him but then turns against him."

"Watch your pronouns, Billy. For clarity's sake, use nouns, in this instance proper nouns. Again, how would you describe the relationship of Claggart and Billy?"

Billy had to do a little juggling. Then he said, "Claggart seems to like Billy but then Claggart turns against Billy."

"A bit heavy. Why does Claggart turn against Billy?"

Billy shook his head. "I don't know. It didn't make sense."

"You like Bzy, don't you?"

Billy didn't get the drift of the question. "Yes."

"What would cause you to dislike her?"

"Are we talking *Billy Budd* or Bzy, Dad?"

"All human nature is the same when it comes to likes and dislikes."

Billy said, "If she hurt me, I could get to dislike her, I guess."

"Then you might say bad things about her, am I right?"

"I could."

Jacob spread his arms, not wide. "Billy hurts Claggart, did you consider that?"

"Billy doesn't hurt Claggart! It's Claggart who hurts Billy!"

"To Claggart, Billy is evil," Jacob said.

"Dad, it's like you're talking in riddles!"

Jacob smiled. "Doesn't Claggart give Billy a slap on his rear at one point?"

"That's what I'm saying. That he rats on Billy doesn't make sense."

"Men through the ages have been scornful of women," Jacob said. "They punish women. Do you know why?"

"No." Billy was stirring uneasily in his chair.

"Women have what men want; it gives them power over men. Just like Billy has power over Claggart."

"Both are men, Dad."

"What Claggart wants he can't have," Jacob said, "but he can't stop wanting Billy. The slap on the young sailor's bottom is as close as the master-at-arms will ever get to expressing himself physically for the handsome, young sailor."

"Something isn't clicking for me," Billy said.

Jacob considered his son. Without so much as a knock, nature would come storming in and start making demands on Billy, causing him to either take a shine to girls or, as could happen, boys. "Some men like men, especially at sea when women aren't around. I'm not saying Claggart is a confirmed homosexual but he certainly has tendencies. He's attracted to the 'handsome sailor.' And he's angry at Billy for denying him what he'd like to have. Do you follow that?"

"I think so," Billy said.

"In your opinion," Jacob said, "did Captain Veer do the right thing sentencing Billy to hang from the yardarm?"

"What else could he do?"

"Why at the penultimate moment—look up 'penultimate'—does Billy say: 'God bless Captain Veer!'?"

"It's not clear to me."

"Next week I want an essay on Melville's novel, and you can

answer it there," Jacob said. "Good discussion."

****

After supper on Sunday, Jacob gave the kids their allowances and left for New York, and Hedi went about her business of taking care of her children and the house they lived in. Jacob wasn't a father coming home for the weekend, he was a guest arriving at a clean, comfortable dwelling with a well-stocked pantry and bar, the woman in charge and her children tip-toeing around so as not to get in his way, to disturb him in his quiet readings and writings. On a warm day perhaps a watering of the lawn. He arrived as a guest and left as one, leaving everything for the help to tend to. A quarter for you, you, and you. Nice children, well-mannered. And this same man, very soon now, would be coming here to live. He would give up the guest role and become a real husband and father. Hedi could only hope. But one thing she knew with certainty. She was tired of weekends!

On Tuesday Hedi was in the process of making what her family called "best soup" for a midweek dinner, cubes of beef in a large pot of water; onions, small potatoes, carrots would go in later. She gave it a taste, added a pinch of salt. Billy came in from school, dropped the day's mail on the table and gave his mother a greeting. He cut himself a slice of her bread, spread on peanut butter and sat down with a glass of milk. Five minutes later he was out the door, telling his mother he was going to the Cayuga Quarry to work on William D.

Hedi looked at the envelopes, hoping to get a letter from Germany...that never came and never would, until the war ended. She bowed her head thinking of mother and father, brothers and sisters, hungry, frightened, living day by day, praying for the war to end. Here in America, war, for most people, was an inconvenience. "Out for the duration" was a sign you saw everywhere. Food and gas were rationed, but major hardships? The Maverick Theater was starting a new season. Jacob had left a secure, good-paying job to write a novel, they were having both a basement and central heating put in. America didn't have time for war. Germany didn't have time for anything but war.

Her daughters were coming in from high school. Holly had a

lesson with Mr. Bagovitch in fifteen minutes and went upstairs to her room to change, and Rachel stayed in the kitchen. Hedi gave her a quiet look. Ever since Andy had left, she seemed a different person. Quieter, almost to the point of not talking at all. Something had happed that night. Hedi had been getting ready for bed at 10:30 when Rachel had come in, taken a shower, and gone into her room. All Hedi knew—from what Rachel had told her in the morning—was that the evening with Andy hadn't gone as planned.

Holly came tripping down the stairs holding a gym bag and gave her mother a kiss; then she was out the door at something of a run, a girl hard to keep up with. From her earliest years, Holly came and went as she pleased, answerable to no one; no one bothered her. Hedi had always likened her to a cool breeze that came in when you opened a window.

"I'm making myself a cup of tea. Can I make you one, Rachel?"

"Yes. Thank you."

Hedi put on a kettle. "How was school?"

"Getting better. Andy was taking up too much of my time."

"Do you miss him?"

"Yes, but I'm trying to forget him."

Hedi fixed two cups of tea and set them on the table with a piece of strudel. "Is there anything you want to talk about?"

She looked at her mother and hesitated, had a sip of tea.

"What is it, darling?"

Rachel said, "We were kissing. That was nice, but he wanted to go further, I told him no, he said I owed him something. To go all the way, was that what I owed him? Things went from bad to worse."

"Were you afraid?"

"I was, Mom. It was so quiet where we were. Big Bear is wilderness. He came out and drove me home. We didn't say a word." Her eyes filled with tears. "Like that, it was over."

Hedi squeezed her daughter's hand. "I'm sorry, Rachel. It could have been much worse."

"And now I'm going to college." Rachel used a paper napkin on her eyes. "How many years of school did you have, Mom?"

"Seven."

"Did you have a favorite teacher?"

"I did, Frau Bloomer."

"Frau *Bloomer*?"

Hedi smiled. "We loved her. We were in a terrible war and she made us feel safe and protected. She taught me how to add and subtract in my head... fast. I still use it."

"What was it about Heini that you really liked? Maybe loved. You were going to marry him."

"He was awfully kind, he had a good heart. He was the better of two worlds open to me at the time."

"I can see him standing there on the pier, waving goodbye," Rachel said.

"So can I."

Suddenly mother and daughter were embracing.

****

Later, as darkness settled over Bluestone Road, Hedi sat in the living room reading *Buddenbrooks,* liking the story and wanting to keep up with the language; through disuse, like precious plates in a closet never used, it had gathered dust. Slowly the pages of the Thomas Mann novel turned, then not at all, and finally she surrendered to memories of her trip to Germany in the fall of 1930, a trip Elsie Livingston, a patron of the arts and Jacob's good friend in Woodstock, had paid for. Hedi and daughters had gone first, with the plan that Jacob would join them for a couple of weeks at Christmas. On one occasion, shortly before Jacob arrived, she had paid Heini a visit with Rachel and Holly. He had left the coal mines and was, at her visit, chief of the Biskupitz Fire Department. Married, father of two sons, he was the kind-hearted man she had always known him to be—and no longer had horrid etchings on his face.

Jacob and Hedi's father took long walks in the German countryside, and Ignatz would proudly claim, on coming in, of keeping up with the young Boston-born American step for step; but later in the day (Jacob liked telling), Ignatz would excuse himself to take a nap. Hedi smiled at the thought of her father and husband striking it off so well; but the most memorable part of the visit occurred ten days before Hedi and daughters left Germany. Lying in a hospital bed, she watched a woman in white coming toward her bearing an infant snugly wrapped. Beaming, the woman sang out, "Es ist ein Junge!"

They were the most beautiful words Hedi has ever heard.

She closed the Mann novel and set it on the coffee table...as the phone rang. By the tone, the time, she knew it was Jacob wanting to say goodnight, the caring, responsible husband fulfilling a role; even as Hedi fulfilled a role herself of faithful, obedient wife.

They greeted each other, then Hedi asked him how the novel was going.

"I'm finally adding pages."

"Wonderful. Your hands are getting better."

"My hands are out of it entirely," Jacob said. "It's a whole new way of writing for me."

"How so?"

"I thought *The Red Hat* would never see the light of day, Hedwig. Now I'm on a breakaway pace, three to five pages a day, crisp, professional copy."

"What's going on?"

"Betty takes dictation," Jacob said. "In addition to my Reader's Digest secretary, she's typing my novel."

Hedi seemed to hear muted drums in the deep recesses of her heart; someone, somewhere, had died. "If you aren't finishing any pages, what are you giving her to type?"

"I'm dictating my book. What I say, she types," Jacob said. "It's demanding on both of us. Each day the curtain goes up. What are my characters doing today, where were they yesterday? All in my head, in the wings of my memory—the preparation is huge. Hours of it. Can I hold up? I don't know, Hedwig. So far Betty and I are on a great roll. If all goes well, *The Red Hat* will be out by the spring of next year."

No response.

"Hedwig?"

"That's great, Jacob."

"How are you, Hedwig?"

"I'm all right," she said.

"You sound tired."

"It's been a long day. I've been thinking of my parents."

"Well, of course. See you Friday."

"Good night, Jacob," she said.

Hedi turned out the light in the kitchen and went back to the Mann novel in her first tongue.

Chapter Nineteen

Chips had lent the boys a galvanized 24-gallon trash barrel and a large funnel. From time to time, once rain had collected in it, they had emptied it into the boiler. They were doing it now, mid-week after school. Water splashed but most of it found the funnel and went in. Serge had a handy measuring stick, a piece of broken molding from his father's studio; using it, he estimated the water level at one third. Plenty. The idea was to build up a head of steam sufficient to blow the whistle, then let the fire die. How word had got around that "Operation Rumble" in the Maverick Art Colony was a must-witness event, Billy and Serge didn't know; but people were talking about it.

Taking a break, their legs dangling over the side, Serge asked Billy if he was getting cold feet.

"A little. I think about it. How about you?"

"No. I'm afraid it'll be a dud," Serge said.

"If it's a dud, no one can say we didn't try. Harlan told me Thoreau burned down the woods once, as a boy. Camp fire got away from him and a friend."

"Good old Thoreau," Serge said. "He died a virgin, for chrissakes."

"What do you mean?"

"He never had sex with a woman."

"Oh."

Serge scraped a speck of paint off the floor with his thumbnail. "I remember thinking, when we first started on the crane, that we could chug around the colony in it when we got it going. Now we're going to give William D.'s whistle a blast, that's it."

"How come you changed your mind?"

"Reality set in."

From Quarryman came a shout. "Serge! Are you there?"

Hands at his mouth, megaphone style, "What is it, Mom?"

"Leon just won the competition! Come up to the house!"

Serge smacked a fist into the palm of his hand. "Wow! Great!"

"That's wonderful," Billy said, trying to show enthusiasm.

Serge lowered his feet, dropped to the ground, and ran. Billy stayed on William D. a while longer, letting the news sink it. He wasn't immediately involved but he still felt let down. Someone always had to lose. Even in a noontime baseball game, winning felt better. He took the same path as Serge. Crossing in front of Quarryman, he heard the family's excited voices. "San Francisco!" Billy hurried by and out to old Bluestone Road. He glanced at Aurora; an afternoon shadow was falling across it. He didn't want to even imagine what was going on inside. The life of an artist seemed like the best of lives—freedom, no one to answer to, doing what you loved. If you could stand the rejection. Billy imagined Wes would take the rejection OK, a setback yes; but nothing to keep him down. When Billy had posed for him, Wes would tell stories of his halfback days on the Dartmouth team—you played until the last play and sometimes you won on the last play. It was Julia who would be hurt. Same with his own family. Jacob wouldn't give it much thought. Hedi would feel like Julia, the awful blow of it, the loss—

Intelligentsia was open, several people were sitting on the bench on both sides of the long table. Christine, the woman who ran the place, saw Billy and came over. She had on an orange peasant's blouse and leaned over to give him a hug and her breasts rolled forward as if to smack him in the face. As the season moved on, she said, she'd have jobs for him and she planned on paying him this year in money. Two men were exchanging viewpoints at the table

144

and one of them was saying that Angus Beck's vote for Rustovsky was pure politics. Jamison was clearly the finer artist. How politics ruled the day was enough to make a painter go into real estate. Billy told Christine he'd come by soon again and continued to his own house...where he took a carrot from the refrigerator, green top still on, cut it into three pieces and shoved them into his pocket. Outside, he jumped on his bike and started pedaling, ditching it to one side of the mountain-pasture gate and going in. He walked along, carrot in hand, holding it high. Who knew but Champ might get a whiff. He investigated isolated grassy coves. Nothing. The higher he climbed, the stronger his fears that the slaughterhouse gang had already done its work.

"Where are you, Champ?"

He was now at the thick stand of pines where he and Bzy had first spooked the pony. Silence. Why would a pony choose to hide away in a lightless stand of evergreens? Next he came to the broad expanse of gray, rounded stone, hollowed out and holding water. Intrigued as he was, he didn't stop. Just ahead was the broad, ramp-like entrance to the plateau. Clearly he had come too far. Part of him thought to turn back; he had no pressing need or wish to see the cabin so soon again. He was on a mission to find Champ. The thing to do now was to retrace his steps. Clearly he'd missed the pony on his way here, unless—Billy dreaded the thought of it— Champ was no longer in the mountain pasture.

He shook off the idea. He'd look extra hard on his way back; there were many coves and mini-pastures where Champ could be hanging out. But instead of starting down immediately, Billy went up the wood trail deciding, while he was here, to have another look at the cabin.

And there it was, but his eyes immediately went by to the far end of the plateau. Champ was standing there, head buried in the long grass. The pony looked up, snorted.

Flashing the carrot, "Got something for you, Champ."

The maple on the plateau stood between Billy and Champ. Instead of going to the pony, he stopped at the tree. He kept holding the carrot, shaking the green top.

Champ snorted again. Restless, ill-at-ease, trying to figure out

145

what was going on. I've seen this kid before, what's he up to? What is he holding? Hmmm.

Billy spoke quietly, "Come on, Champ. You know I have carrots."

Pony tossing his head, keeping a distance. Boy wants to bring me back to the barn where a man, when he isn't butchering, stands on a stool behind a Holstein heifer saying Wilbur he doing you good, hanh?

Billy settled against the maple, thinking he had nothing to do but wait. He should've brought a notebook and pencil and scribbled a few lines. Anything to get started on it. Like how Claggart patted Billy on the butt, then went and ratted on him to the captain. Nobody is safe. Billy the sailor isn't, Champ the pony isn't, Buck the dog isn't—

"If Wilbur he shake oats at you, stand your ground, Champ," Billy said. "Don't fall for Wilbur's oats! My job is to rescue you. It's like trying to rescue lightning. Wilbur, if he shake oats at you run the other way. Because Wilbur he'll put a rope on you and drag you down a long dusty road to a place made of cinderblocks. This is good living here in Ohayo Mountain Pasture but if you stay here it's over for you, Champ. Mr. Osterhoudt is calling it a vendetta, that's like a feud, he has it in for you for kicking him in the balls. I'm sure he had it coming to him. What I'm trying to say is, if I get you away before Wilbur he get a rope on you, I'll take you home with me. I'm asking you to trust me, Champ."

The pony was still at the far end of the plateau; they had just stopped paying attention to each other. Billy got to his feet and started going closer, talking to him, shaking the carrot so as to make the greens flutter. He stopped ten feet away. "Champ, this is for you but you have to come and take it."

He kept talking, speaking quietly. The pony came closer, then closer, and took the carrot from his hand. Billy pulled out another piece. Champ made it disappear, nuzzled around Billy's pockets—

"That's all I have for now."

He gave the pony's forelock a ruffle; beneath coarse, tangled hair, in need of a serious brushing was a white, perfectly formed check mark. Billy scratched Champ's ears, stroked his neck, then walked away. Going by the cabin, he felt the need to stop and have a closer look—to go inside. He tripped the latch and nudged the door open and went in, stayed perfectly still, hesitant to move, to make any noise. He touched the back of both chairs, crossed to the west window. Lying on a narrow shelf beneath it was a dry, yellowed copy of the Woodstock Record, dated September 1933. He stood there reading a few lines of a story by Barbara Ann Bullock on Angus Beck, a Maverick Art Colony artist who was having an opening in the Woodstock Art Gallery on Labor Day. Billy had the feeling of being an old timer, instead of a kid. He set the paper down, at that point deciding to check out the loft. Why, he didn't know. Cautiously he took four rungs of the ladder up and looked in. A filthy, nasty-looking blanket lay in a wrinkled heap over a thin, foul mattress. He gave the blanket a tug, tossing it over the top of a crude, six-inch-high rollout barrier, then tossed the mattress as well. Billy dragged the grubby items deep into the woods off to one side, checked the front door, and started for home.

****

He rolled down the driveway to Canal Boat and let his bike fall to the grass. "Bzy?"

She came to the door. "Hi."

"I stopped by the theater. Mia said you were home."

"I want to show you something," Bzy said.

"What is it?"

"You'll see."

He followed her across the grassy yard in the direction of Ohayo, then through some trees before the mountain started to rise. She ducked under the branches of a huge pine and, right away, they were in a clearing the size of a living-room floor. In the middle of it was the trunk of the tree, nothing else. Just pine needles. The size, the darkness of the overhanging limbs was like a perfect roof.

"It's my secret place."

"I like it."

"No one knows about it," Bzy said.

"I know."

"You're different." They sat down on a thick bed of needles. "What have you been up to? I thought you'd gone away."

"Where would I go? There's just a lot going on. Champ is in danger."

"What kind of danger?"

He told her about Donny Osterhoudt's father, who owned the slaughterhouse at the end of Bluestone Road. Donny couldn't handle Champ, the pony was too ornery. Mr. Osterhoudt was trying to sell him but when interested fathers came by with their kids, Champ wasn't the pony they wanted. To get his money back, Mr. Osterhoudt was aiming to sell Champ to a dog-food company.

"How awful!" Bzy cried out, her eyes pinching shut.

"I have to rescue him," Billy said.

"I want to help."

"It will be like rescuing a storm cloud, Bzy."

"Let me know." She moved in, putting her arm around Billy; whatever she was feeling, she expressed it fully. He didn't want her to let go. She asked him what was new on his father's regimen.

He told her about *Billy Budd,* emphasizing the part about Billy the sailor and Claggart, the ship's master-at-arms. It was a really good story, but now his father wanted a 500-word essay on the book and Billy couldn't get anything down on paper, and it was due tomorrow.

"What's the problem?"

It was hard to explain. He told her he would sit there looking at a lined piece of paper and nothing would happen. The words weren't there.

"You just told me the story. I wasn't counting the words but it was more than 500."

"That's speaking, that isn't writing!"

"Billy, forget writing. Pretend you're talking to me and scribble words."

Chapter Twenty

Jacob was pacing the floor in his New York office, thoroughly immersed in his work. He donned the mask of his characters as they talked and moved about and interacted with each other or their environments. Fingers skimming along on the keys, Betty took it all down. He talked, she click-clacked, and before Jacob knew it, she was setting a page aside and rolling in another sheet of paper.

He stopped suddenly. "Read me that last sentence, Betty."

She read him the last sentence.

"I really did say 'pellucid,'" Jacob said. "Change it to 'clear,' and keep me apprised of 40-cent words!"

Page by page *The Red Hat* was taking shape. In a crucial scene, Stephen was hearing the confession of a young woman who was sleeping with a married roofer in Medford. Jacob endeavored to put himself in Stephen Rossel's shoes, but whether he was putting words into Stephen's mouth that were truly Stephen's or merely words that priests were supposed to tell wayward young women, Jacob didn't know. Then he realized he wasn't hearing the click-clack of a typewriter.

Jacob looked over. His secretary was pressing a tissue to her eyes.

"Betty, are you all right?"

"I was, and then suddenly I wasn't."

"What's the problem?"

She dropped her tissue into the basket. "In a word, you."

"Am I working you too hard?"

"I was taken on as secretary to the roving editor of Reader's Digest!"

"He went on vacation."

"I might be suing for a breach of contract, Jacob."

"Read me the last line," he said.

****

Later that day, alone in his office, Jacob sat at his desk engrossed in notes, outlines, reference books, the while jotting down talking points—descriptions, snippets of dialogue, stage directions—for tomorrow's session. Maybe another thirty minutes before going out for a light dinner. His phone rang. It was after hours but he said, "Roving editor, Reader's Digest."

His mother was calling from Green Harbor. "How are you, Jacob?"

He sat back, unable to recall when they had last talked. "I'm fine, just finished up a good day's work. Things are going well. How are you, mother?"

"I'm doing nicely, son."

"And father?"

"Your father fell in his room yesterday after coming home from work. He felt dizzy and passed out."

"From drinking?"

"He seemed perfectly sober when he walked in the door."

"What was it?"

"Dr. Monahan is monitoring him. He was dehydrated and had a mini-stroke, perhaps from fatigue, from the God-awful hours he keeps. As for today, he's lying quietly in bed."

"Good, let him rest."

"John is basically running the business anyway."

"Of course," Jacob said, hearing the inflection in his mother's voice.

"The children, how are they?" she asked.

"Rachel is missing her boyfriend who enlisted in the navy. Holly is taking ballet lessons from a Russian impresario but she seems more interested at the moment in modern dance. Billy is fine, always into something—"

"And your novel of a young priest who rises to the high and holy rank of cardinal, how is it going for you, Jacob?"

She knew of it, how well he didn't know; clearly she was excited by the Catholic theme. As for the Jewish father in the Rossel family—

"I'm moving along with it, Mother."

"It sounds like a great book."

Jacob made himself a rye and ginger ale, sat down with it in the interview room. Why the hell had he asked his father for a blessing? Fucking Jew had held his son's feet to the fire. Want a blessing, my son? Pay for it. His father was a shylock reincarnated and would have his pound of flesh. Maybe he should tell his mother of the stress he was under at the time, the pressure to bring in the Jewish father. Don't apologize, Jacob told himself, just level with her...

****

Jacob was in his Bluestone studio that weekend. He had just gone over the essay his son had written, making good use of the pencil in his hand. Billy sat in the chair at the corner of his desk. "All right then," Jacob said. "You have some mistakes here, mechanical errors. But this has an easy quality about it, a nice rhythm. Writers can write a lifetime and never find their voice. The voice here is good, it's you. Perhaps too heavy with adverbs and adjectives."

"What's wrong with adverbs and adjectives?"

"Try to use verbs and nouns that speak for themselves. Sit closer so we can go over some mistakes."

Billy pulled in his chair. Jacob went over every error. In the first paragraph there was a noun-verb agreement, or disagreement. Always go back to the subject. Is it singular or plural? Then use the verb form that agrees. Jacob pointed out faulty parallel structure in one sentence and an instance of a "comma splice"—the use of a comma where a period is required, as between two independent clauses. But Jacob was quick to point out strong sentences as well.

"Spelling. Any question, check the dictionary. One of your

misspellings is more grievous than the others all put together. The way you have it here, Billy, 'it's' is a contraction for 'it is,' as in 'It's a time of rebellion in the British Navy.' Correct. But then you say: 'The ship flew *it's* flag at half mast.' Do you mean that as a contraction also? Because that's the way you've written in."

Billy looked at the sentence. "No."

"It's an easy mistake to make, so always ask yourself, do you want to show contraction or possession."

Jacob nudged aside the composition. Casually, he asked Billy what he thought of the outcome of the San Francisco mural competition.

"It didn't make me happy."

"Too much was riding on it," Jacob said. "Do you understand humanism? The painting of you in football gear is a perfect example. It's alive, it's real, there's a boy there. And Wes's sketches of San Francisco have that same quality. I've seen some of them. By comparison Rustovsky's work is cold, excellent draftsmanship, but where's the heart, the soul of his people? There's really only one way to account for his taking the prize, politics. The third judge in San Francisco is well-known for his leftist views, and Angus Beck is a self-proclaimed fellow traveler."

Billy was getting ready to leave. On his father's signal the boy would bolt. Jacob liked slowing him down; a reckless running about indicated a life without purpose. "Make the corrections in your *Billy Budd* composition," Jacob said. "I'm giving you a new book, *Huckleberry Finn*. Next week we'll talk about Mark Twain's novel and in two weeks I'll want a five-hundred word essay, much like your essay on *Billy Budd*."

He handed Billy his marked-up composition and a copy of the Twain novel. Grim-faced, the boy left his father's studio, and Jacob picked up a section of *The Red Hat* that Betty had recently typed. It happened to be the part of the novel where Stephen is contemplating having more than a friendship with the beautiful Sophia. Stephen is thrown back on his faith, tried as never before to stay loyal to his priestly vow to serve God, to resist the urgings of the flesh....

****

He awoke with a start, sitting upright in bed in the master bedroom of the house, making high-pitched sounds of terror, hands pressing his head. Hedi reached over to comfort him. "Jacob, what is it? You're here, it's all right."

"I—I had a terrible dream."

"Breathe, take deep breaths," Hedi said.

"Hedwig, it was awful."

"Lie back down, Jacob. Can I get you anything?"

He sank back, struggling to clear his mind of—of—

"What was it, darling? Tell me," Hedi said.

"It's gone now. God help me."

But it wasn't gone. Desist, desist! the voice in his head was screaming. She brought you into the world, she gave you life. What did the cranky old Jew ever do for you? Forget your pledge. It was made in a stupid, sentimental moment. Go back to O'Rourke, the Irish trolley conductor, Desmond O'Rourke of the Gaelic clan Ó Ruairc, historic rulers of Breifne, proud father of the young parish priest Stephen O'Rourke...and one day Cardinal O'Rourke.

"Close your eyes, go to sleep now," Hedi said.

Chapter Twenty-One

Billy braked to a stop and stood astride his bike at the gloomy Osterhoudt barn. Had Donny said "at" or "in" the barn? He kept looking at Donny's house, hoping he'd come out; when he didn't, Billy shouldered the sliding door a little and went in. He didn't see any animals in the gloom but heard sad bleats and moos and the muffled snort of a workhorse. A tremor in his voice, "Donny?" No answer. Thinking to leave, he saw the shadowy figure of a man at the opening to a box stall. Smiling, he was making little motions with his fingers for Billy to come closer.

"I'm looking for Donny."

"He ain't here. I got something nice for yez."

His eyes adjusting, Billy recognized the man. He had something in his hand and was shaking it, like you would if you were about to roll dice. "Come on over, hanh? Wilbur he'll let yez hold it."

Shaken, Billy turned and went out. Donny was just leaving his house; he crossed Bluestone Road and went up to his friend. "Hey, Billy. I'll only be a minute." He headed for the barn.

"Wilbur's inside."

"So?"

"Nothing."

He waited at the side of the road, thinking the whole deal with Champ was getting more and more out of hand. Donny came out of the barn with a coiled 8-foot lead line and a halter of black leather with brass rings linking the individual pieces.

"Any trick to putting it on?"

"The strap goes behind his ears. Then run it through the buckle." Donny dropped both items into the basket on Billy's bike.

"When are they coming for him?"

"I heard my father talking. It could be soon."

"Donny, that doesn't help. You have to give me a day, a time."

"If I knew, I'd tell you. I think you should go into the upper pasture and take Champ," Donny said.

"Take him?"

"Before it's too late!"

"I don't know, Donny."

"You'll rescue him, you told me."

"There's rescuing and there's stealing." Billy said.

"They plan to shoot him," Donny said.

"Shoot him?"

"My father's got a .30-30 and Wilbur is a crack shot."

"Jesus Christ, Donny! Don't bullshit me!"

"I'm not, they're gunning for him."

Billy felt a great weight on his shoulders. "Keep an eye on your father and Wilbur. Give me a thirty minute heads-up on the phone. I'll get Champ. But carry through on your end!"

"OK, Billy."

"Right now I'm going into the pasture," Billy said, and got on his bike.

Finding Champ was never an easy matter; he could be anywhere, and Billy wanted to put the halter on him now. The pony was in one of the pastures near the gate and he went over to him, carrot in hand. Easily done, and Champ had no objection to having a halter put on by Billy, whom he trusted. Then Billy had a thought. Take the pony now. You have him, walk out with him while you can. Tomorrow could be too late. But just as quickly he changed his mind. Billy scratched Champ's ears and left the pasture.

****

Billy was talking with Chips in Carpenter Shop, saying how he had put the halter on Champ in the mountain pasture but hadn't taken him away, rescued him from two men who were coming for the pony with a gun. If not now, soon; and it was weighing on Billy that he'd had the opportunity to walk off with Champ but hadn't.

Chips was tossing around the predicament Billy found himself in when a man showed up at Chip's door. "I'm Nick Bonino, violist with the Maverick quartet," he said. "Excuse me for cutting in. Our music director got his car stuck at the concert hall, mud up to its hubcaps. Can you give us a hand?"

"Sure."

"Thanks." The man went away.

"Billy, come with me," Chips said. "We'll do this together."

They got in the merchant seaman's pickup. "I think leaving Champ in the pasture was the right thing to do," he went on. "If Mr. Osterhoudt and the creep, this Wilbur character, come after him, you've done all you could. I believe in carpe diem—seize the moment—but impulsiveness presents problems, and the two are closely related."

"I wanted to run it by you," Billy said.

"Glad you did. We'll finish after we get the music director out of the ditch."

At the concert hall, Chips skirted some muddy-looking areas and pulled up shy of the stuck car, a two-door Chevy. Fifteen people were standing around.

A large man with a lined face and full head of white hair came over and introduced himself as Lucien Cox, music director of the Maverick Summer Concerts.

"I'm Chips, and this is Billy. Is your car in neutral?"

"It is."

"Emergency brake off?"

"Yes. Is this your boy?"

"Billy Darden is my assistant."

"Nice meeting you both."

Chips and Billy went to the front of the Chevy and Chips pointed to the ground in front of each wheel. Billy should take the shovel and loosen the dirt and stones, make a clean run for each wheel. Minimize resistance. Billy started in. A boy from the group came over and started to chat—blond hair, taller than Billy, maybe a year older. He said his name was Austin.

"I'm Billy."

"My father is the Gregory Fromm, the cellist with the Maverick String Quartet. "

Billy continued undercutting the tires. "OK."

"I play the cello. Do you play anything?"

"Baseball."

"I love baseball!" Austin Fromm said. "Can I help you with anything?"

"There's a four-by-four in Chips's truck. Bring it over."

He went for it. "That's your fulcrum," Austin said, laying it down under the rear bumper of the Chevy.

The way he said it reminded Billy of Serge. Then Chips came out of the woods with a sturdy 20-foot sapling, trimmed of branches. He inserted the thicker end of the lever under the bumper of the car and told Billy to request volunteers.

"How many do we need?"

"Five altogether."

Five men came over. One, a man of considerable weight, went with Chips. The other four split up with two on each side of the car. When everyone was set, Chips and the heavy man bore down on the end of the lever, and the rear of the car went up. Chips yelled "Push!" and the men at the car put their backs into it—and the car rolled forward to solid ground. People clapped and cheered.

Lucien Cox shook hands with Chips and Billy and drove away, and Billy and Austin began filling the hole, using a shovel and rake. Then they put the tools and four-by-four in the truck.

"Thanks," Billy said.

"I'll bring my mitt," Austin said. "Where do you live?"

"White house, next to Harlan's Field."

Back at Carpenter Shop, Chips cut the ignition on his truck. "Billy, the channeling you did made us look good. Any resistance, Lucien's car wouldn't have rolled. As for the pony, I hope you catch a break. In so many cases in life, that's what it comes down to. But you did the right thing."

****

Hedi wheeled the contraption in from the back hall, then over to the kitchen sink where she attached a pair of hoses, both patched with tape, to the corresponding faucets at the sink. Before she turned on the hot and cold, she plugged the cord into to a wall socket and shook in a powdered detergent. With the water running, Hedi emptied the family hamper into the drum and clicked the on/off switch on the machine. Laundry underway, she set about making a new batch of dough. It was Thursday afternoon, Jacob was coming home tomorrow, and he had made it known that he'd like one loaf, at least, with raisins in it.

She started in, following her tested recipe, toward the end of the process sprinkling in raisins, then smoothing the dough into buttered pans and sliding them into the 350 degree oven. The washing machine came to a stop with such a clanking and violent discharge of water that she always had the feeling she was witnessing its death. Work on the new basement was beginning in a couple of weeks. With the furnace she also wanted a new fully automatic washing machine. Jacob was very strange in what he believed were necessities, important additions to a household. Central heating, yes; new washing machine, no. In their car, bought last year, a heater was a key option. Jacob had flatly refused to have one put in. Use a car robe, put on extra socks. A gasoline-powered lawn mower. Why? It was what sons were for. So much of their lives—her life especially—was under his control.

That she and the children went unfalteringly to Mass was of prime importance to Jacob, whereas for him it had meant nothing for years. His mother had insisted the family go to Mass, no question asked, no excuse tolerated. For all its hypocrisy, Jacob chose to follow in that tradition. Not once, in all their years together as parents, had Hedi ever heard him speak of his father as Jewish in front of their children. Perhaps she simply lacked the courage to go behind her husband's back. If Jacob wanted to keep it a secret, she'd keep it a secret, knowing full well it was wrong; it was a weak link, of several, in their marriage.

Hedi picked a pair of Holly's damp blue slacks from the conglomeration of wet, dark-colored clothes and passed them through a pair of rollers that sat atop and to the rear of the washing machine. They squeezed out excess water from laundry so you could then take it outside to dry on a line. If your fingers or something you were wearing got pulled in, there was a quick-release bar right there, so unless you were fast asleep or terribly preoccupied you weren't going to get yourself "squeezed." Last week, with the news that Leon Rustovsky had won San Francisco, Hedi could hardly think of anything except Julia and Wes. The disappointment they had to be feeling when the prize had gone elsewhere, when their dream had come crashing down. Her doctor had feared she might lose her baby and recommended rest and quiet at her parents' country home outside Harrisburg. She had come in to say goodbye to Hedi. Wes was staying behind to consider new avenues to up their income. Then Hedi and Julia were hugging and it was later, doing laundry, that her washing-machine rollers had snagged her hand blacking the nails on her first and index fingers, and she had hit the release bar so hard with her other hand that she'd injured it, and it still hurt....

Holly's pants, sapped of water, fell into the sink. Next through the rollers was Billy's shirt, followed by Jacob's pajamas. He'd worn them twice, Friday night and Saturday; then into the hamper. He liked putting on a fresh pair when he came home. As for *The Red Hat,* he had said on his call two nights ago that it was spinning right along. Hedi found herself fighting to keep a positive outlook, an equilibrium, on the book; and on Jacob himself. Having him at home fulltime for the first time in thirteen years—how she had looked forward to it!—and now that dream was fading. He was no longer capable of sitting down and writing by himself, he had to have someone—well, an attractive woman, typing pages as he spoke, as he paraded and performed and pontificated! And telling Hedi *they* now had 240 pages. Not he; not we. *They!*

Just two days ago, Julia had talked to her about the verdict, two to one in favor of Rustovsky. She was a trouper about it but Hedi had seen the pain etched on her face. She and Wes had taken the win for granted, Julia had said, and had made plans to establish themselves in San Francisco. Now where were they? Not much beyond the early, hand-to-mouth days in the Maverick Art Colony. How clever, how insightful of Jacob to sign on with Reader's Digest! Now, Julia said, you can live comfortably in a thoroughly restored house with full basement and central heating soon going in and Jacob can write without the debilitating stress of keeping the household together. Jacob had a plan: to sacrifice ten or twelve early years of his life so he could then give himself fully to his work. Wes did not have a plan other than painting. Honorable, yes! But where are we now, even with the little family money I have?

Hedi wouldn't have answered even if she knew what to say, though it occurred to her that Julia and Wes were the lucky ones. They had a marriage, respect for each other, trust.

Rachel's blouse, Hedi's skirt, Billy's jeans—through the ringer. When all the laundry was roller-flattened, Hedi tossed it into the hamper and carried it out the kitchen door to the backyard, setting it on the round stone table and pinning to the line one article of clothing after the other. It seemed to Hedi an exceptionally fine day, what with lilacs just coming in and the deep privacy of the West Hurley woods. What could be finer? It was interesting how even your closest friends would comment if you managed to somehow pull ahead. And of course she, the German girl, had latched onto Jacob's "insightfulness" and success.

Hedi felt like crying, at how sad it was that once you were branded, the brand stayed. You couldn't outlive it. When Rachel was born, it made a full house in Bird's Eye and when Hedi had then become pregnant again, they would not be able to spend still another winter in the two-room house against Ohayo Mountain. But they had a problem. Money. Jacob had an account in First National in Kingston with $350 in it. That was the extent, the breadth and width of what they had, and with Baby Two soon to enter the world, and ice, snow and frigid air out there lurking— Jacob had written a poem with a haunting refrain, *It comes, it comes, the cold, the cold*—Jacob and Hedi's options were limited. No way would he write his father and ask him for a loan. A man had to be willing to stoop, but that was a stoop too low. Hedi took it upon herself to start looking for a house and she didn't have to look that far. There was a ten-year-old farmhouse on old Bluestone Road that had its own well, an unfinished attic, and an indoor bathroom. As Hedi was soon to find out, it was for sale by the current owner, one Archibald Barnes.

"It's perfect for us, Jacob," she reported.

"I'm glad. Out of curiosity, what is he asking for it?"

"Four thousand dollars."

"Hedwig, how many times do I have to remind you—"

"I have the money," she said.

"What?"

"It's the exact amount I saved working for your mother."

"My God, I married an heiress!" Jacob exclaimed. "Hedwig! Hedwig!" She smiled at the memory.

Without delay, they moved. Did Jacob mention, had he ever mentioned to anyone, that Hedwig had bought the house with the money she had saved in America for her return to Germany, perhaps to buy a house with her fiancé. She had bought one here instead. She hadn't done it for the accolade. But sometimes she asked herself why Jacob had never referred to it openly, had never acknowledged her contribution. It had occurred to her, in those early years, that Beth and Rod Holloway of Reader's Digest would have still taken Jacob on if they had found the Darden family in a crowded two-room bungalow, but sitting in front of the fireplace, here in their house on Bluestone Road, on that cold November day, had certainly made an impression.

She was pinning clothes to the line when she saw Raphael Hagar crossing Harlan's Field. The biweekly visit. What did he want, what could she give him? It was tedious, but at the same time she was charmed. She liked his company...as long as he didn't overstay.

"Hedi, good morning," he said.

"Raphael, how are you this fine day?"

"I am doing well. Today I feel like a new person."

"How wonderful. Sit down, Raphael. Would you like a tea?"

"That would be very nice. Would you happen to have an old hat kicking around?"

"What kind of hat?"

"It doesn't matter. Just not a watch cap."

They went into the kitchen. She put a kettle on the stove and spooned tea leaves into a ceramic pot. "With a brim?"

"Don't know. But with character."

"We'll have tea, then I'll look around."

He talked about his new sculpture; it was coming along really well, he said. She was happy to hear it. What was inspiring him?

"Sometimes it's just the way you wake up."

She made two cups, adding a little sugar and milk. Raphael had a taste. "You make a fine cup of tea, Hedi."

"It's all in how you pour it."

"Then you pour it well."

Raphael said he had a nephew visiting him later this summer and he was counting on Billy to take Aiden fishing in the Ashokan Reservoir. Hedi said Billy would be more than happy to do it. She mentioned the competition between Wes Jamison and Leon Rustovsky. Raphael hadn't given it very much thought. Judges. It's never about quality, it's all politics. It corrupts good intentions by government on all levels.

Hedi said she thought he was right. Then she excused herself and walked through the house to the master bedroom where she opened Jacob's closet. On the top shelf were seven or eight hats. Two fedoras, a blue winter cap with earflaps, a Panama hat with a lime band, an old straw hat he had worn long ago at a Maverick Art Colony Festival—and then she saw the one she wanted. A black wool yachtsman's cap with gold leaves on the visor and an anchor on the front wreathed in gold leaves; it sat close to the head. Jacob had bought it to wear on a schooner he had chartered for a cruise up the Atlantic seaboard; it was the only time they had all vacationed together as a family. Hedi didn't take it from the shelf easily. By giving it to another man would she be wronging her husband? Then, on impulse, Hedi took it from the shelf, gave it a dusting with her fingers, and went back to the kitchen.

"Oh, yes!" he cried out, taking it from Hedi and putting it on. It appeared to fit perfectly. "What do you think?"

"It's becoming on you, Raphael."

In the doorway, as he was leaving, he gave Hedi a kiss that by increments was becoming a real kiss. She read his thoughts. *Take a man's hat, his wife's next.* Unless it was her own thoughts she was reading. She watched Raphael as he crossed Harlan's Field doing a mini-jig, hat jauntily perched.

****

162

In the kitchen—where else would she likely be as the sun began falling?—Hedi was starting dinner for her children and herself. Knockwurst, baked beans, sauerkraut. Jacob would be here tomorrow and she had one of his favorite Friday-night dishes planned. Fish chowder. Holly was upstairs doing homework and Billy was in the library room reading *Huckleberry Finn*. And the German girl was putting together a meal...and fighting her thoughts. Jacob would come home tomorrow saying they should pack a picnic lunch and sit on the shores of the Hudson watching the Poughkeepsie Regatta, as they had done a few years ago. Columbia's shell was one of the favorites. Then Jacob would tell her what to prepare for the picnic, as was his custom: crabmeat sandwiches and, of course, her home-style potato salad with a nicely chilled bottle of Riesling. And what a perfect time to don his yachting cap! Dust it off for me, would you, Hedwig?

The phone rang. She mumbled under her breath in German. She was dying for a smoke but her hand was shaking and she couldn't get a cigarette out of the package. Finally getting one, not lighting it, she picked up.

"Hello.

"Hedwig, how are you?"

"Just starting to put together supper for the kids—hold on."

"Where are you going?"

"Something is boiling on the stove." She set the receiver on an upstairs step, lighted a cigarette, inhaled. "Yes, Jacob."

"I got a letter from Wally. He'd seen the Barbara Ann piece, as predicted, and had a few things to say about it. The Reader's Digest was mentioned. Nothing wrong with that per se. But he wasn't pleased that an editor's son had rooted for one boy, son of a Russian-born Maverick artist, and not other boy, a local kid. The 'American.' He implied that Billy had taken a wrong step somewhere since our family visit with the Duprees. But no damage to our relationship. The door is still open. He all but invited me to do a story on 'Our Wandering Children.' He'd give me a bonus on top of my pension."

"Will you do it?"

"I'm working well on my novel, and doing an article of that

163

scope—it would take me well into June," Jacob said. "I'm just so relieved, delighted really, that my relationship with Wally is still solid. In all honesty, I saw him axing my pension—thanks to our impulsive son. But I dodged the bullet. Forgive the mixed metaphor."

She hadn't picked it up. "It's wonderful news."

"I won't be home until ten o'clock tomorrow night," Jacob said. "A well-established literary agent has invited me for a drink and an early dinner. Luther's meeting me in town."

"That's very exciting, Jacob. I'm making fish chowder tonight."

"Have a cup ready for me when I walk in," he said.

Chapter Twenty-Two

He was in his room with eight pages to go in *Huckleberry Finn,* at 10:45, when a car pulled up in front of the house, its headlights brightening the path. Car door opening, closing. His father walking on the curving stone path. In his mind Billy slides a bullet into his .22, pokes the barrel over the windowsill, takes careful aim—

He broke away, clasped his hands over his eyes, horrified by what he'd just envisioned. Had he pulled the trigger? It had just happened but the moment was gone. The front door opened and his father came in. Made a drink for himself and set it on the mantelpiece. Started telling Hedi about his meeting with Emily Neher, the agent, who wanted to see any portion of the novel he cared to send along. He told her he wasn't ready to show anything but he'd get in touch with her when the time came.

"It's a good start," Hedi said.

His father's words drifted through the register. "Latest word from Reader's Digest, I'll be able to keep my office. No breaks, same monthly rent. With a caveat: because I'm a private individual I'll have to put down a first and last month plus a returnable fee against 'damages.' I objected strenuously to no avail. I almost called Wally, decided against it; so that's that. It was almost laughable. Can't you hear Harlan saying to Raphael Hagar, 'I'd love you to come to the Maverick. The rent is fifty dollars. But you have to pay another fifty with your first payment, plus fifty to cover whatever you break or destroy. Altogether, $150 up front. Would you like to think it over, Raph?'"

"You might have to come home, Jacob."

"When this book is done, Hedwig, I'm coming home and never going anywhere again. Did you say there might be a little fish chowder waiting for me?"

They went into the kitchen.

Billy undressed and crawled into bed, still shaken by the image of himself loading, pointing his .22, unable to recall if he'd fired. Surely the crack of the rifle would have stayed in his memory, but all was silent. Billy began the Lord's Prayer, fell asleep in the middle of it.

It was light when he woke to the ringing of the telephone. What time was it? Who could it be? Then, all at once, he leapt out of bed and went quickly down the stairs, picking up the receiver just outside the stairway door. "Hello."

"I heard them talking," Donny said. "Wilbur's got the gun."

"Have you seen it?"

"It's leaning against the wall. They're having breakfast."

"Donny, you have to delay them," Billy said. "It's a big pasture, Champ could be anywhere."

"I'll try."

"Do it!"

Billy hung up. In his room he threw on his clothes and made sure his sneakers were tightly tied. In the kitchen he reached in the refrigerator for carrots, grabbed the last two, cut each into three pieces and jammed them into his pockets. Then he was out the back door. Hanging on the wall in the shed was the lead line. He dropped it into his basket, backed out his bike and coasted out to Bluestone Road, pedaled past Mr. Bagovitch's house, then steadily on, reaching the pasture gate in three minutes. He yanked the lead and pushed the bike into the bushes, then slid across the heavy timber in the gate, opened it and walked in.

"Champ?" He began looking, running. "Champ? Where are you?" The longer he spent looking, the greater the chance Osterhoudt and Wilbur would come in. Billy's heart was racing.

"Champ, where are you?" Then he heard a whinny. Champ was standing in a patch of grass. Billy pulled a chunk of carrot from his pocket and held it out and the pony snorted and came toward Billy, taking it from his hand. Billy, talking all the while, snapped on the lead line and gave Champ a second piece of carrot. "Now we're going to walk," he said. "To the gate and out to Bluestone Road. Are you ready?" He scratched Champ's ears, made to lead the pony, but Champ had another idea. Why is he doing this, where is he taking me? Right hand on the halter, Billy gave a little tug. "Come on, Champ. You can do this."

They walked along, Billy half-expecting to see Osterhoudt and Wilbur already in the pasture. What would he do then? "Nice and calm now, Champ. We're almost there." Billy kept talking, chiefly to calm his own nerves. He pulled on the gate and they went through. Champ appeared to be getting antsy as they drew near Bluestone Road. Then they were on it, heading in the direction of the art colony. Anyone coming along would see them, couldn't miss them. Maybe fifty yards ahead the road turned and once around the small bend they would be in the clear. Billy kept looking over his shoulder. Just as he figured that he and Champ had escaped, he caught sight of a dark red pickup making a sharp right turn into the upland pasture. Billy felt dizzy at the close call and was afraid he'd never be lucky again. He kept talking to Champ, scratching his cheek. He wasn't using the lead, his hand was tight on the halter, and he kept glancing back. Where old Bluestone Road, the spur, branched off they walked along and then they were at the house. At a small maple on the boundary line with Harlan's Field, Billy wrapped the lead line around a branch, then stood there talking to Champ in quiet tones, patting his muzzle, relieved to have made a successful getaway. He had rescued Champ but now what? He didn't have a plan, had no idea of what to do next. Treats were fine but a pony needed food, water, shelter. Champ was out of his element; this wasn't the pasture on Ohayo; and Billy was feeling uneasy as well.

The door to the front hall opened and his father came out carrying a notebook. He had to keep up with Betty, which meant rehearsing, having scenes fully in mind, the characters involved;

the more he could do in preparation, the more pages they could produce. About to cut across the terrace to his studio, he spotted Billy standing on or near Harlan's Field with—he looked closely—a pony. What the hell is going on here? The boy had an incredible ability to disrupt his father's day. Jacob hated interruptions, uninvited guests. He set down his notebook, walked off the terrace and went closer, speaking loudly, flailing his arms.

"Billy, what in hell is going on here?"

"Dad, no! Stop!"

Too late. Whinnying sharply Champ reared, tore the lead line loose, Billy made a two-handed lunge for the halter, grabbed it, locked on. Champ running onto Harlan's Field kicking, tossing, dragging him along, running across the spur then across Bluestone Road onto Maverick Road, past Harlan's place, Billy bracing his legs, yanking on the halter, Champ at last slowing, then stopping, pony and boy breathing heavily. Billy hung on to the halter, more to keep himself from collapsing than to control Champ. They started back, a whinnying from different horses on Bluestone Road, Molly and Betsy clomping along pulling Sherman and his brother on the buckboard.

"Billy, what do we have here?" Sherman asked, leaning down.

"Pony bolted."

"Do you need a hand?"

"I'm doing OK."

"We'll follow right behind you, we're meeting with your mother."

Billy led Champ off Bluestone Road onto the spur. Parked in front of the house was a grimy red pickup. Jacob, standing at the driver's side window, was talking to Rolf Osterhoudt. Billy had a notion of what was going on, and his heart sank.

Osterhoudt was saying through the open window to Jacob, "Here they are now."

Jacob turned to look, disappointed to see his son *and* the pony coming up old Bluestone Road. He had hoped Billy would return, from wherever the crazed animal had dragged him, alone. Billy was walking slowly; both he and the pony were looking weary, done in. Following closely were the Marshall brothers and their team.

168

"Like I was saying, Mr. Darden, your boy stole my son's pony."

"What do you base that on?"

"We saw Billy's bicycle at the pasture gate. Now the pony is here, on your property. Do I call the police? You tell me."

"Wilbur he says call the police, hanh?" A rifle was tucked against his leg.

"It's up to you, Mr. Darden," Rolf said.

"There's no reason we can't discuss this further," Jacob said.

"Good point." He looked Darden up and down and paused. "I'll sell you the pony."

"What do you want for him?"

"A hundred and fifty dollars."

"That's goddamn steep," Jacob said.

"Steep for a pony like Champ, Welsh through and through? Stands thirteen three, six years old. That's an excellent price."

"You can do better than that," Jacob said.

"What I can do is call the police," Osterhoudt said.

"Let's keep the police out of this," Jacob said.

"My offer to sell Champ is good until 9:00 a.m. Monday."

"What happens then?"

"I'm slaughtering two steers on Monday," Osterhoudt said. "Champ will be next."

"Next for what?"

"Butchering."

"Wilbur he cut pony's throat, hanh?"

Jacob felt his mind spinning in ever-tightening circles. *Turning and turning the widening gyre. The falcon cannot hear the falconer; things fall apart.* "Can't you find someone to buy Champ?"

"I've tried, so far unsuccessfully. I'm trying right now," Mr. Osterhoudt said with a smile, his thick lips never parting. "Horsemeat is in demand."

"Give me a little time to think about it," Jacob said.

"Good enough," Mr. Osterhoudt said. "I'll come by at nine Monday morning."

"Wilbur he cut pony's throat, hanh?"

"Shut up, Wilbur!" Mr. Osterhoudt yelled. Then to Jacob, "Have

169

a check for me—make it out to Siegfried Osterhoudt; or I keep the pony."

"All right."

They shook hands. Osterhoudt and Wilbur drove away, and Billy came over favoring his right leg, holding his shoulder. Jacob gave his son a close look. "You all right?" he asked.

"Champ stomped on my feet a couple of times."

"It's a wonder you're even walking! What happened just now?"

"You scared Champ, is what happened," Billy said. "He thought you were Mr. Osterhoudt."

"Am I supposed to be impressed?"

"Did you have to come over storming and yelling, waving your arms?"

"I woke up intending to go to my studio and here we have a pony in the yard. Should I have tiptoed?" Jacob said. "Billy, we have a lot of things to go over. How I approached Champ isn't one of them."

"Common sense would tell anyone not to wave their arms and yell."

"Don't lecture or judge me, Billy," Jacob said in a threatening voice. Pony or boy, what was the difference? "A couple of slaughterhouse heavies were here, and this Mr. Osterhoudt you speak of said you stole a pony and he threatened to call the police."

"I didn't steal the pony."

"You took Champ from someone's property and brought him home. That is stealing!"

"I had to rescue him," Billy said.

"Voices were commanding you. Is that what you're saying?"

"Donny told me his father and Wilbur were gunning for Champ. After they shot him, they'd drag him to the slaughterhouse."

"So this is a moral issue for you," Jacob said in belittling tone.

"I wasn't going to let it happen," Billy said. "I first saw Champ in the Osterhoudt upland pasture a year ago—oh, can he run! His tail, his mane, and my heart were flying. No way was I going to let Mr. Osterhoudt butcher Champ for dog food! They were coming for him just now and I had to get to him before they did. God Almighty, Dad! Can't you understand that?"

Jacob was moved by his son's comments, and he had to respect his courage—a courage he himself had little of—in the face of two disreputable and unsavory men who were gunning for the pony Billy was set on rescuing. "You have a number of regimens, now you have a pony regimen," he said. "Don't let it go to your head and start thinking you're suddenly on your own. I was going to start you on violin lessons with a new teacher here in the Maverick."

Amazingly relaxed after so stressed a morning, Jacob looked at his son peacefully, thinking he could almost hug the kid. "I'm putting off the violin for now," he said. "I'm buying Champ. Clearly we'll have to board him at first. Go tell Sherman that I want to see him; his barn would be perfect."

Chapter Twenty-Three

Jacob was at his desk in his Bluestone studio, rehearsing passages he planned to dictate to Betty Monday in New York. In a flashback scene, Milton Rossel, in his dry-goods store in Boston with Stephen, wanting to interest his teenage son in the business. Imported fabrics. Then a family scene showing an open, give-and-take relationship—

Knock on studio door. "Come in." His son walked in and sat down. "How are you, Billy?"

The boy took in a deep breath, just now coming back to earth. "Champ likes where he is. It's a great barn, Betsy and Molly and Champ, how they whinny back and forth. All kinds of animals wandering about. I was there for two hours this morning, working in the barn, grooming Champ at a hitching post. His mane and tail are thick and rough, full of burrs and tangles. One way to do it would be to shear them down and start over, Sherman said. I said I'd rather work on them day by day."

"Did he say anything about saddling Champ, actually riding him?"

"Soon, in a couple of days, when he's more settled in," Billy said. "He lived in the mountain pasture for so long he's near wild. But he followed the buckboard on a lead line when we took off yesterday—no problem. Sherman said that was a good sign."

Jacob nodded. "Having those workhorses here had to have had a calming effect on Champ. Getting down to brass tacks, Billy. I agreed with Sherman to a two-week board. I don't want to make it any longer. It's reasonable but that isn't the point. I want you to get hold of Chips and tell him you want to make a stable out of the tool room. Of course, use my name."

Billy wondered if he'd heard his father correctly. "I will, Dad. That's wonderful."

"As for *Huckleberry Finn,*" Jacob said, "what's your overall take on the novel?"

"On the raft with Jim, all the adventures they had. It's a great book."

"What was Jim escaping from?"

"Miss Watson."

"Be more specific."

"Slavery."

"Yes. Was he treated badly?"

"No, but he was a slave."

"Why was it so important for him to get down the river? The name of the town escapes me."

"Cairo. If they got to Cairo, Jim would be free."

"No one wants to be owned," Jacob said. "For your essay next week, I want you to compare Jim and Huck. Both were unhappy. Jim was a slave but well-enough treated. Huck was free but treated brutally by his father. Make a case as to who has a worse life, or a better life, as you choose. Now, as to this 'three-mile run in West Hurley.'"

The look on Jacob's face hardened; he was annoyed, troubled. "We have a problem here," he said. "Telling Serge to kick, when I told you to flat out ignore him; that was unforgivable. How could you have forgotten, for chrissakes?"

"Him and Jimmy—he and Jimmy—were drawing near the finish. I wasn't thinking."

"Billy, that's easy to say. I'm not moved by it. Wally wasn't happy about Barbara Ann's column but he let it slide. I should give Billy 'better guidelines,' is what he said."

"Better guidelines as to what?"

"As to the people you know, your friends."

"My friends are OK."

"I think you're too easily influenced. Too quick to join in someone else's game," Jacob said. "Take the crane. You had fun playing on it as an 8-year-old. Then Serge comes along and has the simplistic, outrageous idea to get it running again. There are creative ideas and crazy ideas. The crane is a crazy idea; Champ is a crazy idea but we have him now. It was courageous of you to rescue the pony. That halfwit Wilbur had a gun between his legs! I'm ashamed of myself that Osterhoudt got the better of me. My father would have killed him. I don't mean literally. In closing the deal. The kraut knew he had me—one, by threatening to call the police; two, blackmail. Pay the one-hundred-fifty or that pony is dog food. Sometimes I think I became a writer to make up for my failures," Jacob went on. "Creativity has strange motivating forces. I put down the money for Champ for less than fatherly reasons, but I'm glad you have him nonetheless."

****

It wasn't quite like asking what the Gospel was about or what Father Riordan said in his sermon, but asking his children to speak at Sunday supper when silence or a simple chit-chat was what they really wanted, was close to it. Hedi had made a ham casserole and sharing a quiet meal would have concluded the weekend in the nicest possible way, but no. It always struck Hedi as odd. Jacob had a lot of secrets; secrets made up his life; but he wanted his children, those closest to him, to speak openly.

"Rachel, let's start with you," he said.

"Dad, please."

"How is Andy liking boot camp?"

Hedi looked over at her daughter. Rachel said, "I haven't heard from him recently."

"I would have thought you wrote back and forth each day."

"No."

"What is there to do in Big Bear once you get there?"

"Not much."

"Well, if you like somebody, that's not so bad." Jacob smiled, then to his other daughter, "Holly?"

Mr. Bagovitch had praised her on her last lesson; her barre work was excellent, he said. She was starting to think she liked modern dance more, however.

"What brought that on?"

"The idea of dancing your own way instead of everything just so established. The positions. I thought Mr. Bagovitch might yell at me when I told him."

"Did he?"

"He encouraged me," Holly said. "He even knew the name of a teacher."

"That's wonderful," Hedi said.

"He said all dance owes form and grace to classical ballet, and discipline too."

"I thought you didn't like discipline," Billy said.

"Discipline means a lot of different things, I think," Holly said.

Jacob took in his son. "Billy, how about you?"

"This is the week I learned the brain is like a steam engine."

"What kind of nonsense is that?" Jacob said to his son.

"Freud said it."

Hedi and the girls laughed spontaneously.

"Freud said the brain is a steam engine?" Jacob queried.

"It's what Serge told me."

"Aha! The truth comes out. Under what circumstances did Serge say the brain is a steam engine?"

"We were working on William D.," Billy said, "standing in the cab looking at the off-center shape of the eccentric gear. What it does, why it's important. Without the eccentric, steam would keep coming in and the piston would never get back for a new power stroke. The eccentric cuts off the flow just long enough. With a crack express crossing the Great Plains doing eighty, think how many times in a second the eccentric is called on. We were there looking at one, had our hands on William D.'s eccentric, thinking about what it does. It's never late, it never misses! Isn't that great? Then Serge says to me, 'Billy, Freud called the brain a steam engine.'"

Luther Ryan arrived, beeped his horn. Jacob distributed allowances to the children, kissed Hedwig, and was gone.

****

On Monday morning, after the kids left for school, Hedi cleaned up the master bedroom and bath. As she was putting loose items away in the kitchen, she heard a knock on the front odor. She had never met Mr. Osterhoudt but had seen him from time to time on Bluestone Road. Thick-bodied, full-faced, blue-eyed, he had made her think of a young man she'd known in Biskupitz. Shortly after she and Heini had become engaged, Kurt Bauer had smiled at her outside the butcher shop where he had just started working; his father was the proprietor. She preferred his looks more than her fiancé's, a lot more actually, and Kurt wasn't a miner. But she was spoken for and, in any case, would soon be on a steamer bound for America...to learn English.

She opened the door. "Good morning, Mrs. Darden," he said. "I'm Rolf Osterhoudt. I don't know if we've ever met."

"Good morning, Mr. Osterhoudt. you've come for the check."

"Or the pony. Whichever."

"I have a check," Hedi said.

It lay under an ashtray on the mantelpiece. She handed it to Mr. Osterhoudt, who glanced at it, folded it and slid it into the pocket of his loose-fitting shirt. He looked, she imagined, about how Kurt Baucr would look today; she liked the look.

"I have the saddle Donny wanted Billy to have," he said.

"That was nice of your boy."

"They're good friends, they play baseball together. Plus a saddle pad, bridle, and some brushes and currycombs."

"Thank you, Mr. Osterhoudt."

"Please, call me Rolf."

"I'm Hedi. You can put the saddle and other stuff in the tool room next to the garage."

"Thank you, Hedi, and thank your husband."

"I will."

"Good to have met you." Osterhoudt smiled and went out.

Once every two weeks Hedi did a cleaning of Jacob's studio, usually on a Monday. She gathered together what she would need in a pail and carried it outside, walking to the small, shingled building in the remote corner of the property. Why should she think that Jacob's studio would be neat, pulled together? It never was. She picked up items on the floor, mostly crumpled sheets of paper, stuffed them into a large paper bag with string handles and emptied the wastebasket, then gave the floor a thorough sweep. Three years ago, while they were visiting Green Harbor, a red squirrel had gained entry to Jacob's studio, likely via the chimney; with no way to get out, it had gnawed away the putty and lower frame on the southern window. The squirrel lay dead on the floor when they got back. Hedi had swung the poor animal by the tail into the woods, then had cleaned the mess it had made trying frantically to escape.

Jacob liked that she tidied his studio during the week, but please, he had instructed her, don't toss anything on top of the desk away. Coffee mugs half-filled with coffee and rancid milk didn't fall under that request; neither did cigarette butts in a brass ashtray. Maybe he'd taken a single puff from any of the half-dozen. Hedi emptied the mugs outside and the ashtray into the paper bag, then began a quick dusting of the book shelves...and found herself thinking of the similarity between Rolf Osterhoudt and Kurt Bauer. A question came to her: would she have refused Jacob if *Kurt* were waiting for her in Germany?

She may have thought twice but Jacob's proposal was too all-consuming, too wondrously unreal. How often in a young woman's life did opportunities like that come along? Now, seventeen years later, Hedi was still taken by that moment on the Green Harbor dunes. But sometimes she would wonder what living in a quiet German town with someone like Kurt Bauer would have been like. There was more to it than that. What she missed, on those occasions when she would allow herself the privilege of missing, was living with a man, in Germany or America, with whom she felt loved. Jacob was a great provider, he took care of her and the children, loved her after his fashion; but did he love her? Oh, to be loved! Just this past Saturday morning he had reached out intimately in the early June light of their bedroom. With Betty Trill tending to his needs—secretarial, yes, but not exclusively—what moved him to reach out to his wife of an early morning? Love? Passion? Much as Hedi wanted to think either, or both, she knew what it was. Obligation. She supposed, in the realm of married life, it could be worse. You could be forgotten, castigated, abused. As it was, this past Saturday morning, just as Jacob was reaching out to her affectionately and they were about to make love, the phone had jangled and Billy had come noisily down the stairs to answer it. Jacob had sworn under his breath (not wholly under his breath). A minute later Billy had stormed downstairs again and out the back door, slamming it closed with a kick, and Jacob had thrashed about in bed castigating his son for selfish, thoughtless behavior.

"Where the hell is that boy going?"

She had tried to calm Jacob down. He was making too much out if it, she told him. It wasn't personal.

"It is personal," he came back. "All *too* personal. 'Having a little fun with Mom, are you? Not today, Dad, sorry.'"

She was hoping he might calm down and make a second advance but it wasn't going to be; he wasn't thinking of her, how *she* might be feeling. Obligations were by rote; they signified a duty.

Hedi ran her dust cloth over the legs of Jacob's chair, then sat in his chair and gave a brass pull on the main drawer a quick polish. A thin edge of paper protruded over the top of the drawer; thinking to slide it back, she pulled the drawer open and tucked it back in, her eyes drawn to the opposite side of the drawer—to two small bottles containing pills. In one bottle, they were yellow; in the other, red.

Near the bottles lay a hand-written note on a doctor's prescription, the top portion scissored off. "Jacob, this should keep you for now. Harry."

Closing the drawer, Hedi sat at her husband's desk, troubled. He wasn't a drinker like others in his family; he might make himself a rye and ginger ale, often not finishing it. Pills were something else.

Chapter Twenty-Four

When all seats were taken, a special bus rolled down Hammond Street that Saturday and turned onto Rt. 28 for the eight-mile trip to Kingston. As planned, Billy sat with li'l Jill Santarelli, who had on a peach-colored dress with a lace collar and shiny black buttons down the front. When you had a date for the roller-skating party, you were expected to hold hands on the bus. Who reached out to start it, however, he didn't know. Not one mile into the ride, li'l Jill's hand moved quietly across the seat. Billy saw it coming, scarlet polish on her nails, and reached out, meeting her halfway. Ice broken.

He wasn't unhappy holding hands with li'l Jill. She was awfully pretty, but if you held hands with a girl, you were supposed to talk to her, to start a conversation at least. Billy couldn't think of anything to say. Then he told her that he now had a pony. He had found him in a thick woods on top of a mountain. It did nothing for li'l Jill. She made a face as if wondering why anyone would want a pony anyway. She'd rather talk about going steady, all the great and wonderful things about it. When you were going steady your problems were over. That was it. Nothing to worry about now.

Billy sat back a little in the bus seat, still holding li'l Jill's hand. Might she be interested to learn that he and Chips Doolin had driven to the Willowtown Pond lumber mill and taken away a dozen untrimmed two-by-eights for the floor in Champ's stable, once the tool room? She would listen, but would she reply or comment? She did have a nice way of holding hands, he had to say. Instead of holding his hand like an old sandwich, she held it like a piece of workable clay and kept molding it ever so lightly, as if to fashion a cup or a bowl. Then every few minutes she would look at him with her sleepy browns in a way that made him think she was saying things that kids shouldn't say. Elsewhere on the bus, Clarence was sitting with Henrietta Joy. They didn't appear to be holding hands; she had her head on the geek's shoulder. Billy saw it as an advanced step in sitting together.

He glanced out the window. They were on the main viaduct heading into Kingston and soon were pulling up to the Hudson Valley Roller Rink, a huge shell of a building with a red roof.

In the first twenty minutes of skating, Frank Santarelli and Clarence Bumgardner were "flagged down" and given warnings for excessive speed by the rink traffic cop, a young man with a scrawny mustache and severe crew cut named Zeke who had a whistle around his neck. If he pulled you over twice you were considered a menace to other skaters and the third time you had to surrender your skates and you lost all privileges at Hudson Valley. Plus your name was sent to your principal. Evidently Billy was skating at an OK speed even though he envisioned himself stepping on it, hoping to get flagged. Zeke wasn't interested. Kid. Trying to show off. He had his eye on Clarence. Only when the tall, gangly eighth grader sideswiped Billy "accidentally" and sent him sprawling, did Zeke blow his whistle. Clarence said he'd learned a lesson. When he passed Billy again he smirked and said, "Sorry, squirt."

Seeing li'l Jill sitting on a bench looking lonely, Billy went over to her and asked her to skate. She was only a beginner, and he wasn't appreciably better, but after a while they stayed more or less together to the strains of "Love Me Tonight." Clarence was also skating with Henrietta, and smoothly too. At one point Billy thought to skate away a little and then come back in, like he'd seen Clarence doing, but he lost his balance and went down and Jill, stumbling, landed smack on top of him and everyone laughed and clapped. Then someone said, "Now you guys *have* to go steady!"

180

Somehow word had got out—he didn't remember saying anything—that Billy Darden was going to "break a dollar" on li'l Jill Santarelli on roller-skating day. A couple of kids glanced at the two who had just embraced on the rink floor and were now heading for the privacy of a booth, one of six booths off to one side. Billy asked her what she would like and she said he should surprise her. He went to the food counter and ordered two cheeseburgers, two Royal Crown Colas, and two bags of chips; got a dime back and left it on the counter. Cool. Tray in hand, he went to the booth where li'l Jill, raven-haired princess of West Hurley, awaited her suitor.

****

Billy and Dom, with casting rods and a tackle box, were walking on a cinder roadway that ran straight back three-hundred yards into the city. On either side of the roadway lay woods, thick with live trees and fallen ones too. Clearly no one tended the land; no one had to. It was wild, but wild in a way that indicated it was also forgotten. Its purpose was to act as a buffer between Rt. 28 in West Hurley and the Ashokan Reservoir, New York City's far-reaching water supply. By any name or description, the Ashokan was a magnificent, freshwater lake.

A small brick telegraph station stood alongside a single track of the Ulster and Delaware Line. Twice daily a slow-moving freight would rumble by, first in one direction, then the other. A man inside the station was tapping out Morse Code as the boys walked by. Billy always stopped for a couple of seconds to watch him sending a message in dots and dashes. He and Dom crossed the track, climbed a small rise and were standing atop one of the great stone dikes that kept the water contained. They made their way down the dike at an angle; at water's edge, they ducked into a stand of pines. Overturned rowboats were scattered about like cars parked randomly in a tree-dotted lot.

"Billy, see that big stone there, looks like a pumpkin?" Dom said.
"I see it."
"In case you come by yourself sometime, that's your point of reference."
They walked to the stone. "It's the third boat on the right, aluminum, number ends in 431." They went over to it. "Ain't she a

honey? Like I was telling you, the padlock—just walking by—looks locked."

"It does," Billy said.

"It ain't."

Dom leaned down and gave the padlock a tiny pull; it opened and the chain slipped off. They flipped the boat, laid the oars inside, then dragged it to the water's edge. Dom knew a cove, just around a point in the shoreline, and began rowing. "See how nice she glides through the water? And the oarlocks. Hear any squeaks or groans?"

"No. Quiet. It's a really nice boat."

"Toss in your Red-Eyed Wobbler," Dom said. "It's a good bet right here for walleyes."

Billy let out the lure and twenty yards of line and trolled while Dom rowed. No hits. Once in the cove Dom set aside the oars and began fishing. He had a tin box, curved to fit the hip, packed with dark soil. One of the times Billy had spent the night it had rained, and after dark Dom grabbed a can and a flashlight and they went hunting night crawlers. You would spot one in the grass but if you were slow, it would disappear in a flash. "They're out tonight, Billy. But you have to pounce."

He reeled in and took off the Red-Eyed Wobbler. From an old tobacco pouch in his pocket he grabbed a hook and tied it on. Rock bass, sunfish, yellow perch. Dom landed a smallmouth that went sixteen inches, open season hadn't started yet. Billy didn't say anything. His father had once used the expression "moral compass." Billy didn't remember how, in what context; but he liked the phrase. It occurred to him that a person had a moral compass or he didn't. Serge had one. Hedi had a beautiful moral compass. His father talked a good moral compass. As for himself, Billy wasn't too sure. Sitting here in a boat that "belonged" to a dead man, looking the other way on a friend's less than honest read of fish and game regulations—it seemed to him his moral compass needed improving.

Billy oared the boat going back. Dom did some fancy wrist-action trolling with a silver minnow and damn if he didn't get a big hit, almost to yank the rod from his hands. Did Dom play the fish for three or four minutes, let out line as necessary, tighten the drag on his reel? No, it wasn't how Dom Santarelli worked, it wasn't who he was. He horsed the fish in, delighted with himself as an eighteen-inch brown trout lay flopping in the boat.

Billy started rowing again, thinking what he already knew—Dom had something going for him. Who could explain it? They dragged the late Mr. Wilbraham's boat out of the water and up to the pumpkin and flipped it, shoved the oars beneath. Dom attached the padlock to the chain and, with a light-fingered touch, closed the lock without really closing it. "Billy," he said, "if you want to go fishing on your own, take the boat. Leave the padlock under some leaves. When you're done, use the padlock but don't lock it. Once locked, we'd have to break the chain and, like you said, we're not breaking no chain. That's stealing. Stealing is a mortal sin. Borrowing something from somebody is a venial sin and you don't go to hell for it."

They left the wooded area and climbed the dike, Billy carrying the stringer, Dom the trout, hooking a finger through the gills. By the sun and light, Billy had the time at about five or five-fifteen. The telegraph operator had left for the day; not much business for the Ulster & Delaware. Coming along the track was a man in a yellow handcar, working the arm, propelling the cart along. The boys stepped aside and he rolled by, hardly a nod, a man with a long weary face. Billy thought he might've been nodding off; with no traffic to worry about, safe enough to do. They followed the cinder roadway down; as they stood on the side Rt. 28 waiting for a milk truck to go by, Billy said he had to be running.

"Call your mother at the house and tell her you're stayin' over."

****

Having had a great dinner of spaghetti with sweet and hot sausages, the Santarelli family gathered around, Billy was starting to feel sleepy. Li'l Jill was sitting next to him on a large, four-cushion sofa in the parlor, a room considerably longer than deep just off the large dining room/sitting room. The parlor had no doorway, just a framed opening with a curtain; anyone in it had some privacy, not a hell of a lot, unless the curtain was drawn. Billy had the feeling if he were to lie down, li'l Jill would lie down next

183

to him and no one would mind or care. Mrs. Santarelli poked her head into the parlor and told her daughter it was time to go to bed. She gave Billy a hug and told him privately she'd see him later. Did that mean later tonight?

Dom, whose mind was like a #1 Oneida jump trap, was saying to Billy, "Let's check out the action."

"Whereabouts?"

"In the bar."

Billy had never set foot in a bar; he knew the big, main-floor room, but not the bar itself. He didn't think his father would approve. Other than that, he saw no reason not to go along. Dom opened a door off the kitchen to a dimly lighted corridor. They walked to a door that had a window in its upper half. Dom pushed it open and they went in. Ten or twelve people were sitting at the bar and two couples were dancing to "Tangerine" on the jukebox. People were doing a lot of laughing; the setting down and picking up of glasses and the making of drinks kept Mr. Santarelli and another young bartender busy. Two barstools were empty and Dom and Billy sat down.

Mr. Santarelli came over. He was a big man, thick dark hair low on his forehead, eyebrows that seemed to crash into each other over a big nose. He asked Billy what he would like. He said a ginger ale and Dom had the same. Some of the people at the bar seemed young, maybe Rachel's age; others were a lot older, more like Billy's father. Billy picked up his glass like a big person, had a drink, and set the glass down. Dom asked his father for peanuts and he brought over two small bags.

"Nice here, isn't it?" Dom said, popping peanuts into his mouth.

"Yes."

"Jeeze, we've knowed each other a few years now, Billy," Dom said. "Like I was thinking just the other day how we was still-hunting for grays—me, you, and Frank—on the city. You had my uncle's old .410 with the double hammers. We was spread out, maybe a hundred yards between us, like in a triangle. 'Boom!' comes through the woods. The .410. Then I remember, Jeeze, we didn't tell Billy it had hair triggers, is he OK? I go running over the ridge and you're sittin' on a downed pine, a big gray layin' at your feet."

"It was my first squirrel." Billy looked around. Then he said, "Where did Frank go? I haven't seen him since dinner."

"His girlfriend just got here."

"I didn't know Frank had a girlfriend."

"She graduated KHS two years ago and is taking flying lessons, or maybe she took 'em and is already a pilot."

"His girlfriend? Frank is fifteen years old," Billy said.

Dom let out a little laugh. "Age ain't got nothing to do with it. My brother's built like a bull." He clenched his fist, stiffened his forearm. Then, hand half-covering his mouth, "Woman halfway down the bar, long brown hair, green dress? Nice woman, has a sick husband, poor guy needs an oxygen tank night and day. I lost it with her last fall."

"Lost what with her?"

"Billy, come on. What do you think? Do you know what she said?"

"No."

Dom spoke through his fingers. "It was the best she'd ever had, she told me there in the backseat of her car. How's that for setting a guy up?"

Billy thought he understood English; his friend could've been talking Greek. "Papa," Dom said, "two short ones."

Mr. Santarelli filled two small glasses and set them down. "How's your mother, Billy?" he asked.

"She's fine."

"Give her my regards," Mr. Santarelli said.

Billy didn't know they knew each other. "I will."

"She's a very special woman," Mr. Santarelli went on. "Years ago—you wasn't born yet—I had a business took me around selling produce from my truck. A lot of good customers in the art colony, none so nice as Hedi Darden. She always come out with a smile, a kind word. They were tough times. People like your mother kept me going."

"That's nice, I'm glad," Billy said.

Mr. Santarelli left to serve a patron and Dom picked up his short beer, had a swallow. Billy picked up his and had, well, less than a swallow. A taste, to see if he liked it. Dom walked down the bar. Just then Frank and his girlfriend came out of the door with the glass pane. They came over and said hello to people at the bar, chatted it up. Then they came over to Billy and Frank introduced him to Gail. "Billy's a good infielder," he said to his girlfriend. "I never seen him miss a grounder."

"Nice meeting you, Billy," Gail said.

She had short dark hair and blue eyes and wore a black jumpsuit; it made Billy think she'd just had a flight. People were talking and dancing and the jukebox was kicking out tunes and Billy was thinking a bar was a fun place—and who came out the family door but li'l Jill. She had changed from her clothes and had on a light-brown skirt and a yellow sweater; hair brushed, lips glossed. She came over to Billy and they sat at the bar with Frank and Gail as if on a double date. Billy had another taste of beer. He didn't particularly like it but wasn't going to let it just sit there. Frank and Gail were dancing and li'l Jill asked Billy if he cared to dance. It wasn't a matter of caring. Did he know how? Last winter around Christmas, Holly had given him a lesson to a Hit Parade song, "Night and Day." But that was it.

He and li'l Jill went out to the middle of the room. He tried to remember what Holly had told him but soon quit trying and gave in to the music, the rhythm of "Sleepy Lagoon." Li'l Jill knew how to cozy in. Frank and Gail weren't dancing unless there were certain steps where your feet didn't move. It was like swimming in place. Billy thought of Gail doing incredible turns and dives, drawing fire but never getting hit, an American ace. Dom was talking with a woman in a silvery blouse with an oval neckline. She was laughing. Dom had never said anything to make Billy laugh. Everything with Dom was serious, like when he said not to snap shut the padlock when he returned Mr. Wilbraham's boat. Because then they'd have to break the chain and that was stealing and stealing was a mortal sin. Would that make you laugh? But the woman with the glistening blouse was laughing.

"I like this more than roller skating, don't you, Billy?"

He told her he did. A lot more than roller skating. Not as much as baseball but he kept that to himself.

Chapter Twenty-Five

Mr. Marr announced fifth-grade geography; they were doing New York State, but, before starting in, he gave a look around the classroom. In the seventh-grade row Dom Santarelli was nodding. If his head touched his desk, he'd give the boy a shout-out and have him stand. As if reprimanding Dom would do any good. He'd laugh it off. Mr. Marr thought Dom would likely drop out at the end of the school year. His sister Jill wasn't falling asleep. She had her book open—sixth-grade social studies was next. She was Dom's age and Billy's and should be in grade seven but Mr. Marr had held her back two years ago so now she was a year behind...academically. She was reading her book now as a cover so she could dream. Mr. Marr hated when a kid under his tutelage quit school, even disinterested kids like Dom. But he really worried about Jill Santarelli. He was afraid he might have to hold her back again. If it happened, that would be it for the girl's education. The girl was sweetness itself but her mind was elsewhere. Yearning had taken over her brain.

Billy Darden was writing in a notebook; in the past two days he'd taken it out while Mr. Marr taught other classes. He seemed to think it had nothing to do with schoolwork but it kept the boy busy.

"Now then, our topic of the day in geography is our own Hudson River," the teacher said to his class. "How did the river get its name, and what was the occasion?"

****

Serge and Billy were sitting on the fallen tree halfway home talking about their plan tomorrow to put William D. under its first (and very light) head of steam; to get a fire going under the boiler and watch and listen carefully. They had to graduate, Serge said, from the theoretical and take their first step into the practical. They had slightly over two weeks before the Rustovsky going-away party, their well-established date to show the world the rejuvenated William D., and to wait until then to fire up the old crane would be the height of immaturity, silliness, and stupidity.

"We have to start making actual tests," Serge said.

"The least we can do at the party," Billy said, "is give the whistle a good blow."

"If we can do that, you can bet we'll be heroes. In the beginning we had a dream," Serge said. "We were going to chug through the colony on William D. blowing that whistle, remember?"

"I thought you were crazy," Billy said.

They began walking again. Two water pails sat on the Quarryman driveway and Billy picked up one. They crossed the pathway to Bluestone Road and walked toward the mountain. Billy gave the Jamison house a slow, uneasy look. To get away from the Maverick, the disappointment of losing the Rincon job in San Francisco, Wes and Julia had loaded up their station wagon and were now in a peaceful town in New Mexico. For how long, Billy didn't know; but he understood something for the first time. Painting, writing, sculpting had always seemed perfect way to make a living. You were your own boss and didn't have to drive anywhere to go to work. What recently had started sinking in, for Billy, was how greatly artists suffered. The joy of creating, yes; and the anguish.

He helped Serge at the long-handled pump fill both pails, said he'd see him later, and took off at a run. Chips was working on making a stall for Champ, and Billy was curious to see how it was going. But first he ducked into the ticket office at the Maverick Theater and into the theater itself. Actors—Billy recognized Mia Littlebird—were doing a rehearsal on stage; but that same moment a man stood up in the front row and said, "That's it for now. Excellent!"

Someone near the back of the theater clapped and a girl shouted in a young, familiar voice, "Bravo!"

Billy looked over; it was Bzy. He had hoped to catch her here, and there she was...sitting next to the new kid, Austin Fromm.

"Billy!" she said with delight in her voice.

"Hi, Bzy. Hi, Austin."

"Hey, Billy."

"Then you know each other," Bzy said.

"We do," Austin said. "The other day we practiced the pivot in a double play."

She had on a yellow cotton dress with a blue ribbon at each sleeve. "How are you, Billy?"

"I'm OK." He didn't at all like the way Austin's arm lay on the backrest behind Bzy. "My father bought Champ from Mr. Osterhoudt. We're building a stable at the house."

"Wonderful!"

Austin's hand had slipped a notch on the backrest. Billy had the feeling that it would drop all the way once he left and end up around Bzy's shoulders. Austin didn't seem at all concerned that Billy was feeling uneasy; either that or he didn't care. He asked Billy if he'd ever kept track of his batting average over a season.

"No."

"Last year I hit .409," Austin said.

"Is that good?" Bzy said.

"I guess! Ted Williams hit .406, the highest average since Rogers Hornsby in 1924."

"I have to be running," Billy said.

"I'll stop by again," Austin said. *Right now, go away.*

"See you, Billy," Bzy said.

In a minute Austin would have his arm around her; they'd likely start kissing. He went out. Minutes later he was walking on old Bluestone Road nearing his house. When the smell of fresh-cut lumber came into the air, he started to run, skirted the garage. Chips was standing at the door of the tool room sawing a rough-cut two-by-eight. Piled neatly to one side was the old floor.

Chips stopped sawing. "Billy," he said, "glad you're here."

"How's it going?"

"See for yourself."

Billy looked at the empty tool room, new floorboards all in. "Chips, this is beautiful!"

"Do you want me to build a manger?"

"Is it important to have one?" He was thinking of his father; could see him blowing a fuse.

"I think so." They went inside the box stall. "Without a manger, hay gets all mixed up with bedding," Chips said. "In a manger, it stays fresh and clean." He pointed to the front wall, to the right of the door. "Here's a perfect place for one. Now something else. Where are you going to put your bridle and saddle, your brushes and currycombs? The hay and straw?"

"In the garage."

"If your folks agree to it, fine. But do you know how inconvenient that's going to be," Chips said, "walking through rain and snow and icy wind to open the garage door every time you need something for Champ?"

"I've thought about it."

"I have too," said Chips. "I never had a horse. Well, I used to ride a donkey we had. Where I grew up near Boise, Idaho, we had a farm, a lot of workhorses, saddle horses too. Both my sisters ride to this day. They had a way of cornering me and asking, 'Bob, can you do this? Bob, can you make that?' They wanted a tack room, I made them a tack room. I carved a yoke when I was fifteen and fashioned an oxbow to go with it. My father wanted me to become a civil engineer, a designer. After high school I joined the merchant marines. No one could understand why. What had got into Bob Doolin? When I was fourteen I made a boat. There was a lake near us and I fashioned a sail. I had a girl that used to go out with me, just like your friend, Bzy. I've sailed the Seven Seas, more than seven of them, and visited ports of call around the world."

"Are you missing it?"

"You can't deny something when it's in your blood," Chips said. "But right now I'm happy doing what I'm doing. Taking care of Harlan's buildings and making a stable for a young friend's pony."

190

****

After almost a week of letting the pony settle down in Sherman's barn with easygoing Betsy and Molly, Billy was going to saddle and ride Champ at last. It was a tough pedal to the crest of Bluestone Road but then it was downhill the rest of the way to Sherman's long dirt driveway; he coasted to the barn. A huge maple was in the yard with a bench beneath it. Who should come out to greet him but Buck. Billy gave him a hug and, in return, got a wet tongue on his ear. It was amazing to him that pony and dog, almost from the start, had become friends, long lost. Sherman had no problem with the extra tenant. If it amounted to anything, he'd add it to the boarding fee for Champ.

Molly and Betsy made warm, ruffly noises when he went into the barn. Kink, the goat that roamed the barn like a free agent, came running up and gave Billy a head butt—a friendly reminder as to whose turf this was. A rabbit hutch stood at one end of the barn and a big yellow cat got up from napping on the straw in front of a chestnut mare and her just-born filly. Bantam chickens, in a close circle, moved freely about like a colorful pinwheel looking for a place to roost. Inside the barn, across from the Percherons' stalls, was a room with all manner of harness in it, including Champ's tack. Fastened above the entrance to the room was an old wooden yoke; a pair of crafted oval-shaped collars hanging down to circle the neck of each ox, keeping the yoke in place. Above the stalls was a great loft brimming with hay. The pony was looking at him from his stall.

Billy walked over. "Champ, how are you today?"

He opened the low door to the box and led Champ to a stand-by-itself post in the middle of the floor. He snapped a line to Champ's halter, stood there scratching the pony's ears, talking to him. "Wait till you see your new stable. The tool room had a single door but Chips is making a double door out of it so you can see over the top. And your own manger. Oh, and the farrier is coming to see you. Next week sometime."

From a nearby shelf, Billy got a brush and a currycomb and gave Champ a grooming. Compared to his first day in Sherman's, his forelock and mane were fuller, free of most burs and snags; but they still needed a lot of work. So far, Billy hadn't touched Champ's tail; he wasn't yet comfortable working on or near his back legs. But soon. Perhaps even...now.

Sherman Marshall came into the barn, staying busy for a while tending to his draft horses and the mare and filly; then he ambled over to the hitching post. "How are you, Billy? Ready to ride?"

"It's why I'm here."

"What experience have you had?"

"Donny Osterhoudt used to have a Shetland pony. I saddled her and rode her maybe five or six times."

Billy went into the harness room. The saddle, a dark-brown western, lay on a stationary wooden barrel. Billy picked it up with the accompanying saddle blanket, then grabbed the bridle from a wooden peg and returned to the post. Sherman took the bridle, held it in one hand, his free hand on Champ's halter.

"Always work on the left when saddling," Sherman said. "Same for mounting. OK, set the saddle down. Lay on the pad. Keep talking in an easy manner."

"OK, Champ. Here we go. We're going for a nice ride, you and me. Steady now." Billy put the pad on the pony's back.

"Praise him, Billy."

"Good pony, Champ. You're doing great." He picked up the saddle.

"Now remember," Sherman said, "you have to give the saddle a good swing to get stirrup and girth across his back."

Billy moved in close, gave the saddle a swing. Champ moved sharply aside. With nothing to land on, the saddle thudded to the barn floor.

"Try again," Sherman said, hand firmly on the halter. "If he shies, stay with him, stay in position to throw on the saddle."

Billy lifted the saddle, took a step nearer. "Easy now, Champ. Here we go."

He moved in and made to toss on the saddle but had to wait; even with Sherman holding Champ's head, the pony sidestepped. Seeing an opening a second later, Billy threw on the saddle, then reached down and drew in the girth, ran a leather strap on the near side of the saddle through the ring and pulled up snugly.

"Well done, Billy."

The bridle posed an even greater problem. Champ wouldn't accept the bit. His jaw was locked. Time and time again Billy thought he had it past his clamped teeth but before he could fasten the cheek strap, Champ would spit the bit. Finally it stayed in long enough and Billy managed to secure the bridle.

"Let's go outside," Sherman said. "Unfasten Champ."

Billy wanted to take a three-minute break. He led the pony out; in the barnyard was another hitching post. "As for mounting," Sherman said, "hold the reins in your left hand, put your foot in the stirrup, then up and over."

"OK."

"I'll hold his head."

Billy had the reins. As he was trying to slide his foot into the stirrup—not easy, it was a stretch—Champ's back leg shot sideways, and a bit forward, in a quick awkward jab—like a boxer with his back turned striking an opponent with an elbow—almost catching Billy. Sherman said, "When you go to get on, face his rump, not his head. With nothing to kick at, he won't kick. Try again."

It wasn't what Billy wanted to hear. Eyeing the pony's back leg, he managed to catch the stirrup with his hand and slide in his foot; then he swung up and over and was in the saddle.

"Well done, " Sherman said. "Stirrup length seem OK?"

"Seems fine."

"Take him out to the field, the gate's open," Sherman said. "Show him who's boss. Just an easy walk to start."

Billy touched Champ with his heels, jiggled the reins. They went along for fifty yards, came to the open gate, and went in. It was a great, flowing field with a huge old oak in the center of it scarred by lightning. Question was: How did you get a mean-assed Welsh pony to understand you were the boss? Because right now he was an 82-pound sack of beaten-up potatoes which, at any moment, would topple if Champ got it into his head to buck, rear, or take off on a run.

Astride, Billy was trying not to feel hurt, but he was hurt—like the daily visits in the mountain pasture, what did they mean? It was crazy but he felt deceived. The pony had turned on him. Lashing out with hoof. Sure, I'll take your carrots, just don't ask for any favors. Like wanting to put a saddle on me and a steel bar in my mouth.

Billy pulled on a rein and steered Champ through the open gate. In the field, Champ lowered his head as if to get a scrunch of grass. Not only was his head dropping, his legs were bending, his body sinking. What was this? Next thing Billy knew, Champ was on the ground starting to roll. Billy cleared his feet from the stirrups and moved quickly away. Deed accomplished, the Welsh pony got up as if to run, to make dust. On his feet, Billy grabbed the loose reins and tried to get back on. Champ, wanting no part of it, kept backing away. Stirrup too damn high. Twice Billy tried getting his toe in, third time he lost balance and pitched forward, breaking his fall with folded arms. Tears streaming down his face, he clutched the reins together at the pony's muzzle.

"Champ, what are you doing? Stop!"

There was no way he would try to mount again. Scraping his eyes with the back of his hand, Billy led Champ back to the barn. Sherman took the reins and told Billy to sit on the wooden bench. He sat, leaning forward, head bowed. He was short of breath, eyes puffy, forearms bruised. Sherman took the pony into the barn, came out and sat next to the boy. "That didn't go so well," the man said. "He's a tough one, you were great to hold on."

"What the hell, Sherman. I—I thought we were friends!"

"Billy, let me tell you something," Sherman Marshall said, hand affectionately on the boy's shoulder. "I love Molly and Betsy. They'll do anything I ask of them, haul, draw, plough 'til they drop. Would a friend do that? A friend will say I'm tired, I want to rest, I'll do it tomorrow. Treat Champ well, take care of him, he'll give his life for you, Billy. But if you want him as a friend, forget it. He'll break your heart."

Chapter Twenty-Six

They were moving along at an excellent clip, doing three pages a day on average. Jacob was pleased—more than pleased, he was ecstatic—by his ability to talk his novel and Betty's skill in transforming his words into crisp, error-free copy... as he spoke them. When he considered the abysmal pages he'd struggled to write, not that long ago, on his typewriter, it seemed to Jacob that he and Betty, as a team, were practicing nothing less than literary alchemy.

He was so impressed with the way things were going that, in a weekly session, he'd mentioned it to the therapist. Jacob had thought he'd come to the end of the line with *The Red Hat*, he had started off saying to Smiley. The book he'd wanted to write since his first days in the Maverick Art Colony wasn't going to get written unless, or until, his arthritis went away; and it kept getting worse.

"Virtually overnight it changed," Jacob said. "All my life I've equated writing with the physical act of putting words on a page with a pencil or on a typewriter. Well, there is another way and the hands have nothing to do with it."

"You understand why arthritis hit you when it did," Smiley Blandon said.

"Smiley, we kicked it around. I don't buy it." Jacob was tired of the psychiatrist's obsession with psychosomatics. "For the artist, the work takes precedence. To spare my mother's feelings I was going to scrap my novel?"

"It's what your hands were telling you to do, Jacob."

"My arthritis was real!"

"How are your hands now?" Smiley wondered.

"They've calmed down," Jacob said.

"Take to using your typewriter tomorrow and give me a call," Smiley Blandon said.

"Why, to settle an academic point?"

"I wouldn't call it academic, Jacob. It cuts to the core."

"Betty and I are doing three pages a day, sometimes more," Jacob said. "You don't mess with something that's going well."

Smiley Blandon gave his client a penetrating look. He had a narrow face made up of sharp, incisive angles—the jaw, the cheekbones, a sharply hooked nose. "I'm thinking of the ends, clearly you're wrapped up in the means."

"Goddammit, Smiley, the ends, the means or anything in between, I'm going to finish this novel," Jacob said.

****

Later in the week, shortly before Betty would be leaving for the day, she and Jacob were sitting in the interview section of his office. Fifty-one pages of newly written and typed pages lay on the author's desk. "My mother would like to meet you," Betty said. "Drive out with me someday after work."

"Sure. I'd love to. Does she know that you and I—?"

"She knows. She's happy for me."

"Does it bother her that I'm married?"

"She's never said anything. Ask me if it bothers me."

"Does it?"

"No."

"Tell me about your mother," Jacob said.

"Melissa is a Whiteley from Merion, a 'Main Line girl' all her life," Betty said. "Went to Miss Porter's, debutante of the year—she appeared on the cover of Life—spent a year in Paris studying art; but paramount on her mind was getting married, grabbing a guy with a good name from an Ivy college. From her early years, society played a huge role. Her parents didn't own a telephone book; they didn't have to. The only people the Whiteleys knew, or cared to know, were in the New York Social Register. Appropriately, my mother got involved with a Harvard Wall Street lawyer; good while it lasted; it didn't last. She met a super-rich polo player with impeccable credentials. Dirk Burlingame was a great sport, wonderful fun—they followed the polo circuit around the world with his string of ponies. Ultimately, there was no future in it. Mom wanted to settle down with someone and have a home and a family. Finally she met someone with the unlikely name and background of Mike Benitez, who had gone to Irvington High School and three different colleges before graduating. Zero social bona fides. Her parents—two stuffier people than Reginald and Brooke Whiteley didn't exist—snubbed the Benitezes from the beginning. Their precious Melissa had married down to the extreme and they never really forgave her, or let her forget it."

"In a way that's to your mother's credit," Jacob said. "She broke the mold."

"Yes. But she never really outgrew her cotillion days," Betty said, "even when my father Mike was alive. Now that he's gone, she's desperate to get back in, to reclaim what once was hers."

"Why did she marry him, really?"

"The first time they slept together, Mom once told me, she crossed off anyone else. They had great sex. But for all the zing in their love life, she only conceived once." Betty tossed up her hands. "Yours truly."

He laughed. "Does she work?"

"No. Never has. Painting is work, she says, but she's never had a paying job. Which reminds me, Jacob—we'll both be out of a job at the end of the month."

"I feel like saying 'Don't remind me.' I'm thinking of picking up the lease right here, where we are." After a pause he said, "I need you to stay with me, Betty."

"You know I'll stay with you."

"I didn't know. I was hoping. I'll pay you a good wage."

"Jacob," she said, "I'm not worried. Here's a thought. Mother has a cottage on her property. It's very quiet, well-removed from the main house."

"Does she rent it out?"

"She never has but I imagine she would. I'll talk to her."

****

Back in his 63rd Street office after a quiet dinner out, Jacob wrote chapter headings on a pad, added notes beneath each heading, listed the characters that would be on stage, settings, bits of dialogue, descriptions; exposition in certain instances, but always at a minimum. Best if no "explaining" at all. It was death to a story. Skillful "planting" was the answer. After two hours of putting his mind to the task, Jacob estimated he had seven pages tucked away ready to deliver. He stood up, talking points in hand, and paced the floor, rehearsing a few lines. He was in command, grateful that Betty had committed to staying on.

Time for sleep. In his bathroom Jacob popped two Nembutal, showered, slipped into a pair of pajamas, then reached for the phone on his nightstand and dialed long distance, gave the operator a number, and crawled into bed.

Hedwig, always and forever home, picked up. "Hello."

"Just turning in. I wanted to say good night," Jacob said.

"How nice. How are you, darling?"

"It's been a long day. I added seven pages to *The Red Hat*. It's coming along really well."

"This is your important book, Jacob."

"What's been going on?"

She mentioned the Woodstock Library Fair, preparations for it well underway. As in years past, she was in charge of clothing. The contributions this year were falling behind last year's. What with the war, people were holding onto coats and shirts and the like, but it was still early. Yesterday Billy and Serge had a second rehearsal for William D.," Hedwig went on. "I wasn't there but Billy said they blew the whistle, very faintly. On Saturday at the Rustovsky going-away party they'll give it more steam, he said. I think we should go to it, Jacob."

"We'll drop by. How are the girls?"

"They're fine. Holly's having a rehearsal in Mr. Bagovitch's studio. And Rachel had a talk in high school with a college counselor."

"Good."

He had a wonderful thought of his children and Hedwig in their house; then he said he loved her, good night. "Good night, Hedwig," he said again. "Good night, Jacob," she said. Then he put down the phone, closed his eyes, and was out.

Chapter Twenty-Seven

It wasn't quite like the Maverick Art Colony festivals of old, Hedi was saying to Mrs. Rustovsky, who was hosting the goodbye party with her husband Leonid; but the feeling was similar. Almost everyone in the art colony was there, artists from Woodstock and Byrdcliffe as well. Serge Rustovsky and Billy Darden in engineer's caps were walking around answering questions about the crane, when it first came to the Cayuga Quarry, then about the bluestone industry itself. Bluestone was as resilient to time and weather as glass but would break if dropped, so it had to be handled with great care. The single largest piece of bluestone ever removed from a quarry in Ulster County was taken here at Cayuga in 1892, measuring nine feet three inches by four feet nine inches. William D. had carried that record-sized piece out to a buckboard on Bluestone Road.

Chips and several others in the colony had cleared away brush and trees so that people could view the steam-driven crane from almost anywhere on the lip of Cayuga Quarry. Mr. Rustovsky had mixed up a bowl of punch made with Russian vodka and Beatrice was serving her own recipe of borscht with chunks of braised beef, each serving getting a generous dollop of sour cream. A group of four—guitar, washboard, bass fiddle (large metal tub with a single string), and bongo drums—banged out rhythms. Most of the people had likely supported Wes Jamison in the recent competition, but no one at the party was holding a grudge against the winner. The punch and borscht were plentiful and good.

Half of the people were in get-ups. Rustovsky left no doubt as to his role in a braided vest, ballooning knee-length pants, and wooden sword in his belt. Raphael Hagar, smart in his yachtsman's cap, had somehow got hold of sneakers and a crusty pair of white duck pants. Jacob had thought of going as a yachtsman but couldn't find his cap and went as a poet, white shirt with a red and black neckerchief. Hedi had on what was known as a Woodstock dress, full length, a colorful print trimmed in rickrack, and sandals. Holly and Rachel were helping Mrs. Rustovsky carrying around trays of Russian finger food. Harlan didn't have to don a costume; compared to Rustovsky's get-up, his tan Cossack shirt was what he always wore. Bzy and Mia Littlebird were there and Jacob made sure he went over and engaged the actress while Hedi and Mrs. Rustovsky were talking. Mia's opening in "Boy Meets Girl" was this Friday, and Jacob said he would definitely be there. With an hour to go before the main event, Serge and Billy took stations on the crane.

As the party continued apace, Jacob saw Raphael in the cap he had looked for earlier. He went up to the sculptor and, casually enough, asked him how he happened to have it on. "That's an easy question to answer, Jacob," the sculptor said. "Your wonderful wife gave it to me."

"Hedwig let you have my yachtsman's cap?"

"She did. I asked her if she had any sort of old hat laying around, and she came back with the one I now have on my head. Do you want it back?"

Jacob would have a talk with Hedwig. It seemed like something she'd never do. "It was given," he said. "It's now yours, Raphael."

"Thank you kindly, Jacob. It's a splendid cap."

At about five o'clock Chips, standing on the lip of the quarry, announced that smoke was coming from the crane. Everyone, now in high spirits, streamed over for the show and stood around the edge of the great excavation. The Maverick Band took a position on the edge, and the excitement mounted as the old crane, under

201

rising pressure, began shaking.

"This is crazy," Jacob said.

"They're only going to blow the whistle," Hedi said.

"I don't like it, Hedwig."

In the cab, Billy was looking at the gauge. The needle kept rising and Serge said William D. was really kickin' ass now, but he was going to throw on two extra logs for good measure. Billy yelled, "No, not necessary! We can blow the whistle, as is."

"Without a full head, it sounds like a tired old hoot owl. We have to give these people something, Billy!"

Serge jumped down and threw in logs and came back to the cab. Everyone was watching from the top of the quarry, from wherever they could see. William D. was trembling, shaking. Billy kept looking at the safety valve atop the boiler.

"I'm blowing the whistle," he said.

"Not yet, in another minute." The fire was roaring. Smoke was pouring out of the chimney.

"Here goes," yelled Billy, yanking at the overhead cord.

The whistle was almost deafening. Everyone at the quarry clapped, cheered. Billy kept checking the gauges—water temp and steam PSI. The needles were going up but the safety valve wasn't blowing. He looked at Serge. The plan, made at the last run-through, was to leave the crane after the whistle blast, then to let the old fellow cool down on his own. Serge had both hands on the steam inlet valve and he was making to crank it open.

"What are you doing?"

"We haven't come this far just to just blow the whistle. This is history we're making!"

To lessen the pressure, Billy blew the whistle again. Then, in a stuttering jolt, William D. came awake. It bucked, it groaned, it jolted.

"Serge, stop!"

"Great, isn't it?"

He gave the steam valve another crack. The crane lurched forward along the broad, bumpy path; its jib, bouncing up and down on its cable, drew ever-louder cheers. The screeching of steam, the wrenching of great knobbed wheels turning for the first time in forty years, William D. bucking, advancing—

"Cut the steam!" Billy shouted.

"I'm trying!"

"We're heading for the quarry!"

"It's stuck!"

Billy wedged himself beside Serge and together they made to close the steam-inlet valve; it didn't budge. Then, at an especially sharp jounce, the cable holding the jib snapped, and the jib crashed down, the top of it extending over the lip of the quarry.

William D. ground on and pushed the jib over the edge. The cab was ablaze, smoke was blanketing William D., and William D. was about to go over the edge of Cayuga Quarry.

"Jump!" they both yelled.

Billy hit the ground hard, dazed, knobby rear wheel coming at him. He rolled, wheel missing his leg by inches. On fire, the cab followed the jib over the edge; in a great rumble and tumble William D. toppled into the great excavation, a fiery ball; then a huge explosion. The air was thick with smoke and the smell of fire and Billy didn't know where Serge was. Then he saw; Serge was three feet from the edge trying to free himself from a nearby bush.

"Billy?"

"Yeah."

"You OK?"

"Seem to be. How about you?'

No cheering, no shouting from the crowd. Just silence. Complete and utter silence. "I think my arm is broken," Serge said, sitting beside Billy on the ground.

"Well, we're still alive."

"According to the poet," Serge said, "the world ends with a whimper. Not so! William D. just proved it ends with a bang!"

"We made it, we're here," Billy said.

"You could sue me for breach of contract," Serge said.

"What would I get?

"The Principles of Steam Locomotion."

"I saw it burning, Serge."

"There's nothing else I can think of."

"I won't sue you," Billy said.

They began laughing. Billy was also crying—crying and laughing at the same time. Billows of smoke were rising from the excavation. Then Jacob and Hedwig, Leon and Beatrice, and three men from the Colony—Chips, Raphael, and Nick Bonino—came pushing through brush and trees to check on the boys.

****

Later that day, Jacob and Billy were walking outside the house, talking over what had happened at the Rustovsky party. Jacob was upset, deeply troubled that Billy had gotten himself mixed up in a situation so top-heavy with danger. That he had come away with a bruised hip and Serge with a bump on his head and a broken arm, when they could've been burned to death, crushed, blown up, verged on the unbelievable. You could both be dead! What did you prove by doing it?

"The world doesn't end with a whimper. It ends with a bang," Billy said.

"Eliot wasn't talking about two dumb-ass kids risking their necks in an old steam-driven crane. That's a false equivalency. You blew the whistle, then what happened?"

"People were cheering but they wanted more. So we gave them more."

Jacob gave his head a dismal shake; he picked up a pinecone on the lawn and tossed it onto the spur. "Whose idea was it to activate the crane, to actually get it moving?" he asked his son.

"Serge opened the steam-intake valve and the crane gave a wild lurch, the wheels turned, we were moving. When the jib crashed, Serge made to close down the throttle. We were near the edge. But it was stuck."

"Did you take Serge's word on that?"

"I tried it myself, then the two of us together. It didn't budge."

"Whose idea was it to jump?"

"We both called it."

Billy and Jacob had walked the length of the lawn and were now at the new box stall. "Luckily no one in your careless little game got himself killed," Jacob said. "Your mother was beside herself with anxiety and Mrs. Rustovsky thought she was having a heart attack. You had no thought for anyone else; it was you—you and Serge—

and your escapade."

Billy hesitated a moment. "It got away from us. We knew it was serious."

"What you and Serge did was a blatant disregard for human life. Like giving a loaded gun to a child." The top door to the new stall was open and Jacob peered in. "When are you bringing the pony back from Sherman's?"

"The farrier is coming on Tuesday afternoon. Right after. Champ needs shoes."

"Has he ever had them?"

"I don't know, Dad. He was without shoes in the pasture."

"But now he needs shoes. Is that what you're saying?"

"For hard surfaces, horses should be shod."

"What's your source for that?"

"My source?"

Jacob's eyes momentarily lidded. Did his son understand anything? "Who said horses should be shod for hard surfaces?"

"Sherman."

"Well, the boarding, the farrier, the general upkeep, it's all adding up," Jacob said. "But I want you to understand one thing. I will not have that pony eating hay in the summertime!"

"I'll be tethering him out."

"How's he doing under Sherman's care?"

"He's doing OK. It's a friendly barn," Billy said.

"What is it with Buck and Champ?"

"They like each other."

"No mystery there," Jacob said. "Two of a kind. One's ornery, the other's a simpleton."

"They're a dog and a pony," said Billy. "It's what they are. A dog and a pony."

****

On Tuesday afternoon, with Billy riding and Buck tagging along, the trio moved at a steady walk on Bluestone Road. "Boarding-school days" were over and they were heading for home. Champ was eager to break loose (flash a little steel), but Billy kept a firm hand on the reins. He could feel the pony's pent-up energy and was nervous he might run on his own. Not an hour ago, Champ had had a tough go around with Will Kinkaid, the farrier, at Sherman's outside hitching post. The full-length leather apron Kinkaid wore had served him well, lessening the impact of several sideways kicks. He had worked patiently, shaping, rasping each hoof. He wasn't having a down-and-out fight with Champ but shoeing him was hardly routine. When he was done, Kinkaid said he was more upset by those who hadn't cared for the pony's hooves than by the pony himself. Now Champ was shod with light, racehorse-type plates. He said he'd like to see Champ in four to five months to check on how he was doing.

"Keep his hooves clean, especially the frog," the farrier had told Billy, picking up the pony's front hoof to show him what he meant.

Instead of branching off onto the spur when they reached the Maverick, Billy kept on the main road— less likely someone would come over to talk and maybe spook Champ. Buford, hoeing his corn just starting to grow, took a long look, held his hoe high. Nearing his house, Billy reined the pony off the spur onto Harlan's Field. He felt like shouting; no one was around but it didn't matter. It was how he felt, proud of Champ, of himself. They were home. Champ lowered his head as if to sample the thick grass on Harlan's Field. In deference, Billy let up on the reins. Except that wasn't it. He had the sensation of sinking, getting closer to the ground. Snapping to just in time, he yanked up hard on the reins, blocking the pony's tactic to get the rider off his back.

At the outside wall of the garage, Billy dismounted and snapped him to the hitching rope. "What is it with you, Champ?" he said, taking off the saddle. "Deep down, what kind of pony are you?"

****

He worked on Champ for thirty minutes, getting up the nerve to brush his back legs and begin de-burring and untangling his tail, always checking on his ears. If they started going back, watch out. Buck, observing the care and attention the pony was getting, lay there quietly. What was good for one was good for the other. Billy brought Champ water in a galvanized pail, first setting it down to give Buck a chance to drink from it. Dog wasn't interested. Mostly, if Buck wanted a drink, he'd find a puddle somewhere, a trickle. He was a "no upkeep dog." The only time they had a vet come to the house was the day Buck was foaming at the mouth. A kid in the colony scared Billy into believing his dog had rabies. If he bit you, you could get lockjaw and die. Turned out, Buck had gone after a porcupine and had a mouthful of quills.

After the currying, Billy put an armful of hay in the manger, pulled it apart, and scattered straw on the floor. Among the innovations Chips had made was an oak arm you could lower, or raise, in the stable doorway. When lowered, you didn't have to shut the lower door; the stall always had a free flow of air. When Billy left, he lowered the arm from the outside and walked across to the house.

Inside, his mother was sewing a strip of brown cloth into a carpet lying on the sunroom table. "Hi, Mom."

"Billy. There's new raisin bread in the kitchen. Wash up before cutting a loaf."

Something about her voice seemed different to Billy. She was working on the rug but her thoughts seemed to be elsewhere. As he washed with soap and water, he thought maybe she'd had news from Germany. Three loaves lay on the counter under a thin white cloth. The one he picked up was still warm. There was a trick to cutting a fresh loaf: don't force the knife. Break the crusty surface with the point, then use a firm but gentle ripsaw motion. Billy put a thick slice onto a paper napkin and sat down with a glass of milk at the kitchen table.

He was pleased that he'd finally got up the nerve to work on Champ's back legs and tail. Just keep talking. Words, it didn't much matter what you said. Like how Jimmy McMullan chattered at third. Tone, that was the important part. Don't let doubt or fear creep in. Billy had felt both earlier. How was it possible to be relaxed and easy going, when Champ had tried rolling on him? Twice now! How could you trust an animal who basically didn't want you around?

Sounds were coming from the sunroom. Not loud. Maybe a leaf was brushing against a windowpane. There, again. He stood, leaving his last bite of bread on the napkin. Hedi was standing at the table sewing on a long strand of braided material, except she wasn't sewing. Her finger was bloody and tears were streaming down her face.

"Mom, what's the matter?"

"I pricked my finger. It's nothing. Bring me a napkin from the kitchen."

He brought her two. "Did you get bad news from Germany?"

"No."

"Mom, you're sad about something."

She dried her face, pressed the other napkin to her finger. "Your father just called."

"OK."

Hedi pulled out a chair and sat down, "He...his..."

"Mom, go slow. What's going on?"

"His plan, the plan we had—it won't be happening."

"What plan are you talking about?"

"To live with us fulltime...once he left Reader's Digest."

Billy wasn't exactly crushed but seeing his mother upset blocked out everything else. "Why?"

"He can't write without his secretary, he says."

Billy looked at his mother closely. Her face was drawn, gray; she wasn't old but suddenly she looked old. "Since when does writing take two people?"

"Evidently for your father it does. It never did before," she said.

****

Luther Ryan was getting out of his car and walking on the pine-needle driveway to pick up the Rustovskys. Standing with them was Billy, and no one was saying very much of anything. Luther and Rustovsky each took a bag to the car; then there was nothing else to do except...say goodbye. Mr. and Mrs. Rustovsky gave Billy big hugs; then they walked to the car and got in. Serge lingered at the house.

"Keep walking the trail, Billy," he said, arm in a cast. "Sit on the old oak."

"OK."

"It was a great year. One day you'll write about it."

Why he would say that, Billy didn't know. "So long, Serge."

"So long, Billy."

Serge walked out to the car and got in the passenger seat in front. Then Luther was backing away; Serge waved and Billy waved, raising his arm high, and the Rustovskys were gone. Billy had a strange feeling of not knowing which way to turn. Hoping to shake it, he sat on the sagging 8-inch plank, his back against the stone siding of Quarryman. Then the urge came to him to look at William D. or what was left of him. He went to the spot where the crane had once stood, then followed the access path to the quarry and gazed down. Along the whole downward tumble, the crane had left bits and pieces of itself. A knobby wheel had come loose, as had the fly wheel—it was wedged between pieces of bluestone like a starfish—as had a ragged section of the boiler, a portion of the chimney, and, at the inner circle, the pond at the bottom of the great excavation, the jib lay like a shipwreck on rocks.

A question arose in Billy's mind. If given a do-over for the day, would he choose a simple blowing of William D.'s whistle? It was what people were expecting and it was what he had genuinely thought would happen. Then the crane would stay in the same spot for another forty years for new kids to see, play on, tamper with. Or would he choose what had actually happened? That William D. would go down in a proud, a memorable way as befitted a hero, in flames. Billy didn't know if he would ever have an answer. Maybe when he was seventy-five he would stand right here and know. He picked up a piece of bluestone and hurled it into the air over Cayuga Quarry.

Chapter Twenty-Eight

Using a reward incentive, Billy gave Champ a chunk of carrot for standing still at saddling and another chunk for accepting the bit; by the end of the first week, when Champ saw Billy coming with bridle or saddle, his jaw seemed to loosen in anticipation. Billy rode every day, gained confidence in his ability; he found dirt roads where he could give Champ a touch with his heels and let him flash his shiny new plates. Billy also became adept at using currycomb and brush and finally got Champ's tail free of burs. Brushing it gave it a wonderful shine, made it fuller. Soon he lifted each front hoof and took a screwdriver with a short handle and thick blade and cleaned the underside, especially the frog. He got his courage together and reached for a back hoof. He wasn't in any leather apron and a sideways kick would surely hurt. You were leaning over low, hand on the hock sliding down to the pastern and fetlock; then you gave a little tug, and lo! you were looking at the underside of a rear hoof. More work with stubby screwdriver. Billy gave the pony a carrot chunk and told him he had the cleanest frogs in Ulster County.

The colony was known for rocky outcroppings, not pastureland; except for Harlan's Field and Buford's garden, where did anything grow other than weeds and trees? His father's words a command, Billy had no choice but to search out areas for Champ. The meadow by the red, long-handled pump had good grass but was too remote. What if Champ got himself tangled in his tether with no one around? There was also a small meadow at Canal Boat but staking out Champ on it, even if Mia and Bzy agreed, put too much responsibility on them. Not fair, not a good idea. Mr. Bagovitch had untold acres of meadow all of it posted (Hedi picked wild strawberries in certain fields, an exception). If the impresario saw a pony grazing on his land he'd sure as hell call the sheriff. Billy, thinking on the topic nonstop, concluded that the only "pasture" in the Maverick was fifty yards along Maverick Road as you headed into the colony.

Billy was tethering Champ on it now, the pony's third successive day on this parcel of gnarly grass flavored with sumac leaves. Most distressing for a pony snatched from an upland pasture (his home no less) of the thickest, greenest, coolest grass imaginable. Billy snapped the thirty-foot length of rope to Champ's halter, made to scratch his ears, but the pony wanted no part of friendliness. Billy walked away and Buck stayed; clearly the two had plenty to talk about, to plan. Was a conspiracy in the making, a rebellion?

Harlan was outside Morning Star in his Russian-style over-shirt when Billy passed by. They exchanged greetings and Harlan invited him to sit. Billy was ready to hit the Woodstock Golf Course and make a half-dollar for a quick nine, but he put caddying on hold and grabbed a chair. Harlan said he was still taken by the sight of a pony going by at a gallop and Billy holding on for dear life.

"Your feet were off the ground," he said.

"If I let go, he'd be gone." Trying to find a comfortable way to sit in the chair pieced together with tree branches and vines, Billy related how his father had come out of the house and didn't like what he saw—a pony, a team of horses, a buckboard, people moving around. He saw it as an interruption to his day and came over, arms lifted, demanding to know what was going on.

"The pony saw him and took off like a bat out of hell."

"He knew Jacob?"

"No. My father reminded him of someone Champ hated, likely feared," Billy said. "By nature, Champ is edgy, suspicious."

"He had fire in his eyes when he went by. Well done, Billy."

211

"You had a horse," Billy said.

"I did. There was no other way to get around."

"What was he like?"

A small, reminiscent smile came to Harlan's lips. "Gentle. A friendly old mare. My boys, three and five—I'd get on, pull them up. She'd take us into Woodstock or around. I was at Byrdcliffe at the time."

"I know where her grave is," Billy said, "in the woods below my house, at a stonewall."

"She pulled up lame one day," Harlan said. "No minor injury. A friend and I walked her into the woods. He had a gun and that was it."

"You put up a stone," Billy said. "Painted on it, 'Here Lies Ronnie, a Horse.'"

"It was the least I could do," Harlan said. He poured himself a little more coffee from an enameled pot. "I was on Ronnie one day and she took me down a nameless dirt access to the quarries in the area—later, Bluestone Road. We got to this exact spot when we stopped. This was it, the home to be of the Maverick Art Colony."

"How did you know?"

"I turned to look back, and Mount Overlook was shining on me, the full effect of it. In Byrdcliffe, it's too close. You're more *in* Overlook than seeing it. And the sky. It was a blue I'd never seen before, the purity of it. I might have called my colony the Overlook Art Colony. So many overtones to the name 'Overlook.' I felt the power of it, the beauty of it that day. But I already had a name. It came to me as a young man looking through a train window at the Great Plains, watching a stallion racing across the prairie answering to no one. A maverick. That is art, Billy. That is the artist. Untamed, unbranded, unbeholden."

Harlan was looking down, and Billy seemed to see him recalling those early years of the Maverick Art Colony, sadly slipping away. "Harlan, isn't Byrdcliffe an art colony? What made you want to start a new one?"

"Yes, but it was Richard Whiteley's art colony, not mine," Harlan said. "I helped pull it together with Barton Browne, chose the land we had to buy, built the structures and houses. Almost

212

from the start I could see it wasn't my idea of what an art colony should be. It was organized, it was structured—furniture making, fabric weaving, metal workshops, jewelry making and the like. Painters and writers, yes, but as one of several pursuits one could have. Daily tea with Richard and Sandra. Lovely. I wanted an art colony for poets, painters, sculptors, musicians, a place where an artist could live cheaply and work. I had to get away from Byrdcliffe. Richard was a wonderful man, and generous; he poured his heart and money into Byrdcliffe. Too quickly it began failing. Furniture making, one of the key elements in the early Byrdcliffe, too quickly died. The overhead, and the finished pieces didn't sell. By comparison, what is the overhead for the writer, the painter? In the Maverick Art Colony you paid for your house if you could come up with fifty dollars. Life is short, art is long. Your mother and father came to the Maverick. What souls they were! Jacob untied himself from Columbia because he felt himself becoming beholden to it. An artist has to be free. Which brings me around to Champ. I see him as the second coming of the Maverick Horse. Billy, unsnap him from that tether. Think of making a fence around Harlan's Field. Until then, let him have good grass at least."

"My father isn't going to go along with that," Billy said. "It's not why—"

"Billy, kindly remind Jacob as to who owns Harlan's Field," Harlan said, in a matter-of-fact voice, as of a teacher. "If he kicks—not Champ, Jacob—send him over."

****

Upstairs in his room, Billy added to the dollar tip he'd made caddying for Mr. Spector, giving him a total of $8.50 in his savings box. Fat chance his father was going to pay for a fence. He had already complained about shoeing Champ and had made it very clear as to how he felt about other "extras."

Billy was in his room for another reason as well—to finish his report on *Robinson Crusoe,* due Saturday. Another paragraph or two would bring the word count to approximately 450. What was wanting was a conclusion, a final thought on Crusoe and his man Friday. He had an idea but the words for it were jammed like logs in a river and weren't breaking loose. He wrote a few words

213

anyway, as to give himself a prompt when he came back to it, then set his pencil down and went out.

Champ was tethered on Harlan's Field, doing a very nice job, thank you very much, on the grass. To prevent too harsh a circle from developing, Billy had decided to rotate the placement of the stake every other day; this was only the second day of the new regimen (that word wouldn't leave him alone). Tomorrow he'd choose a new spot. He felt a whole lot better now that Champ was getting some decent grazing, but a tether was a tether. The idea that Harlan had floated wouldn't leave him alone.

Billy unsnapped the rope from Champ's halter and led him to the hitching ring on the outside wall of the garage, then ducked into the tack room for brush and currycomb. He worked on the pony's coat, then his mane and tail. Next, put on the saddle: piece of carrot followed; put on the bridle: piece of carrot. Then came mounting. First you unhooked the pony, then attempted to get on. But Champ wouldn't stand still. He backed, shied away, as Billy—ever mindful of the pony's hair-trigger left hind leg—tried to get his foot in the stirrup. No one was watching but it was still embarrassing. Here he had his own pony and had trouble getting on. "Steady, Champ." He kept his voice low but dearly wanted to shout. On his third try—it was as if Champ had teased him enough—Billy snagged a stirrup, got his toe in, and was up.

He gathered the reins, and as a unit—dog, pony, boy—they went to the spur and stayed on it into the colony until they came to the crossover opposite Ohayo Road. On Ohayo, Billy made a clicking sound, brought in his heels, and Champ broke into a canter. He had the feeling that Champ wanted to gallop but he kept the pony reined in and slowed him to a walk as they neared the intersection with Maverick Road. They continued on Maverick—someone's pail sat on the stone base of the long-handled pump—passing several cabins and coming to the Canal Boat driveway. He started down at a walk and who should come out of the house just then but Bzy...and Austin Fromm.

What's going on here? Billy asked himself.

"Billy, you have Champ!" she said, walking up quickly.

"I do, yes."

"Billy, how are you?" Austin said.

"I'm doing all right. How about yourself?"

"I'm doing OK," Austin said.

Bzy came close, giving Champ's forelock a ruffle "Did you ever think this would happen?"

He wasn't sure what she meant. He said, "No."

"Where are you keeping him?"

"Chips made a stall out of a tool room we have." Then he said to Austin, "I haven't seen you recently."

"I'm around. My father has me practicing three hours a day."

Bzy said, "Opening night for Mia is Friday."

"Tell her I said 'break a leg.'"

"She'll appreciate that."

"Well, see you."

He turned Champ and they went away at an easy walk. Then, venting his emotions, Billy sucked on a corner of his tongue, brought in his heels—and Champ broke into a run.

At the bottom of Ohayo Road where it hit Bluestone, Billy crossed to the spur. A station wagon with wood siding was in the Rustovsky drive. Two very large women—they had on men's clothes and had men's haircuts—but Billy knew they were women, new residents. A good crowd was gathered at Intelligentsia, no kids. Maybe Bzy and Austin were the only kids in the Maverick Art Colony this summer. Standing outside Bearcamp was Raphael Hagar. Billy knew him better than anyone else in the Maverick except Harlan. He was always coming to the house for a leftover snack or something to use or wear. Right now he had on Jacob's yachting cap. The sculptor and ex-cavalryman waved him in and Billy rode onto the property. The house had a strong look to it. Quarryman, the Rustovskys' old house, had bluestone siding, random pieces linked like a puzzle. By contrast, there was nothing fanciful about Bearcamp. It had a brick lower half; the upper part was solid wood; a gabled, wood-shingled roof. Billy knew the house well. Harlan had lived in it for twenty-five years and the room, now Raphael's studio, had housed a printing press. Billy would wander over to watch Harlan set type and activate the great rollers, glossy with ink; and then, a miracle, you would have a printed page!

Harlan's novels and plays, poems by Billy's father and others, short stories and essays, a monthly magazine called "Maverick"—all had come out under the stamp of the Maverick Press.

"Chips said he was making a stable at your house," Raphael Hagar said. "You were boarding your pony at Sherman's. Now that's a fine-looking animal. What's his name?"

"Champ."

"Nicely groomed, well shod. I like when a horse's tail touches the ground." He ran fingers through the pony's forelock. "Who had him before you, do you know?"

"A friend of mine, Donny Osterhoudt."

"What about the saddle?"

"When my father bought Champ, Mr. Osterhoudt threw it in."

"Did you adjust the stirrups?"

"Was I supposed to?"

"Billy, look at the bend in your knees!"

"Sherman didn't say anything."

"He has workhorses. Let's get this right, Billy. Get down."

He dismounted and held Champ while Raphael unbuckled the heavy leather straps on both sides and dropped each stirrup two notches. When Billy was ready to get back on, Champ sidestepped; what was once a challenge now, with the stirrup lowered, was made simple. In a quick, easy move, Billy got his foot in and was up.

"What a difference!"

Raphael said, "I used to be able to mount a galloping horse, no stirrup at all. Where are you grazing him?"

"I'm tethering him on Harlan's Field."

"I don't like tethering. One day he'll get spooked and lassoed by his own rope." Raphael was looking at Champ's front legs, chest, neck. "Do you know what I'm thinking, Billy. This pony is a jumper. I see it, just by how he stands there."

"Is that good?"

"It's fantastic." Raphael's voice suddenly took on a warmer, more intimate tone. He asked Billy how his mother was.

"Last I saw, she's fine."

"A wonderful woman! Has she been making a lot of great things recently?"

216

"There's always something cookin', Raph."

"Give me an example."

"Earlier, just now, she had bread in the oven."

"What kind of bread, Billy?"

"Raisin."

"Raisin bread, you're saying?"

"It's what I'm saying."

Chapter Twenty-Nine

Time was running out on the lease on the 63rd Street office and Jacob still didn't know where he and Betty would be working when it expired at the end of the week. Reader's Digest wasn't going to lower the rent; it was "nonnegotiable." Jacob could not let go of the feeling that the intransigence was payback for a certain newspaper column on a three-mile run in West Hurley. Wally had let it pass when he'd first seen Barbara Ann's story but nothing ever really passed Wallis Dupree. Go write your book elsewhere, Jacob. Good luck. Tracking down an ad in the Times, Jacob had looked at a studio on 67th Street near Third Avenue. Manageable, but the nearby elevated train was noisy and the neighborhood wasn't conducive to writing. That left the cottage in Morristown. Betty had driven him to see it last week, parking to one side of the main house. Now here they were in Betty's car again, this time to meet her mother.

They left behind the unattractive, congested part of New Jersey and were now zipping along country roads in a part of the state Jacob didn't know. Financially, things weren't going well for him. His Reader's Digest quasi-pension wasn't kicking in until September 1st. Jacob had a rush of paranoia and began to think that Wally was making him sweat after so abruptly jumping ship. Emily Neher, his agent, had called to say that after reading the 100 pages of *The Red Hat* she had decided it was insufficiently "filled out" to send to Richard Stein at S&S. Jacob's first novel, *If Winter Comes,* had sold 200 copies. It wasn't as if Stein or any publisher was waiting impatiently for his next book. Emily suggested that Jacob buckle down, add another 100 pages. She found it interesting that he had made the future cardinal's father Jewish. You only saw the Jewish father on a close reading but it added a dimension to the novel nonetheless.

Jacob couldn't get his mind off his financial morass. Starting with the proposed basement at home. The Brothers Marshall were anything but exorbitant, but labor was labor; hours had a way of piling up. And when it came to shoring, you could bet they were going to take their time, not wanting the excavation to cave. Then with a new basement you had to have a new washing machine. Jacob didn't want to insist that Hedwig get along with the one they presently had. It was a threat to fingers and hands and posed a danger of strangulation, but it got clothes good and clean. She knew how to handle it and he was hoping she'd rescind on her request. The furnace and concomitant radiators were a must, except in Billy's room where the register in the floor allowed warm air to flow up, maybe enough to keep a glass of water from freezing. Eschewing a radiator in Billy's room represented a big saving and he didn't want to pamper the boy in any case. Normal household items—food, power, gasoline—were going up. Think supply and demand: war effort, rationing, availability. More and more you saw notices: Out For The Duration. The *un*-normal costs were killing Jacob, like the upkeep of a pony. Not to mention the initial price. Buy Champ for $150 or tomorrow he's dog food. Your call, Mr. Darden. The demented Wilbur making gross sounds in the passenger's seat with a deer rifle between his legs. Jacob felt it all piling up. And now Rachel, after breaking up with Andy Sickler, was picking up the pace of her college-application process. Hedwig had told Jacob about their evening at Andy's camp in Big Bear. Rachel had come home two hours early. Jacob had a good idea of what had gone wrong. Son-of-a-bitch was insisting she sleep with him! Sorry, Andy. Anchors Aweigh. Jacob wasn't unhappy about it. Now his daughter was "talking Smith." Holly, next, would be opting for a college like Bennington. Then Billy. In Jacob's way of thinking, his son needed a push, a path to follow, more urgently than his sisters. Enough of Ulster County with its benighted, reactionary mentality. Jacob saw Billy in a New England prep school where he'd meet the right boys from good families, future leaders of America...

And he would be paying Betty a salary. Senior vice president G. F. Kidd had specifically requested that she come to his office as his secretary, now that the Roving Editor was leaving; but she declined the offer, citing other arrangements. Her priorities were elsewhere. Jacob felt an indebtedness. Betty Trill was nothing short of the *sine qua non* of any literary resurgence he might have, and he desperately needed her.

"Here we are," she said.

They parked at a split-rail fence directly in front of an imposing barn-red house with dark brown shutters and white trim. A brick path led to a heavy oak door flanked by potted geraniums. Betty lifted a polished brass knocker and let it drop. "It's not the way I normally enter my house," she said. "My mother likes meeting new people at her door. She's very traditional."

"I've a strain of that myself," Jacob said.

"You'll get along famously."

The door opened; standing there was a woman in a blue print dress and matching heels with dark-blond hair carefully set falling short of her shoulders. She was smaller than Betty but the resemblance was striking, yet Jacob detected differences. Betty's mother had a certain allure, perhaps that of an older, more knowledgeable woman. She knew something but wasn't afraid to learn more. Jacob didn't know if they would get along famously; possibly they wouldn't get along at all. "Mother, I'd like you to meet Jacob," Betty said. "Jacob, my mother, Melissa."

They exchanged pleasantries. "Betty tells me you're writing a best-selling novel."

"Every writer who ever put pen to paper thinks he's writing a best-seller. I'm working on a book."

"It *will* be a best-seller," Betty said.

"Well, please, come in," her mother said.

It was a large front hall; a crystal chandelier hung from the ceiling. To her daughter, Melissa said, "I thought we'd have drinks by the pool."

Betty and Jacob followed her through the house. Everything in it, like the front-door knocker, had a shine to it—the baby grand in the living room, the parquet dining-room floor, wine glasses sparkling on an antique sideboy, counters in the kitchen glistening like black ice. Jacob had the feeling he was walking through a movie set: "home of top business executive." A round-faced zaftig woman in her thirties was cutting vegetables at the stainless-steel sink.

"Wanda," Melissa said, "I'd like you to meet our guest, Jacob Darden."

"Good afternoon, Mr. Darden."

"Hello, Wanda."

They continued to the door. "She's a wonderful cook, gives a great massage too," Melissa said.

They stepped out to the patio. The pool was smaller by half than the Olympic-sized NYAC pool he was used to but plenty large; in short, it was perfect. He sat next to Betty, Melissa across from them at a glass-topped table. The patio had extensive stonework, a small pool with goldfish in it, many plantings. In landscaping, if you gave Jacob a terrace and a lawn, he was happy. Hedwig made the paths, odd-shaped pieces of bluestone with a quiet curve between points A and B. Never a straight line. Smiley Blandon had once told Jacob it indicated she was in no rush to get anywhere, she liked where she was, while Jacob couldn't get there fast enough. Wanda came out with a sterling tray of hors d'oeuvres.

Betty made drinks at a poolside bar—Scotch for Melissa in a rocks glass, rye and ginger ale for Jacob, gin and tonic for herself. Wanting to hear Melissa talk (when you asked a question of someone, you couldn't be accused of staring), he said he found the patio marvelously done. Had her late husband had a hand in its design?

She didn't answer the question, she ran with it. More than any man alive, he considered his home his castle. She was now devoted to keeping it up in Mike's memory. For how much longer, she didn't know. Maybe when Betty left she'd sell the house; until then, having her here was everything. For these past three years Melissa said she'd lived in a safe environment and was looking forward to getting out into the world again, to spreading her wings.

Jacob liked hearing an attractive woman say she wanted to spread her wings. Of all delightful euphemisms, that was his favorite.

Betty made drinks anew. Accepting a second rye, Jacob observed Melissa bringing the Scotch to her lips. The way she crossed, then re-crossed her legs, played with her fingers, nudged her hair away from her face, he would venture to say that Melissa Benitez was suppressing a great deal of sexual energy. At any moment, the thought came to him in a fine metaphorical flash, she might spontaneously combust.

She asked Jacob to tell her about his novel. He mentioned the title. It was the story of a young priest who rose in the Catholic Church to become a cardinal. Thinking to talk about the theme of abortion in the book, he realized Melissa was on a different tack—her own—leaving the poor author stranded on the dock. "Mike was raised a Catholic," she said, "and he wanted me to marry him in St. Ignatius Loyola in Manhattan. I didn't want to marry him in his church and he didn't want to marry me in the Episcopalian church. In a compromise, to show unity, he gave in and came over to St. James' on 71st in Manhattan. From that day on, organized religion had little or no influence on our lives. I taught Betty prayers and sometimes took her to church, but we weren't a religious family. Personally I think it hurt us. Having faith in common can hold a family together. I imagine you're a Catholic, writing a novel about a priest. Were you a unified family, mother and father and children?"

"We were. Strong Catholics, all of us."

****

They were in the smaller everyday dining room in the house, having "Wanda's own pot roast" for dinner, a fine Chianti in their glasses. Jacob was at the head of the table, where his hostess had graciously instructed him to sit, when she surprised him by saying, "Betty told me you'd seen the cottage."

"Yes. She drove me out last week."

"You found it to your liking," Melissa said.

"I did." Jacob was relieved to be discussing the reason for his visit at last; he had thought the topic would come up immediately. It hadn't. The only emotion that played on him more heavily than anxiety—he had two days left on his Reader's Digest lease—was impatience. "It would be a great place to work."

"Are you interested in living there as well?"

"Yes. To be discussed, of course."

Melissa carved a piece of a roast potato and brought it to her mouth, followed by a swallow—no mere sip—of wine. "Mike built it as a get-away house, a change of pace. For himself, the family. Betty would often go there as young girl and spend the night. My husband worked hard," Melissa said. "Morehead Fasteners was getting tough competition and Mike worked ten to twelve house a day to keep the lead. Then he'd disappear to the cottage for the weekend. Monday morning he'd be a new man."

At the end of every sentence Jacob was hoping she'd come back to the subject of the cottage—and the writer who was knocking on its door—but she kept on telling seemingly endless anecdotes and reflections on her life with Mike. They were willing to give up formal religion by way of having a more unified household, but politics had nearly killed it, regardless. Melissa and her parents were for the New Deal, loved FDR, and Mike hated the president and prayed some nut would save the country by assassinating him. Income Tax, Social Security, regulatory laws. Many a good fight, but we finally learned to accept each other for who we were, and the love we had for each other never went away. Mike had some really tremendous qualities. He was a man of principle and in the business community he was loved. Hundreds turned up at his funeral to pay their respects. She went on and on—Melissa and Mike, Mike and Melissa—but then she turned to Jacob and asked him what he liked about the cottage.

"The quiet, the isolation. It's perfect."

"Mike loved it for those same reasons. Do you have any questions?"

"Is it available? I guess that's number one."

"Of course it's available."

Jacob reached for the wine bottle. Melissa watched him carefully, pleased that he motioned to her glass first; she gave her head a small shake. He poured an ounce into his own glass. Looking at Melissa, "What are you asking?"

"I'm not asking anything. There's no rent. It's not a rental property," Melissa said. "I've always been a supporter of the arts. In his own narrow way, so was Mike. A team of horses couldn't drag him to the opera but he'd open his wallet if he saw a painting or sculpture he liked. The cottage is yours, Jacob, while you're working on your book."

"That could take another year or more."

"However long."

Jacob hesitated; no rent to pay would help him financially. He could give Betty a well-deserved bonus and Hedwig could buy the best washing machine Montgomery Ward made, not its bare-bones model. He had flaws, God knew, a character badly scarred, but this made him uncomfortable. How could he accept living rent free in Melissa Benitez's cottage? It would be giving himself over to her, making him beholden. His father's philosophy—take the money—still held but not so it made you indebted. If taking the money made you a pawn, your only move was walking away.

"That's more than kind of you, Melissa," Jacob said. "But—I wouldn't feel comfortable unless we drew up a lease."

"It's a grant I'm giving you as a man of letters."

"That's a kind interpretation," he said, "but to me it seems too much like a gift."

Melissa bridled. "What is your pleasure then?"

"Even Harlan Gray, the founder of an art colony in upstate New York, charges for a cabin," Jacob said. "It isn't much, but it establishes a relationship. A cosseted artist gets lazy."

"I have no intention of cosseting you, Jacob."

"I'll pay you twenty-five dollars a month for the use of your cottage, where I would live and work."

Jacob thought Melissa might lash out at him but she was silent. Wanda cleared the table, then served an apricot tart and coffee. Melissa folded her napkin and they repaired to the living room where Betty, at the baby grand, played a Mozart and a Chopin, impressing Jacob greatly. Every so often he would glance at Melissa who, he seemed to think, wasn't paying that close attention; something else was on her mind. When Betty finished, they both applauded and, shortly after, Melissa said she was turning in.

"I would've been a good neighbor," she said to Jacob. "You want an old grouchy landlady instead, you'll have one. Bring me a lease and a check."

****

From his first visit, Jacob remembered the path of white pebbles. Now, with the aid of a flashlight that Betty was holding, they walked on it and came, after a minute, to the cottage. They went in via a screened-in porch.

"Here we are, Jacob."

He liked the good-sized room: two easy chairs, a bookshelf, a fireplace, a couple of lamps, a hardwood floor—great for pacing. In one corner stood a desk; on it sat a full-sized typewriter. Jacob said he didn't remember seeing it last week.

"It wasn't there last week. In the drawers are all kinds of secretarial stuff. Let's sit on the porch."

They went back out and sat on a settee with a yellow cushion; suspended by chains, it rocked easily. Straight out, a quarter of a mile away through a number fields and isolated trees, the fairway of a private golf club shone softly. Of a summer evening, she said, her father would take a wedge and a few balls and practice pitch shots.

"I loved the Chopin," Jacob said. "It couldn't have been nicer."

"Thank you, Jacob."

The cottage had the aura of an island about it. Under ordinary circumstances he might feel hemmed in, restricted, deprived even. With Betty, it wasn't a problem. She asked him if he was surprised that Melissa had changed her mind.

"I didn't expect her to," he said.

"It's not like her, but your reasons were convincing, I thought, and honest."

"There was no way I could I live off your mother's generosity."

"You made that very clear." Getting up, causing the bench to jiggle and jounce, Betty said, "I hope you work well here, Jacob."

"I hope we both work well here. It's a joint effort. Where are you going?"

"Home."

"You're home now."

"Jacob, apart from having a two-minute walk to work instead of a forty-minute drive, nothing has changed. See you in the morning."

She gave him a hug and a kiss; to Jacob, both seemed uncomfortably patronizing. Then Betty walked out to the path and disappeared.

The bench rocked quietly. He stayed seated, trying to understand what he was doing in this private little house. Then he recalled. He was working on a novel, trying to finish it with the able assistance of his secretary. Jacob went inside, at the desk finding what he needed. He turned on the lamp and, pushing all else from his mind, started jotting down ideas, bits of dialogue, notes for tomorrow's session.

Chapter Thirty

Rachel got off the No. 7 bus at the intersection of Bluestone Road and picked up her bicycle in the garage behind Blatz's Bavarian Inn. Holly had left early—last day of school was a half day—but Rachel had stayed on at the request of her advisor to have a final review of the colleges she'd applied to. Now, pedaling for home, she was still thinking of the meeting. She'd seen no reason for it when she was perfectly happy with Smith, Mt. Holyoke, and Elmira. Mr. Abbot was an ex-football player from Fordham, with a master's in education from New Paltz Normal, coached JV football and taught American History, married, father of two preteen boys, and— using a term other girls were saying about "Derrick"—a hunk.

Rachel had to pedal when she turned off Bluestone Road and picked up the unfinished, slightly uphill spur to her house. Mr. Abbot had smiled at Rachel in his KHS office, then said the last time they'd talked she had seemed preoccupied; something was bothering her. She'd told him she'd broken up with her boyfriend of almost two years who was now in the navy; and Mr. Abbot wanted to know, at today's meeting, how she was doing.

"Better."

"I'm glad of that. What happened? Can you tell me?"

"We had a misunderstanding."

"My wife's Catholic, I'm a Protestant. It's always been a bone of contention for us."

"That wasn't the reason."

"Of course not."

"I think I should be going now, Mr. Abbot."

"I've kept you over. Can I give you a lift anywhere?"

"It's OK. I'll catch the late bus."

"Have a great summer, Rachel. Any problems, ideas about colleges, give me a call."

At his office door, she sensed he was going to make a move on her. That didn't bother Rachel; what bothered her, as he reached out to bring her in, was her reaction. Kissing Derrick Abbot would be very nice and she had a notion to go along, even to kiss him back. How she managed to say goodbye, to thank her advisor and slip quietly out of the room, she didn't know. All she knew, as she caught her bus for Bluestone Road that afternoon, was that she had to be stronger, clearer. Mr. Abbot had made a move on her because she'd led him on, flirted with him from the start. Right now he was likely thinking of senior Rachel Darden as a C.T. Was that who she was? Was that the woman she wanted to be?

Coming along on the spur, on Champ, was her brother.

She couldn't think of anyone nicer to meet at that precise moment; it filled her heart with quiet joy seeing him on his pony with Buck following along.

"Hi," she said, "how are you, Billy"?"

"School's out," he said. "Mr. Marr gave a talk and let us out an hour early."

She reached out and patted the pony's mane. "It's a great feeling, isn't it, having the whole summer ahead of you?"

"Nothing like it." A horsefly landed on Champ's ear. Billy leaned forward and swatted it away.

"Have a good ride," Rachel said.

She continued on old Bluestone Road. At the house she leaned her bike against one of the tall pines and went in. There was a difference between empty and quiet and this was empty. The back door was open and looking through the hall window she saw her mother hanging up a wash on the line. Rachel thought to make herself a snack.

On top of a chest to the right of the refrigerator lay any recent mail. She gave it a casual look, then a closer, sharper look. In hand writing she recognized, one of the of the envelopes was addressed to her; on the upper left corner: Andrew Sickler, Recruit Training Center—

Rachel snatched it up. Her room was out the back door, then across a small hall to a door. She opened it, went in, and sat down in a blue-upholstered easy chair. Her mind raced back to the log cabin and how, in a minute, their evening together had so horribly ended. Her hands were shaking as she opened the envelope and took out a sheet of plain white paper and began reading.

> Dear Rachel,
>
> Boot camp is over next week and I have done well, was named Division Leader of the 80 recruits in Fox Company. I have a week's leave coming up, then will pick up my ship in San Diego.
>
> I have thought endlessly about our last night together. I have nothing to do now but to tell you the God's honest truth. Only the Lord would know if you would've become pregnant, but how else could I keep you for two years or more? I wanted to give you our child to hold a place for me in a life with you when the war ended. It wasn't laziness or forgetfulness or selfishness on my part, it was a plan and it backfired. I outsmarted myself. I lost the girl I loved (still love and always will).
>
> I will be home next week for several days before catching a destroyer bound for the Pacific. Part of me thinks it would be a bad idea to see you, just too painful for both of us. On the other hand I'd do anything, Rachel, to hold you in my arms, if only for a minute, before shipping out.
>
> Love,
> Andy.

The rear window in Rachel's room looked out to the backyard

and all of Harlan's Field. Coming across it, seeking a bit of strudel or a pair of socks, was Raphael Hagar.

****

After talking to his sister, Billy held Champ to a steady canter. Close to the end of Bluestone Road, he slowed to a walk and went up the wide entrance to the mountain-pasture. He dismounted, opened the gate, led Champ in and pulled it closed. As he gathered the reins to mount, Champ backed and sidestepped. What, me cooperate like a tame, well-mannered pony? I've succumbed to saddle and bridle but I'm not giving up all of my old self. You're on your own, Billy. With stirrups lengthened, it was no longer a problem. Up and in. Play tough all you want, Champ.

It was a great place for riding, rocky, isolated, like a scene in a western; but right now he wasn't into riding for the sake of it. He was here to investigate, to track down the lumber he'd stumbled on with Bzy on their hike. On Champ's back, now, he had the benefit of a little extra height. He searched a couple of mini-pastures, finally finding the one he wanted; and there they were, the stacks of criss-crossed lumber. Billy rode about, eyes lowered: old, weathered chestnut, by and large the pieces looked solid. Billy was pleased. He rode to the Osterhoudt house and Donny came out, happy to see his friend and Champ.

"What's up, Billy?"

"I'm looking to build a fence for Champ and saw a lot of post and rail timber in the upper pasture. What can you tell me about it?"

"I never knew it was there."

"Is it your father's?"

"Well, he owns the land," Donny said.

"Is he around?"

Just then Mr. Osterhoudt pulled up in his red pickup and walked over. He patted Champ, and Donny told him about the posts and rails in the upper pasture. Billy wanted to build a fence for Champ.

"Great."

"I can buy the wood from you, Mr. Osterhoudt."

Billy could see him thinking it through, juggling responses. Was something to be gained? Then he said, "Billy, it's yours. I made a dollar on Champ, no complaints." He fluffed the pony's mane, checked his tail. "He's lookin' real good, Billy."

"Thanks, Mr. Osterhoudt."

Billy and Champ headed for home at a run, slowed to a trot but didn't stop at Champ's stable. Still with Buck, they kept on until they came to Rocky Hill Road where it came crashing down from the upper reaches of the art colony. At the base of Rocky Hill, on a lane that jutted off from it, Billy peered down at Carpenter Shop but didn't see a dark-green pickup anywhere around. "We have to go looking for Chips," he said. He loosened the reins and they started up. Billy leaned forward, low over the saddle, as Champ picked his way around rocks and gullies.

"Steady, Champ," Billy said. "This isn't for a car, but a Welsh pony? Your new shoes, glad to have them, right? Almost there now, easy does it."

When they made it to the top of Rocky Hill, Billy had a thought of popping into Canal Boat, but getting hold of Chips was topmost in his mind and they started along Maverick Road, Billy on the lookout for a certain truck; and there, at Salamander, he spied it. Chips was working toward the back of the narrow house. Billy reined Champ in. Immediately, an Airedale-Doberman mix resting at the door got to its feet and streaked across the yard, head low, no barking. Billy saw trouble. Fangs bared, the dog attacked Buck. From silence, all was chaos. Pony spinning around in a tight circle, Billy having no control, only wanting to stay on. A little man in a paint-smeared smock came running from Salamander.

"Elek, no!" he shouted. "Stop!"

It was difficult for Billy to see what was happening, but he knew the Airedale-Doberman was on top of Buck, mauling him. Champ, still twisting about, suddenly stopped; full weight on his front legs, he let fly a vicious kick. Billy was tossed forward, saddle horn smacking him in the stomach.

"Elek!" the man cried out, dropping to his knees. "Elek! Oh, God! No!"

The dog lay on the ground, bleeding from the mouth, chest smashed in. Still saddled, Billy was struggling to take a breath.

Chips came up. "Billy, I'll take care of this. You OK?"

"I—I had the wind—knocked out—of me."

"Well, take it easy. You sure you're OK?"

"I—I want to see you."

"I'll stop by later. Easy going home."

The man with a paint-smeared smock was kneeling on the ground next to his dog, blood dripping from the animal's mouth. Buck, wobbly on his feet, able to walk. A battle-weary troupe, the three passing the theater and concert hall. People wanting to talk to the boy on a pony with a dog limping along. A frowning Harlan Gray waved when they went by his house. They crossed Bluestone Road to the spur and went in at the garage. Billy hitched his pony, took off saddle and bridle, filled a bowl with water and set it down for Buck who lapped nonstop. Champ also had water, a whole pail. Billy tethered him in Harlan's Field, then gave his dog a careful look. Hair at the neck matted, pulled out, left front leg badly bruised, skin broken...blood.

"You're going to be OK, Buck," he said, patting his dog's head. "I'll be right back."

Inside, he told his mother he needed a basin of warm water. A ferocious dog in Salamander had attacked Buck and a skinny little man with paint on his shirt came running out shouting at him and his pony to get off his property. Champ had kicked the man's dog. Mom, I can't talk anymore. She set him up with a basin and washcloth and held the door; when he went back out, Buck was gone. He looked around. Where are you, boy? Then Billy saw him lying in the sun, licking his leg in Harlan's Field near Champ grazing on his tether. Don't interfere. Leave dog and pony to themselves. Who knew what they were saying?

****

He was mowing the front lawn when Chips came by an hour later. Billy stopped cutting and greeted him at the stable door.

"Good to see you up and about, lad."

"Holy mackerel, Chips. That was something!"

"How's Buck?" He saw the two in the field.

"Licking his wounds."

"Elek died, then and there."

"He died?"

"Hoof caught him square in the ribs. Gyuresko—Bertok Gyuresko—went to pieces. He was still beside himself, ranting and crying over his dog, when I left."

Billy had nothing to say; he was numb and saddened.

"He's claiming you intentionally positioned Champ to give him a better angle," Chips said.

"Chips, I was lucky to stay on!"

"I saw the whole thing." Then he said, "You came looking for me. What's up?"

"Harlan doesn't think Champ should be tethered. He said I could fence-in Harlan's Field."

"He should have room to run, no question. But building a fence is a project and a half," Chips said, glancing inside, admiring his work; the last thing he'd done at his own choosing was nail vertical wooden strips, three at each window, as protection against broken glass. "First of all, it's going to take a lot of material—who's going to absorb the cost, your father? I did the stable, he paid me well. A fence? I have my job in the colony, busy every day at it. I couldn't take the time, Billy, even if you had the material."

"I have the material, it's just someplace else," Billy said. "It's in the Osterhoudt upland pasture."

"What is it?"

"Chestnut posts and rails."

"How much of it is there?"

"Don't know."

"Ten pieces, a hundred?"

"Closer to a hundred."

"Maybe it's enough," Chips said. "Here's something else to consider. How are you going to get all this material down to Harlan's Field?"

"I was hoping on your truck."

"You're honest anyway," Chips said with a grin. "The max for this old truck would be eight rails and eight posts. Plus loading and unloading. A chestnut post isn't light. And on top of all that, building the fence. Billy, I'm exhausted just thinking about it."

"It's not right putting champ on a tether," Billy said.

"I agree with you there." Chips Doolin smoothed his mustache with thumb and forefinger, nodded, liking his idea. "Do you have any money, Billy?"

"Eight dollars and fifty cents."

"That should be more than enough. Here's what I want you to do," Chips said. "Get on Champ right now, go see your friend, Sherman. Betsy and Molly, can they haul? Just bring the money."

Chapter Thirty-One

Preparing for his trip from the cottage in Morristown to his home on Bluestone Road, Jacob slid the twenty-three new pages of *The Red Hat*—from 231 to 254 into his briefcase—to look over and edit if necessary. Already in his briefcase were five carbons of the one-act play he was planning to put on later in the summer. When he talked to Hedwig last night, she told him that an irate artist in the colony had come by the house asking for Mr. Darden. I told him I was your wife and you were away. "Well, your son's pony kicked my dog and I'm bringing charges against you for loss and suffering. Your son spun his pony around on purpose so he could deliver the fatal kick!"

"Champ killed the man's dog?" Jacob asked her over the phone.

"Yes, according to Bertok. Jacob, the man makes me nervous. Will you try to get home a little earlier than usual on Friday?"

"There's a West Shore train that gets into Kingston at 4:21."

Other than that, Jacob's first week in the cottage passed exceedingly well. Early chirpings outside his bedroom window. He awakened a couple of times thinking he was in Bird's Eye in the early years. Sound of footfalls on the path: "Rise and shine, Jacob. Coffee and croissant!" He had gotten quickly up, thrown on a robe, and met Betty at the door. Breakfast on the porch. Yesterday, she had come in while he was still in bed and he had suggested she jump in. Chiding Jacob, Betty reminded him that work came before play. In principle he agreed, but how could he dictate his novel with his mind stuck on "play?" It wasn't a difficult sell. Watching Betty undress was, of and by itself, a pleasure. How well her thumbs suited the purpose of taking off her panties. Hedwig tended to insert her entire hand at the waistband, as if grabbing the handles of a lawnmower. Instead of a slide, it was more of a shove.

Now it was Friday, and Jacob was getting ready to catch the 1:25 out of Weehawken. He adjusted the water temperature, then walked into his confessional-sized shower as the pelting water performed, he sincerely hoped, its priestlike task of pure ablution. He toweled, shaved, put on a suit and tie, and had all of two minutes to meet Betty at her car. Approaching the patio, he made to take a narrow path of slate to the parking area, only to have someone on the patio, straight ahead, catch his attention. Melissa was getting up from a chaise in a lilac-toned see-through chemise, in other words, naked for all practical purposes. He had no way of knowing but was inclined to think she'd got up at that precise moment to send a signal, knowing her new tenant was walking by. Jacob himself took a good look, then veered onto the narrow path through a charming little copse, arriving at his secretary's car in the parking area as she was leaving the house.

She got in, slid behind the wheel, and Jacob closed the passenger-side door. "This is kind of you, Betty," he said.

"I'm helping you write your novel. I can drive you to the station."

"If there's a link between 'secretary' and 'chauffer,' I don't immediately see it," Jacob said, "but thank you."

"It's called currying favor," she said in full bantering mode. "I'm looking for a raise."

"You've had one week on the payroll."

"How about a perk then?"

"Ah, perks! My amanuensis nonpareil is most deserving. What would she like?"

"That you come back to the cottage after your weekend at home."

"I don't think that's a problem."

"Still and all, how may I entice you? Secretarial skills aren't very sexy."

Jacob had to laugh. "Maybe that's what *you* think."

Early afternoon traffic was light and they were moving right along. "You've led me to believe that Hedwig is an excellent cook. *That's* an enticement."

"One of our neighbors in the art colony, an Armenian ex-cavalryman, would kill for a piece of her raisin bread."

"My point exactly."

"Betty, you might not make raisin bread but you offer other delights."

"Is this Armenian cavalryman a threat to you, Jacob?"

"That he would run off with my wife? No."

"Is he an artist?"

"Sculptor. Great pieces of wood, the size of large easy chairs, rounded and polished—it's hard to say what they are. They're nonobjective forms. As for making a living, he lives hand to mouth. Artists of all stripe go to the Maverick Art Colony to live cheaply. If a poet, painter, or musician can't afford a fifty-dollar annual rent for a two-room cabin, Harlan will accept an I.O.U., which he hardly ever collects on."

Betty kept her eyes on the road, conscious of what drivers were doing or had intentions of doing. "Jacob, I'm curious. I imagine your house is comfortable, up-to-date. Isn't it awkward for you living in an art colony?"

"Our house is across the art colony line, so the answer is no—technically. The art colony is a different world."

"But in the beginning you lived in the colony."

"Yes, for almost three years," Jacob said. "It was a struggle; without Hedwig I couldn't have done it. We were never out of debt. I didn't go looking for a 'day job' but when one came my way I grabbed it, the gold ring on the merry-go-round. There are people who say I sold out. They're entitled to their thoughts. If I'd given up on myself as a writer, I'd say it too. Reader's Digest gave my family and me a good life but it never took the place of a 'calling.' I don't mean to sound stuffy but it's the truth. Behold, the day arrived when I closed the door on Reader's Digest. I slipped my hobbles only to discover I could no longer type. Excuse the mixed metaphor. How close I came to knocking on Wally's door and telling him I'd made a mistake. But I was spared the humiliation, the embarrassment, thanks to my secretary who offered to take *The Red Hat* down in dictation."

"I wasn't going to let you throw in the towel, Jacob."

"We should be working right now," he said.

"Everyone needs a break," Betty said. "That little one-act play you wrote, by the way, is charming. It will be the hit of the year in the Maverick."

"You'll have to come up when we put it on."

She smiled at the idea. "As just your secretary, of course."

They were in Weehawken, moving toward the river. He asked her what her plans were for the weekend.

"Melissa and I have a date to see Casablanca," she said. "I'll practice a Debussy etude I'm trying to learn. If the weather holds, she'll likely drive someplace with her easel."

"How about the secret lover you were telling me about?"

"Hers or mine?" Betty maneuvered her car to the curb. They had arrived.

"I meant hers. If yours, everyone's allowed a private life."

"You are most understanding, Jacob."

He gave her a quiet embrace. "See you, Betty."

"See you."

Jacob got out and walked into the sooty station to his train.

****

He sat on the right side of the car, preferring the Hudson River on the way north over the backyards of station-stop towns, but just as many passengers seemed content to look at the rocky cliffs and dispirited backyards. When he and Hedwig had lived in Bird's Eye and afterwards in the then brown house on Bluestone Road, he had taken the West Shore line to meet with editors and publishers on average once a month. It took him into New York via the ferry.

That was then; it was easier then. Now it was a dull, boring trip. The passenger car he was in had a foul odor—cigarette smoke deeply embedded into the rough, green-flecked fabric on each seat. Whatever company had manufactured the material had given it a lifetime warranty against tearing or failure. Hedwig knew about

238

making things last, the importance of getting the last ounce of use out of an item. During the first World War in Germany, she'd told Jacob, her mother had made them wear the left shoe on the right foot and right shoe on the left foot. Not all the time but twice a week for a full day. It doubled the wear. It didn't make any difference what happened to your toes. You had to save your shoes!

As the train rattled along, Jacob thought about his decision to become a writer. His instructorship at Columbia wasn't doing anything for him, wasn't satisfying him in any meaningful way, but did he have the courage to give up a paycheck and prestige and go to Harlan Gray's art colony in upstate New York and proclaim himself a poet? What path did a man choose who wanted recognition, greatness, success— the study and teaching of literature... or the creation of it? Fall semester classes at Columbia were starting in two weeks and Jacob was compelled to act, to decide. Which would it be? In the Maverick Art Colony he could live cheaply and write, but he didn't have it in him to go there alone. Who would go with him to a drafty two room house in a rocky, heavily wooded setting and fight the elements, struggle to keep warm, to stay alive, so he, Jacob Darden, could commence a career as a writer? How about Rose McBride of Malden? She would last three weeks before going start raving mad. Three weeks. Who else had Jacob known who might consider it? And then he thought: the German girl. Would Hedwig say, when he asked her to marry him, that she was engaged to a boy back home? She was sorry, she wished Jacob all the luck in the world. Or would she say, Yes, I will marry you, I will go with you to the art colony. You will write wonderful books in the Maverick and we will have a life together, we will raise a family. Yes, Jacob! Yes!

"Haverstraw!" the conductor cried out. Then, sequentially, "Bear Mountain!" "West Point!" "Newburgh!"

Jacob loved the idea of going home; always had. To see his wife and children, his house. But he knew, even in the early years, he wouldn't stay, wouldn't settle in. Ulysses, away for ten years fighting the Trojans and another ten returning to Athens, embraced his faithful wife, scattered her suitors and sailed off the next morning on new conquests, adventures.

239

A line from Tennyson ran through his mind. That which we are, we are—to strive, to seek, to find, and not to yield.

"Kingston!"

The train came to a jerky stop. The hissing of steam, Jacob stepping onto the platform, Hedwig standing at the station door.

"Hello, darling," she said.

"Hedwig." Briefcase in hand, he gave her thin lips a kiss.

The ride home to Bluestone Road began, Hedwig fighting the gearshift, Jacob determined not to comment, to judge. "How's everything at the house?"

"Yesterday Sherman and Ben started digging," Hedwig said.

"Is it noisy?"

"You know they're there. Of interest, they don't work on Sundays."

"What about Bertok Gyuresko?"

"Nothing further. He mentioned stopping by this weekend to see you. He's determined to get some compensation."

"Is he now?"

"Billy said he cried and cried," Hedwig said.

"Billy cried and cried?"

"Bertok cried."

Jacob thought to instruct on pronoun-noun relationship but quickly changed his mind. "Why was Bertok crying?"

"For Elek, his dog. He's saying that Billy positioned Champ—"

"Do you believe it?"

"I know there are two sides to every story but how could a boy who's just learning to ride manage to do something so—so—?"

"—so unbelievable," Jacob said. "But I'm not absolving Billy, you understand that."

"When have you ever?"

"Many times, you just like to forget."

They were in uptown Kingston, near the massive brick viaduct, not a sparkling part of the city. Most of the shops, dismal to start with, were shuttered. People were taking defense jobs at the Mead Plant on Lucas Avenue. Ray's Taxidermy was "Closed for the Duration." Jacob remembered driving Billy, then eleven, to pick up his "first gray squirrel," dropped off at Ray's a week before. Why

240

Billy had wanted it done, Jacob hadn't had a clue. Still didn't have one. He had handed Ray, a well-stuffed individual himself, five singles.

Once across the viaduct, Hedwig headed west on Rt. 28. Eventually she asked Jacob if he was getting used to his new environment. "A little, not much. When Betty leaves at about 3:30 or 4:00, I walk into the village, check out the Morristown Library, then spend the evening prepping for the next day."

"Where do you have your meals?"

"I grab what I can. My time is pretty much taken up by the novel, moving ahead with it, dictating."

"Well, I have one of your favorite meals for you tonight," Hedwig said.

"Am I right thinking it's a New England fish chowder?"

"With bread just baked."

"Drive a little faster, Hedwig."

She laughed. She had always had an easy laugh, a good sense of humor; it did wonders to make up for a less than striking appearance: hair that had no natural brightness, no shine—she wore it hastily pulled together in a bun with pins sticking out of it like porcupine quills on the scruffy head of a dog. Hedwig was clueless in matters of dress, of style, but if you wanted someone to laugh at a joke, tell it to Hedwig Darden; and she told a good story too, had a natural sense of timing. Jacob despised the shallowness of the saying, said by a man of a woman, "I wouldn't turn around if she passed me on the street." Unhappy for Jacob to admit to, it applied to Hedwig.

She turned off Rt. 375 onto Bluestone Road, down-shifted to keep from stalling, then back to third. No problem. Maybe she was getting the knack. Almost home, she eased onto the spur, bounced along for two hundred yards, and parked in the driveway. They both got out and headed for the house. Jacob inquired if Billy was around.

"Last I saw him he was working on Harlan's Field."

"Doing what?"

"He seemed to be digging."

Inside, Jacob took off his suit, shirt and tie in the master bedroom, let them drop where they would and flung them carelessly to a chair, and put on casual clothes and an old pair of Johnston and Murphy shoes. He had the feeling that Billy was onto something and Hedwig was covering for him. Mother and son against husband/father. He went out of the house to the small back terrace. Standing there he could see the work Sherman and his brother had done on their first day on the job: dug a bathtub-sized hole at the original cinderblock foundation that tended inward even in its initial stage. The brothers had constructed a wooden framework to keep the excavation from caving. Directly overhead, Jacob noted, was the sunroom. The Marshalls weren't licensed engineers but Hedwig felt confident they would do the job and do it well; and Jacob had to admit that she had a great sense of people—knew who was genuine, would keep his word.

He went down stone steps to ground level. The house stood on a plateau that extended some fifteen feet to an escarpment, wheelbarrow tracks indicating that Sherman and Ben had emptied wheelbarrow after wheelbarrow of rocks and dirt over the edge. Jacob circled around to the side of the house and continued out to Harlan's Field. His son wasn't around; what *was* around surprised Jacob, stunned him. Post and rail timbers lay in three large stacks along the edges of the field. Clearly plans were in the air to transform the only open parcel of land in the colony into a grazing ground. Jacob noted two large, perfect circles where Champ had eaten grass at the end of a tether. Harlan's Field was for baseball, football, any outdoor game that kids wanted to play. Not to provide a mean-spirited pony with grass! How did this get started? Why wasn't he informed? Harlan's Field wasn't his, but goddammit to hell he'd made it what it was! Who was behind this effort to change its nature, to pervert the open, poetic culture of Harlan's Field, of boys at play, of the great tradition of athletics, of the Olympiad?

Just then Champ and Billy came at a lively trot down Maverick Road, crossed Bluestone Road and followed the spur to the hitch behind the garage. Jacob stood there, anger mounting, watching his son take off saddle and bridle and slip on the pony's halter...as Buck, a mixed-blood member of this unholy troupe, limped in and sank to the ground near Champ. Billy carried the tack into the stable, in a minute returning with a brush and currycomb; he began working on Champ's coat, his mane. Jacob might have respected the boy for his attention, the caring he showed...if he hadn't felt like beating him!

He made for the front door of the house. Passing behind his son, who was giving the pony's tail full, husky strokes, he said, "When you're finished, Billy, I'll be in the library."

The boy turned. "Hi, Dad. OK."

Jacob went inside. Dinner wouldn't be for another two hours, Hedwig said to him in the kitchen. Would he like something? She had a new batch of raisin pumpernickel. With a cup of tea, he said. He'd be in the library. Then he asked her if she knew of any plans regarding Harlan's Field. He'd noticed a lot of lumber kicking around.

"Billy said he'd found it in Mr. Osterhoudt's upland pasture."

"Found it?"

"So he said."

"Did you question him on it?"

"No. It sounded genuine."

"You at least called Mr. Osterhoudt," Jacob said.

"I didn't."

"How could you be so unconcerned?"

"I knew he hadn't stolen it."

He went into the library, looked at his complete Dickens, pulled down *A Tale of Two Cities* at random. The novel of the French Revolution. "It was the best of times, it was the worst of times. The age of wisdom, the age of foolishness." How perfectly the words fitted what he was going through. In his mind he could hear, would always hear, the rickety sound of tumbrels rolling down Paris streets carrying loyalists to the guillotine. Hedwig came in with a tray—slices of pumpernickel on a plate, butter, knife, napkin; and a cup of perfectly steeped Earl Grey tea—setting it on a small round table between two easy chairs.

"Thank you," he said.

She left and Jacob closed the book, tucked it back in its stiff, well-regimented file, and sat down in the wing-backed chair. So much to talk over with Billy, first the problem with Mr. Gyuresko and his dead dog. Kicked to death by Champ. Clearly there was a question of responsibility. Had Billy handled his pony well or had carelessness and ineptitude contributed to the accident? Not secondarily was the fencing in of Harlan's Field. Actually, it went more to the heart of the matter, was more of a violation—

He heard Billy's footsteps walking into the house; then the library door opened and he came in. He sat in the second easy chair, uneasily.

"I saw you riding up on Champ," Jacob said, "then currying him. His coat has a good shine, and his tail! Does it really touch the ground, or was I imagining it?"

"It touches," Billy said.

"Have you heard from Serge?"

"No. He's not one to write."

"Why is that, Billy?"

"We were friends but he was always someplace else."

Jacob thought it time to end the chitchat. He had a taste of tea, then said, "I understand you had trouble the other day with an artist in Salamander, Bertok Gyuresko."

"Champ kicked his dog," Billy said.

"Hedwig said Gyuresko came looking for me."

"I wasn't here. It's what she said."

"What were you doing at Salamander?" Jacob asked his son.

"Looking for Chips. I had something to tell him but I never got the chance. This dog, a really big police dog named Elek, came streaking across the yard. I was on Champ. We were minding our own business and Elek went straight for Buck. He had him down and was going for his throat."

"Did you position Champ so he could kick Elek?"

"Dad, it's a wonder I wasn't thrown! He was spinning around like a top."

"In other words you'd lost control of Champ."

"Yes, but it was a good thing."

"Why is that?"

"If I'd kept control, Buck wouldn't be with us today."

"Billy, I'm an editor," Jacob said. "I'm pretty good at untangling the knots that writers tie. Please, slow down and tell me again why losing control of Champ was a good thing."

"He knew what he had to do," Billy said.

"Which was?"

"Save his friend!"

"And who, if this dimwitted editor might ask, is his friend?"

"Buck."

Jacob nodded. "So you're telling me that Champ had it in his mind to kick Elek. Is that about it?"

"Yes. To save Buck. Elek was killing him."

"That clarifies a lot for me, Billy," Jacob said. "Now, what in hell is all that lumber doing on Harlan's Field?"

"It—it's for making a fence."

"A fence," Jacob said.

"For Champ. So he can run."

"He runs when you're on him! Isn't that enough?

"Dad—"

"Don't 'dad' me. How did that lumber get there?"

"It was on Mr. Osterhoudt's mountain pasture," Billy said. "Hiking with Bzy was when I noticed it, a whole stack of old posts and rails. He said I could have them."

"Just like that." Jacob shook his head, highly annoyed. "Did he want money?"

"I said I'd pay him. He said take the wood."

"There's a quid pro quo there, Billy."

"I don't know what that means."

"It's a this for that. Mr. Osterhoudt is not a generous man."

"I don't know, Dad."

"There must be a ton of wood out there. "How did it end up on Harlan's Field?"

"The Marshall brothers took their team into the pasture and we chucked on every last piece."

"No, I don't believe that," Jacob said. "They're fine men but they're busy. They work for a living. They're not going to take a day off doing a favor for a kid!"

"I paid them," Billy said. "They figured the job would take five hours, both of them at it. I gave them three dollars and an extra dollar for the horses."

Jacob found himself wondering if his father's business acuity had jumped the son to the grandson; it was really quite remarkable. But he wasn't happy; there was nothing about the fence on Harlan's Field he liked. "Now all you have to do is build it. Who do you have in mind?"

"Chips loaned me his posthole digger."

Jacob liked that his son had shown resourcefulness but the good feeling didn't tamp out the smoldering feelings he had of anger and disrespect. "This time next year you might be halfway through. You've administrated nicely. But come on, Billy. Building a fence takes brawn. No way will you do it yourself. Am I upset? First off, Harlan's Field is not yours to make a fence on. You understand that, I'm sure," Jacob said.

"It was Harlan's idea. I wouldn't have done it just on my own."

"That's very hard for me to believe," Jacob said.

"It's the truth."

"Well, you shouldn't have taken him up on it. Harlan owns the land, yes; but Harlan's Field was a contract between you and me," Jacob said, "to create an open space in this rock-dominated community for the simple beauty and joy of playing games. I love my daughters but I did it so my son could learn to field a grounder and throw a pass. And tackle. One thing the Maverick Art Colony doesn't have is a place where you can take a spill and not bash your head against a rock. In my opinion, a pony's 'freedom' isn't as important as a boy's development. You remember how good we felt when the job was done and we started throwing a baseball, kicking a football?"

"Yes."

"So keep digging postholes if you like," Jacob said, stepping away ungraciously. "You had a plan, but a plan with no conceived or plausible end is no plan. If you were so interested in giving Champ freedom, you would've allowed him to run in the mountain pasture. That's it, you may go. Oh, if you think I'm letting up on our regimen, you have another guess coming."

Billy went out. Jacob picked up the freshly typed pages of *The Red Hat* and started to read.

****

He had his own bread and butter plate, salt and pepper shakers; as always, Jacob thanked Hedwig for preparing and serving a lovely meal. He lifted his glass of chilled Chardonnay to his family, sipped, set the glass down, and had a taste of New England chowder.

"Oh, yes. Just wonderful, Hedwig."

After another spoonful, he said, "Well, a new summer is here. The opening of the Maverick Theater is tomorrow night and the first concert is Sunday."

"When are you coming home to stay?" Holly said.

"Not until I finish my novel. I'm dictating it, and that requires a secretary," Jacob said. "As I speak, Betty types. It sounds easy but it requires serious preparation."

"To speak requires preparation?"

"For me it does. It's like laying out a course before setting sail; otherwise I'd be all over the place." Jacob paused for a moment, had a taste of chowder. "Our basement is going in. This winter we'll have central heating and plenty of hot water. It's considered insensitive to tell your wife you're giving her a new vacuum cleaner for Christmas. So, let me be insensitive." He looked at his wife. "With our new basement comes a new washing machine. The very last one for sale in this great country we're in. Part of the war effort. Montgomery Ward has diminished its inventory of such appliances to zero."

No one commented. Hedwig ladled chowder into Jacob's bowl. "Anyone else? There's plenty here."

Billy had a second helping.

Jacob shook in a little pepper, then said, "We're slowly getting back on our feet as a country. FDR and the New Deal got us through the Depression but it's the war that's really doing it. Is it a good time to bring out a novel about a Catholic priest? The themes of the book are faith, inner strength, love. Where does art fit in when a nation is at war? You could argue that it should stay in the shadows, tucked away in a corner for safe keeping."

He put the last dab of butter on a piece of bread. "But war is exactly the time to paint, write, dance; art is an antidote to war," Jacob went on. "I awoke in my rented room in Morristown two days ago with a wonderful idea—not new, we've talked about it, but suddenly it seemed like the perfect time—to produce our own play. Let's put our minds to work and produce 'The King's Pork Chops' on our terrace to a gathering of Woodstock and Maverick guests. It will be the keynote of our summer...and we'll have a party too. Harlan put on great festivals late every summer for ten years. They were magnificent affairs. Igor Bagovitch—your teacher, Holly—put on a ballet performance that people who saw it still talk about! Our party won't be of that scope, but in spirit and fun it will equal any party of an earlier time. The Darden family will stage entertainment and merriment to make people say, 'We are engaged in a World War but the Maverick spirit is alive and well!'"

Faces broke into easy smiles.

Jacob took in his two daughters, spoke to Rachel first. "I'm putting you in charge," he said. "When you apply to Smith later this year, how magnificently that will stand out! 'Produced and directed by Rachel Darden.' I have five copies of the play. Holly," Jacob continued, "I'm naming you stage manager and chief of casting. Read the play, think of kids you know who could play the parts. You'll also be in charge of props, the individual items for every scene. Billy, between caddying and Champ, and the fence you'll be building, I hope you'll be able to find the time to take over as chief announcer."

"What does the chief announcer do?"

"You'll welcome the guests, talk a little about the play, how you happen to know the playwright, and so forth. You'll be great at it." To his daughters he said, "I'll be coming up on weekends and we can go over the production, any problems you might be having. As to our party, Hedwig, maybe we can work our way around rationing and put on a good spread. A pot of baked beans, potato salad. Possibly a Virginia ham. A gallon of lemonade. We have until Labor Day. Start tomorrow, I wouldn't let another day go by. Set a date for the first reading. Costumes: tell Hedwig what you need. I'll make a contribution to the Woodstock Library Fair. Any questions, comments?"

"What's a 'first reading?'"

"The cast sits around and reads the play," Rachel said to Holly.

"It's step one."

Jacob was pleased. "Check in with me whenever you want and certainly on weekends, but I want you to understand this is your production. I have my own work to do. Let's make this a Darden family summer to remember." He looked at his beautiful daughter. "Rachel, how is this sitting with you? Am I asking too much?"

"Not at all."

"Wonderful. If there are parts in the play you don't like, feel free to edit," Jacob said. "The King's Pork Chops isn't written in stone. It's—"

There was an aggressive knock on the front door. Jacob took a deep breath, cursed under his breath. Hedi went to see who it was. Coming back, she told Jacob it was Gyuresko.

"He didn't waste any time."

"What did you want me to say to him?"

"Nothing. I'll take care of it," Jacob said.

"What's this about?" Holly said.

"Billy, you tell her."

Jacob walked through the sentry box hallway. A man was standing on the terrace looking at Mount Overlook. "May I help you?" Jacob said.

"You are Mr. Darden?"

"I am. And you are?"

"Bertok Gyuresko."

He came closer—short, in his late forties, didn't weigh 130 pounds. Stringy dark hair gathered behind his head. Light on his feet. Jacob had the notion he was an ex-bantamweight fighter. "I heard you might be coming by, Bertok," Jacob said.

"If you have a few minutes, I realize it is late in the day." Thick, middle-European accent. Jacob guessed Hungarian.

"I'm here. What's going on?

"My dog was killed. I'm sick about it."

Wanting to get away from the house, Jacob walked off the terrace to a bench and chair between two young oaks. "It's hard losing a dog," he said. "If my son had lost Buck, there at Salamander, we would have lost a member of the family. We'd still be grieving. Please, sit down, Bertok."

They sat between the young oaks. Jacob knew he was after money. Champ had delivered a kick that had killed Elek, and Bertok wanted restitution. He was within his rights. It was absurd to say that Billy had "steered" Champ into a favorable angle for kicking Elek. What wasn't absurd was that Billy's inexperience as a rider had played a role in the "Salamander Affair." Part of Jacob wanted to apologize, to take the blame, to pay Bertok a reasonable amount (preferably $10, at the most $20) and wish him luck in finding another nice dog.

For a few minutes the two talked generally. When Bertok offered that he'd grown up in Budapest and had held the national title in his class for boxing, Jacob quietly congratulated himself on his powers of perception. Afterward, Bertok had taken an interest in art and had studied in Paris.

Deciding to get down to business—Hedwig had dessert waiting for him and a fine cup of coffee—he said, "Bertok, this is all very interesting and I hope we can talk again. And I look forward to seeing your work. Right now, let's wrap this up. What do you have in mind?"

"To compensate for the loss of my dog and the sorrow I'm feeling, a hundred dollars."

The tone of their talk changed immediately. "Bertok, that's way out of line," Jacob said.

"I think it's very reasonable."

"Well, there's no way I'll pay it."

"I'll take you before a local justice," Bertok said. "Your son maneuvered his pony so as to—"

"That isn't true."

"I saw it myself! I'll take it to court."

"Fine, I'll meet you there," Jacob said. "I'll have a witness with me. You know Chips. He'll tell the judge how Elek shot across the yard and went for a perfectly quiet dog. Getting him by the throat. Who will be your witness?"

Bertok didn't counter and Jacob knew the left hook he'd just thrown had landed squarely. "I'm sorry about Elek," he said. " I have twenty dollars on me right now." Jacob pulled the bill from his wallet. "This is not hayseed, Bertok. It'll get you through the whole summer. Let's put this incident behind us."

The ex-fighter, now artist, gave it a little thought, then took the money and walked away. Jacob's attention was drawn to Harlan's Field where Billy was unsnapping Champ from his tether.

****

At 9:15 that evening, all but dark outside, Jacob told Hedwig he was going out; he didn't say where because he never had and saw no reason to start now. He pulled a sweater over his shirt and walked on old Bluestone Road into the colony, passing Bearcamp and Quarryman, a lamp in the window of each. Soon, through trees, he could see lanterns glowing, heard people talking, laughing, the happy sound of a piano. The country was in a war getting ever closer to home, Jacob was thinking as he drew near Intelligentsia. Artists did not easily lay down their tools. Talk had the Maverick Art Colony on its last legs, but so far it was alive and well.

The place had no door, no windows; a section of it over the table and benches had a roof. Jacob walked in. A woman with jet black hair streaming down her shoulders was sitting at a miniature piano banging out "I've Got A Girl in Kalamazoo." The only person Jacob immediately recognized was the woman he'd hoped to see, Christine. At the moment, she was serving a bowl of chili to a man, then wine to another man. She had on a purple, full-flowing Woodstock dress that clung to, or revealed, the shape of her body. The light caramel shade of her skin was enticing by itself. Bertok Gyuresko, Jacob noted, was at the table spending his money. Christine gave his glass a refill, then, looking about, spied Jacob.

She came over and gave him a full hug, her body making contact with him in a couple of strategic places. "It's so good seeing you," she said. "I was wondering if you'd ever come by."

"The season is young."

"I've seen Billy. Up and about with his pony."

"He gets around," Jacob said. He didn't say "gets under my feet" but it was what he was thinking.

The song of the moment was "I Don't Walk Without You." He asked Christine who was playing.

"Beryl. I asked Harlan what he thought of the idea. He loved it."

251

"You're doing your part. It's great."

"Have you had a good year?" she asked.

"I quit my job at Reader's Digest. I'm writing a novel."

"Good for you! Let me get you something. Wine?"

"Please."

She came back with a blue throwaway glass. He gave her a dollar and she put three quarters on the table. "Don't make yourself so scarce," she said, and left to serve another customer.

Jacob sipped from his glass. At the other end of the table the man, whose name, but not his face, had escaped Jacob, was looking over; and immediately the name came to Jacob. Nick Bonino, lately of the Pittsburgh Symphony Orchestra. Jacob beckoned him over. The seat next to him was open, and Nick sat down with his wine.

"Jacob," he said. "Good seeing you again."

"Nice seeing you, Nick. Big day for you tomorrow."

The man had drooping eyelids, a deep tone to his skin, and a large impressive nose. Of all Bonino's characteristics, his eyes—their sadness, sleepiness, what Jacob could only call their dark seductive nature—dominated. "We have a lovely program this summer."

"Will you be going back to big-time concertizing in the fall?"

"I'm finished with it," Nick Bonino said. "I've saved a few dollars. If I have to take a defense job, I'll do it; but I want to start writing, teaching, with the hopes of getting pupils. You said you were interested in having your son pick up the violin."

"I am. It would be great for him. My father's brother was a violinist of some note," Jacob said. "I've played, never well though."

"What kind of a boy is he?" Nick said.

Oh, to answer that question easily, Jacob thought. "Billy has a good mind," he said. "I've been encouraging him to read, he loves to hunt and fish. I think the violin would be great for him."

"Send him over. If I don't teach Billy the violin, I'll teach him how to cast a dry fly," Nick Bonino said, "and to tie one."

Jacob laughed. "Do you have a family, Nick?"

"A twenty-year-old daughter, pretty much on her own; another daughter—" he had eyes that couldn't grow sadder; they grew sadder, "—died a couple of years ago. I've had family. Father who

252

beat me with a stick if I didn't practice four hours a day."

"Where did you grow up?"

"Rochester."

"Great old town. Nice talking with you, Nick," Jacob said. "Have a great concert tomorrow."

Nick Bonino got up from the table and blended into the night. Jacob sat there quietly, remembering how, even last year, he would wait for Christine to close up Intelligentsia and walk her to her place; actually he'd done it twice. Now he wasn't up to it. Was he slowing down? More likely it was the novel, prepping for it, the necessity to stay sharp. Before, what had held him to the task? The Reader's Digest? It was editorial work he'd done many times in his sleep. But creative work, no faking it there. Jacob had himself a last look at Christine. High yellow. He gave his lower lip a slow lick—

A group of seven or eight people walked across the Intelligentsia yard and flowed in. He assumed they were actors. Artists tended to have a more scraggly appearance. The next moment, among them, he saw someone he knew. Their eyes met—

"Jacob!"

"Mia, my goodness. Hello."

"I think your son and my daughter may be getting married."

He laughed. "May I buy you a glass of wine?"

"I'm with my friends, but thanks. We just had a dress rehearsal."

"How did it go?"

"Not too well."

"Isn't there a saying in the theater? 'Bad rehearsal, good opening night.'"

"Anything will be an improvement. How's *The Red Hat* doing?"

He liked that she remembered. "Moving along with it."

"Great. Awfully good seeing you again, Jacob."

"And you, Mia," he said.

****

He did not tiptoe into the house like a husband coming home late; hardly an hour had passed. And what had he done? He'd had a glass of wine, chatted with a couple of people. Harmless enough. But another voice spoke to him. Jacob, whom are you kidding? You're still keeping your college notebook with a list of girls you

253

knew, had dated, had recently met. Now and then you thinned it down but basically you added to it. In baseball talk, you like having a good bench.

Everyone was asleep; at least the house was quiet, dark. Hedwig had left a nightlight on in the hall leading into the bedroom/dressing room. Jacob undressed, gave his teeth a brush, and got into bed. She was a good sleeper, occasionally snored, not the heavy house-rumbling snore of his brothers Donald and Percival; much quieter, as if, Jacob had once commented to Hedwig, a single cornflake was stuck in her nose. Whether she knew he was in bed, he couldn't tell. In a gesture of husbandly affection, his eyes closing fast, he wrapped an arm around his wife...

He was in Canal Boat sitting with Mia discussing the various ways an actor can show emotions. She was actually giving him a tutorial. Writers have the same problems, difficulties, as actors in this regard. Action, movement were key, Mia was saying. The initial move has to be subtle. Quietly take your partner's hand. Good, Jacob. Move slowly. Suggestion is a prime element. Nothing kills intimacy like coarseness, nothing enhances it like mystery. The crucial point is to know when to abandon nuance and when to start going deep, to plumb the heart of the emotion. Very good, Jacob. Oh, yes, I like how you plumb. Oh, yes! Suddenly realizing it wasn't Mia. They weren't in Canal Boat. He was in bed with Hedwig, making love to her here in their bedroom at home.

****

Now it was morning and the smell of fresh-perked coffee was in the air. Jacob washed up, pulled on clothes, a sweater over his shirt, and went into the kitchen. He said good morning to Hedwig, helped himself to a steaming mug.

"You should go out more often, Jacob."

He laughed lightheartedly. "I'm going to walk around for a while."

A smile in her eyes. "Breakfast in twenty minutes. Bring Billy in with you."

He went out the kitchen door to the small, rickety terrace, then to the back yard. Every ten steps or so he stopped to sip his coffee.

When he came to Harlan's Field, Champ was tethered and Buck was lying close by still licking his foreleg. It wasn't a sight that pleased Jacob. A hard-to-come-by grassy plot in the Maverick Art Colony was a rarity; in fact, anything comparable to Harlan's Field didn't exist. A pony had taken over their lives, was dictating the use of land. Then he saw Billy. Champ and Billy, throw in Buck. The Troika of Bluestone Road.

Jacob walked over. Boy was impossibly involved in making a fence. Like with the steam-driven crane. Jumping in, not thinking. Damn near getting himself killed.

On the ground close to Billy lay a posthole digger. The post was in but it wasn't vertical, and Billy knew it was wrong. Jacob stood there holding his mug, not saying a thing. He wasn't sure his son knew he was there. The post had to be removed. Billy hugged it, lifted, but couldn't get it out. Then he sank to the ground with his back to the post. All around Harlan's Field, in small piles, timbers lay; bleached by the sun, bone hard, well-seasoned posts and rails. Jacob was in a disapproving frame of mind, but he could find nothing wrong with the material. It would be a classic chestnut fence—if and when it ever became a fence. "Billy, it's a big undertaking," Jacob said.

"Dad, I'm tired. I just want to sit here."

"I mentioned that you needed a plan—"

"Harlan said the best plan is do it yourself."

"Good, within reason. But if hard physical labor is involved—"

"Thoreau built his own cabin," Billy said. "No help from nobody."

"Billy, watch your double negatives," Jacob said. "'*No help from anybody.*' Thoreau wasn't thirteen when he did it. He was a strong, full-grown man."

Jacob set his coffee mug down and picked up the hole digger. Just holding it, as if to use it, put a strain on his back. Considering what it did—dig a round hole and pick up the displaced dirt at the same time—it was a great utilitarian tool.

"You need someone to help you, Billy. You moved too fast, you didn't think it through."

On Harlan's Field, Champ went closer to Buck as if to see how he was doing.

"Learn from this," Jacob said.

****

Sunday afternoon Jacob met with his daughters in the library. They had both read the play, liked it, and had some good ideas. In a few places Rachel thought the language seemed forced. Jacob said the period of the play was the 17th Century and royalty spoke in a stuffy kind of way. Rachel understood but the lesser characters should loosen up, she thought; and Jacob went along with it. She should make pencil changes. Holly mentioned that she and Mr. Bagovitch had been working on the dying swan from Swan Lake, and he was of the opinion that she might perform—it was only seven minutes—as a prelude to the play itself. Jacob thought it a splendid idea, but who would supply the Tchaikovsky music? She definitely should keep after it with her teacher. Father and daughters were about to end their meeting when Rachel said no play was complete without a program, "I was talking to Terry about it—Terry, who'll be playing King Thaddeus—is studying civil engineering, and he said he'd design it, single sheet of paper folded lengthwise to give it the appearance of a book. I see it as very important, handed out like at a real theater when people arrive."

"Splendid," Jacob said.

"I've seen his work, his sketches, they're really good," Rachel said, "but we have no way of putting it together. First, the paper, then the printing."

"You've come to the right man," Jacob said. "Send me the sketches, the players and their parts in the play, credits you'd like to give. But wait a couple of weeks, let things settle down, then send it all along and I'll have it put together for you. How many do you need?"

"We have the number of people coming at thirty-five."

"More than that. I'll have sixty made up," Jacob said.

****

They sat quietly in the Kingston station waiting for the 6:15 to Weehawken. There was so much he had to tell Hedwig and he didn't know how to start. Of course, he knew very well how to start. He would sit her down and tell her the truth about Morristown and

Betty Trill. Hedwig was sitting down now, so tell her now. But there was no way he'd do it. They talked about Rachel's leadership quality. Ever since Andy left for boot camp, Jacob had noticed a change in her. She seemed freer, more herself, less preoccupied. If Andy hadn't gone off to war, would Rachel be taking it upon herself to direct the play? She'd want no part of it.

"They've broken up," Hedwig said.

"When did this happen?"

"Sometime just before he left."

"Do you think they had sex?"

"I wouldn't know, Jacob. You're right, she is acting differently."

"God bless that girl."

At last the 6:15 pulled in, well after 6:15. "Will you be up next weekend?"

"Hedwig, what a question. Of course I will."

He kissed her, waved once at the track, and boarded his car with five other people. Only one seat had two open places on it and he went to it quickly and sat at the window. Hedwig was just leaving and he watched as she drove away into the Sunday dreariness of downtown Kingston. Then, finally, he opened his briefcase and pulled out the last ten pages of *The Red Hat* he'd dictated. How out of it, how removed he felt from his work. It was what a weekend at home could do to you. Jacob began reading the pages; by the time the train pulled into Newburgh he felt caught up. He had feared he might not be able to extricate himself from everyday life, but clearly he had. Now all he had to do was prepare for his session with Betty in the morning.

New passengers were streaming in; and then someone was standing by his seat and asking if he was saving it for someone. Jacob decided if he should have a look. The person making the query was a decidedly lower-level executive who saw no reason why anyone should be taking up two seats in the first place. Jacob got the impression that the man didn't want to return to the metropolitan area and likely hadn't had a good weekend at home.

"Let me clear up my papers," Jacob said.

The man sat down, made a lot of fuss going over a colorful brochure and put a stick of spearmint chewing gum into his mouth.

257

Almost to annoy the man, but wanting to get himself into dictating mode, Jacob spoke a few lines out loud, if subdued. Then he gave up and scratched a few notes but it was a terrible ride. When he got off the train in Weehawken, the street was a mob scene. Traffic, people everywhere. Then he saw Betty on the far corner. She had spotted him and was waving her arms in a kind of happy-go-lucky semaphore.

"Over here, Jacob!"

Dodging cars, he ran over to her.

Chapter Thirty-Two

Billy saddled Champ Monday morning and went out to Bluestone Road, thinking to stop and have a serious talk with Buford. The man wasn't anywhere about and Billy rode to the head of the garden and gave a shout...just as Buford was coming out of his house.

"Hey, Mr. Billy."

Billy drew on the reins, tied Champ to a garden post, and walked across the top of the garden. "Good morning, Buford."

"Wuz on you mine, Mr. Billy?"

"I have something to ask you."

"Den come in."

The room had a board for a bed, a rickety wooden chair, something that resembled a table; a one-burner kerosene unit and a small drum stove were in the corner. The walls were covered with broken-down cardboard boxes and layer after layer of newspapers and posters. On one side of the room was a small window, the size of a porthole. Billy thought of Harlan's house, only because Buford's was so, well, the opposite. Harlan's house was made of trees and air; Buford's house was more of a nest in an old oak that squirrels would be happy going into on a winter's day.

"Sit down, Mr. Billy," Buford said.

He took the chair, Buford sat on the narrow bed. "I need your help," Billy said.

"Tell me how."

"Right now I have Champ on a tether. The rope is killing him," Billy said. "Can you help me build a fence?"

"Yes I will."

"I have the wood and a posthole digger—"

"When you wan' dis built, Mr. Billy?"

"When can you start?"

"I's ready in da mornin'." Buford's eyes were glowing in the dusk-like atmosphere in the room.

"I'm paying for this with my own money," Billy said.

"No. I'm doin' it cuz I wan' to," Buford said. "You's da first person ever set foot in dis house. En sometin' else. You's da first person ever give me a smile here in da Mavik. Woman wheelin' her baby, not three weeks ol, here on Boostone Road. She say Buford dis is my son, Billy. I say to da chile, Please t'meet you's, Mr. Billy. Woman a li'l shy, and da boy he smile at me!"

"I'm happy to know that, Buford."

"We gwyne to make a very good fence fo Cham," Buford said.

"Thank you, Buford."

They shook hands. On Champ, he gave a tug on his western hat on his head, and stayed on Stage Door to the theater, then past the theater to Maverick Road. He had told himself that he wouldn't act like a hurt puppy showing up at Bzy's door but here he was showing up at her door. With the barest of news. He would say he was building a fence for Champ and it was something he thought she would like to know. Brought to her personally via the Pony Express. And something else too. More important. So important he'd forgotten what it was.

At a fast canter he rode by the red pump and several houses; people new to the colony were milling about. Gyuresko was standing at an easel in front of his house. With the sound of hooves he turned to see who it was, as if he didn't know. Billy gave the insect-faced little man in paint-smattered smock an easy wave, then drew Champ in and entered the Salamander drive.

"Bertok," Billy said to the artist, "I'm sorry about Elek, unhappy you lost your dog. I hope you're doing OK."

He waited for Bertok to say something but he said nothing and Billy reined Champ around and was back on Maverick Road and was soon clattering down the Canal Boat driveway, and who was sitting in the yellow grass before the house but Bzy...with two boys. They were playing "Rock, Paper, Scissors" and were laughing and carrying on. One of the boys was Austin Fromm, Billy's new baseball pal, who was also making moves on Bzy as if Billy wasn't otherwise in the picture. He'd talked to his sister about it. What had Rachel said? "You have to roll with it. Billy. It's the way it is."

Now, Austin was in the process of taking Bzy by the forearm and striking her wrist with two fingers pressed together. His "paper" had covered her "rock." But not too hard, as Billy judged. As for the other kid, he had a lot of dark hair and sharply cut features: nose, cheek bones, chin. Older than Billy. Maybe older than Austin. As Billy rode up, all three got to their feet and came over.

"Billy, how are you?" she said, delighted to see him; it didn't seem put on.

"I'm OK. I have a message for you."

She patted the side of Champ's face. "What is it?"

The boy Billy didn't know appeared to be giving him and Champ a serious onceover. "Rachel and Holly are putting on a play later this summer," Billy said to Bzy. "They want you to come over and audition for a part."

"I'd love to. When?"

"They're having a reading at the end of the week. So, soon."

"Hey, Billy," Austin said.

"Hi."

"This is Keith Langley."

"OK," Billy said.

"We've known each other for years," Austin said. "Keith's father is a famous impresario."

Billy didn't know what an impresario was but it sounded important. "Where are you staying?"

"With Austin, for a couple of days. Until my dad gets back," Keith said. He kept on talking. "I can't decide if you remind me of Tom Mix or the Lone Ranger. Tell me your pony's name is Silver, I'll know."

"It's not Silver."

"And you're not wearing a mask. That makes you Tom Mix."

"Keith goes to Deerfield," Austin said.

"What's Deerfield?

"It's a prep school," Austin said.

Keith gave Billy a slow, judgmental look. "Where do you go?"

"West Hurley."

"Never heard of it. How old are you anyway?"

"Is that important?"

"You have a pony," Keith said. "Children nine or ten have ponies."

"Champ is no ordinary pony," Bzy said.

"When I was your age, we had horses," Keith said. "My brother carries a five goal handicap. Right now he's captain of the Yale team."

"In what, field hockey?"

"I'm talking polo," Keith said. "I'll be playing at Meadowbrook all of next month. Why do you keep Champ's halter on when you take him out?"

"I never thought of it."

"Well, it's very déclassé," Keith said. "Let me have a ride."

"Champ has a mean streak," Billy said.

Keith laughed. "I started riding when I was five.

Billy dismounted and handed over the reins. "When you go to get on—"

"Go away, cowboy."

Champ did his usual backing and sidestepping, and when Keith finally grabbed a stirrup he was facing Champ's shoulder. Mean-assed rig reacted with a sharp sideways kick, narrowly missing Keith's knee. Shaken, off balance, he fell, lay flat on his back.

Billy grabbed the loose reins. To Keith, "You OK?"

He was getting to his feet. "You and your goddamn pony can go to hell!"

Champ wouldn't stand still; eyes wide, he was ready to bolt. Finding the stirrup, Billy made a quick move and was up.

"Stand back," he said to Bzy.

She gave him a look he'd never seen before.

Billy gave Champ his heels, a shake of the reins; in a clatter of pebbles, they were off.

****

The next morning, he changed Champ's tether on Harlan's Field. It wasn't that the pony had eaten all the grass in the circle; it was the wear and tear he'd made walking around and around and the constant dragging of the thirty feet of rope. Billy chose a new spot and hammered in the iron spike. Looking up, he saw Buford shuffling along on old Bluestone Road, in one hand a hoe, a 6-foot rusty pry bar on his shoulder. He let it fall to the ground, and Billy gave him a rundown on the fence, how he saw it. Unfortunately, the number of rails was short, not enough of them to fence in the entire field. Also true for the posts. It was Billy's idea to make a corral in the middle of Harlan's Field. It wasn't what he wanted, but what else could they do?

Buford nodded, kept looking around. Giving no clue as to what he was thinking, he started walking east toward the West Hurley woods until he came to the cliff that ran along the property. After a good bit of study, Buford said, "You doan' need no fence here, Mr. Billy." He pointed south along the lip of the cliff. "Where Cham gwyne to go? Do he fly?"

"No."

"Over dah also." He indicated the southern side of Harlan's Field, an impenetrable tangle of sumac, early-growth trees, bushes, vines, briars. "You doan' need no fence dah, Mr. Billy. Now you ken give Cham da whole field!"

They walked back. By Buford's calculation, the fence was already half built. He needed a measuring stick and string to lay out a straight line for postholes. Billy went inside. Hedi had three yardsticks and numerous spools or balls of twine.

"Is he going to start today?" she asked

"He's already started."

Billy went back out. Buford was looking at the timbers lying on Harlan's Field closest to Champ's hitching post. He took the yardstick and end-for-ended it on one rail, then another. Then he tied the twine to a stone and Billy went with it to a tree near the edge of the cliff, wrapping it low around the trunk. Buford had already begun making the first hole. He cleared away tufts of grass and loose soil with his hoe, then began with the posthole digger. Getting started was the hardest past; then it was just a matter of pressing the tool into the ground, spinning it about, and pulling up loose soil. Buford fell into a rhythm, a way of working that made it seem like he wasn't working at all. Hole made, he dropped the digger and picked up a post. He examined several, chose one, positioned it over the hole and, instead of letting it drop, pushed it in hard.

"Dah we go, Mr. Billy."

It was only then that Billy noticed the post had two openings, two see-through slots in it, one on top of the other. Buford had a rail in hand. Like the post, it was more or less round, except both ends were flattened, thinned down, three or four inches. Buford slid the end of the rail into the lower slot. It poked through slightly on the other side. He then went to the other end of the rail; holding it level, he eyed a line straight down to the string and yanked out several tufts of grass. With the tool, Buford started a new hole, and right then Billy saw how the fence would take shape, step after step. With the second post in, Buford slid the rail into the lower slot and Billy did the same with the top rail. The first section of the fence was done.

They worked steadily, putting in section after section. Every other hole Buford would strike a stone or boulder. That was where the pry bar came in. It had a squared-off tip like a supersized screw driver and Buford immediately started "worrying" the stone, driving the bar into the dirt on either side of it. Sure enough the stone began to loosen; you could hear it say "enough." Buford dropped to his knees, got his hands on it, worked it, tugged at it, and finally came out with it.

Buford left at 5:15; he would be back early in the morning. Billy brought a pail of water for Champ and, in the house, told his mother and sisters about the new fence. Rachel and Holly hardly looked up; they were talking about the play. Stepping in, he said he'd talked to Bzy about a part. She was interested and he told her to come over for an audition.

Holly was amused. "Is that what you said?"

"That's what it is, right, an audition?"

"If it's a big production and actors want a part, they audition for it," Holly said. "It's a competition. If Bzy wants the role, it's hers."

"Who all is in the play?"

"Six altogether," Rachel said. "Terry Monroe and I are king and queen. Holly, Woodrow O'Mara, and Bzy are the farm family, and the king's envoy—who searches the kingdom each year for the perfect pig for the king's perfect pork chop—is Austin."

"Austin Fromm?" Billy asked.

"Your baseball pal. Also Donny Osterhoudt—"

"How long has he been in the play?"

"From the very first. When he said he could bring over a real pig—"

"I mean Austin."

"Yesterday Terry and I were walking in the colony and saw a boy playing his cello on the concert hall stage. When he took a break, I told him about the play. At first he hemmed and hawed but when I said we were hoping to enlist Bzy, he jumped right in."

"Thanks, Rachel," Billy said with sarcasm. "I mean, what the hell!"

"I needed an actor," she said. "That was my priority."

****

The fencing needed to hem in Harlan's Field bordering the spur was considerably shorter, and Billy and Buford, the next morning, were moving right along on it. Billy asked him where he'd lived in the south and Buford said Aynor, South Carolina. His father was born a slave just before slavery ended. One of Buford's brothers was seen talking to a white woman and they lynched him. Had him sittin' on a mule and kicked the mule away. "My pap died in jail, beaten up by guards, kicked and punched for talkin' back. Nobody could do nothin' except pray. I had another brother, he was dragged, they dumped his body in a ditch. Mr. Billy, I say to myself, I have to get away. With a dollar in my pockets, I started walkin'. A white woman in Conway foun' dead, and people is sayin' a Negro done it and skipped town. They's comin' for me. I keep walking, and den a car stops and peoples is sayin' hop in. They's going to an art colony in da north. Ever' morning since I wakes up an' counts my blessin's an' my lucky stars, Mr. Billy."

In succession, he hit stones with the digger. He banged the pry bar almost like a well-driller—bang, crack, slam; then Billy took over. He didn't "worry" the rock like Buford but eventually it loosened and he dropped to his knees and wrestled with it. At the end, from both holes, Buford freed the rock.

The final posthole presented a different problem. Eight feet from the current post took you well into the jungle of brush, vines, sumac. Ground cluttered with roots: trying to dig a hole would be a huge effort, Buford said, but he was willing give it a try. Billy kept looking around. A young maple grew on the fringe of the barricade. By angling the last set of rails toward the tree, and nailing them, it could serve as the final post. He set off at a run for the back hall of the house.

Buford liked the idea. From an old brown cupboard Billy got a hammer and shoved a dozen ten-penny nails into his pocket. Old chestnut was rock hard and nails squirted away on bad strikes but at last the final rails were in, to both post and tree. The fence was done. Together they crossed to the north side of Harlan's Field. Buford drew the lower rail from its post, then the top rail, lowering both to the ground; it created a narrow space to walk through. At the stall, Billy took hold of Champ's halter and led him across the yard, through the opening and into the middle of the field. Just walking up from his house and standing at the fence, looking on, was Harlan.

"Whoa, Champ. Steady," Billy said, trying to calm the pony down; impossible to do. His hand tight on the halter, Billy let go, having the good sense to step back and away—to get clear. Champ bolted, silver-plated hooves whizzing back and high, then breaking into a gallop straight for the fence, either to jump over it or ram into it, swerving at the last moment in front of Harlan and tearing the full length of the field, still with a buck and a kick, then coming back at a full run—his tail, no longer freighted with burrs and knots, really flying. Billy had the unhappy notion that Champ might head for the opening in the fence and take off for parts unknown. Signaling to Buford to reset the two rails, Billy thought to make himself scarce. What was he doing in the midst of the kicking, running world of an animal celebrating its freedom? Then, at once, Champ came to a stop in the center of the field. He stood perfectly still. Billy breathed a little easier, then began to laugh...as Champ, head lowering, knees bending, sank to the ground: rolled all the way over, then all the way back. Getting up, shaking himself. At the fence Harlan clapped enthusiastically, as did the Marshall brothers at the other end of Harlan's Field.

Billy went to the fence and ducked through the upper and lower rails. Buford was hesitant to show his emotion but Billy saw joy in his eyes, success in the open, easy way he stood looking out at Champ. "He be a happy pony now, Billy."

"Thanks to you, Buford." Overcome with gratitude, joy, love— Billy wasn't sure what it was—he put out his arms and gave Buford a hug. The man's hands fell loosely over Billy's shoulders. "I figured five days to make the fence," Billy said. "I want you to have what I set aside."

"Nuffin fo' me."

"Buford, take the money."

"Well, OK. I puts in two days, das two dollars, Billy."

"I'm giving you two dollars and an extra dollar." He handed him three singles.

"Thank you, Billy."

Grinning, "Why am I suddenly 'Billy?' Where's the 'Mister?'"

"The 'Mister' went somewhere. You come back my fren."

Buford put the money in his pocket. Billy gave him a hug and Buford walked out to the spur with hoe and pry bar. The brothers Marshall, looking on, gave their heads a shake and went back to the basement.

****

Later that day, Hedi and her children were sitting down to dinner at the kitchen table: hash, boiled potatoes, steamed carrots. "Your father called earlier," she said. "So much happened last week that he had trouble getting the ball rolling again. Now he's back to work and wants to stay with it through the weekend. So he won't be coming home."

Billy didn't clap but the relief was tremendous; he was yet to begin a reading assignment.

"He misses us very much," Hedi said.

"Where is he actually living?" Rachel asked.

"In a rented room in Morristown, New Jersey," Hedi said.

"Is that also where he works?"

"Yes, his secretary comes in every morning."

"Do you know her?"

"I know of her," Hedi said. "Her name is Betty."

"What's their relationship?"

"She's daddy's secretary, Rachel."

They continued with their meal. Rachel said that tonight was Nickelodeon Nite in the Maverick Theater. She and Holly were going. "It's always great fun," Rachel said. "You coming, Billy?"

"I'm behind on *Robinson Crusoe*."

"That doesn't sound like you, come on."

Billy didn't reply, and Holly said, "I have a friend at KHS, Olga Tate, who's read *Robinson Crusoe*."

"Did she like it?"

"She loved it. She told me about the 'naked foot.'"

"The naked *what*?"

"Foot. Crusoe wakes up one morning after a good many years and sees a human footprint. It jolted Olga out of her chair. Someone else was on the island! How far along are you?"

"I'm on page 2," Billy said.

"In the library Daddy has a bunch of reference books," Holly said. "Check one out on *Robinson Crusoe*. Who's the author?"

"Dan Defoe."

"Daniel Defoe," Rachel said.

"That's what I said."

"Billy, why is it you make everyone sound like a baseball player for the Yankees?"

****

After dinner, Billy found a reference book in Jacob's library and took it upstairs; it gave a full description and analysis of *Robinson Crusoe* and when he started reading the novel it went along at a better pace and after a while he got into the story and began enjoying it. At one point he heard his sisters leaving the house and read for an hour, then went downstairs and grabbed a carrot from the refrigerator and walked out the kitchen door, eager to see how Champ was doing in his new freedom.

Hs stayed at the fence a good while. It was a gorgeous evening, stars just coming out, tunes drifting down from the theater. Champ was grazing at the far corner. By degrees, he seemed to be getting closer, and after a while he was standing there with Billy. "How do you like it, Champ? Any complaints?"

Billy fished into his pocket for a carrot. Champ took it from his palm. In the stillness of the June evening, darkness falling, tunes streaming down, Billy pressed his face into the pony's mane.

Chapter Thirty-Three

Items for the Woodstock Library Fair—old tools, sporting equipment, art supplies, clothing and footwear, books—were stored in a large barn-like structure behind the library, and every day new stuff would come in. Three large bins: acceptable, not acceptable, undecided. The idea was to use discretion in putting items on display. Would it likely sell? Thelma Timmins, president of the library, said that "clothing" kept the library going; and she would always single out Hedi Darden as being in charge of that department.

On this Wednesday morning Hedi was going over clothes that had recently come in. She had a detailed list of "costume" clothing Rachel needed for the play and she was on the look for other items as well. Jacob always made a significant contribution to the library, so Hedi didn't feel guilty she was grabbing anything inappropriately. His check would more than double whatever the items may have brought. Like a rich-looking extravagant robe for the king in Jacob's play. That went into a separate pile. As did the cowboy boots for Billy, brown leather, slightly worn, "Lone Star" design stitched into the sides. The boots would likely sell for two dollars. Hedi took a dollar from her pocketbook and put it into the big glass jar on the table and tucked the boots away. A peasant's dress for Holly, the farmer's daughter in the play. She worked for another two hours, accepting, discarding, putting aside.

At home, she washed up and went out the kitchen door, then circled around to check on the basement. The Marshalls were well along on it, an area opening fourteen feet deep and as wide as the floor overhead. At the moment the brothers were putting in the second of two 4x4 posts to support the sunroom.

"Mrs. Darden," he said, "how are you?"

"I'm doing fine, Sherman. Yourself?"

"No complaints. We're keeping to the schedule. I was hoping we wouldn't have to blast," Sherman said. He pointed to a solid mound of stone, the size of a bathtub. "That's about where your furnace will go."

"Well, if you have to."

"We'll keep banging away at it but I'm thinking a few sticks of dynamite will be needed."

"However you see it, Sherman."

"That's a fine-looking fence in Harlan's Field by the way," Sherman said. "They—they worked together really well, Billy and the colored man."

****

Jacob was staying in Morristown for the weekend but Hedi still decided to make bread, which was what she was doing. Kneading dough, working in raisins, buttering the pans, then carefully shaping the loaves and presenting the pans into the pre-heated oven. She was missing Jacob and was uncomfortable about the particulars of his weekend but she wasn't going to alter her routine. Why, at this point in her marriage, she was suddenly feeling threatened, she didn't know; why she was awakening in the morning and reaching out to the empty side of their bed when she had awakened alone many times before, she didn't know. Maybe it was simply that she was getting older, this November she would never see her thirties again. Last night she had dreamed she was back in Biskupitz and Kurt Bauer, the butcher's son, was asking her to leave Heini and come with him. It had surprised Hedi how quickly she had accepted. How good it had felt to exert herself, to pursue what she wanted without guilt or repercussion. That had been then, in a dream no less. What about now, awake?

One of the several money-making ideas for the library was the making and selling of women's aprons. As a girl she had made aprons for a church bazaar in Biskupitz from her own design. Here, many years later, she had talked up the "apron theme" and it had taken hold. It was Hedi's idea that the making of aprons shouldn't be left to one woman, namely herself. Women in the community would form an apron-making union. Last year seven were in it, now there were eleven. Everyone followed the same pattern but the choice of material was each person's to make. There were those who thought the design of the apron was too suggestive, seeing it more as a sexual enticement than a utilitarian necessity, but a pro-design group argued that men were taking interest in the item for that very reason. The topic was never raised again. Aprons sold for $2 each and last year 207 had sashayed happily off the shelf.

Since May first, Hedi had made fourteen and was now running a new apron of cool, sky-blue cotton through her pedal-operated Singer. After this apron, she had one more to go to match last year's number but she was having second thoughts about doing it. Her energy, her interest, had begun fading. She broke off the blue thread just as her inner timer, corroborated by a keen sense of smell, told her that her bread was done. She took out her pans, rubbed butter sparingly over the light-brown loaves, then let them cool on the kitchen table. The sound of kids on the front terrace, assembling (noisily) for rehearsal, broke into the silence of the house. At first Hedi had thought that Jacob had given Rachel and Holly too great an assignment. He would supply the key ingredient but they would have to do everything else. Hedi hadn't said anything; it was not her nature to speak up; but she saw the production of *The King's Pork Chops* as too burdensome a task for her daughters to take on fully by themselves. Jacob wanted to bask in the success of his children's creativity; yet Hedi knew that his own success as a writer was far more important to him. Working with Betty on *The Red Hat* was the number-one priority in his life. Hedi took a pack of Camels and matches and went out the kitchen door and sat in a canvas chair in the back yard.

She lighted the cigarette. On a nice day like this, she liked sitting here more than on the fully exposed front terrace. It wasn't necessary to have privacy to have private thoughts, but it helped; and with the main terrace now taken over, there was no choice anyway. It was thoroughly pleasant here, with a forest on one side and Harlan's Field on the other, now handsomely fenced with natural timbers. And Champ in the middle, grazing. What an achievement for Billy when his father had said, in a dictum, that the pony would not be given hay in the summertime. That Buford had supplied the muscle and no little amount of know-how, had struck Hedi as beautiful. She was sure the Lord had blessed them, a white boy and a black man working together in the field. Jacob had not commented but she had seen a skeptical look in his eye. Who *had* commented was Sherman. It was one thing to take Buford on as a laborer, but to embrace the man? Sherman said he wasn't happy seeing it. Hedi found herself in a predicament. Sherman was working for her, doing a very important job, putting in a basement with explosives necessary. Should she apologize for Billy? Call it a boy's enthusiasm? Tell Sherman that Billy had not done anything wrong? If anything, she was proud of her son. Hugging Buford was both right and Christian. Furthermore, Sherman—

But that was the end of it. She said nothing, and Sherman went back to work.

In the field, as if startled, Champ looked up, moved quickly to one side as a man ducked through a far corner of the fence and began angling across the field for the back yard of the Darden house. Hedi knew him by the bulk of his shoulders and his dark, unruly hair and, of course, the yachtsman's cap. The shirt he was wearing was open a few buttons revealing a mass of chest hair, thick as interlocking ivy on a wall. She was always of two minds when Raphael Hagar came by. One was tiresomeness. Always wanting, asking. She didn't believe he had ever walked away from her empty-handed. And two, she had to admit she often felt a certain—but she wouldn't say it to herself. Hedi, come on, tell yourself the truth. But she wouldn't say.

"Hedi! I was hoping I'd catch you in."

"Where else would I be?"

"You do go places. On days when Jacob is coming home you're

273

frequently out, picking up a special something for the table."

"Raph, sit down."

He sat in the second chair; it was perfectly fine for a man to sit with his legs apart but in Hedi's opinion, Raphael Hagar overplayed it. "How have you been?"

"What changes for the artist? Day in, day out, he struggles."

"How is your 'black walnut' coming along?"

"It's the greatest thing I've ever done."

"That's good to hear."

He sat there sniffing the air. "Could that be—?"

"It is, and I'll cut you a piece. It's likely still warm."

Inside, Hedi took a loaf from its pan. Newly baked bread was difficult to slice; it tended to buckle. You couldn't press, you had to saw. She sawed two pieces, put them on a plate with a little butter on the side, a kitchen knife and a paper napkin. She went out and set the plate on the table.

"Hedi, what would I do without you? I'd die."

"That is untrue, Raph."

He buttered one of the slices, had a bite, closed his eyes in savoring it. "Delicious. Jacob is a lucky man. Coming home to a beautiful wife, fresh-baked bread on the table, dinner with his family. What more could a man want?"

"I'm not sure."

"You're a good woman, Hedi."

"It's always nice to be appreciated. Thank you."

Raph wondered what all those kids were doing on the terrace. Was it someone's birthday, a party?

"Rachel and Holly are producing a play, written by Jacob, that they'll give later in the summer."

"Isn't that fine. And is Billy in it?"

"He's too busy, he says. But he'll be riding up on Champ to make an introduction."

"I love that pony," Raphael said. "I was telling Billy I think he's a jumper."

"Meaning?"

"A horse that jumps—fences or ditches or hedges. One of my mounts won first prize in a national competition in Armenia."

274

"That's wonderful."

Raphael finished his bread, scraped a rough sculptor's hand over his mouth. He wasn't quite through. Might Hedi have an item about that he could wear?

"Recently I came across an old vest," she said.

"A vest?" Raphael puffed his chest. "Why, I love a vest, Hedi."

"It's leather. You probably want one in cloth."

"You have a vest in leather?"

"Yes. Let me get it."

In the house, she went into the master bedroom; the vest was draped over the back of Jacob's favorite reading chair. Earlier, after she had already "bought" Billy's boots, she spied the vest. Raphael would love it and she put another dollar in the jar. For a moment she stepped back, as if asking herself what she was doing, why she continued tending to Raphael's wants and needs. She didn't know. Maybe it was simply to make him happy. She went out with the vest. "I'm not sure this will fit, Raphael. You may not even like it. But here it is."

He stood and Hedi held it for him and he slipped into it, wriggling his shoulders until it settled.

"Hedi, this is magnificent! It makes me young again. Look at me, Hedi." The vest had two low buttons and small pockets on either side. Raphael buttoned the vest and hooked his thumbs into the pockets. "What do you see?"

"A proud Armenian cavalryman."

He went closer to her, took her in his arms and kissed her full on the mouth. It was the kind of kiss a woman, of the better kisses in her life, would remember; or wouldn't forget. He strode across Harlan's Field, gave the pony's rump a slap, then ducked through the fence to old Bluestone Road. Hedi thought she should sit down.

Chapter Thirty-Four

Almost every afternoon after Betty left the cottage at three-thirty or four—she had a life to lead apart from taking dictation from Jacob Darden—he would either lie down or walk to the golf course, depending on the day. Sunny and bright, walk; dismal and rainy, nap. He had found Mike Benitez's pitching wedge in a coat closet and always took it along on his walk. Sometimes he would find a golf ball in the woods near where the path came out; he would pick it up, add it to the bowl on the porch and bring them home to Billy.

Tuesdays a women's league played and on two previous occasions he had helped a long-legged woman with smooth, comely arms look for her ball here on the thirteenth hole using the Benitez wedge in his hand to push aside grass and leaves. And again today. On her second shot, she told him, she had tried to hook her ball into the green but she had double-crossed herself and the left curve she wanted became a right curve she didn't want and the ball ended up in the area where they were now standing. When, after digging around in tall grass he actually found her ball, she was really pleased; a lost ball was a nasty penalty and the girls she played with gave you nothing! She set up to the ball, giving Jacob a good opportunity to admire her swing and her body. She pitched the ball to the fairway, thanked him, and rejoined her fellow players.

She said something to them that brought a laugh, and Jacob started back to the cottage. Seeing it ahead, he found himself comparing it to one of Harlan's cabins. When Hedwig had first seen Bird's Eye, she'd said nothing, perhaps struck dumb, but he knew she had expected something much different, far nicer. A strong wind might topple the house, and the outhouse was thirty yards up a narrow, ungainly path; but this was where they were going to live, this was their home. With night falling and cold weather already here, he would make a fire. Once he got a blaze going in the drum stove, he tossed in an old tire to keep it alive. Alive? Stove got so hot it almost exploded. He could have burned the house down. But no complaints, no judgments from the bride. Just a scare. Things can only get better for us, Jacob, was how Hedwig had put it.

In the cottage, he dialed the long-distance operator to call his Bluestone home. A familiar voice, blurred with German inflections he'd never taken to, came on. "Hello, Hedwig," he said.

"Darling, how are you?"

"Finished a day's work, three full pages, just had a walk to the golf course here. Tell Billy I'm bringing some golf balls home with me, including a Spalding 'dot.' I'm doing well, missing my family." The easy chair had an ottoman, and Jacob stretched out his feet.

"I'm glad you're getting some exercise," Hedwig said.

"Dictating, I pace here and there around the room," he said. "The walk I take is a nice change of pace. Good news, Emily Neher finished reading 265 pages of *The Red Hat* and loves it. She's sending it to Richard Stein at Stein and Sugrue. Depending on what he says—"

"Jacob, he's going to love it!"

"—she thinks she'll be able to get a good advance. So things are looking up. On the strength of it, I called Luther. He'll be meeting me here from now on. I'll be home by seven on Friday."

"Wonderful."

"How's Billy's fence coming along on Harlan's Field?"

"It's done."

"Hedwig, please."

"Buford and Billy finished it in two days."

"They did not fence in Harlan's Field in two days!"

"They did. They only had to do two sides."

"I can't talk anymore," Jacob said. "Things like his infuriate me, Hedwig. I'll see you Friday."

He hung up the phone and sat there with his eyes closed, for how long he didn't know. Familiar footsteps on the path snapped him to. A tap on the door. "Yes, Betty."

"Sorry to disturb you, Jacob," she said, walking in. "Melissa is having a couple of old friends that she and Mike knew years ago. It's spur of the moment but she'd be happy having you come over, say at six-thirty, and join in."

Jacob took his feet off the ottoman, sat up a bit. "Sorry to say, I have to decline. I'm having a problem with the scene where Stephen gives the key address at the Brotherhood Conference."

"So far, in my opinion, those pages are going nicely for you," Betty said. "I don't see it as a problem." She knew the details, the ins and out of his novel as well as he.

"I'm rethinking the scene," Jacob said. "I wouldn't be a good guest."

"She'll be disappointed."

"My apologies."

"What are you making for yourself?"

"I'm not worried about it."

"I might have to come over later," Betty said.

She walked back to her house, upset; not at Jacob but with her mother. Next time she'd tell Melissa to call Jacob herself. For a good while now—well, since Betty had started working for Jacob— her relationship with Melissa was reverting to an earlier day when Melissa had judged her daughter's successes, accomplishments, almost cruelly. Betty had what her mother had never had, what the debutante of the year was entitled to. Melissa loved Mike Benitez but their marriage was a hiccup compared to Betty's. She and Jonathan Hewlett Trill III walked in circles here and abroad that she and Mike never saw...and it was killing her. And now there was Jacob Darden, Betty said to herself, the scholar, the writer, the intellect. There were affairs...and *there were affairs*. Once again Betty shone, came up a winner, and Melissa scraped along on the fringe of New York society as one who had made the horrid mistake of...marrying down. Once Jacob finished his novel, Betty would get a place of her own. If he had other plans, say to return to his family on Bluestone Road, then she would do something else. She wasn't afraid.

The path terminated at the patio, and Betty went in the back door of the house. Her mother was in the kitchen helping Wanda plan the dinner. Betty walked by but Melissa caught her eye. Well?

"He's staying in," Betty said. "He has a lot of prep for tomorrow."

She continued into the living room where she sat at the piano and ran through a few major scales. Then she began a Debussy etude she was working on, a truly lovely piece. She was still making mistakes but was improving each time—

Melissa walked into the living room, interrupting her daughter. "What did he say?"

Betty continued a few moments, then stopped playing and looked at her mother. "He has to prep for an important dictation in the morning."

"Three hours out of his life and he wouldn't come for dinner?"

"He said he wouldn't be a good guest."

"And what part did you play in that decision, if I might ask?"

Flaring, Betty said, "Melissa, from here on you call Jacob. I'm not his social secretary!" She stepped away from the piano. "We have a month to go to finish his book, and that's a priority."

Melissa snickered. "I forgot." And left the room.

****

At about the time guests were arriving at the main house, Jacob searched the refrigerator for a meal and somehow managed to fashion one for himself, actually one of his favorites: franks and beans. When he finished, he rinsed his dishes and went into his living room/office. The first thing he did, as on previous evenings, was read the last few pages of *The Red Hat*, not as a copy editor looking for errors or inconsistencies (if by chance one popped up, he circled it) but as the author who would be dictating new pages in the morning and wanted to continue on the same narrative thread.

He began quick-reading the typescript: in the main ballroom of the hotel, Stephen Rossel, bishop of the greater Hartford diocese, is standing at his table to give the keynote address at the Conference on Brotherhood. Eight months after Pearl Harbor, largely due to the war effort, the country is beginning to pull out of a great Depression. Race relations in the South and in major cities like Philadelphia, New York, Boston, are fraying badly. The Ku Klux Klan is alive in America, anti-Semitism is rampant. Stephen looks out at the assembled clergy, political leaders, dignitaries. No single speech will bring about the necessary changes, will do away with prejudice and bigotry. Civil unrest in America is a discussion we must all have, and churches of all denominations have a prime responsibility to subdue rancor and bring peace and acceptance to their congregations.

Jacob laid down the last pages of his dictation; the next couple of pages would be Stephen's talk, which, as Jacob thought about it, would be in the form of a homily. He spent the next two hours crafting it, scribbled the last sentence, and sat back, considering it one of the finest pieces of writing he'd done in a long time. Clear, strong, on point, precisely what a rising leader of the Catholic Church would say at a conference to promote brotherhood.

Jacob stood, poured himself a rye and ginger ale, read Conrad's *Nigger of the Narcissus* until almost ten. Then he took a couple of downers and crawled into bed.

****

Betty came in at 8:35 the next morning, as always smartly put together. "Good morning, Jacob."

He had showered and shaved and had put on his last fresh shirt; he was badly in need of clothes and would restock this weekend at home. "Good morning to you, Betty."

She set a crisp paper bag on the kitchen table and they pulled up chairs, partook of the coffee and cherry croissants. Betty talked about the party. Melissa was terribly disappointed that Jacob wasn't there. She had expected a slow evening—William and Darlene Krupp from Duluth, Montana, were fine people but oh so dull—and had hoped her tenant, novelist Jacob Darden, would supply the spark to keep it going.

"One can hope," Jacob said.

"I told her next time she should contact you herself."

"Thanks." He closed his eyes and gave his head a little shake.

Finished with croissants and coffee, hands rinsed, they were ready to start. Jacob gathered up his notes, talking points, the text he had written last night. The Hartford bishop expressed the honor he felt standing in for Francis Cardinal O'Connor who had recently fallen and broken his hip. Our prayers for a quick recovery are with his Excellency. Then the Bishop of Hartford began addressing the assembled conferees.

"I speak to you today on the topic of brotherhood and of the human failings and weaknesses we are prone to."

Betty typed. Click clack, click clack.

"In the efforts to accept, to embrace someone else's race or religion, we must look at ourselves first. Prejudice, bigotry, hatred are learned at home."

Click clack, click clack.

And so it continued. Bishop Rossel spoke with compassion and eloquence. The theme was home. Time and time again he referred to it. "To overcome ill feelings, prejudicial beliefs, cruel disparities, we must overcome these failings where we live. This is not easy to do. Once ingrained in a family, judgment of those who are different is hard to shake. We nurture hatred and fear, disparage someone for the color of his skin, someone else for her religious beliefs—it all starts in our own living rooms, at our kitchen table. Bigotry starts at home and is perpetuated at home and must be eradicated at home."

The homily went on for another forty minutes, becoming increasingly warmer, more heartfelt. "Introibo ad altare dei! Let us approach the altar of God together, asking for His divine help in bringing people together...everywhere. Dominus Vobiscum. Amen."

Sitting in the chair at the main desk, Jacob stopped, his head rolling back. It hadn't been a difficult session but he felt exhausted.

"Beautiful!" Betty said. "God, you can pour it!" She glanced at her watch. "Here's what I'm thinking. It's a beautiful day. You go to the pool, have a swim. When I get back—"

"Where are you going?"

"The dentist. I'm sure I told you."

She gave Jacob a kiss and left, and he made his way into the bedroom, stretched out, closed his eyes. He felt restored when he came to 40 minutes later, gathered himself together and went out to the white-pebbled path, following it through a tunnel of heavy hemlocks to the patio and pool. As he stood there looking quietly about, the house door opened and Wanda—Jacob remembered her cheerful moon face, her wonderful pair of bouncy tits—came out with a thick white bath towel folded over a pair of navy blue trunks.

"Mr. Darden, hello," she said, coming toward him. "I have this for you."

"Wonderful."

"Betty said you might have an appetite."

"She was right."

"I can bring you something."

"Make it simple, Wanda. A beer if you have one."

"Whatever you might need by way of lotions or creams you'll find in the bathhouse."

It was on the far side of the pool, a well-designed little structure that reminded him of the sentry box at home, just much larger. Everything a person needed, changing to or from a bathing suit, was in it, plus a narrow bed against one wall if said person wanted to nap or simply lie down. Stripped of clothing, rather alarmed at how white he was, Jacob stepped into a pair of navy trunks, pleased that a lightweight, silver-gray robe hung on one of several ornate brass hooks. He chose a sun lotion and smoothed it liberally on his head. Then, outside, he went to the nearest of several poolside chairs, thinking to sit, only to decide to swim first, then to relax. He laid the robe on a chair, stood on the edge, and dove in.

Jacob swam in his own version of the crawl to the deep end, then the shallow, where he stood in chest-high water taking in the patio and the whole rear of the house. Whoever Mike Benitez was, he certainly had a good idea of what comfortable living was all about. For a moment Jacob thought of the Maverick Art Colony and what Harlan considered comfortable living. What more did a man want but a roof over his head and freedom to paint, write, sculpt? Of all professions since the dawn of modern time, what profession was more crucial, more important to an enlightened civilization than the arts? Jacob grabbed hold of a chrome hand railing and helped himself out.

He dried with the big towel—thick, fluffy, like those at the NYAC—then draped it over the back of another chair and slipped into the robe. He hadn't sat for ten minutes, just long enough to feel warm and dry, when Wanda came out with a tray. Did Mr. Darden wish to sit at one of the tables or have the tray near him on a private little stand? Knowing himself to be a messy eater—a deference he didn't show at home—he said the table. She set it down, then poured beer into a glass.

"Thank you, Wanda."

"Anything else, give me a shout."

"I will. Much obliged."

She smiled at Jacob, took leave. She was a sexy little number; astraddle, she'd bounce around delightfully. Jacob examined his tray. Side of potato salad, small bowl of chips, a finely sliced chicken sandwich with tomato and lettuce. He tasted the potato salad, had a slurp of beer, then picked up the sandwich. He indulged himself in the pleasure of the moment—basking in the sun, enjoying the food, the sudden laziness of the day. Enough to make any man feel amorous. Were Betty here, he would tell her he was feeling sleepy and they should take a nap (code). Jacob was thinking to give Wanda a shout. He would tell her he needed a massage. Was she available? There was a daybed in the bathhouse —

Just then the back door to the main house opened; only it wasn't Wanda who came out but Melissa. "Jacob," she said, "I hope Wanda has taken good care of you."

"Oh, she has. Excellent care." He stood to greet Melissa. "But I must say I'm feeling guilty about it."

"On what score?"

"After turning down a dinner invitation, to have a swim in your pool."

"Jacob, I'm glad to see you relaxing."

"Will you join me?"

"I'm just out the door, meeting a friend. There's a show at the

Morristown Art Gallery we want to see. A young artist named Vernon Sabarese is getting a lot of attention."

"Have you ever had a show of your own?"

"I have. Possibly this fall I'll have another."

"I'm looking forward to it."

"One day you must see my studio."

"Definitely."

"Well, I'm off."

"Good seeing you, Melissa."

She walked away; what he saw was pleasing to the eye. A French expression came to mind: *La jambe, c'est la femme.* The leg is the woman. Jacob finished his lunch, took off the robe and sat for another ten minutes in the sun. Then he changed and went back to the cottage and found himself suddenly curious to read the last pages of the typescript, to see if he would have a different take on Stephen's homily. But he felt that it worked, it was exactly what a bishop would say on such an occasion. He returned the pages to their place, having a positive feeling that he was on track to a successful ending—

The phone rang. Picking up, "Roving Editor, Reader's Digest."

"Are you required to say that forever?" Hedwig asked.

Jacob squeezed the back of his neck. "Sorry. What's happening?"

"A couple of things. One of the girls in the play, who plays the daughter of the king, a piece of bluestone broke loose on the terrace and she fell off it and sprained her ankle."

"Any repercussion?"

"Doctor's visit, I said we'd pay for it. Then the fence Billy and Buford built, someone pulled down a section of it last night. This morning when Billy went out, Champ was gone. He came in the house, as angry, as upset as I'd ever seen him. I asked him if there was anything I could do. He said call Mr. Spector and tell him Billy can't make it. Then he grabbed a bunch of carrots and left. That was eight o'clock. He just got home, leading the pony. Now it's two-fifteen."

"Who knocked down the fence?"

"Don't know yet. Billy is sleeping."

"Goddamn pony has disrupted our family," Jacob said.

"I need you here," she said.

"Hedwig, I happen to be in a life-and-death struggle with my novel," Jacob said. "It could be getting away from me. I'll see you Friday."

"I'm running out of patience."

He heard her hang up the phone. He put down his own phone and decided to sit on the porch, and had just settled into the swinging couch when he saw Betty coming down the pathway. "How was it?" he said as she walked in.

"Don't ask. Did you have a swim?"

"I did. And lunch. Melissa stopped by. She gave me an open invitation to use the pool."

"She likes having you around," Betty said. "I almost fell asleep driving home."

"I'm glad you didn't."

"You're looking kind of sleepy yourself, Jacob."

"Beer at lunch will do it."

"It's naptime, I'm thinking."

When they awoke, it was after four o'clock—and Jacob wondered out loud if they should make an effort to write another page.

"It's up to you."

"The hell with it. Let's go out."

****

They went to the Morristown Art Gallery, the former mansion of oil tycoon Winston J. Millerton III, and viewed the work of nonobjective expressionist Vernon Sabarese, whose work Melissa had gone to see. Try as he might, Jacob found nothing in the paintings that he liked, let alone understood. This man calls himself an artist? Standing back, Jacob told himself that anyone who picks up *Finnegans Wake* might say, this man calls himself a writer? Any artist deserved his due. Sabarese...maybe not.

Later, in the restaurant, Jacob brought Hedwig into the conversation. She didn't want him staying away for another two-week stretch. Too much was going on and she wanted him home on weekends.

"What did you say?" Betty asked.

Jacob had a taste of the veal parmesan, one of his favorite dishes at Chico's; a sip of a fine Chianti. "I said it was something Hedwig and I had to talk over. Basically, it had to do with the novel I was writing. Truth is, Betty, I don't like leaving you at all."

"Do you think I like it?"

"I wasn't planning to fall in love with my secretary."

"I wasn't planning to fall in love with my boss."

"So here we are," Jacob said.

"Foggy little fella, drowsy little dame," she said.

"I want to marry you, Betty. I'm planning on divorcing Hedwig."

She took in a deep breath. "Let's hope we're both still kicking by the time it goes through."

Chapter Thirty-Five

Directing "The King's Pork Chops" might help her get into Smith, but Rachel wasn't happy about sacrificing the entire summer for the dubious boost it might give her application. Certainly her father left her with more than she could handle while he *dick*tated his novel to his *sex*retary in Morristown. Holly had an early lesson with Mr. Bagovitch, and now Rachel was alone on the terrace—the stage to be—waiting for the *dramatis personae* to arrive for rehearsal. It was a glorious summer morning. Robins hopped about; not so far away, Mount Overlook had on a lovely blue shawl.

Rachel was upset but it was Hedi whom Jacob was really hurting. He was angering and disappointing his daughters, but his absence was taking a deeper, more emotional toll on their mother who refused to acknowledge what Rachel and Holly, and others, suspected. Hedi's philosophy: As long as Jacob came home, she didn't care. What kind of a philosophy was that? Nothing could injure if injury was your life. Like having Hedi's mother-in-law serve Fig Newtons and ginger ale in paper cups at Hedi's wedding reception. Goddammit to hell! What had happened with Andy made Rachel nervous, skeptical, as to what lay ahead for her, how life—real love—would finally play out. She still shuddered at how he had accosted her in Big Bear. He was going off to war and wanted to make sure she'd be waiting for him when it was over, a baby in her arms. Oddly enough, she still thought of Andy in a kind, caring way. At other times, Rachel was glad they'd broken up. Andy Sickler hadn't picked up a book since he'd graduated from KHS. After giving him a couple of kids, then what? Her father was a selfish scoundrel, out for himself, but he had an intellect. He was a writer, loved books, was creative.

Rachel was at loose ends trying to stage the play her father had written. Six characters were in it, seven if you counted the pig. Billy had asked Donny Osterhoudt if it was possible to have a real pig on stage. If Donny could arrange it, the part of "farmhand" was his.

Rachel hoped she could do her father's play justice. People were going to laugh. Twenty minutes, he'd told her—that was all an audience on a Sunday afternoon, intent on mingling, eating and drinking, could take of an amateur production. Cut where you have to, Rachel. Edit freely. Keep an eye on your watch—twenty-five minutes, maximum.

A read-through, without too many stumbles, had taken an hour and a half. Rachel didn't have the faintest notion of how to speed the play along. It was about a king in a faraway land whose envoy would scour the kingdom each year for a pig that would produce the best, most tender, most succulent pork chops. Having enjoyed many an excellent pork chop in his life as king, Thaddeus Nosnibor believed that he hadn't, as yet, found *the* perfect pig that would produce *the* perfect pork chop. He would soon be celebrating the forty-fifth year of his reign and would sit down to a feast on that occasion of the finest pork chops ever served to man. To his envoys he shouts: "Find me that pig or it's your head!"

Just then Terry Monroe parked his 1933 "straight-eight" Packard roadster in front of the house. He came over in a slow, easy walk. "What's cookin', Rach?"

Before she said anything, Terry went to the place on the terrace where a stone had come loose, a potentially dangerous situation. He'd made a repair yesterday. "It's solid," he said, coming back. "You OK? What's on your mind?"

"We have to speed things up."

A car parked and a Woodstock boy got out, Holly's new friend,

Woodrow O'Mara. Then Bzy and Austin came in from the colony. "Today we get serious," Rachel said. "Holly is at dancing class. I'll take her part. The playwright wants Pork Chops started and finished in twenty minutes, twenty-five maximum. Who has a watch?"

Terry Monroe raised his hand.

****

Raphael Hagar was standing with Billy—Billy on Champ's back— in the middle of Harlan's Field. As a trio, they were looking at a sapling, shorn of branches, about eight feet long, lying on top of a pair of cardboard boxes. Raphael was saying it wasn't much of a jump at eighteen inches but he wanted to see how Champ took to it. "In the cavalry you're only as good as your mount," he went on, "and if your mount isn't a good jumper, you'll be in trouble. Champ is small, but some very good jumpers are small. The best jumper I ever rode in Armenia was fifteen hands two, and he flew over five-foot fences."

"What was his name?"

"Nazzi. Two z's. The heart he had! He never balked. When Nazzi missed he missed big, took down the whole damn fence. He wasn't a bay like Champ, he was chestnut. I have a picture of him, one day I'll show it to you, Billy. Here's what I want you to do. Go up to the jump, let your pony have a good look at it, then go back ten yards and come in at a trot. Lean forward, easy reins, let Champ know you're with him. Go ahead, do it."

Billy let Champ see the sapling, then turned away and came at the jump—and he went over it, no problem. Raphael clapped lightly. "Well, done, Billy. Now I want you to try something else, go out a way and come in at an easy run."

Champ got a little testy at a canter—the restraint of it—but he came in and went over.

"Lookin' good, Billy."

Just then Hedi came out of the house with a basket of clothes and Raphael let his eyes wander as she began hanging them to the line.

"Make the jump higher, Raph," Billy said.

"Not a good idea, considering the tack."

"What's wrong with it?"

Raphael reached up and took hold of the horn. "You can't lay close to a horse on a saddle meant for herding. In Wyoming, where I lived before coming to the Maverick, a kid riding western came into a jump. Horse balked, boy went forward, horn smacked him like he'd been punched in the solar plexus by Joe Lewis. Knocked him cold."

"So?"

"So you need a different saddle." Raphael glanced at Hedi pinning away, gave his leather vest a little tug.

"Raph, my father isn't going to buy me a new saddle!"

"You don't need one," Raphael came back. "There's a place in Kingston that sells all kinds of old stuff. I've seen McClellan saddles at Stan's for three dollars."

"What's a McClellan saddle?"

"It's made for the military," Raphael said, "going back to the Civil War. Perfect for what you want."

Finished with hanging up clothes, Hedi wandered over. "What's going on?"

"Raph thinks Champ would make a good jumper," Billy said.

"With practice and training." Raphael said, "Champ could do three feet or more."

"That's exciting." To her son, "How about lunch?"

"Sure."

"Raph, I'm making up some grilled cheese and tomato sandwiches. Will you stay?"

"Hedi, I would like that very much."

****

For the first time in two weeks Jacob was sitting with his family at a Hedi-cooked meal: breaded filet of sole, rice and a tossed green salad. Table perfectly set. He looked at his wife and children and said, for the third time, that it was great to be home. His room in Morristown was feeling more and more like a prison; his only divertissement was a half-mile walk to a golf course. He was turning out good pages on his novel so any hardship—boredom, loneliness—was worth it, he kept telling himself. What was going on in his children's lives? He looked about, taking each of them in.

Rachel got right to it about the play. They were making progress but it was still running too long and she had an uncomfortable feeling that she was over her head. Terry Monroe came up with the idea of cutting everyone's lines in half. Possible or not, it got the kids laughing. Terry was Rachel's schoolmate at KHS, going into his last year, soon to be eighteen. She liked how he participated, seriously but not too. He was a good actor, quarterback on the KHS team—

"Holly, any input?"

"No problem with props, thanks to mom," she answered. "I have a list of 'needed items,' maybe seventy-five percent filled. The play is fun, people will love it. As for editing or cutting, I'm lost. Mr. Bagovitch is after me to work harder. I'm actually doing an entrechat."

"That's exciting."

We have a recital the week before the play," she said.

"I'd say your summer is well taken care of, Holly." Jacob turned to Billy. "Champ's fence looks good. I like how you pursued it, stayed with it from start to finish."

"Buford did most of the work."

"It's the idea that counts. You had the idea," Jacob said. "In my opinion, however, the fence was done at a cost. A pony gets himself an acre all to himself, to run in, graze on. I'm still hurting that you sacrificed the things you and I had planned—throwing a football and baseball with real zing; you're no longer a kid tossing a ball easily with dad. Skeet shooting on Harlan's Field. This was going to be the year when you challenged my record of seventeen out of twenty clay pigeons; the year I handed you my L.C. Smith to take afield. Harlan's Field was ours; now it's Champ's. I commend you on making a fence, but there are more things involved here than convenient grazing for a pony. Now tell me about the boys who pushed over the fence."

"It was only one boy, Keith. He pulled apart a section of it."

"What would motivate him to do that, Billy? Wrecking someone's property is serious business."

"He wanted to get back at me."

"What had you done to him?"

"I didn't do anything, he brought it on himself."

"Billy, you did something," Jacob said.

"I offered to let him ride Champ."

Jacob broke away another morsel of the sole, added a touch of wine to his glass. "Was that a mistake?"

"I didn't think so, I thought it was nice of me," Billy said. "All he did, like from the second we met, was take shots at me. Calling me Tom Mix, with my cowboy hat on and boots, as I clattered down the Canal Boat driveway on Champ. Laughing at me because he went to prep school and I went to West Hurley."

"What prep school?" Jacob asked.

"Deerpark."

"I think it's Deerfield."

"Then he asked me if I was ten. I asked him why he wanted to know. Because I had a pony, he said. Ten-year-old kids had ponies. Then he started talking about polo. His brother was captain of the Yale polo team and Keith was almost a two-goal player. He'd been riding since he was five."

"What's his last name?" Jacob asked.

"Langley. His father is a big-time something-or-other."

"Impresario," Jacob said. "Where are you going with this saga?"

"Do you want me to stop?"

"Keep on, Billy," Rachel said.

He waited a second or two. "Keith said he wanted to ride Champ. I said, 'He's ornery.' But he persisted, like I'd insulted him. So I said, OK. And gave him an instruction how to mount—"

"Is there more than one way?" Jacob asked. "You put your foot in the stirrup and swing up."

"He didn't listen to me," Billy said. "He gave me a look, like step back, kid. He wanted to show off for Bzy and Austin. He made to get on and Champ lashed out with a sideways kick he has. Luckily for Keith he missed. By inches. Keith fell back and lay on the ground like a floored boxer."

"But you said the kick missed," Jacob said.

"It threw him off balance. He got up, swearing at Champ, and I rode away."

"And under the cover of night, Keith came back and sprung

Champ. Is that what you're saying?"

"Yes."

"Do you have proof of that?"

"No, but it's what happened. Then I went looking for Champ."

"Billy, Lawrence Langley is well known in the music and theatrical world," Jacob said. "Can you imagine the lawsuit? That you'd given Keith 'instruction' on how to mount Champ would have no bearing in a court of law. The pony is a menace and he maimed Langley's son."

"Keith Langley got what was coming to him," Billy said.

"You should have said, 'No, you can't ride Champ,'" Jacob said. "He'd already killed a dog. If he hadn't 'missed' Keith with that kick, the boy would've had a crushed kneecap, a shattered shinbone. End of discussion." Jacob wanted a little more wine and, bottle in hand, poured.

"Dad, Billy went looking for his pony," Rachel said, speaking out. "Let him finish!"

Jacob wasn't happy letting his son take over the narrative. With a forced gesture, "Go ahead, Billy."

Billy was silent for a moment. Then he said, "I went to Sherman's first, knowing Champ had felt at home with Betsy and Molly, but he wasn't there. Where was another place he'd go? The Osterhoudt mountain pasture where he'd run wild for so long. I looked and looked, around each bend into another pasture, you never saw greener grass. But no Champ. The trail runs along the spine of Ohayo Mountain. I'm at the spot where Bzy and I had hiked in May, where we'd heard a sound, a rumble, of a large animal in evergreens so thick and dense you can't see in. At that time it was Champ; now I'm at the same place and I know he's in there."

"What did you do?" Holly said.

"I thought he might come out," Billy said. "He had to know I was there. Nothing. No rumbling like before, just quiet. I waited and waited, then pushed aside the thick branches. It's like dusk, just before it gets really dark, thin strands of sunlight shine through the green roof. I go in three or four steps and stop. Looking at me is Champ. Will he bolt, the way he did that day with Bzy? I go closer.

The checkmark on his head is under a strand of sun and looks like a star. Lying right there next to him is Buck. Hey, guys, how're you doing? I fasten the lead to Champ's halter and the three of us go out of that dark corner of the mountain and start for home."

"What a wonderful story!" Rachel said, tears in her eyes.

"Beautiful, Billy," Holly said.

"Well, that's quite the narrative," said Jacob.

****

It was after ten o'clock. Hedi was getting ready for bed and Jacob was in the bathroom washing up, making a general mess of the counters and floor, pissing in the toilet and leaving it. More than once, in late summer, their well had run dry, so he had got into the habit of not flushing except when flushing was an absolute requirement. Jacob had no feel for the workings of a house, for tools; he prided himself on fixing something creatively, coming up with a jury-rig fix that took care of the problem. Walk away with a brush of the hands. There, done. The new basement held no interest for him. He could edit an article, a book, with surgical skill; everything else, he was all thumbs.

Hedi got into bed, head and shoulders propped against a couple of pillows, looking at the bank of windows across the room...remembering how they had talked about the prospect of the early sun shining in on them when the addition was but a plan. Truth was, Jacob liked sleeping late and the curtains were always drawn in the morning. He came in from the dressing room and worked his way clumsily under the covers.

He had a book but didn't open it and after a while set it on his night table. Then he lay there, hands on his smooth round stomach. Then he said, "How are you, Hedwig? Still upset?"

"I am, yes. Another spoiled dinner. We live a life of spoiled dinners."

"So you think what Billy said was truthful."

"It moved his sisters and me to tears. And how you belittled him when he finished. I thought it was awful."

"He needed to be drawn up short. He was playing with your emotions."

"But not yours," Hedwig said, with rare sarcasm.

294

"Mine too, but I'm not prone to sentimentality. You and the girls bought every word," Jacob said. "A pony does *not* resort to dark woods in the middle of a sunny day. Billy was spinning a tale, enlisting support from you and his sisters."

"Jacob! My God, how cruel you are!"

"From what I've seen in his essays, Billy has a gift—I'm not talking vocabulary or choice of words," Jacob said. "He has a way with expression, he has a lively imagination. Problem is, it devolves into superficiality. There's no bigger put down in letters than calling a writer 'facile.'"

"He's only a boy. *You're* the writer!" Hedi spoke with feeling. "I will not cosset my son. You're thinking of yourself and *your* mother, Jacob. She did more than cosset you, she smothered you in her bosom—in bed no less!"

Feeling the sting of the comment, he sat up as if to retaliate physically, at the last moment checking the impulse. He had never hit her, or any woman, and he didn't want to start now with his wife; but he couldn't deny the anger and how deep it went. Time and time and time again he would look at her hoping to see someone she was never going to be, a woman of class, carriage, beauty: only to be disappointed...and angry. She was Hedwig Ludmann, the help, the German girl who would make the beds and wash the floors and do the dishes; who, as his wife, applied lipstick badly, sometimes got a smudge of it on her teeth, and wore awful rayon blouses and her hair in a careless bun as they were sitting down to dinner or going out.

Jacob fell back on the bed, hands pressed over his face, remembering lines he'd written Hedwig, in a poem, when she was visiting her family in Germany just before Billy was born. *"That I might wake from chilly dreams to find you here beside me, blossoms on the bough, winter in flight, and spring not far behind."*

Ah, the poet! The great culler of words, player of heartstrings. Who could make you cry, could seduce women, move a nation. Drop a dime in the slot, get a poem, a fortune cookie.

"I'm under terrible pressure," Jacob said, speaking quietly when all was chaos. "Richard Stein is looking at *The Red Hat.* I have forty pages to write, to finish this novel. I'm at a crucial point in my life."

"You've been at a crucial point in your life for as long as I've known you," Hedi said.

"Try to understand."

"Haven't I always?"

Nothing more was said. Jacob rolled over, eyes still open, seeing the darkness in the room.

Chapter Thirty-Six

The Woodstock Library Fair, held on the third Saturday in July, was great fun. People spent a few dollars for a good cause. Music, games, food, booths to browse in for this item or that—books, appliances, clothes. Hedi's racks of dresses, coats, suits were the busiest spot at the fair and she helped people decide and always gave them a break. Instead of three dollars for a tweed jacket, two and a half. She knew how to sell, to bring in money and make people laugh and walk away happy. Her children were at the fair, and they came by from time to time to see how she was doing. Holly bought a flat box with a velvet cover and in it were hundreds of assorted beads with a booklet on how to string them together and make necklaces. It seemed, to Holly, a wonderful hobby. She would dance, she would always dance, but making beads was a quiet, meditative way to lose yourself. Rachel was at the fair with the young man she was going with, Terry Monroe. Nothing about him you wouldn't like. He was all of two months older than Rachel. Young, but at least *she* wasn't the older. Girls she knew said Terry was a rebound and wouldn't last. Maybe so, but he was fun, agreeable, easy going; and thoughtful.

Billy stopped by to see his mother. He showed her the wrench he'd bought with adjustable jaws that you opened or closed with your thumb on a moving spool. She liked thinking that something of her brother Joe was in Billy, because her brother liked tools and used them well and Jacob couldn't hammer a nail without bending it and then smacking the bent part into the wood. Billy had also bought a wire bucket of "maybe forty" golf balls for a quarter. From caddying, he was learning a lot about golf and was thinking he might take it up. He loved baseball but except for school where could you play? Hedi looked at her son standing there with his wares; she'd never seen him looking so low. Bzy and the Fromm boy were wandering the grounds.

Clothing brought in the most money at the Library Fair that year, $2,355.75, a record, and Hedi Darden received recognition from the president of the library, Elsie Winslow, as the individual who, through her dedication to the library, hard work and positive nature, exemplified the spirit behind the fair's success. An article came out in the Woodstock Record with a picture of Hedi going through a rack of dresses with her old Maverick friend, Julia Jamison.

****

Hedi was glad to have the fair over and done with; it had taken an awful lot of time and her house needed attention. Last year she had decided she wouldn't take charge of clothing again but then she had volunteered; now she was giving herself the same lecture... as she began a thorough cleaning of her kitchen. Refrigerator first, defrosting the freezer compartment; the build-up of frost was taking up half the space. As for next year, the way things were going she honestly didn't know how she'd be feeling when the library fair committee started making plans. America would likely be more engaged in the war in Europe with troops on German soil by then, and Jacob's novel would likely be out. If any of that had a bearing.

Hedi placed a pot of boiling hot water in the freezer unit and shut the door. So much was going on, it was impossible to predict. But not impossible to conjecture. Hedi thought about what it would be like if one of these days Jacob didn't come back at all. She would look at it as a failure, perhaps the greatest failing in a woman's life: failure to hold her man. Like last weekend in bed it seemed as if their marriage was ending then and there. It was so unlike her to throw something so personal up to his face. How Ellen Darden loved her firstborn son. He had such a sweet way of crawling into bed with her, she had once told Hedi, when Jacob Sr. left before dawn to meet an early shipment of flowers. What had made Hedi come out with something so critical last weekend, she still didn't know. Maybe because she was now fighting for Billy. More likely it was out of anger, too long held, at the way Ellen Darden had insulted her at the reception. From the very start, Hedi's marriage with Jacob was on a precarious footing. She began moving chunks of ice and frost from the unit and dumping them into the sink. Ultimately, it seemed to Hedi, it was the woman who kept a house together. She couldn't give in, couldn't give up—her family in Germany weren't the only ones struggling to stay alive. Hedi would keep her family together here in America; in so many ways the house they lived in now was but an extension of Bird's Eye.

Once the freezer unit was frost-free and cleanly wiped down, Hedi began on the refrigerator itself. She could hear the Marshall brothers arriving in the back yard and, shortly, there came a knock on the kitchen door. Sherman gave her a greeting, then said they would be blasting tomorrow morning at eleven o'clock. He told her to remove plates and glasses from shelves, take cups off hooks, and lift any paintings from the walls.

****

The "blast box" on the front lawn (Sherman's scary term for it) had a rod sticking up with a crosspiece on top so you could grab hold of it and push down, like a bicycle pump. But the similarity ended there. With a pump you got air; with the blast box you created a spark that traveled along the wires running across the terrace and snaking down into the basement. Standing at the blast box as if guarding it was Ben Marshall; his brother was in the basement for a final check on the placement of dynamite sticks.

Standing to one side of the box and farther back from the terrace were Hedi and Billy. If her husband wasn't around—he wasn't— then a son could provide the support a wife would want to have if explosives were about to be detonated under her house. Billy was concerned but wasn't worried. With Sherman in charge, it wasn't likely that anything would go wrong. When he and Ben had started setting up earlier, Billy had overheard Sherman saying to Hedi that she might have to replace a light bulb in the sunroom lamp. What Billy couldn't understand was why his mother so anxious. Did she know something that he didn't know?

Someone was walking on old Bluestone Road, coming onto the property. Looking over, Billy recognized Wesley Jamison. He told his mother and she turned.

"Wes, how nice." It was always a pleasure seeing her friend. The last time she'd seen him, he had looked tired, in low spirit, no doubt from the loss of the San Francisco competition. Blows like that didn't disappear overnight. Back from New Mexico, he seemed his old self again. Clearly, however, he wasn't here to socialize.

"Hedi, Billy, how are you?"

"Wes, this is unexpected," she said. "What brings you to our door?"

"I'd like to use your phone, if I might. Something has just come up."

Hedi immediately thought of Julia's failure last year to carry a child to term; it hurt her deeply to think it was happening again. "Wes, is everything all right? You know—"

"Everything is fine," he said.

"Well, right now the phone is off limits," Hedi said. "We're expecting a blast."

"So today's the day. Am I in the way here?"

"Not at all. Please stay," Hedi said.

"I have good news for a change," Wes said. "My dad hasn't been feeling well and I wanted to let him know that Vassar College is taking me on as a fulltime instructor in its art department."

"Wes, how wonderful!"

Just then Sherman Marshall walked around the outside of the house. To Hedi, "We're set to go."

"Oh, God," Hedi murmured. "Billy, hold my hand."

"Sherman picked up the loose wires and, leaning over, attached them to the terminals on top of the blast box. He then gave an OK to Ben.

It was the stillness just before a storm hits, then the first crash of lightning. With the solemnity of an executioner, Ben grabbed the handle with both hands and plunged the rod into the blast box.

300

BOOM!

Hedi lurched. The house staggered, Billy seemed to think, like a boxer whose knees had almost buckled when hit with a solid left hook. He seemed to see objects flying, furniture gliding about—

"All clear!" Sherman cried out.

"Let's go look," Hedi said.

They crossed the lawn and went in. Chairs, sofa, coffee table were, in fact, occupying different places in the living room; bugle had jumped its hook and lay on the stone hearth. How Hedi had forgotten to clear the mantelpiece she didn't know, but she had, and now Jacob's favorite brass ashtray, a box of wooden matches, and a German beer stein lay on the floor, its handle broken. Hedi could only feel they had gotten off light. She told Wes that the phone was in the kitchen. First, he said, he wanted to re-hang the paintings taken down in advance. With Billy's help, he put them back where they belonged.

Wes went into the kitchen, used the phone. In five minutes, he came back out, announcing how happy his father was, then giving Hedi a warm hug and getting one in return.

"How happy I am for you and Julia," she said.

"We caught a break.

Billy didn't follow Wes out the door. He grabbed his football from the front hall shelf and shouted to Wes who was crossing the lawn. The painter stopped and Billy, hoping to put a spiral on it, threw him the ball. It was more of a wobble but Wes Jamison caught it, held it.

"A step up from pinecones," he said. "But they served us well. I haven't had a football like this in my hands since Dartmouth." The artist gripped the ball, his fingers firm on the lacing. "Run out for a pass, Billy. Five yards, then cut."

****

Archbishop Stephen Rossel and Pope Pius XI were in the papal chambers in the Vatican having an intimate, solemn discussion, which (Jacob had well in mind) would culminate when His Most Holy said the words: "My son, I herewith pronounce you a cardinal in the Roman Catholic Church."

The phone rang. Betty looked at him and he signaled "pick up."

"Yes, Emily," she said into the receiver. "Hold on a moment; he just stepped out."

Jacob held a nonexistent phone to his ear, pointed to the bedroom. He waited a moment, then picked up. "Hello, Emily. How are you?"

"I'm fine, Jacob. How about yourself?"

"Hard to say. I'm trying to finish a novel."

She came out with a light-hearted laugh. "Really? Glad to hear it." Then she started in: "Dick Stein at S&S read the 200 pages I sent him. He likes what he's read but isn't ready to make an offer."

"Why not?"

"It doesn't hold together in its present form."

"What's wrong with its present form?"

"It's neither fish nor fowl."

"Is that what he said?"

"It's a quote."

"Emily, maybe we're barking up the wrong tree."

"That's possible but Dick Stein likes this book. With changes, he sees potential here for a bestseller."

"What's the main problem?"

"It has to do with Stephen Rossel's father. The future cardinal's father, Milton Rossel, is Jewish. There's a reason for this, Dick is thinking. This is a Catholic novel and a Jewish father lurks in the background. Conflict, tension. But you let Milton Rossel fade away; he's only mentioned again in passing. As written, it has overtones of anti-Semitism."

"Does he want to work with me?"

"You're a very good writer, Jacob. He sees two options," Emily said. "One is delete the Jewish father altogether, wipe out nuances in the early chapters, and replace 'Milton' with 'Patrick,' an Irishman who loves his church, his local pub, his Irish Catholic wife and is demonstrably proud of his son, Stephen. *The Red Hat* then becomes a strong, full-blooded Catholic novel. Or you can stay with the Jewish father unapologetically—make him a real person, someone who participates in his son's Catholic life—lovingly or not; but is always a man of substance."

Silence.

"Jacob?"

"I'm here, I'm thinking," he said. "Did Dick Stein express a preference?"

"He implied the 'Catholic' version would likely be a popular book. It's quite a journey Stephen is on as he rises through the church. The 'Jewish' version would be a superior novel if done well. He'd like to meet with you and he wants you to call."

"Thanks, Emily."

He put down the phone, ill-at-ease, frustrated. The fictitious Jewish father, in the novel to placate a real-life Jewish father, had turned the tables on the half-Jewish author.

Betty hung up the extension. Coming out of the bedroom with her shorthand pad, she asked Jacob what his thoughts were.

"It's not what I wanted to hear."

"He wouldn't be giving you options if he didn't like the book."

"Betty, he rejected the book."

"'As is,' he rejected it," she said.

"I had a reason for leaving Milton Rossel in the shadows."

"And Dick Stein wanted to know why. I questioned it myself, do you remember?"

His silence meant yes.

"I forget your explanation," Betty said. "It didn't strike me as convincing but I'd said enough."

"I did it to satisfy a pledge I'd given my father."

"And the pledge, if I may ask?"

A voice, deep inside Jacob, told him to pull aside the curtain. He was sitting with a women he loved whose help was all important to him as a writer, and he was still keeping the truths of his family, that he had so assiduously kept secret all his life, to himself. It was time for a change.

"Let's go out to the porch," Jacob said.

They sat on the swinging settee. In the not-too-distant distance, a man and a woman, with caddies, were walking along. Jacob watched for a moment, then told Betty about the lunch he'd had with his father in Boston as he and Hedwig were planning a life in the Maverick Art Colony. "My father believed that I wanted his blessing. It wasn't why I was meeting him for lunch, but yes, his blessing would be wonderful to have. But he made me pay for it, Betty. I owed him, and blessings didn't come cheap. So I told my Jewish father what I'd do in my yet unwritten novel about the Catholic Church. I put it in the form of a pledge."

****

Two days later, Jacob visited his therapist in Manhattan. They sat in silence in Dr. Blandon's office. Unless the patient spoke first, it was how a meeting would go. Once, with nothing said at all, Smiley had called it a "fruitful session" as he was saying goodbye to Jacob at his door. But today Jacob wanted something more tangible to walk away with.

"I'm meeting Dick Stein tomorrow," Jacob said, "and I'm feeling shaky. Don't know where I am, where I'm going with my novel; which is to say, my life."

"Keep talking."

"The promise I made to my father seventeen years ago has caught up with me." Jacob tried to get comfortable in his chair; it wasn't happening. "How pleased Jacob Sr. was when he learned the future cardinal's father in my novel would be a Jewish merchant," Jacob said. "That was my pledge. But I haven't lived up to it. I snuck Milton Rossel into my story through the back, exactly how my mother snuck my father through the back door of our house. Dick Stein didn't offer me an advance, to my great disappointment. He didn't flat-out reject the book; he wasn't ready to commit to it. If I'm willing to make changes, he'll look at it again."

"So—?"

"I'm willing to make changes," Jacob said, recalling the easy, the opportunistic pledge he'd made years ago, remembering how successful, how clever he'd felt.

"That's to your credit, Jacob."

"It happens to be a change that would hurt my father, wound him deeply. I wasn't delivering what I'd promised. He might hurl a Zeus-like curse on me."

"What about the other change?" Dr. Blandon queried.

"If I bring in the Jewish father as a full, round character, unlike the stick he now is, it would likely kill my mother."

"How so?"

"That her husband, my father, was a Jew was never so much as whispered in our house. Did people outside the family know? If they knew, they didn't spread it about. Names don't mean much, but *Darden*? Not Jewish. Jacob Darden Sr. is a successful Boston florist. Cardinal O'Connor considers Ellen Darden a personal friend. Twice in earlier days she won his highly esteemed 'Catholic Mother of The Year' award. Then to have her eldest son publish a novel where the fictional son is a leader in the Roman Catholic church and his fictional father is a Jew? People would read between the lines. She'd never live it down. What would compel a son to expose, for all the world to see, the bigotry, the meanness, the arrogance—otherwise called pride—of this celebrated Catholic woman? What has she hidden all these years? What psychological harm has she done to her children? Driven them to alcohol and drug abuse, sexual hang-ups, self-doubts, fears. How loving she seemed, how controlling she was. How she reviled Hedwig at our marriage, who had made her beds and cooked her meals and cleaned her bathrooms. Did I stand up then and say anything? Take those Fig Newtons and throw them in her face? My God, how could I have let that act of unmitigated scorn go by? I now have the opportunity to pay her back for that most unkindest cut of all by pulling aside the sacred curtain of her life and revealing who this 'Catholic mother of the year' really is! I don't believe a more hubristic woman ever lived than my mother. I drank the milk of paradise—and it killed me."

"You were a child on those early morning visits, Jacob."

"The child is father of the man. Who I was then is who I am now."

"You are forgetting something," the doctor said. "Today you are a writer. Forget your mother, forget your father. It's why you left teaching, why you left editing; it's why you went to the Maverick with Hedwig—to write. Your whole life points to this moment. You are a writer, Jacob. Let the old chips fall where they may. You are here, today, to tell the truth!"

Chapter Thirty-Seven

It wasn't exactly uphill to Bluestone Road from the golf course but going home required more pedaling than coasting. Already bushed from lugging clubs for four and a half hours, Billy had nothing too good to say about it. Get on your bike and start in. Eventually you'd get there. With Mr. Spector on vacation for the next two weeks, Billy thought to quit caddying for the rest of the summer and spend more time fishing, exploring new roads on Champ. What he really wanted to do was take a second hike to the old trapper's cabin with Bzy. But with the play—and Austin—where would she find the time?

Billy came to old Bluestone Road, pedaled on, and dropped his bike to one side of the drive. A rehearsal was in progress; kids, at the moment though, were on a break. Rachel and Terry were walking on the spur, closer to each other than two people would normally walk. Billy liked Terry, an all-around great guy; he thought of him as a brother he'd never had. He'd liked Andy Sickler a whole lot also. He had always given Billy great tips and information on hunting, fishing and the great outdoors. On grouse hunting. But Rachel had never seemed relaxed or happy with Andy. Everything was serious, maybe because he was going off to war. Once it was over and he came home, they were planning on getting married and living in Big Bear. God's country, as Andy called it.

Then, something had happened, and she hadn't spoken of him again. Rachel and Terry Monroe laughed a lot, as if she'd never had any fun with Andy and was now making up for it. Holly and a boy named Woodrow O'Mara were sitting on the edge of the terrace. He was Holly's age, his father, Raymond O'Mara, was a writer, the family had just moved to Woodstock, and Woodrow knew everything there was to know about the "old West," particularly the gun slingers of the era. Not exactly Holly's interest but he was smart and made her laugh. "Woody's a kid who gets it," she'd told Billy. As to what Woody O'Mara got wasn't clear but "getting it" was evidently a very good thing. As for Austin and Bzy: they were sitting together on the lawn near Jacob's studio. Maybe they were holding hands but Billy wasn't going to look twice. As Rachel had said, he had to roll with it. Billy was trying to roll with it. Realistically, Austin Fromm was older, taller, better looking, smarter, and played the cello. And he had cool moves, like his arm on the backrest of a theater seat and casually letting it drop onto Bzy's shoulder. Moves were important, and Billy didn't have any that he knew of.

He checked on Champ in Harlan's Field, filled his pail, and went inside through the kitchen door. Hedi was putting pans of bread into the oven.

"Hi, Mom."

"Billy." She sat down with him at the table. "How are you?"

"Tired. Mr. Spector is always adding a new club to his bag and he doesn't use half of them. But he gave me a two-dollar tip today."

"What got into him?"

"I gave him a read on the last green," Billy said. "He sank the putt and won his match with Mr. Cozzens."

"That's a good reason."

"He and his wife are going on vacation tomorrow."

"Where are they going?"

"To an island off the coast of Maine for two weeks."

"Well, how—how nice."

"He said he wants me to sit for him when he gets back," Billy said.

"That's a feather in your cap," Hedi said.

Billy didn't see why. To get a feather in your cap you had to do something, achieve something. Any fool could sit in a chair and have himself painted.

"He's a very famous artist," Hedi said.

After washing up and having a snack, he went to his room, pulled on his western boots and went out, leading Champ from Harlan's Field to the hitching post near the stall. He didn't like the McClellan saddle nearly as much as his Porter saddle from Phoenix, but he was trying to get used to it, especially because he and Raph now had a course of four jumps that could be set at two feet and at two and a half feet, depending. Sometimes after a session, Hedi would come out with slices of bread with honey and a few sticks of celery and radishes on a plate and cups of local cider.

On Champ, he passed Bearcamp and Intelligentsia and Quarryman on the spur; then it merged with Bluestone Road. They went by Rocky Hill; he pictured himself at the top of it, bearing left, and Bzy running out of Canal Boat and leading him to a secret place under the branches of a great pine. Billy kept going on Bluestone Road, Buck trotting alongside. A dirt road branched off to the right. Unlike Rocky Hill, it didn't head due west and wasn't steep; it pretty much followed in the general direction of Bluestone Road, weaving along through thickly wooded land on a quiet rise and after twenty minutes it leveled off. Quiet, no one around. On the West Hurley school trail you were close to the earth; on the trail he was on now, you were near the sky. When he came to a clearing, he looked down and saw the roofline of a big red barn. A narrow dirt road led to the barn from Bluestone Road and coming along on it was a team of draft horses drawing a buckboard. Champ let out a high-pitched neigh, and neighs came back. Then another exchange between valley and hill, quieter now, more whinny than neigh.

****

Betty and Jacob had never worked together better, nor for such extended sessions, than in the three weeks following Jacob's Century Club lunch with Dick Stein: splicing dozens of new pages into the novel in carefully selected places, including the last chapters of the novel. At their lunch, Dick had said he and Elaine were going on vacation on July 1st and he would love to have the pages to take along. Send them to his home in Riverdale, if they're ready by then.

Jacob made sure they were ready, on some days working with Betty well into the evening. Two days before the Steins were to leave, he sent the completed novel to Riverdale and spent the next weekend at home, working with Rachel and Holly on the play; otherwise it was a weekend he would choose to forget. Not only was his marriage to Hedwig strained to the breaking point, the fear that he'd made a mistake—that he'd given in to Dick Stein's preference for the Jewish father, if not then and there at the Century Club, weighing on him heavily. He was not in a very good place when he walked into the cottage Monday morning.

Betty was in the main house, and instead of calling her he lay down in his room to nap; in time he would call. How long he'd napped he didn't know; but the phone began ringing and he answered it, giving into the modicum of cordiality he had or could muster.

"Hello," he said at his desk.

"Hello, Jacob. This is Dick, calling from Montana."

"Dick, well—I'm delighted to hear from you. Montana?"

"We belong to a fly fishing club. Very quiet, just a wonderful place to get away to. I do some fishing. Elaine casts a mean dry fly. Jacob, I just finished your novel. You know, after our lunch, I wasn't sure what tack you'd take. I was hoping you'd run with the Jewish father—the fully developed Jewish father—maybe you'd go with the surefire Irish father. I had a good talk with Jerry—Jeremy Sugrue—and he suggested we do the Catholic version of *The Red Hat*. Not even the hint of a Jewish father in the beginning. Coming out with a strong Jewish character as the future cardinal's father—he had his doubts. Why complicate a perfectly fine story of a young American priest rising to the rank of cardinal?"

"It's a good argument."

"Jacob, I'm delighted by your decision. Your changes are masterful."

"That's nice to hear."

"Jacob, it makes for a better story," Dick said. "I'm taken with the episodes you use to bring Milton into the story, starting when he asks his 12-year-old Stephen to pray with him in the synagogue. Next, and excellently positioned, is Milton's making it clear to Stephen, a day after his high school graduation, that he wants his firstborn to take over the family business in imported fabrics. Stephen says he has committed himself to joining a seminary and become a priest. What a tender scene it is. Then—Stephen is a bishop now and is making the keynote address before seven thousand dignitaries, heads of state, and leaders of religious faiths around the world—when he confesses to the world what he has never come out and said, publicly: his father is a Jew. Something holds him back; clearly that 'something' is his Catholic mother, as the reader learns from earlier pages. In essence, Stephen shows himself to be worthy of high office in the Catholic Church. Metaphorically, a world leader in peace and diplomacy. Stephen Rossel, of a Jewish father and Catholic mother, is a great character. Jacob, are you there?"

"I am, but speechless."

Dick Stein laughed. "My God, it's a better story, a richer novel, with Milton in it. What the novel will do for bringing Jew and Catholic closer isn't the question. Good fiction moves people deeply, makes them think and feel and wonder; it changes attitudes. You've written a powerful novel, Jacob."

"I'm speechless again."

"*The Red Hat* has a certain charm as a title but does it compel readers to open this book," Dick said, "does it foretell of a journey they are about to make? I want to call your novel *The Cardinal*. Think it over. I'm calling Emily to talk over a contract."

"Dick, you're supposed to be fly fishing," Jacob said.

"The evening rise awaits. In truth, I've already landed a beauty. Goodbye, Jacob."

Head lowered, Jacob sat there succumbing to the joy, the pleasure of the moment. Someone was coming down the path.

"I knew you had to be back," Betty said. "The line was busy."

****

It wasn't late but Hedi had turned in; she was exhausted and hoped to get a full night's sleep. With Jacob's input this past weekend—Dick Stein was reading a revised version of *The Red Hat* and Jacob had been totally preoccupied—they had gone over the names of twenty-five guests already invited (with children of course and any weekend friends) for Labor Day. The number was now 31 but it wouldn't stay 31. Word was going around that the Jacob Dardens were throwing the last of the great Maverick Art Colony parties. The guest of honor would be Harlan Gray himself. Preceding a production of a play written by Jacob Darden, Billy Darden would put on an exhibition of fence jumping on his pony; and, as the lead-in to the play, Holly Darden would give an exhibition of ballet with violist Nick Bonino. All beautifully planned. Jacob liked planning. As for putting the plan into effect, he'd leave the details to his wife and kids.

The phone rang. Hedi picked up, knowing who it was. "Hello."

"Hedwig, how are you?"

Speak of the devil. "We've had a busy day, I'm tired."

"Was the barrel of hard cider delivered?"

"Yes. Sherman set it on a sawhorse in the basement."

"How did the dress rehearsal go?"

"Rachel seemed very pleased."

"Great," Jacob said. "I've good news myself. My agent is drawing up a contract with S&S for forty- thousand dollars."

"That's wonderful! That's a huge amount of money!"

"For The Cardinal."

"The what?"

"It's the new name for the book."

"Jacob, I love *The Red Hat*. Since the day we moved to the Maverick—"

"I know, Hedwig. Names change. I want you to hire someone for the weekend. You need help. It's too much for one woman to handle."

She wasn't replying.

"You deserve it after all these years."

Silence.

"See you Friday about one. Hire somebody! Good night, Hedwig."

She put down the phone, lay in bed staring at the ceiling. *You deserve it after all these years.* As if they were the words she

311

wanted to hear. She knew Jacob well enough to know *those words* weren't in him to say. Maybe to write in poem. She lived as in a dream, and always had.

Chapter Thirty-Eight

On Friday evening of the Labor Day weekend, the Dardens sat down at the sunroom table for a fish chowder dinner. Jacob poured a chilled Chablis and talked about his novel, the contract he had signed with Dick Stein. The great advance. The only thing he wasn't saying was the new title. Hedwig had taken *The Cardinal* as well as a mother would who had just learned that officials had changed her child's name behind her back. Holly wasn't sure about "advance." Jacob explained the term, took pleasure in doing it. An advance was money a publisher gave a writer before—in advance of—actual sales. A writer received no royalties until the publisher made up that amount.

"What are royalties?"

"They are a percentage of profits. A standard contract calls for a ten-percent royalty; that means the author gets a dime for every dollar his book makes."

"Who gets the ninety cents?

"The publisher."

"That doesn't seem fair," Holly said. "After all the work you did, you only get a dime?"

Jacob sat in his captain's chair as if his ship, rich in exotic spices, had just come in. "Ten percent—it can go up to fifteen—of a big number is a pretty big number."

He looked around the table at his wife and their children, one at a time. "It looks as if the Maverick Art Colony might take a final bow at the end of this year," he said. "Things aren't looking good. First and foremost, the war—battlefield or home front—is terribly demanding, preoccupying; and it's only going to get worse until the happy day when it's over. I'm happy we're here now, taking part this weekend in a great tradition of art and artists— dancing, acting, performing—while we're together, healthy, well; while the Maverick is still the Maverick."

Jacob lifted his glass to his family.

****

The curtain on "The King's Pork Chops" was two o'clock on Sunday; at two on Saturday some thirty spectators, guests of the family, were standing at the post-and-rail fence as Billy, on Champ, was getting ready to negotiate a series of jumps on Harlan's Field. Raphael Hagar, holding the cheek-strap of the pony's bridle, was talking to Billy. Training was important but it all came down to the rider. Firmness, confidence. Approach each jump with purpose, he was saying. Give Champ an OK and sail over it. Raphael turned to the gathering, Billy's mother and father and sisters among them. At the side of the fence paralleling old Bluestone Road stood Harlan and several others. First, Raphael gave a little background on who he was, where he had grown up, his early years in the cavalry of the Armenian army, and now a sculptor living in the Maverick Art Colony.

"One of my jobs in the cavalry was training horses to jump," Raphael said. "When you're fighting a war on horseback, your mount better know how to negotiate a fence, an obstruction, a trench. Battlegrounds are tough places. The first time I ever saw Champ this spring, I said to myself this pony's a jumper. I could see it in his legs, chest, his spirit, how he held his head. So we started training. My life's work is sculpting, but working with Billy and Champ has made my summer."

Jacob was not happy at the ex-cavalryman's comments; something about the Armenian's manner, attitude was invasive, too close to home.

Raphael told Billy to give Champ a warm-up run. Pony was edgy

313

and Raph wanted to have some of that excess energy used before the actual jump. Billy reined Champ and they ran at a good clip, not a gallop, the length of the field to cheers and clapping.

"Here's how it works," Raphael went on. "As you can see, we have four individual jumps. The 'posts' are old nail boxes, set on end, with trimmed saplings running from one to the other. Right now all jumps are set at two feet; the nail boxes are two feet. The second time around, the jumps will be roughly between two-feet six inches and two-feet eight inches. If Billy wants to try a single three-foot jump as a finale, he'll go for it. The saddle he's using is an old McClellan saddle from World War I. Unlike his western saddle, it doesn't have a horn and is better suited for jumping."

Raph gave Billy a come-in; he patted Champ's neck and had a final few word with the rider. "You're in this together, it's like the two of you are one. Start when ready."

Billy put Champ into a canter and moved into the first jump, taking it cleanly. Then, on a prescribed route, the second, the third, the fourth, all at the same easy run. Great clapping, Hedi, Rachel, Holly, all clapping, happy. Jacob looked vaguely annoyed.

Raphael adjusted the height of each fence by putting blocks of wood on top of each box and laying the saplings across. He signaled Billy, who circled about, then came at the higher jump. A touch of hesitation in Champ, Billy held him to it—up and over.

"Good pony, good jumping," Billy said. "Three to go."

Champ cleared the remaining jumps.

"Great!" "Well done!" "Encore!"

Raphael asked Billy how he felt about three feet but he said no; he was proud of Champ. Twice around was enough.

"That wraps up the equestrian aspect of the weekend," Raphael said to the gathering.

People were happy. Cheering, clapping. Billy raised his arm. His father was walking away.

Billy dismounted and led the pony to the garage-wall hitch, took off his saddle, switched from bridle to halter, and brought Champ a pail of water. As he was brushing Champ, Terry Monroe and Rachel came over.

He wanted to tell Billy he'd put on a good show. As an athlete, he always appreciated when an athlete gave his honest best. He knew Billy was tempted to try three feet, but everyone respected him for not going for it. To know what you're capable of at any given time is class. Then Austin and Bzy came up. The young cellist just stood there. Champ's taking over Harlan's Field had pretty much cut short their baseball; other than that, they didn't have much in common, unless you counted Bzy. She told Billy she was proud of him, and Champ too. Going around twice without a miss was really something. Austin said they were kids' jumps; it was pretty boring. Bzy took the brush from Billy and used it on Champ's coat. Then she stopped brushing and gave it back. She looked sad. Then she went away with Austin.

Billy gave Champ's tail a few strokes, then led him through the lowered rails and let him go. In a few minutes he was pushing the lawn mower, giving special attention to the area where Holly would be dancing, and thinking, all the while, about Bzy. When he was about two-thirds through the lawn, he stopped to get a drink of water from the outside faucet, then sat on the bench between two oaks, resting.

When he got up to finish mowing, a car with three men in it pulled up to the house on old Bluestone Road. The car was old, dirty, and rundown. A good bit of commotion was going on inside it. One of the men, it would seem, couldn't move; the other two were trying to assist him in some way. Billy couldn't figure it out. First off, why were they here? The doors were now open and two of the men finally had the lower half of the third man outside the back of the car. Then they lifted him to his feet; his legs dangled like stalks of asparagus softly cooked. As a unit, the three moved toward the house, the helpless man between the two who were helping him along. He had a wasted look—grizzly whiskers, ragged clothes, broken sandals on his feet. The other two were better dressed, certainly stronger; the one with red hair had a ragged mustache, the other was heavyset and wore glasses. They went past Billy. The man in the middle was talking, saying things, but nothing Billy could understand. They got to the terrace, entered the front hall, and knocked on the door.

Billy thought of going inside, then changed his mind. His father

315

didn't need a boy standing there to lend a hand. Whatever the purpose of the visit, he didn't imagine it would be drawn out. He went to the mower and started shoving it around again. He was doing the stretch of grass that grew along the spur, almost done with the job when the house door opened and the three men came out much like they had gone in, two helping the one. Billy stood by the mower as they drew near their car. He was looking at the poor wretch of a man straight on, his eyes glazed, mouth open, legs wobbly.

"I'm Billy Darden. I live here," Billy said to the man with red hair. "What's going on?"

"We stopped by to see your father."

"I saw you go in."

"You Jacob's son?" the man in the middle said, words running together.

"I am."

"I'm James Flannery. Always liked your father, he gave me a ten spot—stay on the wagon, he told me, he'd give me a hundred."

"Come on, James," the man in glasses said.

"Did you carve the Maverick Horse?" Billy said.

"I did glad to meet Jacob's son good man your father."

He put out a hand and Billy reached out and took hold of it; thin, sickly as it was, he didn't want to let go, but James Flannery's friends were pulling at him and then were juggling him back into the car.

****

Two important events happened Sunday morning. At eleven Rolf Osterhoudt drove up to the Darden house in his red pickup with Donny, his son. A wooden crate, fresh straw sticking through its mesh-wire sides, lay in the payload area along with a table. Rolf carried it in and Donny followed along pushing the table conveniently on wheels. When father and son were on the terrace, Donny picked up the crate and set it on the table. Hedi came out of the house, a smile brightening her face when she saw who it was. "Rolf," she said, "good morning."

"Good morning, Hedi. I am delivering the Osterhoudt contribution to the arts, such as it is."

She saw the crate, peeked in, and let out a small, surprised laugh. "What a fine contribution it is! I have to get Rachel—"

—who was just coming onto the terrace, a red-checkered neckerchief around her hair; beneath it were curlers. "Mr. Osterhoudt," she said, "what have you done?"

"Take a look."

Rachel peered into the crate and almost screamed. Having an actual pig in the play had made for occasional, and often humorous, talk, but no one in the cast had ever thought of a real live pig as anything more than a joke.

"Thank you, Mr. Osterhoudt. How much does it weigh?"

"Forty pounds this morning. Donny named her Lucinda after one of his cousins in Scranton," he said to Rachel but also Hedi; he wasn't forgetting Hedi. "Note how easily the table moves," Rolf went on. "You can move her on stage and off, whatever is required. Or Donny can reach in and pick her up in his arms. There's a trick to holding a pig but Donny can do it."

"You've thought of everything," Hedi said. "You will be coming to the play with your wife?"

"We wouldn't miss it," Rolf Osterhoudt replied with a smile.

****

Sherman and Ben Marshall lugged the barrel of cider up from the basement and set it on a sawhorse in a shaded corner of the house, near the well. Both sampled a cupful, nodded their approval; had another taste. Just the right amount of "hard." It was going to be a very good party.

Inside the house, Hedi's new helper, Hannah Hardenberg, set out a plate of sandwiches on the sunroom table and a dish of celery, carrots, and apple slices. The idea was to make a snack available. Everyone was scurrying about getting dressed, saying lines, preparing for the occasion.

Chapter Thirty-Nine

Guests began arriving at 1:50 and Austin Fromm, standing at the top of the driveway and looking official, like King Thaddeus's envoy in the play, handed out programs and directed people to the lawn facing the terrace, a.k.a. the stage, handsomely concealed behind a ruby curtain. The program, folded lengthwise on heavy off-white stock, occupied guests. Then at 2:10 Jacob Darden came out of his house and stood before the gathering, now close to forty, welcoming all graciously, even as new people trickled in and took programs. He had on dark blue trousers, white dress shirt and white shoes, bald head glistening in the lawn's quiet shade; a fine country gentleman reaching out to friends who were here to see a ballet performed by his daughter, Holly, and a play written by himself and directed by his daughter, Rachel.

"We are here today," Jacob said, "gathered in the great tradition of the Maverick Art Colony festivals, to express ourselves creatively, to reach out to friends and neighbors—" he caught the eye of Mia Littlebird, "—and to share with you our great love of the arts: dancing, music, the theater. We live in a country at war, a country that allows us to be free. So have fun, enjoy yourselves. When the creative part of our afternoon is over, stay for some good food and cider and merriment."

Jacob gestured with an easy motion of his arm. "Harlan is here today. He has told me personally, and sadly, that the ever-pressing seriousness of the war leads him to believe that a new Maverick season next year seems unlikely. We hope this is not so but knowing of our great national effort to defeat Japan and the need to destroy the Axis, if or when we are called, we can see how this could be the final year of the Maverick Art Colony as we know it. That said, I want to dedicate today's festival of the arts to the man who headed those truly great and memorable festivals of yesteryear, Harlan Gray; but more than that by far. It is unlikely a man will ever appear again to so put his heart and soul into the arts, to give artists the time and the place to practice—to write that sonnet, carve that sculpture, play that score, act that part. I am here today, many of us are here today, because Harlan Gray, my friend, *our* friend these many years, cared for us, invited us into the Maverick Art Colony to work, to be artists, to participate in the greatest occupation on earth. Thank you, Harlan."

Everyone applauded fully. "There are two among us today I would like to personally recognize, both of whom are closely linked to Holly's performance. The first is Igor Bagovitch. Igor played an important part in the early Maverick festivals. As a former member of the famed Bolshoi ballet, he went on to choreograph many acclaimed ballets and now heads the Woodstock School of Dance. Igor has coached, taught, choreographed my daughter for the past two months on the final scene in Swan Lake. Also of major importance in Holly's performance is the former lead violist in the Pittsburg Symphony Orchestra, Nick Bonino, who has agreed to accompany Holly as she dances the dying swan to the heartfelt music of Tchaikovsky. When Nick finishes here, he will join with fellow members of the Maverick String Quartet for a full afternoon of chamber music in the concert hall. One final note before we start. People coming late, kindly stand quietly while Nick Bonino plays and my daughter dances."

Jacob looked over his shoulder. "And here he is. Mr. Bonino," Jacob said, "welcome!"

"Thank you, Jacob."

They shook hands; then Jacob walked out and sat next to Hedwig among the guests. Nick moved closer to the group and said he felt honored to be a part of this wonderful occasion, this lively, free-spirited Sunday at the home of Hedi and Jacob Darden. He paused briefly, then said, "Jacob and Hedi made their first home in the Maverick Art Colony, where their daughters, Rachel and Holly, were born. Needing space—a third child was on the way—they moved, an easy walk to their new home, here where they are now. Certainly, in all manner of art and creativity and freedom of spirit, Hedi and Jacob never left the Maverick. I will be playing the sorrowful last scene in Swan Lake, one of the most beautiful ballets, in which Odette, the white swan, dies. The score, by Peter Tchaikovsky, is a natural for the viola, deep, sorrowful refrains. Mr. Bagovitch, Holly's teacher and a famous participant in the early Maverick festivals, tells us that ninety percent of the dying swan scene has the ballerina on point. Holly does not yet wear the ballerina's shoe and will dance on demi-toe in her performance."

Nick Bonino turned away from the seated crowd. "I see her now! The white swan, Odette!"

In a white flowing dress, a wreath of white flowers in her hair, Holly walked toward Nick. He moved to one side of the lawn, tucked the viola under his chin, and began to play; and Holly began to dance. Her legs trembling, shaking, she made small little steps on half-toe, ankles almost touching, passed close to the violist and out to a narrow section of lawn, arms fluttering, fading, then rising, her wrists and fingers limp but nicely poised, legs constantly moving, weakening. She bent at the waist, legs forever in a spasm, the rich, somber singing of the viola accompanying her, bow strokes slow, mournful, as of a fading heart. The beautiful white swan sinking, falling to earth, failing; but a surge, reaching out, her fingers eager to touch, to feel; she will not die. But then a second falling, a faltering, a folding, a crumbling of her body, head sinking, coming to rest on her knee... and quiet.

No one seated on the lawn at the Darden house moved, overcome. Holly rose, curtsied, Nick wrapped a free arm around her shoulder, and everyone stood up and cheered.

"Bravo!"

Jacob came over, hugged and kissed his daughter, gave Nick a joyous handshake. The two walked off—Holly in a rush to change for the play, Nick to the concert hall. People were still commenting, expressing themselves, wiping away tears. No one seemed impatient for something new to happen; what had already happened had made everyone happy. Then, quite suddenly, the sound of hoof beats. A rider was coming along old Bluestone Road. He cut sharply onto the driveway before the house and rode up to the lawn. Red ribbons in his mount's mane, white ribbons in his tail. In baggy trousers and denim jacket, the rider spoke to the gathered townspeople.

"Hear ye, hear ye! King Thaddeus is on a rampage. He will stop at nothing in his search for the pig that will provide His Majesty with the juiciest, most succulent pork chops ever. If unsatisfied, the king threatens to inflict severe punishment on the people of Zudakistan." The village crier turned his mount and took off for the next town.

Great clapping. Silence. Then...curtain.

It had two parts to it, like drapes on a big window. The curtain on "stage left" opened and King Thaddeus was in his private chambers in the castle with his wife, Queen Isabella, who had on a long flowing gown and a rope of pearls at her neck.

The king, in a purple jacket with medals pinned to it, sat in a king-sized easy chair with a scowl on his face. "One day before I die, Isabella, I want to partake of a perfect pork chop. Is this asking too much? I am the king! I have armies at my command, priceless jewels in my crown, the richest and most beautiful grounds to stroll on, and above all the loveliest of wives. Yet each year I am denied a simple and honest wish."

"I think it's about time you suppress your fantasies, Thaddeus," Isabella says. "You have a notion that a beautiful pig will produce the best pork chops."

"Don't you think there's truth to that?"

"No!"

"I beg your pardon!"

King Thaddeus pulls a bell cord and his envoy (Austin Fromm) comes in from stage rear. "Yes, Your Majesty."

"I am giving you one last chance, Maximilian," King Thaddeus says, "to search the land and bring me the finest pig in the country!"

"Your wish is my command, most noble lord."

"For the past five years, you have failed in this effort, Maximilian. Fail again, it's your head!"

(left curtain closes, right curtain opens)

A humble farmhouse kitchen. Four characters seated at plain wooden table: Mr. Fanshawe, a farmer, Mrs. Fanshawe, a son Otto, and a daughter Sarah are sharing a meal of parsnips, crusts of bread, a mean-looking chunk of cheese. Mumbling, the father bemoans their existence, the struggle to keep going. It is a hard life in Zudakistan. A knock at the door. Farmer Fanshawe rises to meet a stranger, who introduces himself as an envoy to King Thaddeus. The family is stunned. When has anyone of such importance, of any importance at all, ever visited the family?

"I am on a mission from our king," Maximilian announces with a superior air.

"What is this mission?" Farmer Fanshawe asks.

"To bring His Majesty the greatest of joys. I have been traveling the countryside for a week, and just now as I was going by your farm I believed I'd found a candidate."

Sarah (Bzy), the only family member not in awe, confronts the envoy. "A candidate for what?"

"The king's table." Max looks casually around, his presence heavy in the room. "If I could have a closer look at this beautiful pig—"

"But—" Sarah is stammering. She is terribly upset. "The king's table? What are you saying?"

Otto exits to the rear and comes back holding a young, well-scrubbed pig against his chest, squirming, trying to get free. Audience erupts in laughter.

"I will take this pig off your hands. King Thaddeus will have the finest, most succulent pork chops at last!"

"No! Lucinda is a member of our family!" Sarah cries out. "You—you can't!"

Maximilian sees her for the first time as a spirited and lovely young woman. "I will pay you and your family handsomely."

"How much?" Farmer Fanshawe immediately inquires.

"Three-hundred Esties."

That is more than he makes in a year of backbreaking toil. They shake hands, Farmer Fanshawe pockets the money, the envoy says an official carriage will be back in three days to transport the pig to the king's palace. Maximilian gives Sarah a last look and leaves the family.

Emotional storm in the Fanshawe house when they are alone. Sarah crying, yelling. Three members against one. Father, mother, brother trying to convince her that survival—*survival*, Sarah— carries more weight than allegiance to a pet pig. We can hardly feed ourselves!

(Right curtain closes, left curtain opens.)

King Thaddeus and Isabella in private sitting room, two days later. King's envoy has just delivered his report on the pig; former owner is Farmer Fanshawe in the poverty-stricken Zinnastein region of the country. This pig will assuredly deliver superb pork chops. King licks lips in anticipation of the meal. Queen Isabella rides him for his crass, uncultivated enthusiasms. He should grow up! Maximilian, the envoy, back on stage. A visitor from the Fanshawe family is looking to have a meeting with the king.

On Maximilian's request, King Thaddeus consents to a hearing.

Sarah, knees scraped, hair in tangles, curtseys before the monarch. "Most Honorable King Thaddeus, I have traveled the country these past two days wanting to reach you, hopefully in time to save Lucinda." She looks at the king with tearful eyes yet talks in a strong, if quavering, voice. "I rescued her when wild dogs attacked her family. I am here to appeal to your Highness to spare her life." Sarah bows her head, then looking up, "Lucinda is a symbol of our country. If you take her, we die. Give us food, build us schools, give us a better life, King Thaddeus. We beg of you. Save Lucida and save your people." She drops to her knees.

All is quiet. Thaddeus speaks to his envoy, who goes out. Moments pass. Then Lucinda is brought in, wiggling and very much alive. "So it shall be!" announces the king, lifting his arms.

Curtains fully open, music in the air, both sides meet and rejoice.

The audience rose, cheered, applauded.

"Playwright! Playwright!"

Jacob raised both hands, then, gesturing toward the stage, cried, "Director!"

Rachel bowed, and a celebration began. Kids hugging, dancing. Austin jumped around with Bzy on the stage. Billy looked on and felt part of it.

****

Not only was Hannah Hardenberg in the kitchen helping Hedi with food and drink but Hannah had her husband helping her as well. He was a bruiser of a guy, drove the West Hurley "Drift Buster" in the winter, and was chief of the volunteer fire department. Want something done? Call Harold. As it turned out, he had solved the problem of preparing fifty ears of corn, which Jacob had said was a must for a Labor Day party. Harold would cook the corn on the fire house range. The kitchen was well set up for community functions like the popular pancake breakfast and the always successful pot roast supper. If Mr. Darden would care to—

"Please, call me Jacob. Consider it done."

The cider barrel was moved to a more easily accessible spot on the terrace. A jug of red wine and a large bowl of Jacob's own punch, lightly spiked, were on the sunroom table as were a baked Virginia ham, a tray of corn on the cob, and Hedi's own potato salad. Mrs. Hardenberg was very good at overseeing the table as people came inside to help themselves, telling guests that Mrs. Darden had planned for thirty and now closer to forty were here. A person could come back for a seconds, if anything was still available. Then she mentioned the pair of trash barrels at the corner of the house. Just drop everything in when you're done.

Guests took their plates outside and sat on the lawn, picnic style. The punch was going fast and the jug of wine soon had a big dent in it; the tap on the cider barrel was also getting a rigorous workout. After excellent performances, people were now eating and drinking, socializing. Jacob circled about, talking first with Harlan.

"This is splendid," the older man said. "The ballet, the play, Billy and the pony. And excellent fare. The Maverick is alive and well, Jacob."

"If a party can have a theme, Harlan, it's what I wanted."

"It's what you have."

Jacob couldn't walk three steps before stopping and talking with guests. Julia Jamison was clearly with child, glowing in it. She and Wes had high praise for the girls. Swan Lake in the Maverick. What a fine job Rachel did directing your play. And Billy. Great sense of timing, of derring-do."

"I'm glad they didn't run anyone over," Jacob said.

Bzy and her mother were standing on the side lawn and he walked up. It was Bzy he spoke to first. "Miss Fanshawe, I presume."

"The former Miss Fanshawe."

"One's role often stays with an actress," Jacob said. "You were great. I didn't see a dry eye in the house."

"The playwright gave me some good lines," Bzy said. She spotted Rachel and Terry beneath the oak trees talking with Holly and Warren O'Mara; excused herself and went over.

"Mia, how nice seeing you," Jacob said.

"It's good seeing you. What a lovely play."

"I'm afraid the last scene was *deus ex machina* to the core," Jacob said. "Bzy put her heart and soul in it and made it work."

"Having a girl walk across the land and stand face-to-face with a king? It's a great theme," Mia said. "When did you write it?"

"One weekend a couple of years ago, to clear my head of Reader's Digest pabulum."

She had on an ankle-length lemon-yellow dress, cut low across the front, and her eyes—he kept thinking "lake blue"—seemed to be inviting him in for a dip. "You have to be happy with the afternoon, Jacob," Mia said.

"It's been a good summer for the kids," he said. "Mia, I have misgivings. After all my talk of loving theater, I didn't see you in a single play. I owe you an apology."

"Jacob, please. You have a wife and family, you're writing a novel. How's it coming along, by the way?"

"It was accepted by Stein and Sugrue."

"How wonderful! When is it coming out?"

"This spring, now called *The Cardinal*."

"I thought *The Red Hat* was a great title," Mia said.

"I did too, but Dick Stein thinks *The Cardinal* is more to the heart of the book."

"He's probably right." After a pause, "We're leaving in the morning," she said.

"For Boston?"

"It's my home. Most out-work actors migrate to New York, but who knows?" She was speaking warmly, taking him in. "I'm glad we met, Jacob."

"The party is young. Have a drink, some food."

"That's kind of you, but I should be running," Mia said.

In an embrace, his hand rose to the back of her head; his lips touched her ear. Then she drifted away, spoke briefly with her daughter who wanted to stay with her friends.

Thinking to see Hedwig and spend a little time with her, Jacob went inside just as Raphael Hagar, with a generous second helping and a full wine glass, was coming out. They passed with hardly a glance. The food on the sunroom table was seventy-five percent depleted, five ears of corn left, the jug of red all but empty. Hannah Hardenberg was in the kitchen with her husband, as were Mr. and Mrs. Osterhoudt. Jacob didn't see Hedwig. Rolf Osterhoudt's wife, Murgatroyed, was a large woman with an open, uncomplicated face. They were all talking happily in German, plenty of food on the table, beer mugs in hand. As for the beer, Rolf had brought a dozen bottles.

"Lucinda and Otto stole the show," was the first thing Jacob said.

"Donny got a big kick out of being in the play," Murgatroyed Osterhoudt said.

"I felt for sure that little porker was going to get away," Harold Hardenberg said.

"We must've looked at six or eight pigs for the part," Rolf Osterhoudt said.

"She was the right one," Jacob said.

"Every player did their parts real good," Murgatroyed said.

"That little farm girl who confronted the king," Hannah Hardenberg said. "I like that."

"Just don't get too many ideas," Harold said.

"Has anyone seen my wife?" Jacob asked.

"She went looking for you," Osterhoudt said. "She wanted to show you where the real party was."

Laughter. Jacob recalled the day that Rolf had come by looking for Champ; the halfwit with him had had a rifle between his legs. Jacob pushed aside the unsavory thought, the unhappy meeting; but how ready it was to jump in. "Those trash barrels have solved a real problem, Harold," Jacob said.

"It's my pleasure to help, Mr. Darden. When I leave I'll bring them with me. In the morning you won't even know you'd had a party."

"How will I be able to explain a hangover?"

New laughs. Just then Hedwig came into the kitchen to great cheering. "Oh, here you are," Jacob said.

There was, in fact, a chair next to Rolf at the table, and he gallantly pulled it out for her.

Jacob stayed for few minutes and went back out. The festival crowd was thinning. It was down to twenty-five, twenty; a good number had left for the Sunday afternoon concert. Some older people were sitting and lying around on the grass. But for others, the afternoon was still young; the cider and wine and punch, or the combination thereof, was taking hold. Jacob could hear his voice growing louder, words coming out freely, not much thought behind them. Emotions crowding out thought. Edward Harrigan, the writer, was trying to do an arabesque, and kept tumbling. The afternoon had gone from creative expression to the ease and pleasure of a good meal to men acting absurdly in free-spirited competition. The sillier the better. Loony tunes. Women watching, laughing; but it was the males who were acting out. Angus Beck seemed to think he could do a handstand but his arms collapsed in the effort and he fell on his face. People thought they heard the crack of breaking bones and Angus was holding his head in a strange way as if it wasn't on straight. Commercial artist Wyatt Stanton, a golf enthusiast, challenged nonobjective painter Preston Berlin to a footrace to the pine. Preston started out fast but fell after fifteen yards and Wyatt tripped on his shoelaces shy of the finish. Judged a draw. The cider barrel was empty and the object was to see who could stand on it the longest when it rolled. The writer Raymond O'Mara had grown up in the great northwest, among loggers, and he stayed on for three rolls. Harrigan gave it a go. Feet slipped sideways and he fell on the barrel, legs apart. *Thud.* He let out a huge groan. He had hoped to have one more kid, he said. Women laughing. Men never grew up. What the hell did Jacob lace that punch with? Whew! Sweating, panting, Woodstock-Maverick Olympians ready for more. Next event. Billy was standing on the terrace and Jacob yelled over.

"Get your football!"

Billy didn't like the idea but he ducked into the front hall and came out with it.

"Throw it here!"

Billy threw the ball to his father. "Let the real game begin!" Jacob said. "I'll captain one team. Wes, an old Dartmouth footballer, another. Choose up sides!"

Captains shanghaied revelers.

On the first play Jacob told Maverick artist Steve Edie to "go deep." Others should block, protect the quarterback. "Hut!" Jacob spotted Edie, threw the ball—it fell short. A player on Wes's team picked up the football and began running with it. Cries of: "Dead ball, incomplete pass, you can't run with it!" But no one listened. Raphael Hagar kept running and was duly tackled...and fumbled. Ed Harrigan, a proponent of football in the image of Rudyard Kipling, recovered the fumble and ran for what he took as the goal line. Score! He then tried to dropkick the ball for the all-important extra point, and from then on it was every man for himself, kicking, passing, tackling, fumbling.

Billy didn't like seeing full-grown men using his football in a stupid game. Kids in school kicked it around every day but this was different. His father had given him the ball on his eleventh birthday. Coming home late on a Friday, he had laid it on his sleeping son's bed. Now his father and Angus Beck were attempting a statue-of-liberty play that resulted in (what else?) a loose ball. Men were beginning to call for a timeout; a few simply quit. Not Ed Harrigan. He was determined to set the Columbia eleven back to their own goal. One good kick would do it. He punted, plenty of steam behind it, but the ball sailed too high—so high that it hit the middle branches of a pine on the east side of the lawn...and stayed there.

The game now turned to getting the football down. The land on the far side of the tree was rough, uncultivated, terminating at the cliff. You could throw stones and heave sticks and not worry about hitting anyone unless he was walking in the woods below. Revelers gathered stones on the spur or driveway and launched an offensive at the ball that rested in the tree like a sleeping, pregnant marten. Billy hadn't gotten the ball snagged but he was trying mightily to free it. So was Terry Monroe. With his passer's arm, he hit the branch a couple of times with a rock but the football didn't fall. After a while, the challenge wore off; a brisk wind would do the job easily enough. Billy was grateful. Sooner or later the football would come down.

Suddenly a great cheering went up as if the football had decided to fall on its own. That wasn't it. Jacob was coming out the front hall carrying his shotgun. He crossed the lawn to the spot where men had thrown stones ineffectively for the past fifteen minutes. He would settle this little problem with gusto, just watch. He brought the 12-gauge L.C. Smith to his shoulder, took aim. Billy's thoughts were screaming, What are you doing? Dad! Don't do it. No!

BOOM.

The football was propelled through the branches and out the other side, hitting the ground with a barely heard thud, as of something lifeless, dead.

Laughter. Wild cheering. "Well done, Jacob! Bravo!"

Jacob went into the house to store the gun and Billy walked in after him. They were momentarily alone in the front hall.

"Why did you do that, Dad?"

"What are you talking about?"

"That was my football!"

"I'll buy you another."

"I don't want another!"

"Get over it, Billy. It was all in good fun."

Jacob continued inside. Holding back tears, Billy walked out to the terrace, then angled over to the fence and stood there looking at Champ in Harlan's Field. How long he stood there he wasn't sure. It seemed late; the party was over. A few people were still on the lawn, mostly kids. Then someone was coming over, saying his name.

"Billy?"

He turned; standing there in the growing shadows was Bzy. She came in and gave him a hug. "That was an awful thing," she said. "I was very hurt by it. I saw the look on your face, the disbelief. I'm sorry, Billy. I'm really sorry."

"Are you going home?"

"I am. We're leaving in the morning. I want to ask you something."

"All right."

She came in closer and stood with him, their faces touching. "Does the Maverick Art Colony have to be up and running for us to go to the trapper's cabin again?"

"No. We can go whenever we feel like."

"I'm happy you said that," Bzy said.

"I'm happy you asked."

She gave him a kiss. Unlike other kisses he'd ever had, it lasted; then it ended and she pressed a finger to her lips.

"See you, Billy."

"See you, Bzy."

She went to old Bluestone Road, turned and waved; and then she was gone, blending into the night.

****

It was Labor Day Morning and Rachel's crew, and her brother, were taking down the stage with chatter, a lot of laughs. Jacob could hear the kids from inside where he was having breakfast with Hedwig, going over with her a number of book-keeping items.

Like the Reader's Digest first payment of his pension. Jacob still harbored thoughts that Wally had delayed activating it in a grudge, but the money was coming in at last. Unlike the procedure of old, Jacob said, Hedwig should put the retirement checks, each and every time one came in, into her First National account in Kingston.

"What's going on, Jacob?"

"New money means new accounting."

"That isn't what I mean," she said, her frustration, her anger, rising. "You're book is finished. That finishes you in Morristown, as I see it. Are you coming back to live with us or aren't you?"

"I have a few loose ends to tie up. Is there any coffee left?"

She pointed to the pot. He looked at her sharply, then poured for himself.

"How long does it take to tie up a few loose ends, Jacob?"

"It's a busy time for me," he said. "Meetings with my agent, the S&S publicity team. They're all very excited about *The Cardinal.*"

"Fine. So are we. When are you coming back?"

Outside came the beeping of Luther's horn. Jacob sat there, looking at her, sitting very still. Then he said, "I'm not. It's over for us, Hedwig. I'm leaving you."

Her stomach twisted in a severe spasm. Was she breathing, had her heart stopped?

"From here on, I won't be coming back for weekends," he said. "As for the kids, I'll stay in touch, by phone, by letter. As to why I'm leaving you, Hedwig—I'm in love with Betty and we'll be getting married, likely in the spring when *The Cardinal* comes out."

She held her cup, hand trembling, wanting to throw her coffee in his face; but she didn't. It wouldn't quell the anger, the pain, the shock coursing through her body; only killing him would. She felt herself breaking down, buckling. "Get out of my life, Jacob! *Get out!*"

He picked up his grip, walked through the living room, out the Dutch door. He waved to his daughters who were taking down the stage with others in the cast, including Billy. Then he took Hedwig's curving bluestone path to Luther's car.

****

In the parking area before Melissa Benitez's house, Jacob passed Luther Ryan a check for twenty dollars and told him he wouldn't be needing his services for a while. From what Jacob had said during the ride to Morristown, the driver well understood. There wasn't much about Jacob, or any of his clients, that Luther didn't know. He had the reputation of a priest: what you say in this confessional box never leaves. So let it all out, guys, I'm here but to listen. Jacob had told Luther more than once that he had a book in him; all he had to do was change names, hair, heights. Jacob had even come up with a title: *Shrink On Wheels.*

"Give me a call, Jacob. Any time. And good luck!"

"Thanks, Luther."

He had left Jacob off at the slate path through the little wood; it merged with the white, broader path and he was soon at the cottage and phoning the main house to tell Betty he was here—and *dying* to see her. It was her mother who answered, to his great displeasure.

"Melissa, hello. Jacob speaking."

"Are you back?"

"I'm in the cottage," he said. "It Betty there?"

"Did you see the blurb in the book section of Sunday's Times?"

"No. Is Betty around?"

"I have it right here."

"Melissa, I'd like to speak to Betty—is she in?"

"Let me read it to you."

The rustling of a newspaper. Jacob was crunching his teeth. She began reading: "'New York literary agent Emily Neher said she had wrapped up contract negotiations with Richard Stein, head of the publishing house, Stein and Sugrue, in connection with Jacob Darden's forthcoming novel, *The Cardinal.* The contract, Emily Neher said, would give Mr. Darden 'the largest advance ever given an American author.' The novel tells the story of Stephen Rossel's rise in the Catholic Church to become the Cardinal of Boston. It is due out in the spring of 1944."

She stopped reading. "We're so proud, so happy for you, Jacob."

"Thank you," he said. "I saw her car, I'm wondering if—"

"A college classmate flew in for the weekend," Melissa said. "She's getting a divorce and had to see Betty. We weren't expecting you until later."

Her continued use of "we" was troubling to Jacob, somehow putting Betty and her mother on an equal footing. "When will she be coming back?"

"Betty said between four and five," Melissa said.

"Oh." Jacob felt terribly let down, disappointed. "Well, let her know I'm here."

"Of course," Melissa said. "But it's barely one. Come over for a bite and a swim."

He could use a nap. Next to seeing Betty, he would prefer a nap. But it was a long afternoon and a swim and a bite first were hard to turn down.

In fifteen minutes he and Melissa were sitting at a poolside table. She had on a thin, sky-blue robe over a one-piece swimsuit and Jacob was in Mike Benitez's trunks and a white terry robe. They had both had swims and were now waiting for Wanda to bring in lunch. Melissa was delighted with the program that he had brought over: **A Summer Afternoon of the Arts: Dance, Music, Drama, and Horsemanship at 71 Bluestone Road, the Maverick Art Colony, Woodstock, N.Y.**

"Now tell me about 'The King's Pork Chops.' And Holly's dance and Billy, the village crier. I want to know everything."

"I'll tell you everything," Jacob said. "The kids did it all themselves. I pretty much threw the play at them with the instruction: keep it at twenty minutes; and they did."

"How does horsemanship fit in? I'm assuming it wasn't dressage," Melissa said.

"Hardly," Jacob said with a laugh. "Billy took his pony over a number of jumps. Not that high but it was very well done."

"Rachel directed the play, a play you wrote, no less," Melissa said. "How wonderful!"

"She'll be applying to Smith. It will sit well."

"Not Vassar?"

"She never considered it."

"Let me know. I have a strong contact with Vassar."

"I'll keep that in mind."

Melissa smiled intimately. Having a writer in her cottage had always appealed to her; having the author of *The Cardinal,* who had just landed a great advance from an esteemed house—that was something else. "Your other daughter did a ballet to the dying scene in Swan Lake," she said. "It's one of my favorite ballets, and Tchaikovsky! Did you have a recording of it? The score, by itself, brings tears to my eyes."

"A professional violist accompanied Holly."

"His name is here, yes, I see it. Nick Bonino."

Wanda came in with a lacquered tray of tuna-salad sandwiches, coleslaw and a bowl of chips. Is there a preference for drinks? the little woman with bouncy tits and rollicking ass, asked Melissa, who then queried Jacob, "A glass of wine?" He truly wanted to have one but loosening his inhibitions sitting poolside with Betty's mother wasn't a good idea. "Lemonade would be very nice."

"Yes, two of those," Melissa said.

The beverages arrived and they began their lunch. Lovely. But he wasn't at ease; he was, in fact, very ill at ease. The desire—call it what it was, *need*—to have sex had increased incrementally all weekend. Having Mia Littlebird briefly in his arms had only enhanced the urge. That Betty would come tripping along the white-stone path when he arrived in Morristown had kept him going. And here sitting next to him was a neurotic sixty-one-year-old woman who was doing something with her legs: subtly pinching and releasing them as if she were trying to squeeze juice from a berry, or crush a rose bud, between her knees.

"What a great environment for children to grow up in," Melissa was saying, "an artistic environment and fresh air all in one."

"Absolutely," Jacob said. "Just marvelous. But I can't see my daughters settling in or around those same environs. I see them getting away, branching out in the world; and rightly so. My son is just the opposite. He loves where he is, the friends he has, and has no ambition to leave."

"To his detriment or his benefit, as you see it?"

"Detriment. He has to move on."

"Of course."

Wanda cleared the table. Unless Jacob was hallucinating, she gave him a quiet little look when asking if he would like a sweet.

I'd love one for Christ fucking sakes! Jacob's inner voice raged. "What do you have?"

"I could bring you a creamy éclair or a delicious pear tart."

"A pear tart. Thank you, Wanda. And a cup of coffee, please."

Melissa began talking about her painting. She was into a new phase, she said, having set aside her plein air easel for studio work, namely still lifes: flowers, a wicker basket of vegetables, fruit—

"Ah, nature morte. What is so exquisite as a Cezanne apple?" Jacob said.

"Exactly. The concept of instilling life into something that no longer breathes. But I've heard it's better to show than tell," Melissa said.

His sweet arrived. Jacob immediately had a bite of the halved pear touched with a honey-like drizzle. Melissa sipped her coffee. Finally picking up where she had left off, she suggested that she show Jacob her work.

"That would be very enjoyable," Jacob said.

"Shall we go then?"

"Melissa, dressed as I am, it would be difficult for me to concentrate."

"Then undress."

"Now or later?" Jacob said with a laugh, enjoying their epee-like game of thrust and parry.

"Slip into the robe. There is no one here."

"Wanda is here."

"That little wench! Come on, Jacob. You'd be surprised what an old Main Line gal can teach you."

In her late husband's clammy old trunks, Jacob sensed a distinct rumbling, as of cogs turning, engaging. He was very close to throwing propriety to the wind. Why didn't he give the woman what she wanted? But he was still holding on, almost as if proving to himself that he wasn't a complete satyr. "Might'n Betty and her friend be coming in at any time?"

"Jacob, not to argue this point. She won't be back till five, four at the earliest." A smile, not of kindness or love—Jacob was hard-pressed to define it—touched her lips. "I'll be in my studio. Wanda will show you the stairs."

Melissa got up and went into the house.

Jacob stayed at the pool for a moment, then made for the bathhouse; he shed robe and trunks, washed up, pulled on his clothes and went out. Wanda was sprucing up the table. He thanked her for the lunch and continued to the path of white stones

335

and the cottage.

Back in the cottage he undressed, got into bed, and fell asleep. Then someone was shaking his shoulder, saying his name. He woke with a start. "Where am I? What time is it?"

"It's two. Wake up. You're in the cottage."

"Oh. Well, hello. You're back early."

"I am?"

"Melissa said between four and five."

"What?"

"Betty, let's not talk about it right now," Jacob said. "Get into bed with me."

Chapter Forty

On the first day of school, on his bike, Billy turned off Rt. 28 and pedaled down Hammond Street. He had planned, all along, on walking the old trail, then at the last minute had changed his mind. Whether it would become permanent, he wasn't sure. One thing he knew, he missed Serge.

The old schoolhouse sat there empty and sad like a kid who'd just been yanked for fumbling in the end zone. Billy cut onto Bonesteel and there it was, broad-shouldered and shiny, big windows along the front, a large stone pedestal with a tall flagpole on it, Stars and Stripes flapping in the morning breeze. A stone path ran around to the back of the school and a big double door entranceway. Billy parked his bike. He wondered if kids were looking at him thinking here comes an eighth grader. No one seemed to be paying any attention. Inside, three steps took you to the main level and a pair of classrooms, one on either side of a wide hall. The classroom on the right had younger children in it and a number of parents. Looking into the room on his left, Billy recognized kids and went in.

Li'l Jill, sitting at a desk in a sky-blue dress, gave him a wave and a big smile. Her brother was standing in the back of the room against a wall of cubbyhole drawers. "Hey, Dom," Billy said, walking up. "I thought you were quitting."

"Frank hounded me into giving it another shot. What the hell. Did you catch the teacher next door?"

"No."

"With someone like her, I might learn something." Dom chuckled. "Hey, I got me a new boat."

"You already have a boat," Billy said.

"Now I have two."

"Pretty soon you'll have three."

Dom had himself another laugh. "Where's the football, Billy? You always bring it in."

"I don't have it anymore."

"What happened to it?"

"It got lost."

"How can a football get lost? A golf ball, OK."

"Well, it's gone," Billy said.

"I have a football," a new boy said. Tall, reddish-brown hair, a quiet, easy-going look.

"Good. Bring it in," Dom said.

"I'll get it at lunchtime."

"What grade are you in?" Billy asked the boy.

"Seventh."

"I'm Billy Darden."

"Sid Gottlieb," the new kid said.

Dom gave the boy a slow, close look. "Dom Santarelli."

They shook hands all around. Mr. Marr was talking. "Your attention, please. This classroom is for students in grades five through eight. Family members, visitors, kindly leave. School is in." After a couple of minutes, he said, "Eighth-grade students will have the row by the windows, then seventh, then sixth, then fifth. Take to your desks."

"What do you think?" Dom said to Billy.

"About what?"

"Sid."

"He seems really nice."

"You're kidding, right."

"Why would I be kidding?"

Covering his mouth, talking quietly, "He's a yid, for chrissakes."

Mumbling to himself, Dom took a desk near the back of the room. Billy went closer to the front. When all kids were settled in, Mr. Marr made an opening comment. "How grateful we are having a new, modern schoolhouse when so many children have nothing even close to it," he said. "We must not take our education and our school for granted. To do so would be a disservice to our country and the boys in our war with Japan. My son Emmet Jr. is a Marine in the thick of it right now. Let us send all our servicemen a prayer."

The teacher bowed his head. After several seconds he said, "I have selected eighth-grader Billy Darden to lead us in our daily Pledge of Allegiance. Billy, come forward, please."

****

Sid's football didn't need air. It had faux laces and a grainy-sided leather-like cover. Dom said it might work and started kicking it around on School Field. "Seems OK," he said, "let's get started."

Dom and Billy were named captains. On a toss of fingers, odd or even—no one ever beat Dom on a finger toss—he got the first pick and chose Norman Wheat. Billy took Case Vandermark, good on defense and a strong kicker. Then Dom, then Billy again. Dom picked Donny Osterhoudt, not fast but a solid blocker. Now Billy had to make a decision. Should he take Lewis Barona, plenty tall but kind of listless, or the new kid who had brought in the ball?

Billy picked Sidney and Dom took Lewis. With only twenty minutes of recess left, the teams had a "pre-season" game. With the score tied at two touchdowns each, Sid let Billy's pass slip through his hands on the goal line. Sid made to offer Billy an apology and Billy said no apologies, who doesn't drop a pass?

Mr. Marr rang his bell and kids started walking in. "How did you lose your ball?" Sid asked Billy.

"It got stuck up in a tree."

"And it's still there?"

"No, my father shot it down."

"That wasn't very nice."

"Where do you live?" Billy asked.

"In Zinnia. It's a hamlet—"

"I know where it is. What brings you here?"

"My dad's with the Defense Department and he goes where they need him. Right now he's at the plant in Kingston."

When Billy got home later that day, his mother was sitting in a corner of the kitchen at her sewing machine, putting a hem on a navy blue skirt. He seemed to think she looked sad as she sat there, foot on the pedal. Had she had bad news from Germany?

"Tell me about the new schoolhouse," she asked her son.

"Everything is really nice. Real bathrooms, cubbyholes for your stuff, drinking fountains."

"Is Mr. Marr still your teacher?"

"He is," Billy said. "He chose me to lead the Pledge of Allegiance every morning."

"That's an honor, Billy."

He opened the refrigerator door. "There's a new boy in school," he said. "Kids are talking about him. Like last year with Serge."

"What are they saying?"

"They're calling him a yid."

"What's his name?"

"Sidney Gottlieb."

"That's terrible."

"What's a yid, Mom?"

"It's a mean and nasty word for someone who's Jewish."

"How do they know he's Jewish?"

"If your name is Sidney Gottlieb you're probably Jewish," Hedi said.

Billy made a sandwich and sat at the table with a glass of milk. "And that's why they're saying things about him?"

"I think so. It's called anti-Semitism," Hedi said.

"What does it mean?"

She was changing a bobbin on the machine. "It's a term used for anyone, or for whole groups of people, even a country, who dislike Jews, who are scornful of people who are Jewish. No other reason. Some people hate Negroes. It's prejudice, Billy. It's narrow-minded, and it's wrong. Fight it or walk away from it, just don't participate."

Hedi went back to her sewing. Anti-Semitism was a topic that Jacob shunned, and she had adhered to his philosophy of letting a sleeping dog lie. But he was no longer here, and suddenly she saw the necessity of speaking out on her own.

"Where does it start, where does it come from?" Billy wanted to know.

"It starts at home. How people talk. What parents say and believe. When Hitler first came to power ten years ago," she said, "he persecuted people he thought undesirable and he's still doing it. Jews and gypsies and Negroes." Hedi paused, giving herself a chance to reconsider what she was about to say; then she said it. "When you were born, Billy, anti-Semitism was on the rise in Germany. My sisters and mother advised me against having 'Baby Wilhelm'—meaning you—circumcised until we got home. Jews ritualistically have the procedure done. Christians also but it's the parents' decision. In Germany it's the state, the government, that wants to rid the country of Jews. Nazi officials were said to be searching maternity wards in hospitals looking to snatch male Jewish babies from their cribs. Billy, if you had spent any time in a hospital at all, the Nazis might have stepped in and taken you."

"Where?"

"Who knows where? Away."

Billy stared at his mother. "Mom, I don't understand. We're Catholic."

"But the evidence, to the Gestapo officers on a search, was there. Take the infant now, look into it later," Hedi said. "Who cared about mistakes? It would have been very tense, and considering that Baby Wilhelm's grandfather was Jewish—"

"Grampy Darden is Jewish?"

"Yes. Aunt Helen told me in Green Harbor after I'd been there a year that her father was a Jew from Russia. That's how completely and skillfully Grammy Darden controlled the family."

"Why hasn't Dad ever said anything?"

"Ask him," Hedi said.

Billy sat there for a moment, taking it all in...or as much of it as he could, then told his mother he was taking Champ on a run.

****

Hedi had begun serving one-dish meals of late, today's was a tuna casserole, hoping her children would start liking them. So far

341

not much enthusiasm. Certainly a casserole was easier to put together and more economical too. The kids took after Jacob, who liked the meat, starch, vegetable trio with a salad on the side and good bread also; possibly dessert. That was the basic Sunday meal, and who could complain? Usually on Wednesday she might start thinking about what to have on Sunday and would go about checking her coupons and sizing up what was out there. Not next weekend though. In the past few months Jacob's weekend visits hadn't been steady, and from here on he wouldn't be coming home at all.

Hedi was looking at her children, enjoying the brightness of their faces as they spoke and listened and laughed about the Labor Day weekend. All day yesterday she'd thought she had to break the news, but they were still so charged up from their performances that it would have been insensitive, if not cruel of her, to bring them down. She would do it tomorrow. And now she was thinking it again. She could only wonder if, in putting it off, she was protecting herself. When Sarah, the farm family's daughter, had stood up to King Thaddeus, it had made a strong, unexpected impression on Hedi. Never before had she spoken to Jacob so forthrightly as that morning. God, how beautiful to say something and mean it. But was she now fearful she'd collapse in a pile of sadness, grief, bereavement when she told her children.

"Mom, that was pretty good," Billy said, putting down his fork.

"Glad you liked it."

"It was filling," Holly said.

"It's how things are going to be from here on," Hedi said. "Shelves and racks are getting thinner and thinner. What was there today won't be there tomorrow."

"How's the new school, Billy?" Rachel asker her brother.

"There's no comparing it to the old school, especially the bathrooms," he said. "Mr. Marr is still our teacher. He has a new blue suit, shines just like the old one."

"Then how do you know it's a new suit?" Rachel said.

"I don't know, I'm just saying it."

"Do you know what makes a suit shine?" Hedi said to Billy.

"I was thinking the quality of it."

"No. It's been to the dry cleaner too many times."

Billy cleared the table. The girls were putting things away and starting to wash the dishes when Hedi said she wanted to see them in the living room once the kitchen was done.

"Terry is coming over," Rachel said.

"Well, he can wait."

"Mom, of course he can, but what's up?"

"It's something I have to tell you."

"Tell us now. We're all here."

"I know, but the living room is better," Hedi said.

The sisters and brother looked at one another. Holly's shrug of her shoulders spoke for all. When the kitchen was done, they went into the living room. Hedi sat in the upholstered chair, fearing she wouldn't be able to speak. She tried to light a cigarette but her hand was trembling and she couldn't direct the match and finally put it and the cigarette into an ashtray.

The children exchanged looks.

"Your father," she began, looking into the center of the room, focusing on space, "won't be living here anymore. He told me yesterday, just as Luther was driving up to take him away, that he was leaving me. As of now, we're separated. Your father has taken up with someone else—well, Betty, his secretary."

Holly broke into tears, burying her face in her hands.

"I knew it from the start, " Rachel said. "God, how could he? Mom, I'm sorry." She began crying.

Billy sat there perfectly still; it seemed to him he hadn't taken a breath since his mother had spoken. Consciously, he inhaled. *Won't be living here anymore, separated, taken up with his secretary.* Was he feeling free, or terrified? Was it good news or terrible news? His mother's eyes were brimming; she was close to joining her daughters in out-and-out tears, but something was keeping her from giving in, from breaking down. To do something, instead of sitting there like a bump, Billy went into the kitchen and grabbed a bunch of paper napkins. His sisters each reached for one and Hedi pressed a napkin to her eyes.

"I can still hear him saying on the dunes, 'Will you marry me?'" Hedi said to her children. "It was the happiest moment of my life,

343

there on the dunes on Green Harbor beach."

"Had you even kissed?" Holly asked, still sniffling.

"No."

"What's going to happen, Mom?" Rachel said. "You're separated. Is he divorcing you?"

"He wants to marry Betty," Hedi said. "Monday morning Luther was in his car, tapping his horn—it's when Jacob spelled it out. We were through, he was marrying Betty."

"He wasn't thinking straight," Holly said. "Shooting Billy's football out a tree. What a stupid, thoughtless thing!" She looked at her brother. "Did he say anything to you?"

"He said he'd buy me a new one."

"That made up for everything, didn't it?"

"It made things worse." Billy said.

"Your father is a very conflicted man," Hedi said to her children.

"What does that mean, Mom?"

"It means he grew up in a divided family."

"I always thought it was a very strong family," Rachel said.

"That was the impression Grammy Darden liked to give. Jewish father, Catholic mother," Hedi said. "It was the opposite of a strong family. They went to church, they prayed—"

"You can't pray a lie," Billy said, straight from *Huckleberry Finn.*

They all gave him a glance. Then Holly said, "Why are we only finding this out now?"

"When your father was here, it's the way he wanted it," Hedi said.

"I feel liberated," Rachel said.

When they had finished talking, expressing themselves, talked about sticking together as a family, Billy went up to his room and sat in a window seat with a school book in eighth-grade science. His assignment was to read the introduction to the chapter on weather. He liked the topic but his concentration was shot and, after a poor start, he set the book down.

It was the start of a new school year and he decided that his desk was a mess. He began throwing away old tests, reports, magazines, tossing them into the wastebasket. Billy sighed; he was tired, terribly mixed up. Starting with the football, now the breakup of his mother and father. He tossed an essay he'd written for his father on *Huckleberry Finn*, was about to toss one he'd started on *Robinson Crusoe* also for his father but had never finished; he had never so much as asked Billy how it was coming along. On impulse, Billy made to tear it in two as a statement on the "new regimen" his father had started him on; but even with his intention firmly in mind, he decided to read what he'd written. His thoughts came drifting back. He arrived at the sentence where he'd left off, remembering how he'd been unable to express his next idea; he couldn't find the words to do it. Billy surprised himself, now, by finding those words and finishing the idea. All he had left was to write a conclusion. What was the novel really about? What was at the heart of the relationship between Crusoe and his man Friday? Billy sat there passing it around in his head, trying to focus; and then it came to him, he saw it clearly, and he again put pencil to paper.

Chapter Forty-One

After looking for a week, Jacob and Betty miraculously found a second-floor, partly furnished apartment on 11th Street in Greenwich Village—two bedrooms, a good-sized living room, a third room that had "Jacob's studio" written all over it, and an eat-in kitchen. The bathroom was quite ordinary but it had a good tub, pleasing to both.

Furnishings, many of them Betty's from an earlier day, including an upright piano, were trucked in from the Benitez house in Morristown. Melissa said she was glad to get rid of the "extra stuff" and knew Betty would put it to good use in their new place. There were still items they needed but they could at least get started in their new pad with a modicum of comfort and convenience.

On the day they finally left, Melissa gave Betty a tearful embrace. Jacob had the impression of a mother saying goodbye to her twenty-one-year-old daughter who, just married, was leaving with her husband to start a life. It seemed a bit dramatic when the daughter was a divorced woman of 41 and Jacob wasn't taking her to Istanbul. As for Jacob, Melissa put out her hand in a parting gesture. He wanted to believe, while holding it, that their dalliance was a thing of the past. He thanked her for her many generosities; he had never written better anywhere than in her cottage. It was her pleasure, she said, graciously, but as she stepped back, Jacob had the feeling they hadn't played their last game of Touché. The former Debutante of The Year was a woman scorned.

****

Three weeks after moving into their apartment, Jacob and Betty had a routine going. They were getting to know the neighborhood, the local shops and restaurants. Betty was making the place comfortable, wanting to change a dwelling into a home: hanging the few pictures she had brought from Morristown, new lace curtains on the living room windows, scattering about some colorful cushions and generally cleaning and polishing every nook and closet, the stove and refrigerator. Jacob helped here and there but, basically, ensconced himself in the utility room that had wondrously become a study for the man of letters. He, Jacob, author of a great novel soon to appear, was already at work on a new novel on the whiskey business in America.

Betty began to feel she knew something about his novel in progress, *Water of Life*. He was always ready to talk about his work and she liked the involvement. They would go to any one of the small restaurants within two or three blocks of their apartment; of an afternoon she would search shops on 4th Street to see what she might pick up for the apartment. Jacob's agent, Emily Neher, told him *The Cardinal* looked good in the pages of Cosmopolitan. She'd be sending him a check for $15,000, minus her ten percent commission, for the middle of the three S&S advance checks he'd be getting, then added that "Dick Stein said reprint houses were in a bidding war for the novel."

"Terrific."

He took walks up and down the various streets of Greenwich Village. Soldiers and sailors, away from action, were now looking for action. Jacob remembered how he used to think walking in the Maverick Art Colony was the finest walk a man could have. The quiet, the fresh air, the coolness of Ohayo Mountain: a Harlan Gray life devoted to simplicity and freedom. But New York City had something equally great going for it—the pulse, the excitement of endless possibilities.

He was tired when he got home and glad to see Betty in the

living room reading in the big easy chair. He gave her a greeting, said he would be taking a nap, did she care to join him? She didn't answer, but when he was in the bedroom taking off his clothes she came in and took off hers. It was a wonderful nap. Outside a north wind was blowing and they didn't feel like going out, but they got themselves up and went to a cozy Italian place on 4th Street and had spaghetti with meatballs, a Chianti and crusty bread. They were both glad they had come out. A cold wind pushed them along on 11th Street on their way home.

In the apartment they sat down for the evening, in slippers and loose clothes. Jacob picked up a book he'd taken out of the branch library on 23rd Street, *An Analytical Reading of Finnegans Wake* by Julius Farhmer, a professor of literature at Princeton. The New York Times had recently given the book a strong review and Jacob was looking forward to reading it.

He had always liked scholarship, had done some serious work in it at Columbia—first on Emerson's famous letter to Walt Whitman greeting him at the start of a great career; also on Henry David Thoreau and the only young woman he had ever loved. A lot of heavy-duty sleuthing was necessary to come up with something pertinent, significant. But Jacob put a creative work—poem, story, novel, play—on a rung of the literary ladder above scholarship, journalism, biography, essay. He didn't want to investigate, to write about other writers or events; he chose to write. He liked Professor's Farhmer's good intentions but his academic prose began to seriously cloy, and on page 65 Jacob put the book down, sat back and gave his full attention to the Debussy etude Betty was playing on her upright.

When he'd had a place on 63rd Street, he didn't feel free, didn't feel a part of New York. Wally was watching him. He was living in the company house. No longer. Beholden to no one. Philosophically he loved Harlan Gray and the Maverick Art Colony, but this was where he belonged, in New York City, in a Village apartment, with books and art and a lovely woman at the piano—

Betty's hands lay quietly on the keys.

"Beautiful," Jacob said. "Will you do another?"

"I'll play all night."

"Play the Mozart you did earlier in the week."

And she began. He sat there, going over in his mind "Ode to A Nightingale," unsure when Betty finished if, like Keats, he sat there, so taken by the song that he questioned whether he was awake or asleep. At breakfast the next morning, Betty boiled two eggs and made toast, and they were at the small table in the kitchen. Jacob told her he'd be going to the main library later in the day.

"What are you researching?"

"The debate taking place in the latter half of the ninetieth century as to what defined whiskey."

Jokingly, "Do you need research on that?"

"It was a huge issue at the time, and it wasn't until years later that it was finally settled," Jacob said. "As for *Water of Life,* it's the heart of the novel—the truth of a product, the character of a man, a family steeped in the lore and legacy of Kentucky bourbon."

Betty lifted the coffee pot, added to his cup, then her own. "Jacob, this sounds fabulously interesting. Where and when did this idea come to you?"

"I grew up in the middle of Prohibition," he said. "People talked booze, they made booze. Rich Stilwell, a bootlegger in Woodstock, pushed white whiskey or, as he called it, 'white dog.' He was a great raconteur and told me about a lawsuit in the last century over whiskey; his father had testified in the trial. The argument was this: Could the term 'whiskey' be used on a bottle of a crafted four-year-old bourbon *and* a bottle of tasteless neutral spirits made that day and topped with 'whiskey flavorings?'"

"Could it?"

"Yes, and it was."

"Was a decision made?"

"Yes, but not for years and years, and unsatisfactorily at that."

"What was it?"

"Whiskey made with neutral spirits and artificial flavorings had to have the word 'blended' on the label. 'Blended whiskey' as opposed to 'straight.'"

"That's something, I suppose," Betty said.

"The novel will take a lot more digging and research than *The*

Cardinal," Jacob said.

"How can that be?"

"The story of the Jewish-Catholic family in *The Cardinal* is my story," Jacob said, "my family. The Woodhulls in Kentucky? One thing I know about them for sure. They're not Catholic and they're not Jewish."

"This is new ground for you."

"I'm twenty-five pages into the book," Jacob said, "and don't know *what* they are. Just Protestants."

"How about Calvinists?" Betty said.

"A Calvinist works his tail off, because success means you're one of God's 'elect,'" Jacob said. "That fits Anson Woodhull."

"Here's a question for you."

"Go ahead."

"When you were growing up, would there have been more or less dissension in your family if your father had been a Protestant?"

Jacob broke into muffled laughter. "I'd say more. All Catholics I knew as a kid railed against Protestants. *Black Protestant.* To even step inside a Methodist church doomed you to hell. Catholics and Protestants are like roommates who don't get along. They both believe in Jesus but are always in each other's face. A Catholic and a Jew, short of an all-out war, what's the point of disagreeing? The gap is too wide. They put up with each other. That's how it was in our house in Malden and Green Harbor. Disdain? No doubt, no doubt a lot; but they dealt with it. I believe Jews are quieter by nature, less pugnacious. How many, by comparison, go into the ring? Max Baer, Benny Leonard, a few great ones. Barney Ross. My mother could handle a Jewish husband. A protestant husband would have been in her face from day one. It would have been horrendous."

"But she was so—so *Catholic,* how could your mother have dated a Jew to start with?" Betty came back. "Gone to bed with a Jewish man? Is there a logical explanation for it?"

"I think there's an easy one," Jacob said. "Jacob Sr. was good-looking, energetic, generous with gifts; and clearly determined to get this sweetheart of an Irish girl with honey-blond hair and glorious breasts into bed. He succeeded...and knocked her up. I was the product of a shotgun marriage. As to what kept so unlikely a union from breaking up—divorce was a mortal sin, one reason. Another reason, my father started making money. He had a small florist shop, then opened his own business and made real money. Living with a Jewish businessman wasn't so bad. She cursed him by day, fucked him by night. The children kept coming. She was chosen Catholic mother of the year in 1927 by Boston Cardinal William O'Connell and again in—"

The wall phone rang. Closer to it, Betty reached up and removed the receiver. On the chance that it could be his agent or publisher, Jacob's eyes stayed on Betty; but after she said hello and then said nothing for ten seconds, he realized it was for her. As to who was calling, he had a suspicion and left the kitchen. In his study, he looked over the last page he'd written, corrected two typos with a pencil, then crossed out an entire sentence. Jacob rolled in a new sheet of paper. A tap on his door kept him from starting in.

"Come in, Betty."

There was a small second chair with a wicker back but she didn't sit. "That was my mother."

She had never called before to the best of his knowledge. "How is she?"

"She's feeling depressed."

"I'm sorry to hear that," Jacob said.

"She wants me to drive out and see her."

"When?"

"Today. You'll be at the library."

"I will be, yes." He paused; something wasn't sitting well. "When are you leaving?"

"In ten minutes. I'll be home by three."

Chapter Forty-Two

Holly had asked her brother more than once why he liked hunting and trapping. If you love nature so much, why can't you walk through the woods without a gun? Why can't you look at a stream in a meadow without setting traps? Then she would say, "How can you kill animals and cause them great pain for what, after all, is a hobby?"

"Hunting and trapping are not hobbies, Holly."

"They are. You do them for fun."

"I sell the pelts and bring home food."

"Squirrel is not food!"

"Mom doesn't complain, and Raphael loves when I bring him squirrels."

"Boil an old shoe for Raphael, he'd relish it."

Billy moved along, shotgun in the crook of his arm, looking, listening, trying to avoid excessive leaf-cracking. He loved these woods beneath his house and his father's studio, considered them his own. They were a part of the same forest he and Serge had walked last year, but different, as neighborhoods in a city are different. On the hike to school, you had a mix, a family of different people living together, pines and hardwoods, old trees and young, a graveyard where trees went to die, pretty flowers along the way, a solitary pastor in white to bless you in the morning, a fallen oak across the trail on whose solid back you rest. The woods he was in now, everything was somber, dark. It was a land of massive hardwoods and evergreens that had somehow made it through the centuries. Here and there a few younger trees and clusters of brush and bushes, but these were serious woods, well-robed lords looking down at commoners.

Billy moved on, step by deliberate step. A sudden beating of wings, "Rrrrmmmmmhhrrr!"

He thumbed safety forward raising gun too late partridge gone no shot. He watched the direction of its flight through the trees, a brown streak flying low, after forty yards curving, settling. He started after it, this time ready when it took off again. And it did. But where was it? There, ducking behind a tree. No shot. "Rrrrmmmmmhhrrr!" A second partridge. Billy got a better view of it, all of one second. He fired, bird dropped, fluttered in the leaves, lay still.

He went over to it, remembering his talk with Andy Sickler about game birds. The pheasant had more style but the ruffed grouse was the greatest game bird of all. For one, it was a native of the eastern woods, while the pheasant was an import from China. Andy had once estimated that in all his years of hunting partridge, he'd come up empty eight shots out of ten. Billy field-dressed the bird, hunted until coming to a stonewall running east and west. Sometimes he would sit on it when still-hunting grays but mostly it marked the end of a hunt. Last year he had told his father about the wall, still in good shape except for a small section of it where stones were missing. His father had mentioned a famous poem by Robert Frost about a stone wall and had quoted a line: "Something there is that doesn't love a wall." Billy had told himself that one day he'd read the poem and find out what that "something" was, but so far he hadn't.

He stood at the stone wall looking through the evergreens to the boggy field, then turned and started the trek home. At which point, lo! the faithful Buck came running up, wagging his tail, panting.

"OK, how many rabbits did you kick out, how many squirrels did you tree?"

"Roughff! Roughff!"

"Two rabbits, three squirrels," Billy said, patting the dog's head. "Excellent."

At the cliff near his house, Billy unloaded the gun and took the same path up that he'd taken down, in reverse. On the plateau, walking on the narrow path to the house, he kicked something buried in leaves. It wasn't heavy like a stone or a log. Looking down, he saw what it was. He might have kept on walking but leaving it here wasn't right either. He picked up the riddled, sunken, ugly carcass. What had moved his father to shoot it, Billy didn't know and doubted he ever would. Looking at the football now, Billy scrunched his eyes to hold back tears. Then, using a sidearm delivery, he sent it flying over the cliff and into the woods below.

In the back hall Billy stowed the gun, hooked his jacket and opened the kitchen door. His mother was at the table looking pale, lost, and seemed unaware that he had come in. "Hi, Mom."

"Oh, Billy," she said, turning off war news on the radio.

"I shot my first partridge," Billy said.

"That's wonderful."

"Will you cook it?"

"Of course I'll cook it. They're supposed to be delicious."

"I don't want Holly thinking I only bring home squirrels."

Hedi came out with a dry little laugh, but it was a laugh. "A partridge isn't very big. We may have to settle for one bite each."

"Is there a trick to plucking?"

"Dipping a bird into a pot of very hot water helps, but it isn't necessary. Minus hot water, grab feathers and start pulling."

"OK."

"Billy—"

"Yes, Mom."

"You're the man of the house now."

He hesitated a moment, as if to say something, then plucked the bird in the basement, every last feather; covered it with waxed paper and set it in the refrigerator; then went out and saddled Champ. The first hard frost had come to Ulster County; today's temperature hovered around forty degrees, cold but not wintry. Most of the houses were empty. Harlan had left for his winter home in south Georgia but looking at his house now you wouldn't know if he was, or wasn't, in. Closing Morning Star was like closing a stand of skinny trees. The concert hall and theater, a couple of gnarly old bears early into their long sleep, were quiet. Billy had hoped to say goodbye to Chips but one day he was gone; Carpenter Shop was empty. The sea had called him, ports of call. Raph Hagar wasn't leaving the Maverick. Where else would he find a woman next door to keep him clothed and, if not fed, happy with an occasional slice of home-baked bread? For some artists it had been a disappointing season, but diapers on the Aurora clothesline made Billy happy for Wes and Julia Jamison.

When he returned, he tied Champ to the hitching post, brushed his coat, his legs; examined hooves and shoes. Time to call the farrier. He led Champ into the stall, lowering the oak bar on his way out but leaving the door open, then sat on the sill. Buck meandered over and lay down beside Billy, and Champ stood at the bar looking out, presiding at a weekly meeting of "Animals United." Billy raised the first point of interest. How did it look for the Maverick Art Colony next year? And answered, not good, a possibility it wouldn't open. A lot would depend on Harlan. New topic. Abandoned cats in art colony. Buck's forte. Cats were great fun to chase but he would never hurt one. Equine rep gave his head a toss: canine's pants on fire. Champ was declaring Rocky Hill off limits. Too rough and steep. He was a sure-footed Welsh pony, not a Rocky Mountain bighorn! Billy commented that he would take Champ's comment under advisement but couldn't guarantee that Rocky Hill would have an off-limits status. The canine representative of Animals United fell asleep while the equine rep yawned mightily. The homo sapiens rep began drifting off also, only to sense activity on top of his head. Something was nuzzling about. Billy reached up to investigate, his fingers coming in contact with something very soft, velvety smooth. What was the equine rep up to? Was he thinking to have a taste of homo sapiens' hair, or was it more of a game he was playing?

****

At ten minutes after twelve, li'l Jill and Billy walked into the West Hurley Inn. Two men and a woman were at the bar; behind it stood Mr. Santarelli. He waved, pleased to see his beautiful young daughter bringing a boy from the Maverick Art Colony home for lunch. Very nice, the girl knew what she wanted; it was never too early to latch onto a guy. He waved, the kids waved back and walked past the bar to a door at the end of a long hallway. They took off their coats and went in.

The first thing that hit Billy was the delicious smell coming from the kitchen. Mrs. Santarelli in an apron greeted the kids and told them to sit at the main table. Lunch was a bowl of spaghetti and meatballs. A loaf of Italian bread. Grated cheese. A couple of Royal Crown Colas.

Not too bad, Billy thought, and started in.

In a few minutes, Shorty came in. He sat at the far end of the table in his special chair; it was the only chair that worked for a man who was four feet eleven inches tall. He was bald, had small bulging eyes, no shape to his body whatsoever. More like a block.

"Are you liking your lunch, Billy?" li'l Jill wanted to know.

"Very much."

Mrs. Santarelli's brother walked in and sat down. Vince. Neat mustache and dark rich-looking hair but he had a terrible hack and Dom had told Billy that his Uncle Vince, the top mason in Local 19 in Kingston, had lung cancer. They gave him a year to live if he stopped smoking, six month if he didn't. He hadn't stopped. The last time Billy had spent a night with the brothers Santarelli, Vince had awakened at six, hacking badly, and Billy had looked over from his cot and watched as Vince, sitting on the edge of his bed, struck a match, cigarette between his lips, and inhaled like it was the last breath he'd ever take and he wanted to make it a good one. He then got up and dressed for the day. He was now having lunch; a cigarette was burning on a handy ashtray. Even as he had a swallow of food he took a drag. Dom had once told Billy that his uncle was a great hunter and everything he knew about hunting he'd learned from Vince.

"How are you doing, Billy?" li'l Jill asked.

"Doing great. This is wonderful."

Mr. Santarelli came in from the bar and said something to Mrs. Santarelli. She said something back in a low voice; then he came back in a stronger voice; and pretty soon they had a real live fight

356

going on, in Italian of course. It was Mr. Santarelli who yelled harder and more colorfully. Without catching a single word, Billy seemed to think Italian was the perfect language to swear in. He was so taken by the richness and musical sound of Mr. Santarelli's ranting that he began seeing it as a performance in the Maverick Concert Hall: two violins, one viola and one cello, each playing a different composer in a vivacious third movement.

No one at the table seemed alarmed; it was all part of a Santarelli day.

"Do you want anything else, Billy?"

"I'm full. Thanks."

The door to the Santarelli kitchen opened and Dom pushed in. He hadn't made it to school in the morning; deer season was on. His uncle asked how he'd done. Dom said, "Thirteen pointer, trailed him for two hours, brought him down in the big woods east of Bluestone Road."

Dom's mother put a big plate before her son.

"What gun were you using?" Vince asked his nephew.

"My ought 6."

"Where'd you hit him?"

"He took three steps and dropped."

"The heart, good shooting."

For a minute all was quiet, as if in respect to the hunter and his kill. Dom didn't waste any time filling his stomach with spaghetti and meat balls. Billy finished his own plate, then told li'l Jill he thought they should get back to school.

"So soon?"

He thanked Mrs. Santarelli and told Dom he'd see him tomorrow in school.

"Maybe the day after. Maybe not till next week," Dom said.

Billy and li'l Jill went out, passed Lane's Garage—garages weren't the cleanest of places but Lane's had to be among the greasiest—and picked up the path behind Happy's. With the school in view, they stopped walking and li'l Jill kind of looked up at him, eyes closing; he knew what she was asking for and he kissed her; then they moved onto school property.

****

Donny Osterhoudt spotted Billy in the lunchroom a few days later. They had a lot of history between them, events to share, maybe laugh over. They had a catchall term they used, "Adventures of Champ," and one of Donny's favorites was the time he'd shaken Billy out of bed on a phone call with news that his father and Wilbur had left the house and were on their way to the mountain pasture to shanghai Champ. There was always a new wrinkle in telling that story. No story ever got fully told. One of the books Billy's father had listed for him, *The Odyssey,* didn't see print for almost a thousand years after Homer had first started telling it in a poem and new poets had told it over and over through the ages. Sometimes Donny would bring up the story of Lucinda, or The Pig That Stole the Show. That was always good for a laugh; but it wasn't a laughing matter when, one day in early November, Donny Osterhoudt asked Billy if he'd heard about Wilbur.

"What about him?"

"He was in an accident."

"In a car, in a truck?"

"No, not that kind of accident."

"Donny, I'm not really interested," Billy said, "in anything to do with Wilbur."

"Interested or not, he's dead."

Billy let the news sink in. "What happened?"

"He slipped, butchering a steer, blood and entrails all over the floor—knife entered his mouth, came out on the top of his head. He died in a pile of guts."

Billy thought he might throw up if he opened his mouth to say anything.

Donny said, "My father put the slaughterhouse up for sale."

"Because of...what happened?"

"It's what my mother wanted for years, all the screeching of animals and the blood and the god-awful smell. Wilbur was the last straw," Donny said. "They took her away."

"Took who away?"

"My mother. To an institution."

"I'm sorry to hear that, Donny. But she'll come back," Billy said.

"They're saying maybe not." A tremble in Donny's lips, tears building in his eyes.

Billy thought for a moment, then said, "I was thinking of Geraldine the other day."

"She was a good pony," Donny Osterhoudt came back, almost like an old man reminiscing. "They were nice days."

****

On the Tuesday before Thanksgiving, still using Sid Gottlieb's football, Dom and Billy threw fingers on School Field for the last game of the year. Billy, taking "even," threw out one finger. Dom threw out one also. Winning the toss, Billy chose to receive. And so the game—crucial in that each team had won ten times—began.

Dom scored first on a Mack-truck run straight up the middle. Then Richie Fox on Billy's team intercepted a Dom pass and ran it in. Score 6-6. Norman Wheat ran back a Billy punt fifty yards for a touchdown. Billy threw a pass to Joe Smith who dodged Lester Long on Dom's team and scored. Running, punting, tackling. The score remained 12-12. Dom gave a harsh stiff arm to Sidney Gottlieb, knocking him to the ground. Donny Osterhoudt kept Dom from scoring with a good tackle but he scored on the next play. 18-12. Billy threw a pass to Case Vandermark for a score. 18-18. Any minute Mr. Marr would ring his bell. Billy sent Sidney on a ten-yard button hook who then shoveled the ball to Richie Fox, who scored. Billy's Team now leading 24-18. Dom's team had to score. A tie wasn't great but it beat a loss. Dom sent Norman Wheat out for a long pass. Norm was making to snag the ball but Sid Gottlieb reached up and knocked it away.

Mr. Marr was ringing his bell. "Clang! Cling! Clang!"

Billy's team gave a traditional cheer for the losing team and the players began walking in. "That was a great block," Billy said to Sid.

"I put up my arm."

"You saved the day. Take credit."

Dom walked by and Billy said, "Good game."

No comment.

"Dom? You talking?"

"If I have somethin' to say."

"OK, then," Billy said.

"But now that I'm thinking on it, I have somethin' to say. What is it with you, Billy? Last year sucking up to a Commie, now a yid."

Billy felt the sting of the words. "That's a lousy thing to say."

"Both of yez, drop dead!" Dom said.

Chapter Forty-Three

Hedi set her laundry basket on the stone-topped table in the back yard and began hanging up articles she'd just taken from her washing machine. With Jacob gone, it was a lighter load, not by a whole lot but definitely fewer clothespins were needed. The basement was warm and she had put up a clothesline in it. Today, however, was so clear and bright, moderate November temperatures, that she thought to give her and her children's things one last fresh-air flap. Among the items pinned were Billy's red-and-blue flannel shirt and Holly's navy warm-up slacks. She went back inside, hands chilly. Not too many outdoor clothes-drying days were likely until the spring.

In the kitchen, Hedi heated up a cup of coffee, at the table, looked over some bills she had to pay, a delivery of home-heating oil, new shoes for Champ, a bill for an oil change and tune-up from the Woodstock Garage, and a final payment for the new furnace, $115. Not a problem, all manageable, and she was even able to put a little away each month from the Reader's Digest mini-pension of $81 a month. One of Hedi's fears, going back to early childhood, was poverty. She often thought of the chunk of lard that had fallen off the back of a truck in Biskupitz. How her mother had beamed when she went home with it.

Hedi wrote a few checks, addressed a couple of envelopes; she didn't want to think it was how the rest of her life would go—she was only 38. Did she want to go on believing her husband would come back to her? A knock on the kitchen door. She knew who it was, and she wasn't unhappy; it just wasn't Jacob.

"Come in, Raph."

Yachtsman's cap, rough wool sweater, black corduroy trousers: he opened the door. "Hedi, I saw your clothesline dancing, had to pop over. Have I caught you in the middle of something?"

"Nothing out of the ordinary, just a normal hectic morning of a single woman. Sit down, we'll have tea. Will you have a cookie?"

"That sounds very nice, Hedi."

She put on water. While it was coming to a boil she opened a tin and scattered cookies on a plate. He picked one up and popped it into his mouth. "I'm missing your bread, not that I ever had anything but a slice. It always made my day. When will you start in again?"

"I'll know when I know. Right now the inspiration is gone."

"Clearly waking by yourself in an empty bed isn't helping," Raphael Hagar said.

The water boiled and she poured it into her teapot. "Neither would waking with the wrong man," Hedi said. They sat together at the table. His hand descended over the light-blue cup, a dark cloud over a lake. She asked him how his latest work was coming along.

"I think it's my finest piece."

"Billy said he put a very high price on it."

Raphael laughed. "The boy is acting like my agent. Five hundred dollars, a nice price indeed."

"Where did he come up with the number?"

"It's a game we play. Three-hundred fifty is the middle ground, then it goes either way, higher or lower. We've been doing it for years." Raphael tasted his tea, had another cookie. "How's he doing without his dad in the house?"

"He says he doesn't miss him. I don't know if that's true," Hedi said.

"I think working with him over the summer, training Champ to jump, instructing Billy—I never had a better time. When they

362

cleared the higher fences, second time around, I was so proud."

"It woke Jacob up," Hedi said. "And the way Holly danced."

He finished his tea, had another cookie.

"I should be going. Hedi. It was very nice, thank you."

"Could you use a suit?"

"What kind of suit?"

"A man's formal suit, jacket and trousers. With a shirt and a tie."

"Hedi, when would I ever wear a suit with a shirt and tie?"

"They might invite you to the White House one day."

"They might. Sure, I'll take a suit."

"We'll talk about it again. Now I have to bring in clothes."

They went out, went over to the clothesline, and she tested one of Rachel's dresses with her hands. A breeze pressed Hedi's skirt against her stomach and thighs. Raphael Hagar went up to her, buried his face in her neck, kissed her passionately, then brought Hedi to the ground, fell on top of her and reached for her breasts—

"Raph, stop!"

"I love you, Hedi!"

"No. Stop!"

"Let me make love to you!"

"No!"

He was moving on her, tried kissing her again. She pushed at his chest, easier to budge one of his oak sculptures. Unless she stopped him, now, the unimaginable was going to happen. Raphael made to reach under her skirt. Somehow Hedi managed to wriggle free; she got to her feet, ran to the house; once inside she locked the door and fell into a kitchen chair. If he pounded on the door, she would call the police. No pounding came. Then what was she hearing? Was he out there?

Hedi sat quietly, trying to regain her composure. The ringing telephone startled her. What now? She got unsteadily to her feet and went over to answer it.

"Hello."

"Hedwig, this is Jacob."

"I know your voice."

"You sound out of breath."

"I am."

"Are you all right?"

"I'm fine."

"I hope you're taking care of yourself, Hedwig."

"Jacob, why are you calling?"

"Did the Reader's Digest check come in?"

"It did."

"New furnace working all right?"

"It appears to be."

"Hedwig, bookstores around the country are placing advance orders for *The Cardinal* in record numbers."

"Good."

"I thought it was something you'd like to know."

"I said 'good.'"

A short pause. "I'll be up Saturday to see Billy."

"What time?"

"I may be early but he should meet me at one in my studio."

"That won't work." Hedi said. "He's going to a football game with Rachel."

"Then Sunday. Same time. The application for Stover arrived."

"So you're back to sending him away."

"You used to think it was a wonderful idea."

"Things have changed, Jacob, in case you haven't noticed."

"All the more reason," he said. "I will not have my son cosseted by his mother."

"You're thinking of the wrong mother, Jacob, and the wrong son!"

Silence. "I won't be coming into the house," Jacob said. "Have Billy make sure kindling and a few logs are in my studio."

"How long will you be staying?"

"An hour at the most. Do you want me to stop in?"

A selfish, solitary thought passed through Hedi's mind as to why she would say yes; she shook it off, disliking that she'd had it. "The answer is no. Goodbye, Jacob."

****

At eleven o'clock Saturday night, Terry Monroe pulled up his two-seater in front of the Darden house. The front hall light was on, also a table lamp in the living room. They sat for a while looking at the house, not wanting to say goodnight. "What a wonderful day we had," Rachel said.

"It was. It was a perfect day."

"I'm missing you already."

"I'll see you tomorrow. I love you, Rachel."

The small car made getting close difficult but they managed, and then Rachel was walking up the path to the house. Terry flashed his headlights as she got to the door, then drove on. She got ready for bed, going over their day together starting with the football game. With the clock running out, Terry threw three consecutive completions and on the last play ran the ball in on a five-yard quarterback keep. KHS a winner over Tri-County Champion Sawyerton High, 27-23, to take home the trophy. Later at the team party Terry was awarded the game MVP trophy and named Kingston Player of The Year.

The rest of the day had passed dreamlike for Rachel. They had gone to a party, parked on a mountain road overlooking the village of Woodstock, stopped at a roadside restaurant that specialized in ribs, taken in a movie. What she appreciated in Terry was that he never pressured her to go all the way. It would happen naturally, in time.

Rachel went out of the kitchen, crossed the back hall to her bedroom door. Opening it, she went in, changed into pajamas and crawled into bed, looking forward to getting under the covers and rethinking, reliving, her evening with Terry. They were both young, college lay ahead; it seemed to Rachel the world lay ahead for her and Terry. They would make it happen; he was that kind of man, she that kind of woman. On her night table was a lamp and a clock; lying between the two was a small, pearl-gray envelope, her name on the front and address, 71 Bluestone Road. She opened the envelope, pulled out a plain sheet of stationery, and read:

> Dear Rachel,
>
> This is very difficult to write but we had to let you know that our son, Andy, went down with his ship, the USS Schuyler, under a relentless kamikaze attack in the Battle of the Philippines. He was in the gun crew of the ship's 40 mm. battery and fought to the end to

save his ship and defend his country. He always said you were the only girl he had ever loved or would ever love. We ask for your prayers to get us through this dark period of sadness and loss.

Sincerely,

Ruth Sickler.

Rachel read the letter through again, a moan rising in her chest like the coming of a storm; you hear it before it hits. Then, setting the letter aside, she buried her head in her pillow and wept.

****

From his upstairs room, Billy saw the car pull in and park on the spur, not opposite the house but opposite his father's studio; a man, in fact his father, got out and walked across the lawn. Billy had no clear idea of why he was here. All Hedi had told him was that he should put some logs and kindling in the studio; his father was coming to see him, to have a talk, at one o'clock.

When the clock on his desk read 12:57. Billy went down the narrow stairs, tossed on a jacket, and walked out. At his father's studio he hesitated, then rapped with his knuckles.

"Come in!"

"Hello, Dad."

Seated at his desk, a small fire in the stove, "How are you, Billy?"

Taking a chair, "I'm all right."

"How's school?"

"Everything is new," Billy said, "bathrooms, desks, blackboards. Young kids have a new teacher, Miss Kelly. We have our old teacher, Mr. Marr."

"How are you and Sidney Goldfarb getting along?"

"Sidney Gottlieb. We've become really good friends"

"What do you like about him?"

"He's an upfront kind of kid. He gave me his football."

"Why would he do that?"

"I don't know, Dad. He felt like it."

Jacob opened his briefcase and took out several sheets of paper. "I want to talk with you about next year, your education; indirectly, your future. These pages are part of a brochure that was sent me, at my request, ten days ago," Jacob said. "Namely, the history of the school—founded during the Revolutionary War, by the way—its academic curriculum, athletic curriculum, campus life, and an application form. I want you to look over the material, every page, with the idea of filling in the application. With the goal of going there next fall."

Billy felt a chill across his back. "Going where next fall?"

"Phipps Academy in Stover, Massachusetts, north of Boston," Jacob said. "The school goes by 'Stover,' always has. It's consistently the top-ranked school in America."

"Dad, I'm going to Kingston High School next year."

"That's why I'm here, Billy. To get you out of your current dead-end environment. It's time for you to step out and meet new kids, get a solid education—"

"I'll meet new kids in Kingston High. Rachel got a good education there, why wouldn't I?"

"What I'm talking about is more than an education per se. It's the credentials."

"I'm not keeping up with you, Dad. What kind of school is—?"

"Phipps Academy, goes by the name Stover. It's a boys' New England prep school—"

"No way! Dad, I'm not going to prep school," Billy came back. "A boy I met over the summer went to prep school—Deerwood, Deerpath, Deerhaven. Whatever the name, he was the most arrogant, conceited kid you would ever meet. Champ made him look like a fool, and to get back—not at Champ, at me—he broke down the fence—"

"Kids like that are everywhere," Jacob said. "Billy, it's time for you to branch out and have a fuller, a richer education. You'll meet topnotch boys, you'll befriend the future leaders of America. Wouldn't you like that?"

"Not especially," Billy said. "Norman Wheat and Case Vandermark are both good kids, terrific athletes. Last year—well, there isn't a better kid anywhere than Serge Rustovsky. And now there's Sid Gottlieb. He's like Serge, just not so crazy. He makes model airplanes with his father, planes with real gas engines. They fly the planes at the golf course, early morning or late afternoon.

I've been there—planes go zooming around and you're always running like crazy to keep up. Usually they crash into trees."

"Let's go back to the applications—"

"Dad, you're forgetting something," Billy said.

"Am I?"

"Who'd take care of Champ? Is Mom up to it, or Holly?"

After a pause, Jacob said, "Billy, a pony is a time in a kid's life. It isn't like having a dog. Unless someone has a big farm, endless fields and resources, ponies are sold. They are bought and they are sold. As for the application, fill it out accurately and neatly. The school wants to see a sample of your writing, a three-to-five-hundred word essay on any topic. Mr. Grenville, the director of admissions, said it ranks very high in accepting a boy."

Billy was breathing heavily; his lungs were starting to ache.

"The cut-off day for submissions is March first," Jacob said. "That gives you time—not a hell of a lot but some—to complete the application. There's a fee. Clipped to the form is my check for fifty dollars. Send it along."

"Dad, I don't want to go to Stover."

"Stop fighting me, Billy. You don't know what's good for you!"

He wasn't sure whose voice it was when he spoke next but he had to assume it was his. "I know what isn't good for me, Dad."

"What are you talking about?"

"The secrets of Green Harbor."

Jacob throttled the impulse to shake his son violently. "Some things aren't your business, Billy."

"Tell me why my grandfather's religion isn't my business?"

"There's an expression, 'need to know.' You don't need to know."

"Lies are better, keeping Billy in the dark is better. Is that what you're saying?"

"Fill out the application for Stover and send it back with the check," Jacob said.

Chapter Forty-Four

When the phone went silent after the second ring, Jacob knew that Betty had picked up; if the call were for him, he'd soon hear a rap on his door. No rap came, and Jacob went back to the slow, plodding task of writing *Water of Life*, of getting a first draft down of paper...via typewriter. He missed the ease, the pace, of dictation, but his hands were OK now. The rigor-mortis-like stiffness he'd experienced writing *The Cardinal* was not to be easily diagnosed as viral, arthritic, psychological. It had attacked him, made a statement, and now it was gone. Jacob was knocking out sentences again and was hating it.

Fifteen minutes later there came a knock.

"Yes, Betty."

Standing in the doorway, "That was Melissa."

It was no longer a newsworthy item and he didn't understand why she was apprising him of it. She and her mother talked on the phone a couple of times each week. Twice since they had moved to New York, Betty had driven out for a visit and had spent the night. Personally, he was getting tired of her inability or refusal to break away from her mother. They'd left Morristown for that reason, and Melissa seemed more involved in their lives now than when he'd lived in her cottage.

"What's up?"

"Tomorrow she's coming into Manhattan for a matinee with her theater group," Betty explained. "They'd bought tickets for *Oklahoma* in May and are finally seeing it."

He saw what was coming and gave his head an imperceptible shake. "She wants to come by, of course."

"She's yet to see our apartment."

"Then she'll look around and leave in fifteen minutes, of course."

"After the matinee she wants to visit, take us out to dinner—"

"And you said—"

"We had a dinner date and wouldn't be able to do it."

"Spoken like a good secretary," Jacob said.

"I'm not your secretary!"

He was stunned by her outburst. "Well, you were. I didn't mean it literally."

"What I told her was a lie. I'm not happy about it."

"It was a white lie, Betty."

"She's coming into Manhattan again next week."

"Give me a heads-up and I'll make myself scarce."

"Jacob, you have to get over this."

"*I* have to get over this. You're the one who's fixated."

"For a writer, you have the empathy of a stray dog," she said.

He felt like saying something back, not wanting her to get away with the aspersion; but she didn't give him the chance. Brusquely she closed the door, five decibels shy of a slam.

****

In the morning after a silent breakfast, Betty left to re-enroll in NYU's master's program in art history. He asked her when she'd be back. She said she hadn't decided and walked out, and Jacob went to his writing table, adding, after three hours, a page and a half to *Water of Life*. What with the chaff swirling around in his head, he felt lucky to have added anything at all, anything of substance.

Jacob showered, shaved, put on a suit and tie; slipped into his polo coat, placed his favorite brown fedora on his head, and went out; on a cold December day he hailed a cab and stepped out at the public library on Fifth Avenue. He followed up on notes he'd taken for the last couple of days, jotting down words and phrases that would bring a sense of verisimilitude to chapters on Appalachia. The process of making bourbon started with an unlikely gruel of ground corn and malted barley and was called, of all things, the wort. So much to learn, especially compared to how little he'd had to learn on or about the Catholic Church. He'd only grown up in it. Outside again, Jacob headed south on Fifth Avenue, negotiating the large number of men and women in the armed forces walking about, taking advantage of a few days' leave before shipping out to face enemy fire.

He entered the Columbia Club on 43rd Street. Rex, the maître d' in the dining room, came over, always glad to see his friend; they began talking. Uniquely. Years ago they had discovered they both loved Latin and had started conversing in it. Their locutions were brief, uncomplicated, but Latin it was, the all-important verb appearing at the end of a sentence. A smile came to Jacob's face whenever he contemplated that he and Rex were the only laymen, perhaps in the world, who were carrying on in what, after all, was a dead language.

Jacob had a bacon, lettuce and tomato sandwich and a cup of coffee, then walked west to Seventh Avenue, wanting to get home by five to have a nap (hopefully with Betty). Later he would take her to Bartholomew's, a four-star restaurant on Christopher Street. He still felt the anger in her voice, and the annoyance in his, when they had exchanged words over Melissa's post-theater idea of stopping by to see their apartment. Jacob walked briskly, thinking it next to impossible that he and Betty were in serious trouble. They'd had a spat. It was nothing.

On Seventh Avenue, he thought of stopping by the bar in the old Chelsea Hotel on 23rd Street—famous for its artists and writers— but continued south, eager to get back to his place. Again he went over the flare-up he'd had with Betty earlier in the day. He had always thought the love between Betty and her mother was genuine, but recently, pondering the complexity of whiskey-making, Betty and Melissa's relationship had come to have darkly symbiotic overtones; it was a rich and complicated wort. Were he, Jacob, in charge of administering it judiciously to his oaken barrels, he might, after hard consideration, simply toss it as too

371

damn toxic.

The apartment was empty. Jacob made himself a rye and ginger ale and sat down with Julius Farhmer's book. The Princeton scholar made a valiant pitch on the accessibility of *Finnegans Wake,* and perhaps a dozen readers would buy Joyce's novel with the brave intention of reading it, only to stop after five pages by throwing their hands into the air in surrender. Jacob himself could read the novel because he was inexplicably wired to read it. He thought back to his days as a young instructor. How generously, how enthusiastically the Columbia University Press had published his monograph on *Ulysses,* thrilled as it was to have this talented and already proven scholar on its staff. When *The Cardinal* royalties started coming in, he would pledge—that word had gotten you into a honey of a fix, Jacob, be careful—a sum of money double the amount he owed Columbia for his blithe disregard of contract.

He closed the book. No Betty, no phone call. What the hell was going on? Jacob poked around in the refrigerator and found a well-wrapped pork chop (worthy of a king). He sat down with it and a few spears of asparagus. No one cooked like Hedwig but he had to say that Betty was expert in putting leftovers away. As for Melissa—think of Betty, you had to think of her mother—Jacob thought back to the moment she had got up from a poolside chaise wrapped in a lacy see-through robe knowing her tenant was passing. How did she know? She was a woman on the prowl...she knew.

From that day on, Jacob sensed she would be his nemesis. No woman could have wanted sex, good old rock-hammering intercourse, that day more than Melissa Benitez. And, conveniently, there he was, a man of letters no less, there to escort the former, and still quite lovely, debutante to all the openings and high-end galas in New York; and he'd blown the opportunity for that honor on moral grounds. If this best-selling author, famous scholar and renowned poet had fucked Melissa Benitez, he would then have gone down in flames in Morristown, New Jersey, where, for the record, no Maverick artist belonged to start with. But he had nixed the tryst out of loyalty to her daughter no less, and now this—this backlash.

Jacob put his plate and utensils in the sink and spent an hour in the living room making notes on *Water of Life*. Thinking about the story, the best way to tie it together, to present the characters. The novelist was in charge of a world of his own making, and he had a lot of thinking to do, endless decisions to make. In the early drafts of *The Red Hat*, Jacob had pictured Stephen Rossel as a godlike character, tall, handsome, intellectually superior. Where were his flaws? The future cardinal had no flaws. Only after bringing the Jewish merchant fully into the story as Stephen's father, had Jacob recognized what an artificially contrived figure he had created in Stephen in the first place. Throughout the novel Jacob then set out to take the sickening edge off Stephen's leading-man physique and larger-than-life intellect. On official business in the Vatican, the future cardinal meets Sophia, a woman held in the highest esteem in Roman society. In a do-over, he turned her from a bloodless pinup into a living, breathing, and all-the-more intriguing and beautiful woman. Jacob had never made better edits.

Jacob set his pad aside, glanced at his watch. It read 9:40. In his bedroom Jacob thought to call Betty, then decided against it. She had reasons for staying away and he didn't want to appear anxious or needy. Sitting on his bed, he gave instructions to the long-distance operator, then waited for Hedwig to pick up. What were the odds she wouldn't? She was the Penelope of wives—faithful, steadfast, trustworthy.

"Hello."

"Hello, Hedwig. It's Jacob."

"Where are you?"

"In our apartment, Betty is visiting a friend—"

"Why are you calling me?"

"Well, it's been near zero every morning," he said. "Are you keeping warm?"

"Between the furnace and kitchen stove we're comfortable."

"Glad to hear it. Did Billy send out the application to Stover?"

"Jacob, I don't know."

"Is he around?"

"He's upstairs in his room."

"Get him!"

"He's sleeping. He needs his sleep."

"He needs an education. I expect you to follow through on Stover."

"I'll talk to him," she said.

"I'm coming up next week. Any news from Germany?"

"Jacob, you know there isn't," Hedi said. "At best they're struggling to stay alive. But the other evening I had a visitor and we spoke German. It lifted my spirits."

"Hans Hecker, a fine old friend," Jacob said, "and an excellent plumber. I remember the day he told us we should have central heating—"

Hedi thought to let it slide. But then she thought, why? To protect her marriage? She chortled noiselessly. "It wasn't Hans, it was Rolf Osterhoudt," she said. "He brought over a bottle of Dornfelder, a red wine that takes after a pinot noir, he told me."

"Hedwig, what are you doing? That son-of-a-bitch blackmailed me."

"He outsmarted you, Jacob."

"He's a smalltime player. Don't get mixed up with him!"

"We laughed together, had fun with our German. It was a very good evening," Hedi said.

"Where's your better judgment?"

"Holly is calling me. Good night, Jacob."

The line went dead. Jacob jammed down the receiver. Sharing a bottle of wine with Rolf Osterhoudt. What in hell is going on here?

He made to call Betty, then decided to wait until the morning. Jacob made himself a rye and ginger ale and padded into the living room to do what he loved most. To sit down with a book.

****

He awoke at 8:45 in the morning, ample sleep but groggy. Popped a couple of Dexedrine, shaved, showered, pulled on some clothes and made a cup of coffee—checked his novel-in-progress, thought about the current page. Where was he going with the scene? He scribbled notes in the margin—and the phone rang.

It was Betty; he asked her why she hadn't called.

"Melissa and I got talking, suddenly it was twelve."

"It was still the polite thing to do," Jacob said.

"I wasn't feeling polite."

"Betty, we had a spat, for chrissakes! What are you saying? "

"I want to step back and think over who we are and what we're doing together."

"Stop it, this is crazy."

"I'm not happy living with you," Betty said. "You're wrapped up in a new novel and that puts me in the outfield somewhere, waiting for you to recognize me—you know for what. You don't need a wife. You need someone to type your books and fuck you at the end of each chapter. Sleeping in my own bed last night was a pleasure."

"In your mother's house," he said.

"I woke up thinking you were in the cottage," Betty said. "The feeling didn't last but I walked out anyway and looked around. Something once so great for us was now so empty. I was overcome by sadness."

"We can make it work again, Betty. This is new for us; we can adjust."

"I don't believe 'adjusting' is who you are, Jacob."

"I don't want you leaving."

"We owe ourselves a little time, a trial separation. Two weeks, even a month," Betty said with feeling. "Because right now I'm —"

"You're serious, aren't you?" he said, beginning to wonder. She wasn't bending, wasn't coming around

"Yes, it pains me to say."

"Are you seeing someone?"

"That's absurd," she said.

"If that's what's behind this, then—"

"You're projecting, Jacob. From the very first, Melissa said you were coming onto her, looking at her sexually. That day at the pool, she thought you were going to attack her. You sat there leering at her with an erection! Finally she decided to simply walk away for her safety and good name. Otherwise, and without question, she would've called the police."

"Betty, it's me or your mother, not both," Jacob said, "isn't that what you're saying? I could share you with Melissa but would likely end up killing her. So let's leave it there. Thank you for coming to the rescue of *The Cardinal*. I mean that sincerely. Good luck."

Jacob put down the phone, sat there, shaking his head. He had believed they were meant for each other, had believed they'd get married and would have a damn good life together. He wasn't happy breaking off with Betty but, as he reflected on it, he was glad to be free, away from her. Really, away from Melissa. That was at the heart of it. What drew a strong, educated, otherwise independent woman continually back to her mother? He didn't have an answer for it but saw himself, down the line, putting a similar daughter-mother relationship into a novel he was working on. The author didn't have to have answers; let the readers kick it around and decide.

Jacob pulled page 56 from his typewriter; when he pulled page 88, her upright piano and her inlaid coffee table were gone; also a mahogany box of sterling flatware, a tea set of Noritake china, a handsomely framed mirror that had belonged to her father, boxes of personal items including a Webster's she'd had at Bryn Mawr, and a photo album of her mother as a famous debutante. When Jacob pulled page 129 of *Water of Life* from his Smith-Corona, there were no outward signs that Betty had lived in the apartment on 11th Street. He was working well, made trips to the library, started chatting with a comely, dark-haired, 20-year-old Barnard junior who was doing in-depth research on the Lake Poets, Jacob's discipline while he was an instructor at Columbia. Her name was Vicki Comfort and she reminded him of his own beautiful daughter. Twice he took Vicki out for coffee and the next coffee break might suggest continuing their discussion on Coleridge's "Rime of the Ancient Mariner" in his apartment. If he found himself in bed with the young woman—he had reason to believe it would happen—how easy to live out a fantasy he'd had since his daughter so gorgeously blossomed into womanhood at sixteen. But he and Vicki never met at the library again. Jacob was disappointed, but it was for the better, clearly.

Publication date of *The Cardinal* drew nigh. He'd had several meetings with S&S to go over plans on how to get the novel off and running on day one. Publicity. Potential radio interviews, the delivery of unbound copies to major newspapers and journals, the making of ads and the schedule of running them in important outlets, the front and back copy on the cover, photograph of the author. Jacob participated in every way possible. Occasionally he called home, spoke to the kids, with Hedwig. She surprised him by saying they had had a tragedy in West Hurley the other day

A comment not to be taken lightly. "What was it?"

"Two boys, Jimmy McMullan and Clarence Bumgardner, drowned in the reservoir. They were ice fishing and the ice broke."

"In weather like this?"

"In one of those places warmed by an underwater spring, I heard," Hedwig said.

"That's awful," Jacob said. "How is Billy handling it?"

"He's upset. We all are."

Jacob asked her if Osterhoudt had made any more visits with a supposedly fine German red, an oxymoron if he had ever heard one, he added.

"Now just beer," Hedwig said. Fed up with Jacob's judgments, she hung up.

Now, coming in from dinner in a local bistro on a cold, blustery night in January of 1944—no night to be alone—Jacob walked into his apartment. He took off his overcoat, dusted snowflakes from his fedora, put on slippers and his favorite smoking jacket, then sat down with *War and Peace* and a rye and ginger ale in the living room. A man could almost be happy. Recently he had started reading Tolstoy's epic novel again. What with Hitler's invasion of Russia and Russia's back against the wall, how closely history was repeating what Tolstoy had so magnificently written—namely, Napoleon's invasion of Russia in 1812.

Chapter Forty-Five

Billy had never been in a Protestant church before as he and Hedi got out of the car and walked toward the Methodist Church in West Hurley. His grandmother in Green Harbor had told him two years ago: if a Catholic enters any church except a Catholic Church, it was a mortal sin and God would strike you down. Hedi said nothing that would indicate it was a sin, if only a venial sin. The only expression on her face was sadness, the sadness and sorrow that she, and everyone in West Hurley, was feeling on this cold, blustery night as they walked up the concrete path to the heavy church door and went in.

It was crowded and they found two chairs in the back and sat down. At the altar lay the coffins. Jimmy in the one and Clarence in the other. The gloom was like heavy fog. No one said anything but people were crying. A minister came out in a dark robe and began talking and reading from the Bible and from a balcony came a chorus of sad and melancholy songs. Billy didn't have any good thoughts about Clarence but he had learned at Sunday School not to speak against the dead; pray for them that their souls go to heaven. He said a prayer for Clarence. He couldn't think of anything nice to say about him except Henrietta Joy had her head on his shoulder on the bus. Jimmy McMullan was a good ball player and he could chatter. No one could chatter like Jimmy. Billy had lied to him once, saying that he didn't know if Serge was training for the run, and he was sorry about that. And something else. He wanted Jimmy McMullan to look up to him and he never had. He hadn't called Billy "a little squirt" like Clarence had but he'd never told Billy that he'd had a good hit in a game or had made a nice play in the field. And still something else now that he was thinking about it. These two kids were dead and gone, and no one except family members was going to say very much about them from here on, and Billy was—hard as it was for him to admit— envious of Jimmy and Clarence for all the great things people were saying about them here, right now, at this funeral; then Billy had another thought, the deepest he'd ever had: being dead wasn't really so terrible. Look at all the praise and love, the kindness and the caring you got. When did you get anything like that when you were alive?

The funeral ended with music and prayers and finally the "Our Father," which the minister and Protestants ended with a different version, "for thine is the Kingdom, and the power, and the glory, forever. Amen." Billy was used to "deliver us from evil. Amen," but the "Kingdom, and power, and glory" had an upbeat, positive ring to it. The Catholic version ended in a pretty dark word, 'evil.' He wasn't going to start saying Our Father like a Protestant but he didn't dislike their way. He seemed to think words mattered. His grandmother in Green Harbor would probably say if you said Our Father like a Protestant you'd go to hell. One day he would ask Father Riordan how he looked at the Protestant ending of the Lord's Prayer.

People were hugging each other and crying and milling around and Dom came over and Billy thought they would say a few things about the kids they'd known, last year's eighth graders. Something kind, a memory. Billy thought Dom had taken the tragedy to heart. He went to Mass, took Holy Communion a lot more than Billy did—

"Hey, Dom," he said. "It's really sad, isn't it? It doesn't make sense."

"It sure don't." Then, in a low voice, as if passing along secret info, "There's a catamount in the area."

In *Wild Animals of North America* Billy had read about the

catamount, also called cougar or mountain lion; knew its habitat. "Who said that?"

"Tommy Castle, warden in Ulster County and points north."

"No one has seen a catamount in New York State for twenty-five years," Billy said.

"Tommy Castle don't lie. He spied one up near Marion Corners, wandering down from the Adirondacks, he reckoned. Unless you got a 30-30 with you, stay in. How many traps you got out?"

"Seven."

"I'm checking my line with my thirty-thirty on my back. Cat come at me, he'll be one sorry cat."

Billy's mother was walking over. She asked him if he had paid his respects to the families.

"I have."

"Be careful, that's all I'm saying," Dom Santarelli said to Billy in a final warning. "They like layin' on a branch and waitin'."

****

When his alarm clock woke him the following morning at ten minutes to six, Billy hesitated a few seconds, then swung out his feet, put on shirt and pants and laced up his high tops. Downstairs, he pulled on his winter coat; in the back hall Billy grabbed an oak stick with a Y at the end of it, threw his basket onto his shoulders and went out with Buck.

It had snowed during the night, two to three inches. Billy tramped along. Jesus, it was cold; had to be zero. He and Buck had started out together but the dog quickly disappeared, looking to scare out a snowshoe rabbit and have himself a good chase. For all that, Billy was glad having Buck along. These were big, snowy woods. Sunlight, starting low, was climbing tree trunks like glittering ivy. As for tracks, he didn't see any out of the ordinary.

Billy's feet weren't numbing but he could feel the cold through his high tops. He pushed ahead, crossed over the stonewall where it was missing stones. Now he was on Mr. Bagovitch's property. He moved into the scrubby field dotted with cedars, branches decked in white.

His traps lay in the ice-laced stream. In the early sunlight, he spotted his first set, remembering how he'd placed the trap in a channel, a path muskrats used in moving about. There it was, glistening dully in four inches of water. He stomped along the edge of the stream. No disturbance on his second and third traps.

The fourth trap, gone. He had endeavored to make a "drowning set" and thought he'd succeeded, but when he pulled on the chain, an empty trap came in, a bit of skin and hair in the closed jaws. Trap five untouched; setting six, evidence of a struggle, but nothing to show. On Dom's trapline, misses were rare; he knew what he was doing.

Billy moved to his last set. Ahead, on the stream's edge, a muskrat was struggling to free himself from a trap. Billy's heartbeat immediately picked up. In the sun's first rays its coat shone like anthracite coal, like crushed black diamonds, and the size—this was the king of muskrats, a sure contender for the Sears Best Pelt Award. Billy tightened his grip on his stick, moved closer. *Come near me, I'll kill you,* the muskrat was saying, its eyes fiery slits. Billy took the warning to heart. And leave the animal to its misery? Either way, it lost. The trapper had no alternatives. Stick raised, Y pointing down, Billy went closer. He had to make a good strike, catching the muskrat on the neck and holding it under —

Enough said, Billy. Do it.

He heard the sound of a running animal coming nearer. Concerned for his own life—Dom would have his thirty-thirty unslung by now—Billy turned, relieved to see his dog running toward him. Immediately he went back to his job at hand...to discover that his foot had slipped and the muskrat was tearing a ragged hole in the toe of his high top. Billy let out a cry, lunged with his stick, missing the neck and catching the muskrat on his hunched rear leg, sending muskrat and trap into the stream. Billy dropped to his knees. This wasn't over. No way. He pulled at the chain to bring muskrat and trap in; all that came in was the trap.

Billy cried out in anger, in crushing disappointment. *Son-of-a-bitch! Goddammit to hell!* He was looking down at the toe of his high top, feeling a sharp pain; seeping out of the ripped leather was blood.

I better get home, he thought.

He set out on a quick step, at one point slowing, thinking to rest.

Only to realize that Buck—honorable mongrel—was at his heels, barking, nipping his legs. No time to stop.

They continued on. The cliff beneath his house was almost impossible to climb, but the nipping and barking didn't give Billy a choice. When he finally pushed open the kitchen door, Rachel and Holly were having breakfast. Both jumped up—Holly screamed—when their brother stumbled in and fell into a chair. Hedi sized up his face, the tear in his boot, the frozen blood.

"Rachel, call Dr. Krugman. Holly, get some extra blankets in my bedroom closet," she said, then helped Billy with his laces.

****

Two days later Raphael Hagar came rumbling up the stairs, pushed into the room and stood at Billy's bedside. "What the hell happened?"

"I had a fight with a muskrat."

"A muskrat, you're saying. Not a bear."

"It was a big muskrat. Look at my boot."

It was lying in the corner. "How much of your toe did he get?"

"Dr. Krugman said seven stitches' worth."

Raphael glanced around the room, sizing up how his young friend lived. "Are you going after him?"

"Dr. Krugman?"

"The muskrat."

"No."

"Read *Moby Dick*"

"Isn't that about a whale?"

"Read it."

"How's Champ?" Billy asked.

"Loves his stall, hates being boxed in. I'm letting him have a run in Harlan's Field later today."

****

Sidney Gottlieb came by to see Billy the next day. He'd ridden over on his bike from Zinnia, and he had something for Billy. It was in a wooden box that might hold a casting reel or a coffee mug. But Billy didn't think it was either. Sidney told him to open the box. He opened it and took out a Mighty Mouse gas engine, propeller and all. He looked at it for a good while. "Sid, this is beautiful," he said, "but you shouldn't give it away."

"I cleared it with my father," Sidney said. "If it's what I wanted to do, then I should do it. It was the plane we launched last fall—you spun the prop on it, remember, to get it started? Went twice around the golf course and crashed on the ninth green and took down the flag stick. Wrecked the fuselage but not a scratch on the engine."

"That was a great flight." Billy put his fingers on the prop, moved it slightly. "This means a lot to me, Sid. Thank you."

"You're a good friend, Billy."

****

He stayed in his room, resting, letting his toe heal. It wasn't much more than a nip but, as Dr. Krugman had said after seeing the condition of Billy's high-top, it wouldn't have surprised him to find half his toe gone. Billy was only now starting to feel warm, to kick the chill. Both his sisters came into his room, Holly saying maybe he had learned a lesson. Every morning when he woke up, he thought of his traps, several still set. He had to go back. His mother brought him breakfast and on the third day she stayed with him a little longer; his father had called, she said, and he wanted to know if Billy had filled in the application for Stover.

"No."

"Are you going to?"

"I keep putting it off."

"Where's the application?"

"Over there on my desk. With Dad's check."

Hedi gave her head a slow, distraught shake. "Your father is dead set on it, Billy."

"I have to talk to somebody, Mom."

"How about Wes?"

"I love Wes. Somebody younger."

"One of your pals."

"No." He was quiet for a couple of seconds. Then he said, "Rachel."

"She won't be in until later."

"That's OK. I'll catch her later."

****

Kids were still talking about Jimmy and Clarence when Billy went to school the next day, his big toe bandaged but lightly, no lacings in the one shoe. He walked with a slight limp. Li'l Jill was the first to come over to see how he was doing. He was doing OK, he said. He had doctor's orders to take it easy. Then she said she'd missed him. "School's really dull without you, Billy." He had reason not to believe that but didn't say anything. Donny Osterhoudt came over. Now that the slaughterhouse was closed down, they had moved to Zinnia, he said. Not much land but quiet, a lot nicer. Dom Santarelli came by, eyeing his foot.

"Heard you got bit by a muskrat," he said.

"Wrecked my high-top."

"How'd it happen?"

"My foot slipped and he went for me."

Dom Santarelli looked amused.

"Any new sightings by Tommy Castle?" Billy said.

"I was yanking your chain," Dom said.

"Then you made the whole thing up."

A thin smile cracked Dom's lips.

"That was one lousy goddamn trick!" Billy said.

"Cool down, Billy. Who's checking your line?"

"First chance I get, I'm pulling my traps."

Billy walked away. Mr. Marr welcomed him back and asked him to lead the school in the Pledge of Allegiance.

****

Later that day, after dinner, Billy went out the kitchen door, walked across the back hall and knocked on the door to his sister's room. In his hand was a large-sized envelope.

"Come in."

Rachel's room was at the south end of the house, windows opening to Harlan's Field and the Maverick Horse. She was lying on her bed and put a slip of paper in the book she was reading. "Mom said you wanted to talk. What's up?"

"Problems with Dad."

"That's nothing new. What is it?"

Billy kicked off his shoes and sat on the foot of the bed. "He's got me in a corner."

"I'm listening."

"Dad wants to send me away to school," he said. "He sent away for an application for Stover. Last time he was here he told me to fill it out and send it in. Why should I fill it out? I'm not going away, Rachel. He spoke to Mom the other night. He wanted to know if I'd filled out the application and sent it in? She told him she didn't know, but he wasn't backing off. So that's where I am."

Rachel thought for a long moment, tossing around ideas. She wanted to help her brother but she didn't want to flat-out go to bat for him, either. "Is that the application you're holding?"

"Yes."

"Let me see it."

He gave her the envelope and she went over the different items. Billy looked out the window at the cold winter's night and the moon-lighted stable door. After a while Rachel said, "Billy, schools like Stover turn down far more boys than they take. What realistically are your chances? I wouldn't sweat it too much. Dad is so wrapped up in his new life, his novel that's coming out, he has no time for his family. Send this back to the school. Take pride in yourself and do it neatly. When Dad asks you if you sent in the application, say yes. If he wants proof, tell him to look for his canceled check."

Rachel picked up two pieces of composition paper clipped together in the application. "What this?"

"Oh, they want a sample of my writing."

"And this is it?"

"It's a book report on *Robinson Crusoe* I did last summer. Dad never saw it."

"Billy, it has to be typed."

"I don't type."

"Your chances of getting into Stover are slim, at best." Rachel said. "Sending in these pages like this, you can cross off Stover."

She put everything back into the envelope and handed it to Billy. "Send in the application to satisfy Dad, or don't. But don't lie to him, Billy. Tell him the truth."

Chapter Forty-Six

Mostly Jacob worked on his novel; he walked the streets of the Village, and in the evening he read. Actually he impressed himself with his discipline. One morning in mid-March, writing in his apartment studio, his telephone rang. Picking up, "Hello."

"Good morning, Jacob. This is Dick Stein."

"Good morning to you, Dick. How are you?"

"Fine, Jacob. I seem to think you're at your typewriter."

"Why would you think that?"

Stein laughed. "How's it going?"

"I'm along on a new novel."

"That's what I like," Dick said. "What's it on, roughly?"

"The whiskey business in America, working title *Water of Life.*"

"Sounds intriguing," the publisher said. "When you have a hundred pages, let me know."

"Right now I have well over a hundred."

"I want to see them. Let's get this down on paper, Jacob. Has Random House been knocking on your door?"

It was Jacob's turn to laugh.

"Have Emily get in touch with me," Dick said. "Jacob, my wife Elaine and I are throwing a launch party for *The Cardinal.* The book is officially coming out on Tuesday of next week, March 21. The party itself is on Saturday, the 25th, at our house, and we're asking you and your wife to be guests of honor. Twenty-five people in the arts, publishing, public life; it'll be a fine literary/social affair. Cocktails at six, dinner, I'll say a few words, an author's reading—if the author cares to read."

"The author would like to read."

"Terrific! We're at 66 Essex Street in Riverdale. While I'm thinking of it, Jacob, your complimentary copies are available. Should we send them to your upstate address or your apartment?"

"My apartment, apartment C."

"Will do. Now get back to that. I want those hundred-plus pages, like the sound of it. Oh, my secretary will mail you details—address, phone number and the like—in case you want to get in touch with us."

"Thanks, Dick."

Jacob put down his phone. A party to launch *The Cardinal.* Very nice. He didn't see how he could ask Hedwig (or if she'd accept if asked.) Couldn't ask Betty. He could go solo, of course; but the nature of the occasion rather required that the guest of honor show up with a woman on his arm; if not his wife, a significant other.

He went back to his novel, stayed at it until noon, then shaved, changed into a suit. He usually went to the main library, always good for an hour, then wended his way back to 11th Street, each time on a different route, always stopping in a bookstore if he came across one. Many had his novel in the window. "Pre-Publication Special for *The Cardinal.*" People weren't storming the door but it was early. No one knew about it yet, managers were quick to tell him. He liked stopping by the Columbia Club for lunch and a chat with Rex in Latin. Part of Jacob's day. And so it went. A carton of books was delivered to his door and he took one out and held it in his lap, eyes closed. More and more he stopped by the bar in the old Chelsea Hotel. Writers and artists started coming in about 3:30 and Jacob would have a couple of drinks, get into some lively talk and go into the hotel dining room for dinner, then home to an empty apartment where he would read John Milton and always end up with the poem on his blindness.

"...they also serve who only stand and wait."

Three days after his novel came out he called Bluestone Road, and Hedwig, sure as the sun rising, answered. "Jacob, Hello. Your book arrived. I was touched by the inscription and proud of you for the dedication to your mother and father."

"I should have dedicated it to you, Hedwig."

"No, you did the right thing."

"Dick Stein and his wife are throwing a launch party for the book," Jacob said. "You and I are the guests of honor and I thought you might come to the city—"

"Jacob, I don't feel right about it."

"Why not? You are my wife."

"We're a broken couple. It wouldn't bode well for the book."

"Well, I was thinking of you. Is Billy around?"

"He's out with Champ."

"Buck saved his life. Is that what Dr. Krugman said?"

"It's what he said."

****

On a waning afternoon two days before the Stein party, Jacob found himself walking west on 57th Street; just shy of 7th Avenue he came to the dark-green awning of the New York Athletic Club. He pulled open the tall glass door and walked in, went directly to the gym. He donned workout clothes and did light calisthenics, stretches, tossed the medicine ball with a trainer. Then a swim and ten minutes in the steam room. A pelting shower, dressed again, then an easy chair in the club lounge. Reviews of *The Cardinal* in major papers were out, one more glowing, positive than the next. The Jewish Father, Milton Rossel, there for his Catholic son Stephen Rossel in his climb to the rank of cardinal in the church. In the club grill, porterhouse steak, roasted potatoes, a draft Michelob....

As Jacob was leaving the NYAC, a young navy lieutenant was talking with a club employee at a display case in the main lobby. Voices weren't raised but something was going on. They weren't merely chatting. Jacob walked over. The officer had a cigar in his hand taken from a display of cigars. The manager was saying, "We don't take cash, sir. Sorry."

"I don't understand."

"It is club policy, sir. I apologize."

"My ship was torpedoed off Okinawa, we lost seventy-three men, and you won't sell me a cigar?"

"I've tried to explain—"

"I'll sign for that," Jacob said to the manager.

"Thank you, sir," the officer said to Jacob.

"It is my honor," Jacob said.

They shook hands. The naval officer walked out with a cigar and Jacob signed the chit.

When he got back to his apartment, several telegrams were in his mailbox. He carried them up, unlocked his door, and set them on a small table in the front hall. After hanging up his coat, Jacob went into the living room, sat down in his favorite chair and opened the first telegram. From a college classmate and longtime friend, now on the editorial staff of the Times. "Happy for you, Jacob. Saw it coming long ago. Best, Aaron Miller." From a former girlfriend, now a screenwriter in L.A. "Jacob, congratulations! I'm thrilled. Hope one day to see you again. Love, Kim." A telegram from dear friends at Reader's Digest. "Wishing you all the best with *The Cardinal*. We're very proud of you! Beth and Rod Holloway."

One more telegram. This was interesting. From his brother: "Sad to inform you that mother collapsed at home earlier today. In Mass. General for observation. Will call in morning with the latest. Nathan."

Jacob thought of phoning the hospital, wanting to get more information now. Possibly she had fainted: dehydration, a drop in blood pressure. Something of a tippler, his mother had likely passed out. As for his brother, "Nathan the Devout," as their mother had called him, he'd gone to a famous seminary in Boston and had entered the priesthood, only to drop out after three years. No reason given. Talk. As kids, he and Jacob Jr. had fought and Jacob couldn't say they were on a better footing now.

Suppressing thoughts of Nathan's news and wanting to regain the upbeat mood he'd had on leaving the NYAC, he picked up *Leaves of Grass*, hoping to absorb a modicum of Walt Whitman's enthusiasm, delight in living. Oh, to loaf and invite my soul! Jacob thought, opening to the great poem.

He read for forty minutes, never fully giving himself over to the poet; he was worried about his mother, as to the reason for her collapse. He didn't like the sound of it. Jacob made to turn in—brushed his teeth, swallowed a couple of valiums. Bottle getting low. He saw himself wandering over to Seventh Avenue tomorrow to pay Harry a visit. Which, as Jacob thought about it now, was where he'd been heading when the NYAC had beckoned him to enter.

****

A ringing phone woke Jacob. He reached across to the night table and picked up, said something meant to mean "Hello."

"It's your brother, Nathan."

"Give me a minute."

He used the bathroom, splashed his face, grabbed a towel. Then he was again in the bedroom, half under the covers; it was a cold rainy day and the apartment was chilly. "What's happening?"

"Mother is better. At least she's resting comfortably."

"Thank God."

"When I sent you a telegram last night, she was in bed, unresponsive. I was terrified that she had suffered a stroke," Nathan said. "The Globe was open to a review of your novel, *The Cardinal.* I remember thinking the praise, the joy she was having at her son's success was too much for her to take."

"Go ahead."

"Then I read the review," Nathan Darden said.

Jacob said nothing and his brother, in an entirely different tone, said, "How in hell could you sully the Darden family like that, savage your mother's reputation so viciously?"

"Nathan, listen to me—"

"It was disgusting what you did."

"You can't judge a book unless you've read it, Nathan."

"The review tells me all I want to know. The father of the future cardinal is a Jew! That's blasphemous—"

"What's blasphemous is that it was hidden from us as kids!"

"And who is this novel patterned after?"

"It's fiction, Nathan. The family's name in the book is Rossel."

"Say what you want to, it's father and mother and their children—all eleven of them, what a coincidence. And the way she

390

treats her husband—"

"Well, isn't that how it was? Did mother treat father with a shred of dignity? She made us swear to secrecy, to never admit—"

"And you had to spread it around. It's so transparently autobiographical. Christ Almighty, Jacob! I thought being a man of letters was honorable. You stood above everyone else like a doctor and had decency and kindness in your heart. You've hurt the family, Jacob. Nigel is the only one who isn't saying you stabbed mother in the back!"

"*The Cardinal* is a novel. The Rossels—"

"—are the Dardens to everyone in the greater Boston area," Nathan said, finishing the sentence; sticking it to his brother as he always had when they were growing up.

Jacob wasn't gaining any ground.

"What are the doctors saying? Is she going to pull through?"

"Now that you've maligned her, do you care?"

"Nathan, don't be stupid! Tell me."

"The doctor says she'll be home in three to five days," Nathan said. "It's not necessary for you to come, if that's what you're asking. Who wants to see you anyway? You were always for yourself. This proves it. You brought a Jewish father into your book thinking to shake up the literary world and sell more books. The hell with you, Jacob. You have destroyed our mother. May you rot in hell!"

The line went silent and Jacob put down the phone, exhausted, beaten up. Gratefully he was seeing his therapist at three.

****

In his session, Jacob spoke of the telegram and then the accusatory phone call from his brother Nathan. Their mother had seen a review of *The Cardinal* in the Globe and had either had a stroke or a heart attack and was now in the hospital.

"You couldn't have been taken by surprise," Smiley Blandon said. "You subconsciously knew it would happen if you brought Stephen's father into the novel."

"I feared it would happen."

"Did doing it show courage on your part?"

"At first it showed cowardice," Jacob said. "I inserted Milton

Rossel into the book in the first fifty pages to fulfill a pledge to my father. I skillfully camouflaged the Jewish merchant so no one would notice—no one meaning my mother. My secretary noticed it, picked up on it; that's the way it stayed. Until Dick Stein, the boss at S&S, told me he wouldn't publish the book with the Jewish father stuck in the shadows. He was too important a character. Bring in Milton fully fleshed, as someone supportive of Stephen in his career as a priest, he'd offer me an advance unseen in American letters. Dick Stein had me up against the wall. My own father's mantra was pounding in my head: 'Take the money! Take the money!' I accepted the proposal. For money, I was willing to wound, injure my mother, send her screaming into the night. All along, as I made changes in the narrative, I saw myself driving nail after nail into her coffin. And now she's in the hospital. The book is flying off the shelf around the country. My agent, Emily Neher, says she's talking movie with producers; even in war-ravaged Europe, publishers are lining up. Smiley, I have a successful novel, I'm living every writer's dream, and I'm beside myself with unease. Anxiety. Self-reproach. I want to hide in a corner like Milton Rossel in the early draft of *The Red Hat*. Dick Stein is throwing a launch party for my novel on Saturday. Guests of honor: Jacob Darden and his wife."

"That's great," Smiley Blandon said.

"I called her, thinking to have her come to the city and we'd go to the party together. She wasn't interested."

"How did that make you feel?"

"Empty, rejected, angry."

"But you still have Betty," Smiley said.

"Wrong. She walked out on me."

"Add your mother, I'd say you're having a bad run on women, Jacob."

****

On Saturday, walking quietly along in the Village, his mind churning, he heard someone saying his name; not at a distance but close, like right behind him on the sidewalk.

"Jacob, is that you?"

He stopped, turned, and they were face to face.

"It is you," the woman said. "My goodness, hello."

Scrambling, coming up with her name. "Mia."

They hugged; it was a very good hug. "What are you doing here?" she asked.

"I have an apartment on 11th Street."

"With your wife?"

"No, I'm by myself. Hedwig and I have separated."

"I'm sorry, Jacob." Then Mia said, "I have a walk-up here on Bank Street. Actually I just left my building and saw you walk by."

"Chance meetings have always intrigued me," he said.

"Yesterday I read a review of your novel in the Times—and what a review! And here you are."

"And here *you* are, Mia. Have you been working? Any jobs?"

"My last gig was off Broadway, a little known Ibsen. It ran for two weeks. Barely paid my rent."

"Well, you're more beautiful than ever. Where are you going, if I might ask?"

"To pick up Bzy at a Saturday morning art program and, yes, she's in a play."

"The wondrous Bzy."

"Come with me if you like."

"I'd love to." They continued on. "I just had an idea," Jacob said. "It's a shot in the dark but here goes. Tonight Dick Stein, the S&S publisher, is throwing a launch party for my novel at his home in Riverdale. Would you come with me as my guest?"

"Jacob, I'd love it."

"And Bzy too."

They continued on, crossed 7th Avenue and walked down Christopher Street, soon coming to a public school: kids and parents milling around on a broad play area, no grass but plenty of space. And who should come running across it but a beautiful girl in pigtails whom Jacob remembered well. She came up to her mother and gave her a hug. Something important was on her mind but before she got going on it, Mia said, "Bzy, you remember Mr. Darden, Billy's father. We just ran into each other on the street."

The girl shifted her attention. The joy, the excitement in her face, faded.

"Hi, Bzy, good seeing you," Jacob said. "Your mother said you were in a play. Knowing you, I wasn't a bit surprised."

No response.

"Jacob is talking to you," Mia said to her daughter.

She hesitated a second, then said, "That was a terrible thing you did."

"Bzy!" Mia scolded.

"No, it's OK," Jacob came back. "Adults at my party were behaving badly. I know, I was one of them." He paused, then said. "I hope you can forgive me, Bzy."

She didn't reply and they began walking, joining the people leaving the school grounds. She was telling her mother about the play. Maria, the lead, had unexpectedly dropped out, and Mrs. Frank, the director, had asked Bzy to take her part.

****

At 5:50 that afternoon, the three of them were in a taxi en route to Riverdale, Mia between Jacob and Bzy. She didn't ignore him but certainly it wasn't a talkfest on the way to the launch party. Jacob mentioned that Rachel was on tenterhooks waiting to hear from Smith, and Terry Monroe had made it into Yale on a student deferment: a short-term reprieve. Then they were driving through a section of expensive Tudor-style houses, lovely trees and grounds.

The taxi pulled up to one such house. "Sixty-Six Essex Street," the driver said.

Jacob handed him a five-dollar bill, and they got out. Elaine Stein, a woman with dark-brown hair in a blue dress with a V neckline, met them at the door. Introduction. "Come in, come in," Elaine said.

They walked into a very large living room. Two long and narrow tables draped in white ran along the sides of the room, leaving ample space in the middle to mill about and have cocktails. One by one people came over to meet the author and his friend and her daughter. Pretty quickly Bzy met one of the Stein children, Joanna. Jacob was holding a rye and ginger ale, Mia a glass of red wine, and it pleased Jacob that she didn't cling to his side. Guests wanted to chat with the author but it was never a handshake alone.

Occasionally Jacob looked around even as he spoke with others on a personal level. Mia and a man with a reddish-gray beard were clearly involved in a conversation. Lucy Belle Dupree and Wally came over and congratulated him heartily, but both, with Mia elsewhere in the room, were curious to learn about Hedwig. Jacob said she was fine; they were separated but she and the children were doing well. Lucy Belle said the last time she and Hedwig met, at the Breakers, she was the star of the show. Wally seemed happy to see Jacob. He was looking forward to reading *The Cardinal*, and from what he'd read in reviews, it looked like a natural for the condensed-book section of the Digest.

"Nobody condenses a book like you, Jacob," Wallis Dupree said. "Would you consider pinch hitting for Murray Cooper and doing your own novel?"

Jacob had a good laugh. "I'm going to have to recuse myself there, Wally."

Others came up. His agent, Emily Neher, was a small, highly energized woman with a quick smile. She had just heard that his novel was now officially #1 on the Times best-seller list. "We're off and running, Jacob."

At 7:15 Elaine said a buffet was now ready. Guests were asked to pick up a plate, go into the dining room, help themselves and return here to the tables. Jacob, Mia and Bzy took plates, helped themselves, and soon everyone was seated and partaking. There was a buzz in the room from talking and a clinking of utensils.

"This is all very lovely," Mia said to Jacob.

"You've been meeting people," he said.

"I have."

Three carafes of red wine were now on the table and he poured a glass for each of them. They began eating and after a while Dick Stein tapped his glass and made a toast. "To my friend Jacob Darden. It has just been announced in tomorrow's Times that *The Cardinal* is the best-selling book in America."

Guests lifted glasses to Jacob. "Congratulations."

"Thank you, Dick. And everyone," Jacob said, raising his own glass. "I can't help thinking I'm at a rehearsal dinner and tomorrow I'm getting married."

Laughter, clapping.

When everyone had finished the main course, two negro women in crisp blue cleared dinner plates. After a moment of quiet, the host clinked his glass. "We'll be having coffee and dessert later, and then, or thereabouts, we'll have a signing. Stein and Sugrue is presenting each guest here this evening with a copy of *The Cardinal.*"

He then spoke about Jacob's life as a poet, a scholar, a ranking editor at Reader's Digest. After twelve years with the magazine, he had resigned and had devoted himself fulltime to working on his novel. "Jacob," he continued, "we'd love to have you give us a little background on the book and read a passage of your choosing. A copy of your book is at the lectern."

"Thank you, Dick."

Jacob stood and moved to the lectern. "This is a wonderful occasion and I want to thank Dick and Elaine for this party to launch my novel. It is my pleasure and great honor to be here. The book was begun in 1936 when Hedwig and I, on the second day of our marriage, moved into one of Harlan Gray's houses in the Maverick Art Colony. I didn't get very far with *The Red Hat,* what the novel was then called, maybe twenty-five pages, when the need came to make a little money. Living in the colony was inexpensive but we needed food, bills started to pile up, and then Hedwig announced we were 'expecting.' I put the novel aside and began writing short stories and magazine articles, not that all of them sold. The few that did kept the wolf from our door, barely. Then a remarkable thing happened. Beth and Rod Holloway of the Reader's Digest stopped by our house on Bluestone Road and offered me a job. To say their visit was serendipitous wouldn't be the half of it. They are not here tonight but they sent me a warm, congratulatory telegram. Wallis Dupree and Lucy Belle are here to my great joy. It could be fairly said that Reader's Digest is the creative guardian angel of my novel."

Jacob looked out at the people seated before him, his eyes resting momentarily on Mia, whom fate had brought into his life again, for how long he couldn't say; but how pleased he was having her here tonight. "My ten siblings and I were raised in a Catholic household," Jacob continued, "by an American/Irish mother. No one strayed; no one dared to. All quite interesting since our father was Jewish... and kept at a distance. We were not an integrated family. It was those early years that formed us, made us who we are today. My father was a great pickerel fisherman in the many marshy ponds in eastern Massachusetts and often took me with him.

"I love him, I respect him. A hard worker all his life, he runs a successful business as a wholesale florist in Boston; but the conflict of being his and my mother's son at the same time was a great strain and took a toll on me. He asked me to join him in the synagogue when I was thirteen. I wanted to, I looked up to my father; then why didn't I go from Catholicism to Judaism? Because I didn't want to die and go to hell, quote-unquote my mother, a true believer. She was the boss when it came to matters religious. My father was upset, and I felt guilty about turning him down; and I felt guilty when he asked me to join him in the family business once I graduated from college. Father, I told him, I want to be a writer. But I'd make it up to him. In a novel I was planning to write about a parish priest who would become a cardinal, I would make the father of the cardinal-to-be a Jew. He was delighted. And when he asked me what the mother of this cardinal-to-be was like, and I told him a strong-willed Irish Catholic, oh that smile on his face. Did I see a touch of the vengeful in it? I couldn't say for sure, but I thought so.

"I brought the Jewish father into the story but I still didn't want to go to hell. So I played down the Milton Rossel character, knowing my mother would one day read the book. Milton Rossel is a dealer in dry goods, and I tucked him away in the first fifty pages so no one would pick up on it, and you know who I mean. Dick Stein read the draft. He came right to the point. Delete the in-name-only Jewish father who does nothing for the story. Take him out and you'll have a good Catholic novel about a parish priest who works his way up the Church ladder; or—and it's a very big or—make the Jewish father a living, breathing individual who has a distinct part in the book, who helps his son, morally and spiritually, as he rises in the Church. It's your choice, Jacob. It would be a good

Catholic novel or else a great Catholic novel about faith and prejudice, darkness and enlightenment. It's all there. The main character will still be the young priest, but the Jewish father, if well-drawn, will have a great influence on his son's life. Think about it, Jacob, and let me know. Do you want me to go to hell, Dick? I didn't ask him, but I was thinking it. Anyway, to conclude this tale about a tale, I reintroduced a flesh-and-blood Jewish father into the novel. I didn't have to look very far, drawing heavily on my own father. How narrowly I first created Milton Rossel, and now what a role he has! Dick's confidence in me and the novel has dulled the slings and arrows I'm getting from family members in the greater Boston area for exposing their prejudicial and—yes, I'll say it—anti-Semitic views. I'm now called 'Jacob the Betrayer.'"

Jacob paused; nothing worse in public speaking than running on. "So much for background. The passage I'm going to read is where Milton Rossel takes his teen-aged son to the local synagogue. Stephen, already saying he wants to be a priest, feels no pressure from his father to convert to Judaism. What he feels— well, it will stay with him his entire life and enrich his life immeasurably as a priest. But let me read you the scene."

He then read the section where Stephen's mother is unyielding in her insistence that he refuse his father and remain a Catholic. When he finished, guests clapped, shouted approval. Jacob signed thirty books, Dick presented the author with a leather-bound copy of *The Cardinal*. Jacob, Mia, and Bzy were the last ones saying goodbye. Bzy and Joanna Stein promised to see each other soon again. A taxi pulled up. Embraces, many a thank you. Mia commended Jacob on the reading and talk as they headed back to New York.

"It's called the benefit of having a captive audience," he said.

"Jacob, it was wonderful. I was very proud of you."

Nearing Bank Street, Mia said she would invite Jacob to come in but she and Bzy had so scurried around getting ready for the party that the apartment resembled a disaster area.

"Bzy's fast asleep and I'm close to it," Jacob said. "I'd love to come by some afternoon. We could have lunch."

****

On Wednesday of the following week, they were sitting on a blue sofa in the living room of her apartment. The room had the architecturally dull, closed-in dimension of a square, but two windows to the street gave it a certain openness at least. From the pocket of his jacket he took a little silver-wrapped box and gave it to Mia.

"Jacob, what is this?"

"First time at someone's house, it's customary to bring a gift."

"From Tiffany's?"

"It seemed handy."

Mia opened the box and took out a gold bangle bracelet. "This is beautiful." She slid it on her wrist, rolled her hand; it spun easily. "Thank you, Jacob."

"I was torn between the bangle and a diamond-studded brooch in white gold."

"I hate diamonds and white gold together," Mia said. "You chose well. Would you like a glass of wine?"

"Love one."

Mia excused herself and Jacob looked around. In one corner of the ceiling, paint was flaking. She brought in a bottle of red wine, two long-stemmed glasses, then put a dish of crackers and cheeses on the coffee table. He poured, lifted his glass.

"Cheers."

"To you, Jacob."

"To you, Mia. This is so nice, sitting here with you," he said.

"I'm happy."

"I know so little about you," Jacob said. "I don't even know where you grew up."

She began talking. She'd spent her early years in Elmira, New York. Her father was in the city fire department and her mother taught sixth grade social studies in the Stanton Street public school. Traditional family values. Father a sports fan, mother into local government.

"She ran for mayor," Mia said, "lost by 107 votes. The Southern Tier is strongly Republican. She's a great one for bucking the tide. I went to Elmira College and majored in Theater Arts—my top competitor for the lead in 'The Farmer's Wife' was a wonderful actress named Rebecca Shaw, but the director didn't trust her dedication. We were doing the play by Eden Phillpotts for our senior production."

"I think he just liked you more," Jacob said.

"He liked me enough."

"Who was the director?"

"My future husband, Matt."

"Well, imagine that," Jacob said with a laugh.

"He loved directing, loved acting," Mia said. "He had a couple of good runs doing both but after a while his interest in the theater waned. He loved hiking. We hiked as a family here and in Europe. He was well-known as a race-car driver. We didn't have much money but we always made it work. One time the three of us—Bzy was nine—rented a little house on the Shetland Islands. A neighboring farmer raised ponies and she rode the same one every day. Sorrel-coated Nancy. What a sight it was. I remember Bzy saying, 'Can't we bring her home, Daddy?' I swear he thought about it, but all he could say was: 'We'll come back.'"

"Great adventure-filled days," Jacob said.

"Wonderful memories."

"How many rooms do you have here, Mia?"

"This and two small bedrooms. I mean really small," she said. "One of them is Bzy's."

Chapter Forty-Seven

Hedi sat on the sofa in the living room of her house, thinking now was the time to start reading *The Cardinal*. Anxiety had kept her from getting into it. She was totally supportive of Jacob in giving flesh-and-blood substance to the Jewish father; her fear was that he'd pay. She could imagine all hell breaking loose in the Malden/Green Harbor/Boston clan when it came to light what Jacob Jr. had done. The dedication by itself was no doubt causing great upheaval in the family.

FOR ELLEN AND JACOB DARDEN SR., MY MOTHER AND FATHER

On a recent visit, Raphael Hagar had seen the book, had picked it up, turned a few pages and had then made as if to toss it into the fireplace. Hedi had yelled at him and asked him to leave the house, and she hadn't heard from him since. How arrogant, threatened, insecure artists were! A writer has a book published, and another artist, of an entirely different genre, acts out in an angry, envious fit. She had never thought of Raphael as temperamental. Maybe he simply hated Catholics. She had once asked him if he would like a copy of the Bible, they had several in the house; and he had replied that the only "Bible-like" book he'd ever studied, read or believed in, was the Koran. But there was something else at play with the sculptor. Hedi was generous with food, a slice of bread, a mug of soup, articles of clothing from sock to cap; she came across with really good stuff...except what he wanted more than anything. And if not now, when? King Jacob had fled the country; the battle-tested cavalryman would win over the beauteous Hedi. Then some goddamn lead-footed German who made his living slitting animals' throats had pushed his way onto the scene.

Hedi picked up her husband's book, opened it, her eyes going, once again, to the dedication. The setting in *The Cardinal*—to her, it would always be *The Red Hat*—was reminiscent of the Darden family in Green Harbor. The fictional father, Milton, was like Jacob Sr. in many ways—a Jewish merchant devoted to his work (dry goods), who took care of his lawn, supported his family. Jacob Sr. loved his family but was mostly off stage—kept off stage was more like it. Very little time or space was given him, as Hedi knew so well.

The fictional Milton Rossel, as she soon began to see, was like most fathers. No denying of his faith or religion. The mother, Greta Rossel, was a strong Catholic who insisted her children stay with the Church; narrow-minded, yes, but far more open than Ellen Darden who flat out prohibited the words "Jew" or "Jewish" to be spoken in her house. There were disagreements, altercations in the Rossel family over religion; sides were taken, but the children were right there to listen, to make up their own minds. As she read along, Hedi came to see a clear difference between the Rossel and Darden family. Privacy was important in both but the Rossels didn't tolerate secrecy; the Dardens lived by it.

At that point (page 47) Hedi broke away from the world her husband had created. Anxiety came rushing in anew. Jacob, let the Ellen Darden ilk scream, pontificate, condemn, she thought. It's their ignorance talking. You opened up the door to their world of wrongs.

A knock on the front door. "Who is it?"

"Rolf."

"Come in."

He pushed into the house—pressed shirt, creased trousers, brown hair buzzed short—with a package the size of a book wrapped in heavy-duty paper. "Let me put this in your fridge, Hedi," he said, going into the kitchen.

402

When he came back out, she said, "What do I owe you?"

"Nothing. Because of my old business, I have good contacts," Rolf Osterhoudt said.

"Well, thank you." She thought of Raphael Hagar—needy, a taker. Rolf Osterhoudt wanted to share, to give. "Will you have a coffee?"

"I'm fine. Thanks."

"How about a beer?"

"That would be very nice but I have to run."

"Then sit with me for a minute."

"Best offer yet," Rolf said.

They sat on the sofa. Rolf commented on the book on the coffee table. In German he said, with surprise, "This is your husband's, I see."

Continuing in German. "It is. It just came out."

"It's a beautiful book."

"I think so," Hedi said.

"Is there money in writing a book?"

"If it sells there can be a lot of money," Hedi said.

"Is *The Cardinal* selling?"

"Evidently it's off to a great start."

"Wundebar!"

Hedi inquired after his wife. "How is Meg doing?"

"Not well. She has serious diabetes. And she's depressed."

Still in German. "God bless her. I'm sorry, Rolf."

She squeezed his hand. The bulk of it, the thickness of his fingers pressing against her palm, startled her momentarily, caught her off guard. She wanted to get back to *The Cardinal,* but talking German with Rolf wasn't an ordeal. It made her feel like a girl again—Kurt Bauer, handsome son of the local Biskupitz butcher, was calling on her.

"The slaughterhouse, the physical layout, was bought by a Dutch businessman/engineer," Rolf said. "The U.S. Government is behind it. When the deal goes through, I'm looking to buy a parcel of land. I have this great idea."

"Tell me."

"Not yet, Hedi, but soon. When it goes through, I see you as a part of it."

They went to the door. Rolf gave her a friendly embrace and walked out to his truck. Hedi watched him for a for a moment, feeling an excitement in the air; something was happening, but she wasn't going to dwell on it. What had she been doing when Rolf walked in? Oh, right, reading *The Cardinal*.

****

Billy made himself a snack of homemade bread and peanut butter, glass of milk. The day's mail lay on the cupboard and the top letter caught his eye—a formal envelope, his name neatly typed; and, upper left, Phipps Academy, Stover, Mass. Billy picked it up. Did the letter say what he wanted it to say, that Stover had turned him down? He began to read: "Dear William, I am pleased to tell you that I am giving your application to Phipps Academy special consideration."

What? Who's asking for special consideration?

The letter went on for several paragraphs to explain what that consideration was, but he let it slip from his hand, suddenly worn out, as if picking up his traps, all that yanking and tugging at chains, had taken it out of him. Thinking to go to his room and lie down—

Rachel came in with Terry and saw him at the table, sitting there. "What's up, Billy?"

"Nothing."

She saw the envelope. "You heard from Stover."

He gave a nod. She saw how tired, how down he looked. "Billy, they take one in ten. You didn't want to go anyway. May I see it?"

"Go ahead."

She looked at the first couple of lines. "Billy, you were accepted!" She continued reading. "This is amazing. Listen to this. 'The application seems hastily done, as if you didn't take going to Stover seriously. Perhaps you were pressured. That isn't for me to know and I was ready to send you a letter of rejection. I looked at your hand-written essay and found it to be remarkably thoughtful and mature. I am asking you to write me a personal letter saying you have a genuine interest in coming to Stover. Or, after much thought, you have decided to withdraw your application. In either case, I would like it in writing. There is a worthy boy waiting to take your place if you choose not to reply, but my hope is you'll answer my letter affirmatively. With warmest regards, Fletcher B. Grenville. Director of Admissions.'"

After a short silence, Rachel said, "Well, there you have it, Billy. Never let anyone say you weren't given a chance."

****

Hedi had once enjoyed having a phone...as she moved from the living room to the kitchen to answer the ring. Terry Monroe sometimes called twice in the same evening and Rachel might phone him just before turning out the lights.

Hedi picked up the phone. "Hello."

"Hedi, this is Helen, your sister-in-law."

"Helen, my darling, I'm fine," Hedi said. "And you?" She reached for a chair at the kitchen table.

"Not so well."

"I'm sorry to hear that," Hedi said. The truth was, Helen was never well. Of all of Jacob's brothers and sisters, she was the dearest, the kindest, the most beloved of aunts; and the loneliest and unhappiest of people. Taught first grade. Nothing, so far, had ever given Helen cause to rejoice. At one point she'd had a man interested in her; it ended bleakly. She was almost forty, and was convinced she'd go home to an empty two-and-a-half-room apartment in Malden for the rest of her life. "What is it, Helen?"

"Jacob's novel is wreaking havoc in the family," Helen said. "Mother hasn't got out of bed this past week. It's devastating to her that...that Jacob made the cardinal's father in the novel Jewish. Nathan is beside himself with indignation. Why would Jacob do that, Hedi?"

"He's a writer, it's the way he saw the book."

"At mother's expense."

"Helen, Jacob Sr. is Jewish and Jacob, *my* Jacob, didn't want to skirt the issue any longer."

"It's almost as if he consciously was out to besmirch mother's reputation," Helen said. "If she had any favorite it was Jacob Jr. She worshipped the ground he walked on."

"Helen, I know how it looks—"

405

"People are allowed to have private lives. Mother and father have always had private lives. The Jewish thing is old, passé, it's no longer a bone of contention, and Jacob Jr. goes and dredges it up."

"Something that stilted makes a mark forever," Hedi said.

"What does he actually say?"

"We don't talk that much. He's with his secretary—"

"You mean Betty?"

"Yes."

"She walked out on him," Helen said.

Stunned, suddenly short of breath, "What do you mean?"

"Nigel told me. He's a writer himself now, he and Jacob talk all the time. Oh, and Jacob is now 'madly in love' with an actress," Helen went on, "Mia, by name. Hedi, Jacob is out of control. All this success coming his way has done something to him, corrupted him. He's turning on those who dearly love him—his own mother, on you, your marriage. Jacob should be with you, Hedi, not chasing women."

"Helen, I can't talk anymore."

"I love you, Hedi. You're too good for my brother."

She re-hooked the receiver, stood there thinking, awakening. Somehow, at that moment, she'd seen enough, learned enough, taken enough to—to finally kiss the German girl goodbye.

****

Hoping to forget what was nagging him—he was yet to answer Mr. Grenville's letter—Billy made visit after visit to the reservoir, brought back rock bass, sunfish, yellow perch (half of his catch went to Raphael) and cleaned and scaled fish for Hedi. He found old country roads in Zinnia great for riding; he caddied for Mr. Spector, prevailing on him to play a shot from the Sawkill that led to his best score at the Woodstock Golf Course, an even 80. Playing baseball on School Field helped, but when the game was over he found himself once again in a quandary, caught in a predicament. It had gone on too long, and he would end it.

He packed a knapsack with a sandwich, an apple, a thermos of water and, if necessary, a writing tablet and pencil. He saddled Champ, whistled to Buck, and started down the spur to Bluestone Road. When he came to the mountain pasture, he saw the old rickety gate was off its hinges and he rode in, after ten minutes coming to the narrow trail that angled across the face of Ohayo Mountain. It was a climb, nothing steep but a solid uphill slant. When they came to the black-as-night evergreen stand, Champ let out a whinny. Billy would never know what that was about but it was intriguing to mull over, even a little scary. Mist, or vapor, was rising from the large stone area with the scooped-out little basins. Around the next bend, they came to the grassy plateau and the old trapper's cabin. He waited a couple of minutes to see if someone might come out, then dismounted and tied Champ to a porch post. He knocked on the door, waited a second, and looked in.

Nothing had changed. He took a carrot from his pack for Champ, then sat on the bench and looked around. Buck, as always, showed up independently, panting, then lay down on the porch floor. Billy took out his sandwich, ate half of it, then gave the other half to his dog. Champ looked on attentively when Billy pulled out the apple and started biting into it. Pony was getting fidgety. "What is it with you guys?" Billy said. "I'm trying to enjoy my lunch and end up giving away half of it. If you had food, would you share with me?"

He had another bite of the apple, then, without having to stand, reached out and Champ took it from his hand. Apple even beat a carrot! "Look what else do I have here," Billy said. "A Baby Ruth!"

He cut it equally into three pieces. Billy pulled the thermos from his pack and had a swallow. "Now you want water to wash it all down, I suppose."

Somehow he gave them a little—Buck lapping the thermos top set on the floor, Champ from a cupped hand (enough to wet his muzzle). What was left, Billy poured on his hands, drying them on his pant legs. Then the three rested on, or near, the porch of the old trapper's cabin. Buck didn't wait long to fall asleep. Champ's head was lowering, eyes closing. Growing sleepy himself, Billy resisted; he reached inside his pack and took out tablet and pencil and a stamped, addressed envelope. He looked at Champ and Buck, the yellow plateau, cabin door, blue sky, then at his own hands. Picking up pad and pencil, he wrote: "Dear Mr. Grenville—"

Chapter Forty-Eight

Hedi was sitting in the library of her house talking with Rolf Osterhoudt...in German. He was telling her exciting news, a follow-up to the sale of the slaughterhouse. The site would now be the home of a manufacturing facility, Revolvtron, maker of super-quiet, small, powerful fans, the concept and design of a Dutch entrepreneurial engineer and much in demand by the military. With the U.S. Government backing the deal, the check wasn't in the mail; it was in Rolf's hands. He'd made a down payment on 109 acres of land in the town of Glendale, three miles from the junction of Bluestone Road and Rt. 28.

"That's a big parcel of land," Hedi said.

"I have a big plan."

Two bottles of Krombacher stood on the coffee table. Rolf filled his mug, had a swallow, wiped a speck of foam from his lip. "I want to build, create, develop a resort-style dude ranch. I have a landscape architect going over it right now—where the main building will be, the tennis courts, swimming pool and patio, the corral, barn, riding trails and the like. People can come out for a day or a week, however long they want. Friendly for kids and family."

"Rolf, that's big, it's huge," Hedi said, liking Rolf's entrepreneurial spirit. She found that kind of talk, of planning—

unknown to her husband whose ideas on development centered on the written word—very intriguing. "But explain 'dude ranch.' What does it mean?"

"Easy going. You don't have to know how to lasso or ride. A dude ranch has the trappings of a western ranch, but it's show. Wear a western hat around, boots. There will be serious bridle paths, manageable horses. And of course, the kitchen. Do you know how I see it?"

"How?"

"Steaks, chicken, hot dogs. All of that. You bet. But our specialty will be German. That's where you come in, Hedi."

"Me?" Laughter, then suddenly in English, "Rolf, may I think it over for a while?"

"You'd be great at it. 'Rolf and Hedi's Dude Ranch,' I can see it now."

In the kitchen the telephone was ringing. She excused herself, thinking it might be Jacob; whenever Rolf came over, he had a way of calling. It was, in fact, Jacob, and he wanted to bring her up to date on matters financial. The third and last advance money had come in, he said. With my agent's well-deserved cut, the check came to ten thousand eight hundred dollars. He was sending Betty Trill an even thousand, the same amount as on previous occasions.

"Thank you. Does that end the money you'll be giving Betty?"

"Currently Melville Cane is drawing up a plan with S&S. She'll get ten percent of hard-cover royalties for three years," Jacob said.

"What about me?"

"You're my wife, Hedwig. What I make, you make. I'm putting a check in the mail for you for two thousand dollars."

"Suppose we don't stay married," Hedi ventured to say.

"Then my new wife would be entitled—"

"Say I got married again, Jacob." It had never crossed his mind, she realized. "If you ever have a new wife, I could have a new husband."

"Are you seeing Osterhoudt?" he said, gargling the name, giving it a deep German inflection.

"Are you seeing Mia Littlebird?"

"We're friends."

"Rolf and I are friends. I have to go now," she said. "I left him in the library."

"Hedi, I don't trust the guy," Jacob said. "He plays angles, has connections. With you, he's ingratiating himself. He smells money."

"You can't bear it, can you, Jacob, that another man—?"

"Where's Billy? I want to speak to Billy."

"I don't know. I don't keep track of him anymore."

"Did he send in the application?"

"He said he did. Good night, Jacob."

Hedi went back into the library. Rolf had picked up *The Cardinal* and seemed engrossed in the first page; he turned to the second page, read for a while. "I like this. It moves."

"Does Meg like to read?"

"She used to." Rolf stood up. "I'm going to get another. How about you, Hedi?"

"I'm fine."

He went into the kitchen; just coming down the stairs was Billy. They exchanged greetings. Billy said, "Donny told me his mother wasn't doing so well."

"She's pretty ill."

"I hope she gets better."

Rolf opened the refrigerator and took out a bottle of Krombacher Pils, set it down and reached into a cabinet for the opener; he was getting familiar with the workings of the house. "You're going away to school this fall," he said.

"I've applied. I'm not sure I'm going."

Rolf opened the bottle. "Any plans for Champ?"

"Not yet."

"I know a few people who might be interested. I'll see what I can do."

Rolf gave Billy a rap on the upper arm and left the kitchen. "I just had a talk with Billy," he said to Hedi. "He's not sure about going away."

"It's his father's idea. Billy's wrestling with it."

Rolf poured beer into his mug. "What does it cost?"

"Two thousand dollars, but when you figure in transportation,

410

clothes, spending money, it's closer to twenty-five hundred."

"By new clothes you mean uniforms?"

"Kind of a uniform," Hedi said. "From what the Stover brochure says, boys wear sports jackets, trousers, shirts and ties every day except Saturday. Also Sunday, and after religious services."

"What kind of school is this?"

"It's called a prep school. Jacob picked it out."

"It doesn't sound like Billy."

"You're right, it doesn't. Jacob wants to broaden his environment."

They went back to German, spoke quietly. Hedi talked about the visit she'd made to Biskupitz to see her family, who they were, what the town was like.

"When did you do that, Hedi?"

"Thirteen-plus years ago. Billy was born there."

Rolf had a big smile. "He has a German streak. I can see it. He doesn't give up."

"I regret never speaking German to my kids," Hedi said.

"Why didn't you?"

"Everything in me was trying to improve my English."

Rolf laughed; he laughed easily, a trait Hedi liked in someone. He began talking about his life, his early days in Buffalo, New York. His father had a stockyard business; big family, a stay-at-home mother. Rolf didn't graduate from the local college but he was the only one of the seven kids to go past high school. He wanted to be an arborist but there was no money in it. Then he bounced around, doing this and that; an opportunity arose to go into slaughtering, he took it, opened his own business. He made good money but the best part of the last eleven years was the day he sold it. Now the fun starts. He asked Hedi if she'd like to see his new property.

"I'd love to," she said.

"How about I pick you up tomorrow at eleven. Afterwards we'll have lunch in Blatz's."

"That sounds very nice."

Rolf moved closer and took her in his arms. Hedi felt uneasy but prevailed on herself to relax, to give in. Wasn't it time she broke away, jettisoned the image of herself as "the German girl?"

411

Chapter Forty-Nine

After finishing her shift at Charlie's Cafe, Mia would go to her apartment on Bank Street, get her mail, freshen up, then meet Jacob at his apartment for lunch. However they would spend the afternoon, either together or alone, Mia would meet Bzy at her school and return with her to 11th Street around five. Then they would be together, Mia, Bzy, and Jacob. Always dinner, then reading, talking, playing games—charades, cribbage, cards. The apartment's second bedroom became Bzy's room. How nicely it was fixed up—pastel-pink sheets, colorful throws on bed and chair, Degas posters on the walls. On the dresser was a photograph of her father at a campsite in Colorado. Sometimes, when Jacob might peek into the room during the course of a day, the photograph would be on the little end table by her bed.

Whether Bzy would ever come round and trust Jacob fully, was hard to say; she laughed, participated in talk and games. As for coming into his arms for a goodnight kiss, or a morning hug when she left with her mother...not yet. She loved her bedroom, the sunniness of it; but in the past weeks she'd had bad dreams—one of them a nightmare; she'd woken up screaming—of someone outside her door pacing back and forth, wanting to get in.

Who, Bzy?

She didn't know or she wouldn't say. But she was afraid.

412

"Time, we have to give her time," Mia said to Jacob in bed, after the nightmare. "Next week Bzy will be going to her Aunt Pauline's in Connecticut for the rest of the summer. She's happy there. That's all it might take."

He reached across to her. "I hope that more than anything. I love that girl."

"I know you do," Mia said.

****

As was her custom, Mia went to her place on Bank Street when she finished working; and for the first time as she climbed the dingy stairs to the third floor, she thought she might take Jacob up on his offer, made a number of times, to give up her job and her apartment and come live with him in his, at 11th Street. She remembered one such talk they'd had. If she were to give up her apartment, she'd be on the street, she had said. You wouldn't be on the street, you would be here with me, he had countered. He wasn't giving her a line, she knew he was sincere. Still, she had refused to let go of her Bank Street pad. It was a foot in the door of having her own life and she wasn't going to pull away and let it close. About now, however, she was thinking of taking her foot away.

Mia was exhausted and depressed, not nearly so much about her apartment—that sliver of the world she could call her own—as about her daughter: her daughter and Jacob. The anger and fear Bzy had for him had subsided but not entirely; what lingered was enough to keep Mia from making a full commitment. The Bzy-Jacob conflict was a governor on her own emotions, keeping them reasonably in check. In her flat, Mia washed up; instead of changing and going over to 11th Street, she lay down, closed her eyes, and was snapped to by her ringing phone. She picked up, thinking it might be Jacob. It was her agent, Stella Fisher.

"Mia, good morning. Glad to catch you in. I may have something for you."

"Oh?" She hadn't heard those words for a good while. "What is it?"

"David Mallick wants you to come to Cincinnati for an audition. He's Cincinnati Regional's top director—"

"I know who he is."

"His company is in the early stages of putting on 'A Doll's House' and he thinks you'd be perfect for Nora," Stella said.

Mia reined in her emotions. "When's the audition?"

"Monday of next week."

"I'll be there. Send me a note with dates and addresses."

A half-hour later she was walking into the 11th Street apartment. Jacob called her name from his studio. "Mia?"

"Yes."

He came out. "How are you?"

"I've news."

"Tell me."

She told him everything, bringing in David Mallick, whom she'd met at *The Cardinal* launch, as the director.

"The guy with the red beard," Jacob said. "I saw you talking with him, for some time actually. And he wants you for the lead?"

"To audition for it. The competition will be fierce."

"Mia, how wonderful. I'm very happy for you," Jacob said.

They hugged; she was crying on his shoulder.

****

"Mother is in the Green Harbor house, hardly up and about but receiving visitors, mostly family," Nathan was saying on the phone, in the testy voice he always used talking to Jacob.

"So she's doing all right then," Jacob said, alone in his apartment, now for a week.

"I wouldn't say that."

"What would you say, Nathan?"

"Mother's not like she was. They're now saying she had a stroke."

"How does it affect her?"

"She has difficulty blessing herself. It's painful to see."

"Have her use her left hand," Jacob said.

"That's the devil's blessing!" Nathan came back.

"That's bullshit, and you know it."

"Jacob, our mother is a diminished woman," Nathan said.

"Should I come up? Say it and I'll be there," Jacob said.

"She's not near death, but it's hell for her, sitting there all day, father walking by proud as a peacock. The vengeance in that man!

414

Of all the mortifying things you could do to mother, having both their names in the dedication. Good God, Jacob!"

"Nathan, for once, let the old Jew stand tall." Jacob said.

****

Jacob did a double-take as the boy walked off the ferry that mid-July morning. Was it his son? But of course it was. He had on a well-worn sports jacket, same for the pants, a shirt and tie. "Billy," Jacob said, as they shook hands, "I didn't recognize you. How you've suddenly grown! Ready to tackle Stover, I'd say."

"I don't know about that but I'll show up."

"Where did you get the jacket?"

"Mom got it at the Library Fair. Terry says he has one that should fit me also."

"Terry is over six feet tall."

"From when he was younger."

Jacob hailed a cab. "Madison Avenue," he told the driver. "Let us off at 43rd street, north-west corner." Then to Billy, "How was the trip down?"

"I sat next to a man who said he worked on Wall Street. On the ferry, I stood outside on the bow. It was the best part."

"Tell me about your sisters."

"Rachel is psyched about Smith, like she can hardly believe she's in," Billy said. "There's a buzzing in the house. Holly was feeling out of it. She said she wanted to ride Champ. I told her what to do and she did really well, like she was doing ballet. Light in the saddle but in control."

Jacob told Billy that New York was very easy to get around in. Manhattan is pretty much a grid, he said. Right now they were heading east. Streets run east and west; avenues north and south. Then to Billy, "How's your mother? We haven't talked for a while."

"She seems happy."

"Library Fair time—always makes her feel needed, gives her a sense of belonging."

"Mom gave up her job at the fair," Billy said.

"That doesn't sound like Hedwig. How come?"

"Rolf Osterhoudt has plans to make a dude ranch when the war is over and Mom is working with him on it. I don't know what she

415

actually does but she likes the idea, she's interested in it."

"How often does he come by?"

"Two or three times a week. I know you and he got off to a rocky start but he's a nice man," Billy said. "He told me the Schroeder family in Wittenberg was looking for a pony. They have a boy who's eleven and the father and the kid came over to the house."

"Are they interested?"

"I think so."

The driver pulled to the curb and stopped.

"Open the door and get out," Jacob said to Billy.

He stepped onto the sidewalk and his father paid the driver and they began walking up Madison Avenue. Billy wasn't completely naïve about New York City; twice in the many years that Jacob had had an office on 63rd Street, he'd come to New York with his sisters and mother. But it felt different to him now. Visitor though he was, in New York for a day, he didn't feel overwhelmed as he had before. It was a long way from Bluestone Road to Madison Avenue but there was something similar between them too. How much that had to do with the great bookstore window they stood in front of looking at a grand display of *The Cardinal*, Billy didn't know. Probably something, maybe more than he knew.

"What do you think of this, Billy? Makes you feel proud, doesn't it?"

"Sure does."

They walked another half-block, then Jacob said at the entrance to a grand store, "Here we are."

Billy looked at the name on the door: Brooks Brothers. They went in.

A distinguished-looking man with a trim mustache dressed in a gray suit and handsome paisley tie came over immediately. "Good morning. May I help you?"

"I'm Jacob Darden, this is my son Billy. He'll be going to Stover in September," Jacob said. "We want to get a sports jacket for him, a blue blazer also. A pair of gray flannel pants and a couple of shirts and ties. We'll be having them shipped."

"Splendid." Then to Billy, "Off to Stover. How exciting is that?"

In 8th grade English, Mr. Marr had explained the "rhetorical

416

question."

"We have a whole floor devoted to young men. But let me have Alex escort you."

He gave an easy signal and a man about thirty in a blue suit, a pink shirt with a button-down collar, and a blue and gray rep tie came over. Introductions were made. "Very happy to meet you gentleman," Alex said. "Let's go to the third floor."

Billy tried on jackets and flannel trousers, shirts, looked at neckties. He asked Alex about knots. Which did he like? "Four-in-hand is the only way to go. Stay away from the Windsor. It's forced, gross, and has no class."

From Brooks Brothers they went to Abercrombie and Fitch. Billy had had a good bit to say on his sports jackets and pants, but luggage was all Jacob. Billy preferred a duffle-bag variety but his father wouldn't listen. There, right there, he said, pointing to a light-brown leather suitcase on display with solid brass snaps. Two sizes, weekend and full. Please send. Next stop, Spalding sporting equipment. When they walked in, Billy looked around transfixed by his surroundings, a great room of footballs and helmets and baseball bats and fielders' gloves and golf clubs and tennis racquets and hockey skates and exercise equipment and sports-related clothes—

A youngish man with red hair in a Spalding short-sleeved golf shirt asked if he could be of any assistance.

"We're looking for a bulky knit sweater with a loose-fitting neck line," Jacob said. "To be delivered."

"No problem. A varsity sweater."

"Yes."

"In what color?"

"Well, my boy is going to Stover."

"Then you want royal blue. Let's try one on," the man said to Billy. "And when you get your first letter, come in and tell me! What's your sport?"

"Baseball."

"Right now we're headed to Yankee Stadium," Jacob said.

"Dad, you didn't tell me," Billy said.

"Now you know."

"We're playing the Red Sox today!" Billy said.

"That's how I planned it," Jacob said. "One of us will come out a winner."

They had box seats on the first-base side of the field and arrived at the Star Spangled Banner, just in time for the first pitch. To Billy's joy, the Yankees got off to a great start in the bottom of the first inning when Bud Metheny homered with Snuffy Stirnweiss on base. Score, 2-0. Between the third and fourth innings, Jacob hailed a vendor and they had a great lunch, hotdogs and root beer. It turned out to be an exciting game. Martin, Yankee left fielder, hit two homers, driving in five runs altogether, and Pete Fox and Johnson for Boston kept the game close. What impressed Billy the most was the three double plays by the Yankees. The pivot on second base made by Snuffy was beautiful to see. The Red Sox threatened in the eighth inning but the Yankees held on and won the game, 9-7.

As the "winner," Billy shook his father's hand.

Back in Manhattan, Jacob walked with his son into the NYAC. They played pool, had a swim, spent fifteen minutes in the steam room, showered, got dressed, and had dinner in the men's grill—a Porterhouse steak, medium-rare, for two. Mostly they talked about the game. Pete Fox, the Red Sox right fielder, Jacob was saying, shouldn't be confused with another player of the same name, just spelled differently. Foxx. "Double X" they called him. What a slugger. One year for Boston, Jimmy Foxx hit fifty homeruns. They talked about the invasion of Europe in June, how long it would take to defeat Hitler, what a fascist state was compared to a democracy, the difference (in Jacob's opinion) between a Democrat and a Republican. "It's one of the reasons I fell in love with the Maverick Art Colony when I first visited in 1925 and met Harlan Gray," Jacob said. "A Democrat is open, he respects the arts, he cares about people, he wants to protect the environment. A Republican's interest, first and foremost, is financial success. That's it. Make money you're a success, and it doesn't much matter how you make it."

For dessert Billy had two scoops of mint ice cream. He was spooning it into his mouth slowly, thinking what a really great day

418

they'd had. Then he started talking about the only other time he and his father had gone to Yankee Stadium. "We were having dinner in our house, friends from Woodstock had come, and I'd had a dream about Lefty Gomez," Billy said. "I was telling you about it there at the table."

"How well I remember," Jacob said.

"Lefty had come up to visit me in my dream," Billy went on, "and we were tossing a ball on Harlan's Field. Then he decided to throw a few pitches. I was afraid he might come in with a curve and I wouldn't be able to handle it but somehow I managed. I was catching Lefty Gomez. What a dream! You encouraged me to write him a letter, and I did, and holy mackerel if he didn't reply! Tickets for a game with the Detroit Tigers would be waiting for me at the Stadium. He signed the letter, 'Hoping to see you in the Big Leagues soon. Your pal, Lefty Gomez.'"

Billy had the last taste of his ice cream. "I was the happiest kid alive. We went to the game, Lefty pitched, and the Yankees won."

Jacob smiled, more amused than pleased. "You were ten or thereabouts."

"I was, yes."

"Now you're a young man."

"OK."

Jacob inhaled, as if giving himself an extra second. "My secretary wrote that letter."

Billy stared, not at his father, at space; he wasn't breathing. "*What*?"

"Gloria, my secretary, wrote the letter."

"Dad, I—I don't believe it."

"Well, it's the truth."

"Lefty Gomez didn't write me?"

"I followed up on your dream," Jacob said. "We went to the game, saw him pitch—"

Billy pressed a napkin to his eyes.

"Come on, we're in the men's grill," Jacob said.

Billy put the napkin down. Jacob signed the tab and they left the New York Athletic Club.

In the apartment, Billy said he was tired and was going to bed.

He brushed his teeth and went into the small second bedroom. The pillow had a soothing, blossom-like smell to it. He fell asleep but wakened early, not knowing where he was; finally zeroing in. He was in his father's New York apartment. Tears started forming in his eyes when he thought of the letter but he brushed them away. After a while Jacob got up and began clunking around in the kitchen. Then came a knock on his door.

"Get up, Billy. You have a train to catch."

****

After saying goodbye to his son at the ferry, with a firm handshake, Jacob told the driver to drop him off at 7th Avenue and 55th Street. He paid the fare; halfway to 56th he stopped at Dexter's Pharmacy, pushed open the door and went in.

"Hello, Harry," he said.

"Jacob, good seeing you," the pharmacist said. He was a little man with a goatee and a narrow, pinched face. "I see your novel everywhere I look."

"It seems to be doing well," Jacob said.

"What can I do for you, Jacob?"

"Standard."

Harry went inside a back room and came out with a small box which he then dropped into a bag with cord handles. Harry said, "Iris's mother is turning eighty and we'll be spending the day with her and children and grand children in Binghamton."

"Have a great time." Jacob took twenty dollars from his pocket and put the bill in the man's narrow hand. "Thank you, Harry, as always," he said.

****

When his mother met his train in Kingston, Billy told her all that he and Jacob had done on the way home, shopping in three stores, a baseball game and lunch at Yankee Stadium, then a workout and dinner at the NYAC. He'd slept in the small guestroom in Dad's apartment.

"Billy, I have two good suitcases," Hedi said. "They'd be perfect for you and you wouldn't have to worry about scratching them up."

"Dad thought I should have something...nicer."

"He's spending money like a madman."

420

"Mom, every bookstore in New York has *The Cardinal* on display. Twenty, thirty copies in every window."

Hedi turned off Rt. 375 at Blatz's and started down Bluestone Road. Behind the Osterhoudts' old house, at the end of a long straight entranceway, the slaughterhouse was a great pile of rubble, most of it already taken away. Hedi asked Billy what he thought of Jacob's apartment.

"It's a lot bigger than the one he had."

"So it's just Jacob there," Hedi said.

"Mom, I spent one night with Dad, but I think he's leaving."

"The apartment?"

"It's too big for one person, he said."

"Where is he going?"

"He didn't say."

Chapter Fifty

Billy made a few bucks each week caddying for Mr. Spector. Cool mornings he rode Champ on dirt roads in and around Woodstock and West Hurley and Zinnia, on old familiar trails in the colony. How quiet, how deserted it was, most houses empty, the theater, a great wooly mammoth of a building, silent. Billy wondered when, if ever, it would have a new life. Or was its time simply over? Only the concert hall remained active; people drove down Bluestone Road from all over to hear the Maverick String Quartet play on a Sunday afternoon. Music had a way about it; if everything else went, it stayed; you catch random strains of great composers filtering through the trees. And there was Harlan, sitting outside his house tending a little flame, reading. The concert hall did its job well; he was the spark that kept the Maverick alive.

Nick Bonino, leader of the quartet, didn't give Billy violin lessons; that never came up. He gave Billy lessons in casting a dry fly. On two occasions they went to the Sawkill and Billy fished under Nick's watchful eye. "Keep focused on the fly as it floats toward you. If it drags artificially on the current, no self-respecting trout will rise to it."

Billy liked fly fishing and saw himself taking to it seriously one day, but that summer he fished the water he knew. The Ashokan Reservoir. Especially a section of it in West Hurley. It just so happened that a pretty girl with sleepy brown eyes lived nearby in her family's roadhouse.

How happy li'l Jill was to see him stopping by that mid-summer day, shouting his name and giving him a big hug. She hoped he wouldn't forget her when he got into high school, and Billy said he wasn't going to Kingston High. He was going away to school.

"It's not a reform school, is it?" she said, frowning.

He laughed. "I'm not that bad, li'l Jill."

"Come in for a minute, can you?"

"I have to be running."

But she grabbed his hands and they went in and sat on the big sofa in the parlor. Mrs. Santarelli brought in a saucer with three small meatballs on it and a toothpick in each meatball and a can of soda for her daughter's guest and paper napkins. Very tasty. Li'l Jill moved in closer and they kissed and he told her about the school he was going to. It was up near Boston. "Where's that, Billy?" "It's a city in Massachusetts." "Will you come see me when you come home?" "Of course I will."

Later that week he stopped by Bearcamp with two rock bass and a sunfish. Always appreciative of a handout, Raphael welcomed him.

"Thanks."

Billy looked at the huge block of wood in the sculptor's yard; whatever was different about it—shaped, rounded, beveled as it was—he seemed especially to like it. To Raphael he said, "I'm selling Champ."

"How come?"

"I'm going away to school."

"Why?"

"It's my father's idea."

"He's pushing you, Billy."

"He's still my father."

"Stands up for yourself."

"See you, Raph."

Billy got on his bike. On the spur, he saw Buford carrying vegetables wrapped in newspaper to a woman standing at the fence. She paid and got in her car. Then another car swung onto

Stage Door Road and pulled up to Buford's garden. Somehow the word was out: Buford's garden in the Maverick Art Colony was *the* place for fresh produce at rock-bottom prices. Two days ago, when Billy had picked up three ears of corn and a couple of tomatoes, Buford had said to him, "Duh good Lor' be lookin' apter me, Billy. I's gettin' rich!"

****

In time, Billy's new clothes and suitcases arrived—the luggage as a freight item at the Ulster and Delaware depot in West Hurley. It was all very exciting for Hedi and the girls—the sports jackets, pants, shirts, neckties, the blue letterman's sweater. Billy didn't want to even acknowledge the stuff, and when Holly said he'd be the best-dressed new kid at Stover and Rachel said girls at Stover's sister school Adams Academy would be all over him, Billy was troubled anew. The boy he was, and the boy his father was sending him away to be, were different people; it had never hit him so clearly as then. He wasn't going away to school, he was going away to a war. He could live or die.

"Try on the blazer," Rachel said. "Come on, show us!"

But he didn't feel like it and went outside.

****

On Sunday afternoon, Rolf Osterhoudt and Donny came for dinner. It harkened back to Jacob: not quite the tradition of Sunday breakfast but an important family meal. The kids always came to the table well-washed and put-together. The question on this particular Sunday, which had a certain formality about it, was who would sit at the head of the table?

It pleased Billy and his sisters to learn it was Hedi.

The food, German fare that Rolf had helped Hedi prepare, consisted of a platter of creamy mashed potatoes on one side, sauerkraut on the other, and several circles of grilled sausage lying on top. Hedi served and Rachel and Holly delivered heaping plates. Rolf had a beer, and Hedi, looking relaxed and happy, had one also.

In a casual way Rolf mentioned that winning the war was a top priority in the country but his plans for his family-style dude ranch, when victory for America finally came, were underway. That spurred a lot of talk and questions, with Hedi speaking up in a

424

manner that caused her children to wonder who their mother had suddenly become. Donny wanted seconds and Billy asked for mashed potatoes and another sausage. For whatever reason, everyone started laughing. Holly laughed and Donny laughed and Mr. Osterhoudt laughed and Billy laughed and Hedi laughed. It was a chain reaction, then started again. Whatever someone said had a fun, easy-going side to it.

After an apple upside-down pie, and coffee for the adults, Rolf orchestrated a general cleanup. When it was time to leave, he didn't embrace Rachel or Holly but said goodbye with a smile; how nice it was getting to know the Dardens. Hedi, he embraced; thanked for the invitation into her home. She didn't wrap her arms around Rolf but held him nonetheless, and for a while; duly noted.

"That went very well," Rachel said to her mother, when they were gone.

"He sure knows how to laugh," Holly commented.

"I was disappointed he didn't ask me what the day's gospel was about," Billy said.

****

Sometime during the night he was awakened by Champ's high-pitched neighing. He sat up, turned on his light and pulled on clothes, tied his sneakers and went downstairs and out the kitchen door. Champ, in the stable, neighed again. Billy saw the light, as of a fire, toward the colony, and smoke hung in the air. Whatever was burning wasn't far away. He began running. At Stage Door Road, he saw something strange, frightening in its strangeness. In the middle of Buford's vegetable garden, pieces of wood in the shape of a cross were ablaze. That same instant Billy's attention was yanked to the head of the garden. Buford's tarpapered shack was going up in flames.

He ran, prayed Buford had already got out; he was hiding somewhere. Then Billy noticed the heavy log, itself in flames, propped against the door.

"Buford!" he cried out, fists clenched, face twisted in horror.

The heat was too great, and Billy had to back away. At the house he called the West Hurley Fire Department, and soon the blare of sirens filled the air. He went back to bed, couldn't sleep; early in the morning, official vehicles were lining Bluestone Road. Billy led Champ from his stall to Harlan's Field. Pony rolled, got up, shook himself mightily. A deputy sheriff pulled up in an Ulster County car, spotted Billy and came over.

"Did you know the man whose hut burned to the ground?" he asked.

"I did."

The deputy had a large beaked nose and one of his ears looked beaten up, something like a fig. "Anything you can tell us?"

"I called the West Hurley Fire Department. Was...was anyone inside?"

"We found a body burned to a crisp when we investigated. Do you know his name, who he was?"

Billy felt himself choking, could hardly speak. "B-Buford Williams. He—he was a farmer."

They talked for another few minutes. When the deputy left, Billy stayed at the fence, his arm wrapped around a chestnut post, head pressed against it.

****

He wanted to go back, to stand on the road by the burned-down hut but couldn't bring himself to face the brutality, the horrible evidence of the attack, still so painfully fresh—and officials moving about. One day he would go to Buford's house...

Not long after the fire, a van pulled up on the spur, and Billy walked out to meet Mr. Schroeder and his son, Lewis.

"Here we are," the man said. He had a weathered face and thin brown hair and had on faded blue jeans and a denim shirt.

"Hello, Mr. Schroeder. Hi, Lewis. How are you?"

"Excited," the boy said.

Billy remembered him from the visit, when he and his father had come by to check out the pony for sale. Lewis seemed to be a bright, outgoing kid. "We're here for Champ."

"I'll bring him out. Put these carrot chunks in your pocket. Give him one."

Billy went to the stable. The pony was at the oak bar, looking out. Billy stood, hand on Champ's face. "You're going to a new family," he said. "Don't be too ornery, OK? I'll miss you, Champ.

You were the best thing that ever happened to me. Come on. I want you to meet Lewis."

Billy lifted the bar and led him to the van.

Lewis came over and had a carrot chunk for Champ and patted his neck. "Do you remember what I told you, when you were here?" Billy said.

"About how to get on and riding in a field."

"Right."

Mr. Schroeder said, "I'll go over it with him." Pointing, "Is that the saddle?"

"And bridle. Also the pad and a full blanket."

The man went over and put it all in the van, then went to take the lead line from Billy. Only Billy didn't let go of it. He kept looking at Mr. Schroeder, who then went into the cab and came out with a check. "One hundred dollars," he said.

"Right. Thank you."

Mr. Schroeder led Champ into the van, fastened the line. As he was about to lower the door, Buck scooted in.

Mr. Schroeder said, "What's this?"

Billy had to admit he was surprised. "Where Champ goes, Buck goes," he said.

"We bargained for a pony, not a pony and a dog."

"They're friends. It wouldn't be good to break them up."

"What do you feed him?"

"Scraps."

"All right then," Mr. Schroeder said.

They shook hands all around and Billy watched as the van jounced down old Bluestone Road; then he went to the stable door, stood there looking into the empty stall. Sherman had warned him about making friends with Champ. Billy hadn't listened; he was paying for it now. His heart was aching.

****

Sitting with Harlan on rustic chairs outside Morning Star, Billy was saying goodbye to his friend; in no time he'd be leaving for school.

Harlan gave him a slow, an understanding look. He acknowledged the sentiment. Then he said, "You have a lot on your

427

mind. Talk to me."

"I don't know where to start."

"Start anywhere."

Billy gathered together his thoughts. "I'm going to a private school with new suitcases and clothes and I keep thinking of Buford who owned nothing, well, some gardening tools," he said. "I asked him if he'd help me build a fence on Harlan's Field so Champ could run. He came over and sized up the field. I had post and rails but only enough to make a corral. He walked over to the cliff, where it drops off to the woods. He stood there and asked me 'Do Champ fly?' The south side of the field is a wall of brush and vines and trees. Was Champ going to push through? As it turned out, I didn't need a fence all the way around the field, just partially around. Buford signed his name with an X and saw what no one saw. He always called me 'Mr. Billy' from his early days in the Maverick. When we finished the fence he called me 'Billy,' like I was now his brother. I felt honored. Harlan, Buford died a horrible death and now I'm going to Stover."

Billy brushed his eyes. "Something isn't right."

Harlan sat there for a while; then he got up and went into his house and came out in a few minutes with a book. "Billy," he said, "you're a student. You do what students do—they learn, they see, they take in. The man who wrote this book said he wrote it for students."

Harlan handed it to Billy. It was *Walden, or Life in The Woods*. Harlan asked him to open to the last page and find the last three sentences.

He opened the book and found the sentences, and then Harlan was talking: "'Only that day dawns to which we are awake. There is more day to dawn. The sun is but a morning star.'"

"I want to copy those sentences down, Harlan."

"Billy, I'm giving you the book," Harlan Gray said.

Chapter Fifty-One

After getting Mia's telegram that she had won the part of Nora in "A Doll's House," Jacob, delighted by her success, began pondering the effect it would have on their relationship. If a woman's child harbored scary feelings for the man her mother was seeing, that alone spelled trouble. Then have the woman land an exciting new job some 700 miles away and bring a third person into the scenario, say her director. Oh, and consider that the couple's relationship wasn't exactly rock solid when she'd left for the audition.

Jacob wasn't happy with the Mia/David Mallick scenario. Was it a *fait accompli?* One thing he knew, she wouldn't likely come back to the 11th Street apartment, and he couldn't blame her. It almost seemed to be cursed. If he and Mia were to ride out the current tremor, they could find a place of their own, clear of other relationships that had bit the dust and, more importantly, where Bzy wouldn't be so likely to fear that an evil man lurked in the hall.

Jacob started looking around for a short-term solution and found it easily enough at the Columbia Club. He had only one room but a very large room at that on the third floor, with space for a writing table, a comfortable living area with an easy chair and a couple of reading lamps, a bathroom with a full tub, house-keeping services and a first-rate dining room downstairs. In the attractive main-floor lounge, he could have an afternoon drink, quiet conversation, or leisurely read The New York Times. The Columbia Club was a place he knew, where he could work, relax, keep in touch with his family, with publishers and agents and, of course, Mia. He wasn't going to lose her to the likes of David Mallick.

****

Mail sent to Jacob's old address was forwarded, courtesy of the U.S. Postal Service, and one of the first letters to reach him in his new place was from Mia; and he got the feeling, reading between the lines, that she and Mallick had already established a closeness that went beyond a professional bonding of director and actress, a closeness Jacob had seen the first hint of at the Steins' launch party last March. He remembered the red beard, scruffy, needed a trim. In Jacob's opinion—even then, at first glimpse—the director should do himself a service and shave, so close as to draw blood.

He answered her letter warmly. He had left the apartment, he told her, as no longer right for him living by himself. He was now at the Columbia Club. When the time came, they could find a place of their own, one Bzy would hopefully be more at home in than on 11th Street. In Mia's reply, which he received two weeks later, she wrote that Bzy had come out for a few days before starting the Maplewood School in Salisbury, Connecticut. Cincinnati was a warm-hearted city, many fine places to see, to visit. "David" had taken them on a sightseeing tour. A boat ride on the Ohio, followed by a visit to the Cincinnati Museum and Art Gallery, and the famous zoo.

How fine of the good director, making mother and daughter feel so comfortable, so at home.

Jacob bowed his head. Mia had spelled it out, not in cheap words but in physical actions. A boat ride on the Ohio. It hit him harder than he would've thought, and for the next couple of days Jacob didn't do much of anything. Nathan called to tell him mother had had a second mini-stroke. Her speech was affected, noticeably. How sad to see her struggling. Nathan seemed to think she was on a slow decline.

Upset, but not panicking over it, Jacob believed a good workout at the NYAC—throwing the medicine ball as if to knock the young trainer on his ass—was what he needed. The trainer took the cue and threw as if to flatten the angry member. On the street again, Jacob stopped by his favorite pharmacy on Seventh Avenue. Things were getting tight, Harry said. He could no longer do Jacob the service of providing drugs for the established twenty dollars. Jacob said it wasn't a problem. Just get the pills.

In his room, he picked up the phone and placed a call to the house on Bluestone Road.

After four rings, his son answered, and Jacob said, "Billy, hello."

"Dad, hi. How are you?"

"I'm fine, moving along on a new novel. When are you leaving for Stover?"

"Soon, in a couple of days."

"You don't sound too excited."

"I'm not."

Jacob squelched a shot of anger, then said with restraint, "A defeatist attitude isn't the way to arrive in a new place, Billy."

His son didn't respond, and Jacob said, "Put Hedwig on."

"She's in the library."

In the library was a home-spun euphemism for *with someone.* She was slow in arriving, and Jacob tapped his fingers. Kindly break away from the butcher's beefy arms, Hedwig. Finally he heard her coming to the phone.

"Hello, Jacob." Flat, businesslike. 'What's going on?"

"I wanted you to know I'm now at the Columbia Club."

"Oh? Billy liked your apartment. He said it was very nice."

"There was no point in keeping it," Jacob said. "It's too big, too hard to keep up."

"Where's Mia?"

"She's in a play in Cincinnati."

"Well, she's coming back, isn't she?"

"It's questionable."

"You and your goddamn love life," Hedwig said. "You're like a teenager."

He shifted the receiver to his other hand. "What have you been doing?"

"I've been helping Rolf with a plan for a dude ranch."

"A *what*?"

"A resort with the western-style motif. When the war is over, of course; but he wants to get a good jump on it."

To Jacob, it sounded horrible. People running around in plaid western shirts and cowboy hats. "Is he asking you to back him financially?"

"No."

"Not yet anyway."

"Jacob, stop it!"

"Wait and see. I miss you, Hedwig. I'm at a point in my life—"

"I'm going to hang up," she said.

"How are the girls?"

"Terry Monroe's college deferment was rejected," Rachel said. "He's going into a pilot's training program with the Navy. Rachel is beside herself with anxiety, as you can imagine."

"She's not backing away from Smith, is she?" Jacob said.

"No, but the excitement is gone."

"What's gone are the Yale weekends."

"Jacob, I have to go now," she said. "I have a guest."

He felt a sharp pang in his stomach. "Send Rachel and Billy off to their schools with a little extra pocket money."

"All right."

"Hedwig, listen to me for another moment. Are you there?"

The line was dead.

Hs stretched out on his bed for thirty minutes, then stepped into a bath, dressed, and went down to the main-floor lounge for a drink, then dinner. It was called keeping up the front.

****

In Central Park, and elsewhere in the city, leaves started falling; you saw naked branches, the skinny arms of old men with brittle fingers. Jacob followed the poet's dictum: they also serve who only stand and wait. He mostly sat, but he definitely waited. For what he didn't know. He wrote a page of prose. It was like advancing a yard near the top of Mt. Everest. He walked to the New York Public library, a lot closer now. Took notes on the Reconstruction period in the U.S.; much of the novel took place in that era. The lawlessness of the time, the brutality...

Days passed, weeks. Jacob got a letter from his daughter, full of news about college life. At first she had taken it personally and was angry that Terry's deferment had fallen through, it wasn't fair; but now she was proud of him. She was taking a wonderful writing course with a teacher named Brenda Lawless who hoped Rachel's father would come to the campus one day and give a talk and a reading. Billy's letter came shortly afterward. He described the campus and the courses he was taking—Latin, English, Ancient History, algebra. First-year students were arbitrarily assigned to a club: Greek, Roman, Saxon, or Gaul. He was a Saxon. Every weekday afternoon, fully togged, they played football. The letter was newsy but there was nothing personal in it. He might have written it as an assignment in a journalism class, just the facts; but between the lines Jacob read that his son wasn't happy. Send a kid like Billy to prep school, it was to be expected. The change alone. From having a pony and a dog, a life of shooting gray squirrels and trapping muskrats and fishing nearby lakes and streams, how could he be happy? That wasn't Billy.

Jacob returned from a walk on a blustery late-afternoon in November, chatted with Rex, and went into the lounge. With a drink, he settled into an upholstered chair. Of interest, as he went through the pages, was a piece about Erwin Rommel, the great German general known as the Desert Fox, a hero of the Reich but an enemy of Hitler, who had died on October 14. Implicated in the assassination attempt against the Führer, he was given the choice of a trial and certain execution, or committing suicide and having a hero's funeral. He swallowed the poison.

A great amphibious invasion of the Gulf of Leyte in the Philippines, under the command of General MacArthur, was underway. In Europe, the German city of Aachen had fallen, and Hitler was calling into service all males from 16 to 60. Jacob needed a taste of his drink and had one. In less dramatic news, but certainly important, world leaders in the United States, Great Britain, the Soviet Union and China released a statement at Dumbarton Oaks in Washington, D.C. toward the creation of an organization to maintain and restore international peace and security when war with Japan and Germany ended. The organization would be called The United Nations. The words, the phrase, rang gloriously in Jacob's mind. Mired as he was in guilt and in shame, besieged by recriminations, Jacob was immensely grateful to be an American.

In the sports pages, Jacob wasn't surprised to see where the Columbia football team had fallen to Cornell 7-25. Another terrible season in the making. Lou Little, the Lions' embattled coach, was looking for a win over Pennsylvania next week. Dream on, Lou, Jacob thought. As he was closing the second section of the paper, a two-word phrase below the break caught his attention. "West Hurley."

Jacob folded the paper. Why this exemplar of zero towns had made The New York Times, he couldn't imagine, but the headline— *WEST HURLEY PROFITEER ARRESTED*—piqued his interest. He skimmed the story: "Food-stamp scam—West Hurley—FBI arrested Rolf Osterhoudt, 47—key figure in Ulster County ration-stamp program—racketeering—black market in prime cuts of beef and pork—"

At the sheer satisfaction of it, Jacob clenched his hands.

Chapter Fifty-Two

Hedi walked from the mailbox on Bluestone Road to her house on a bitter, late-afternoon day, still feeling the shock, the anger, the sickening pain on learning that federal authorities had arrested Rolf in a ration-stamp scandal ten days ago. He was in serious trouble; a prison term awaited him; their relationship was over. The fun, the clunking of beer mugs, the excitement of having a plan, a goal; the intimacy. She didn't regret that she'd thrown an age-old convention to the wind. She was glad she had. It was like uncovering a bank account that always had money in it.

How could Rolf have permitted himself to participate in so underhanded, so illegal a venture? That was the question that befuddled Hedi.

Some reports were calling Rolf the leader. The prime steaks he'd brought over late last summer had caused Hedi to ask herself questions. She'd felt a twinge that something was off, shadowy. Nothing had ever come of it and she had let it go. And then the authorities had come in and arrested Rolf Osterhoudt on charges of profiteering, of running a black market on food, chiefly quality meats.

She opened the Dutch door and went in, the house smoothly warm, wonders of the new furnace; but for toasty comfort, nothing outperformed the big iron stove in the kitchen. Billy and Rachel were at school, so filling the coal bucket and carrying it inside fell to mother and second daughter. Whenever Holly lugged in a bucket, Hedi couldn't help thinking of the dying swan. How marvelously she had played the role, trembling, near death. Carry in coal? Odette? Never! But here she was, carrying it in.

In the day's mail was a letter from Billy. Hedi opened the envelope at the kitchen table and began to read.

Dear Mom,

I've been here for over two months now and on Wednesday I'll be taking the train into Boston and then a taxi to spend Thanksgiving with Uncle Chick and his family in South Boston. It will be good to get away. It seems like forever since he met me at the station and drove me to the school. The size of the grounds, then and still now, makes me think it's a college. The lawns and playing fields and more playing fields and lawns. And the paths that connect one place to another. A very tall tower called the Memorial Tower strikes the hour and it's kind of lonely walking alone when it happens. Even lonelier are the chimes that sound every fifteen minutes, four different notes in gloomy sequence. How many times did Dad say to me I'd meet topnotch boys at Stover? I've put off saying this but now want to say it. On the first morning in the school I was brushing my teeth in the Willard Hall bathroom and a boy is standing there at the next sink washing up. I'm telling myself I'm about to meet my first topnotch kid. This is it, this is Stover. And he looks at me and says, 'How're you doing?' I say, 'I'm doing OK.' He asks me what my name is and I tell him. 'I'm John Spencer,' he says. Then he says, 'They sure have let the Jews in, have you noticed?'

I didn't know what to say. So I didn't say anything. He comes from Scarsdale and sits at my table in the dining room and we hardly speak. I told a bunch of kids I'd had a pony and went riding with him on mountain trails and they made a joke of it, started calling me 'Hopalong.' There's a lot of razzing going on here, prejudice and the like, slurs and nasty names. Like if they think a kid is a 'homo,' it goes around. There are two kids here last name of Ryan, one of them is referred to as 'homo Ryan' by how he acts, what he does. He's going out for fencing. I don't tell Dad. He'd think I wasn't living up to the standards of the topnotch boys he wants me to meet. We have outdoor sports every day, organized games of football. Kids want to know where I learned to tackle. I'm doing pretty well in my classes. I particularly like my English teacher, Mr. Martinson. He read a story to the class I'd turned in as an assignment, about a boy who has a face-to-face battle with a muskrat. Mr. Martinson asked me how I'd come by the knowledge, the experience, to write the story. I told him I was a trapper and sold muskrat pelts for two dollars each. It got out and the kids started calling me 'Hill Billy.' Kids aren't friendly unless you 'fit in' and I don't seem to fit in. The other day I felt like hitching a ride into Boston, or somewhere, just to get away. I found out where Mr. Grenville lived, the admissions director. I knocked on his door, introduced myself. He thought for a second. Who is Billy Darden? Then he invited me in and said, 'You're the boy who wrote about Robinson Crusoe and his man Friday.' He told me again how special he thought the essay was and we had a nice talk. His wife brought in hot chocolate and gingersnaps. When I left, he said anytime I wanted to come back for a visit, I could. That was nice of him, but I really don't like it here, Mom. I don't feel homesick, just out of place, a stranger. Maybe it's me.

Who's coming to the house for Thanksgiving?

Love,

Billy.

Hedi put the letter back into the envelope. She had objected to

Jacob's plan to send their son to the "Yale of prep schools," as he had called it. Now she wished she'd held out more forcefully. A smaller school would be better for Billy, but she didn't want to step in too quickly either. Fending for one's self was an important element in growing up, surviving in a less than friendly world.

The phone rang, and she went into the kitchen. Picking up, "Hello."

"Hedi. This is Rolf."

Oh, my God, she thought, pressing her fingers to her forehead, wanting to say she'd call back; this wasn't a good time. "Where are you?"

"In Zinnia, they finally granted me bail."

"I'm glad of that."

"I'd love to see you, Hedi."

She had promised herself not to become re-involved with Rolf unless charges were dropped, or a trial found him not guilty. "That would be nice but—"

"I can't leave Ulster County but I'm allowed visitors," Rolf Osterhoudt said. "Seeing you before the trial—they're saying three to five months—would mean everything."

Her left eye began twitching and she covered it with her hand. "Rolf, it's not a good idea."

"Are you believing what they say?"

"I—I don't know enough," Hedi said. "From what I read and hear—"

"Hedi, the feds arrested me on trumped-up charges," he said. "They want to parade 'Rolf Osterhoudt' as the face of corruption. It's all a political setup. My lawyer will prove—"

She tried to light a cigarette but her hands were trembling and she had to blow out the match. "Rolf, I can't see you while you're under investigation—"

"Have you forgotten what we mean to each other?"

"I'm finding it hard to get my thoughts together—"

"Hedi, I'll be cleared. Trust me."

"Seeing you at your house doesn't seem right to me. I really can't talk anymore."

"I love you, Hedi. We have great plans for the future!"

"We had plans for the future. Please don't call me again," Hedi said

She re-hooked the receiver, leaned forward, her forehead against the wall. Did he really believe she'd run over to his house—

The phone rang again. A scream caught in Hedi's throat. Picking up, "Rolf, I meant what I said. Don't call again. I can't see you—"

She stopped talking. The line was eerily quiet.

A man's voice, "Hedwig, this is Jacob."

"Gott im Himmel," she mumbled, terribly embarrassed.

"You did the right thing. The man's an all-but-convicted felon."

Hedi finally got around to lighting a cigarette. She asked Jacob what he wanted.

"I felt like sharing some news," he said. "S&S has published a book of my poetry through the years."

"How nice."

"The Saturday Review of Literature is coming out with a review," he went on, "calling the collection 'lyrical poetry at its finest. Darden's poems really sing.'"

"Congratulations." That topic exhausted, she told him that Billy had written her a letter that had just arrived.

"How is he?"

"He'll be spending Thanksgiving with Chick and family," Hedi said.

"What about Stover. How's he doing?"

"He seems to like his classes," Hedi said. "He likes the sports program. As for the kids, he's uncertain, confused. A classmate told him his first day in the school that Stover sure had let the Jews in. Had he noticed?"

"What did Billy say?"

"He didn't know what to say so he said nothing. What an awful comment!"

"Hedwig, anti-Semitism is everywhere."

"That may be," Hedi said, "but for a boy at the school to accost Billy with something like that? Jacob, it's dreadful."

"It's going to happen," he said.

"Then you're not concerned," Hedi said.

"Billy has to face this and deal with it, he can't run from it,"

439

Jacob said. "I think he's a good judge of character and I know who his mother is. Hedwig, I have news on *Water of Life*. Emily sent Dick Stein a hundred pages and he finally got back to her. In short, he wasn't enthused and saw no reason to give me the advance Emily was asking for. He liked the main themes, the bourbon makers in America, the setting in Appalachia; but the story is flat; it didn't grab him and take him along."

"Jacob, you're breaking my heart," Hedi said. "Good night."

****

In the weeks that followed, he had a number of poetry readings, one at the 92nd Street Y that drew a large audience and got nicely reviewed in The Times. Columbia Pictures—Hollywood had taken interest in *The Cardinal* from the start—was now actively pursuing the property. Local book clubs invited Jacob to their meetings, and members, mostly women, were gracious and attentive. Certainly among them was a woman who would enjoy having a drink with the author. But he invariably went home alone—i.e., the Columbia Club. To bring a woman to his room, then have her leave later that night or in the morning—if it happened more than once, management would have him in for a little talk on house rules. The Columbia Club was a place where a gentleman could securely reside, sign for purchases, once a month write a check. It served a great purpose; a home it wasn't; and more and more Jacob seemed to remember he had a home. Going to his Bluestone studio on a frosty morning and starting a fire in his cast-iron stove: he missed it. Running around to cocktail parties, appearing on Page 6, no wonder he wasn't adding pages to his novel-in-progress. But there was something else he missed, was missing more than anything. He had stayed away too long.

Jacob paused in his ruminations. In the lounge of the Columbia Club, he was catching up on world events in the Sunday Times. His eyes caught a chilling story. The war in Europe wasn't going well. He followed a front-page report. *In the freezing Ardennes Forest in Belgium, a German blitzkrieg was making large gains on Allied forces. Thousands of American soldiers killed and Germans unrelenting in their attack.*

Jacob folded the paper and sat there overcome with urgency. He

had to get home. Then he went out and hailed a taxi. He had a four o'clock engagement. A woman named Laura DeCordova, whom he had met weeks earlier at a gathering in Sutton Place, was hosting a reading/signing party in her apartment in the Dakota.
****

In a simple black dress with a touch of green silk at her throat, smartly cut short dark hair, diamond earrings and a gorgeous smile, she said to Jacob how nice it was seeing him again. He replied it was fine seeing her again, remembering how they had talked briefly at the last reading. And clearly were attracted to one another. Taking Jacob by the arm, she led him into the spacious living room and introduced him to her guests. Already assembled, they were sipping French 75s and tasting delicious cheeses and crackers at the windows overlooking Central Park.

Easy talk, Christmas was in the air. Jacob moved about the room, engaging people, listening to their stories; everyone wanted to write a novel. Laura came over and asked him if he would like another drink? He politely refused; one more he'd be on his ear and he was here for a reading. He thought her apartment was splendid, and the setting. You're in the city, and right across the avenue is a great wood. Had she lived there long? Seven years, she said, and loved it; but since her husband's death two years ago she'd come to think the place was too much for a single woman.

"What are you doing about it?"

"I'm considering a move. There's a two bedroom apartment on Park Avenue I like."

"It would have to be exceptional," he said.

"The East Side appeals to me. Jacob, my guests await you. Are you ready?"

"Let me get my book."

"I have a stack right here."

She went over to a table, picked one up and brought it to him, then announced that the reading would now begin. She introduced Jacob again, with an embellishment that his novel, *The Cardinal*, had been on top of the Times bestseller list for the past nine months. "I'm very happy to have him with us today."

Jacob thanked Laura for inviting him into her home, then said,

441

"Seventeen years ago, my young wife and I lived in a shaky, two-room house in the Maverick Art Colony in Woodstock, New York, annual rent fifty dollars. I'd made a decision to leave the halls of academe and be a writer; and, for richer or for poorer, we started out. For ninety-five percent of the time it was 'for poorer.' We were very hard-pressed to make ends meet. Then, one October day—our piggybank had a few dimes in it—Hedwig said to me, 'How happy you sound this morning, Jacob!' I said, 'Well, I am.' And shortly afterward, I wrote this poem, 'Rich Men Never Whistle.'"

Guests laughed. "I'll read it to you now," he said.

"I am the proof that rich men never whistle!
If you could hear my swift, irregular trill
Blown from my lips like puff-silk from a thistle,
You'd ask: "What turns this fellow's whistling-mill?"
No riches surely! Having skimped and warbled
Through deprivations that would starve a curse,
I hold my song the dearer since ungarbled
By pinch of property or pride of purse.

Minor this music, thin these puckered lips;
Halting these notes and tentative my song:
Yet undefeated, in the cold eclipse
Of poverty, I whistle clear and strong.
Of few things certain, yet of this thing sure:
I am the proof that blessed are the poor!"

The guests clapped, smiled in delight.

Jacob skimmed the contents, some fifty poems altogether, chose one he especially liked. "Indian summer," he said, "is a time of year, more pronounced in the northeast than elsewhere. In Woodstock, in the Maverick, that time of year is memorable. The season is fall, a hundred percent fall; but the mystery is, why is it so like summer during that three-day period in late October? This poem is called, 'Indian Summer—Woodstock.'" He waited a moment, then read.

Fox-grape and Winesap simmer in the haze
Of brown noons steeping in their own slow sun;
The panting beagle guarantees to rise
A dozen rabbits for each new-oiled gun;
Corn is still stubble, and the stoic oak
Secretly mourns the acorns it has lost;
Over the pasture swims a purple smoke,
And the last blue aster waits the year's first frost.

Summer treads gentlest when she breaks her vow
Of green, before the leafless days begin.
"Summer is passing," ruminates the cow;
"Summer is over," groans the apple bin;
Yet here, but for red chevrons on this bough,
I might have fancied June was coming in.

Applause, requests.

He glanced at Laura, who put out her hands, palms up. "As you wish, Jacob. I could hardly agree with my guests more."

He went over titles, nodded. An unlikely choice at a New York gathering but still—

Jacob spoke about a 12-year-old boy he knew who ran a trapline. The boy got up, on the coldest of winter mornings, and disappeared into the woods to "check his sets." One time he asked the boy why he didn't wait until *after* school? When it was warmer, more convenient, plus he'd have daylight. The boy's answer said it all. It was the trapper's code to go out at dawn. For the animals' sake.

Jacob blinked a few times. Then he said, "Forgive my introduction to the poem. Poetry speaks for itself and doesn't need a foreword. I might have simply said this poem is about my son. It's called 'Trap-Boy.'" He began reading.

"Toothy muskrat, striped with ink,
Cunning weasel, wily mink.
Flee, I warn you, pelted pray,
Red-cheeked Boone traps here today!
Soft he comes, knee-deep in snow,

443

A 12-year Crockett, snares in toe,
Reading in the criss-cross book
That creatures write from tree to brook.
See, he bends the steely jaws,
Sets them for unwary paws;
Where the icy streamlet melts
He will trap your sleekest pelts.
So run, furred gentles of the wood,
Or stand—as Fate intends you should—
And match your cunning, life and fur,
Against my trap-boy's character."

Everyone gave Jacob a generous hand. He answered a few questions, signed books, guests started moving toward the door. Scarves and coats, a number of elegant furs. Laura and Jacob stood there saying goodbyes, shaking hands, looking awfully like host and hostess.

"Well, what a really fine party that was," she said when they were by themselves.

"I thought so," Jacob said. "It was delightful. I want to sign a book for you."

"Then come back in."

They sat on the sofa overlooking the park; an all-but-full moon was rising above the trees. Jacob, opening a copy of his book, thought for a moment, then wrote on the flyleaf: "For Laura, at a reading of my poetry at the Dakota, herself a poem."

She was touched, genuinely moved. "Thank you, Jacob. Would you like a brandy, a drink?"

"Sounds nice but I have to be going, I'm sorry to say."

"Oh, I was hoping we'd have a chance to talk."

"I like thinking we'll meet again," Jacob said.

In the hallway, he put on his hat and coat. "Goodnight, Laura, and thank you. It was a great pleasure for me."

"And for me having you here," she said. "Good night, Jacob. You have my number."

"I do."

They embraced and he went out.

444

****

Jacob picked up the message at the Columbia Club when he walked in. "Call Mother." In his room he changed to casual trousers, put on his smoking jacket and slippers, had the front desk put through a call to his parents' winter house in Malden. In no time Nathan was on the line.

"I got your note," Jacob said. "How is she?"

"She's doing well."

"That's wonderful. Put her on."

"She's at Vesper Services at St. Joseph's."

"Well, tell her I called, how pleased I am. Let me speak to Father."

"It's getting late. He doesn't like being disturbed after—"

"Tell him I'm on the phone."

"Call him tomorrow at the shop."

"Goddammit to hell, Nathan! Tell our father Jacob Jr. is on the telephone!"

After a moment, "I'll see what he says."

Jacob held on, thinking Nathan would leave him hanging; he was a master at passive-aggressive behavior. But after a full minute, his father said, "Hello, my son."

Stern as his voice was, it had a melodic sound to it nonetheless, like the creak of an old oak. "Father, hello," Jacob said.

"Are you writing a new book?"

"I've started one. It's on whiskey."

"Now that will be a book. I haven't read your last but I understand it's making money for you."

Jacob visualized the smile on his father's face. "I'm glad mother is feeling better."

"It's a great relief."

"What happened? Can you tell me?"

"I took the blame."

"Father, you've always spoken in a very clear and direct way. What are you talking about?"

"I took responsibility for putting the Jewish father in your book," he said. "At our lunch that day in Boston, I held your feet to the fire."

"So you told her about the blessing," Jacob Jr. said.

"And your pledge. I never thought you'd follow through on it, Jacob. One good deed deserved another."

"How did she take it?"

"She called me a vindictive old Jew, and pretty soon was herself again."

Father and son chuckled. After bidding each other goodnight, the younger Darden called down for a club-sandwich, a draft beer. He partook of his meal quietly, thought of the woman he'd just left in her grand apartment. Were things different, he could definitely see something happening. Laura DeCordova was a fine, certainly an attractive, woman; but things were different, and Jacob was proud of himself for saying goodnight to her when he had, then and there. He did not want a new love affair, only to find himself where he was when it had started, nowhere—living in a men's club in New York.

Jacob carried his sandwich tray to the kitchen sink, washed up in the bathroom, swallowed two pills, then went back to his work table and instructed the switchboard that he wanted to make a long distance call to Woodstock, New York. A pickup in his heart reminded him of a time years ago in Green Harbor when Hedwig's response would have so much to do with the direction of his life; and so it was now. With a difference. Then it was to accept; now it was to take him back. He heard the phone, there by the side of the refrigerator, ringing.

"Hello."

"Hedwig, this is Jacob."

"Hello, Jacob."

By the flatness of her tone, he could be anyone. "I just came in from a reading," he said. "I read a few poems from my new book."

"Which ones?"

"'Rich Men Never Whistle,' 'Indian Summer' and 'Trap-Boy.'"

"Good selections."

"How are you, Hedwig?"

"A friend of mine runs a war-relief program sponsored by the Catholic Church and I've been giving her a hand, two to three hours a day."

446

"That's wonderful."

"With a family in Germany, it's the least I can do."

"Still to be commended," he said.

After a small pause, she said, "What is it? Is some new woman giving you a hard time?"

"There's no new woman. I haven't touched my novel for weeks and weeks."

"That's not like you," she said, perhaps interested but not involved.

"Living in the Columbia Club is catching up with me," he said. "I'm like one of Billy's muskrats, trapped. I want to get out."

"So, get an apartment."

"And take up house-keeping again?"

"You didn't seem to mind when you were on 11th Street, but then you had Betty living with you and then Mia, right?"

"I want to come home, Hedwig."

Silence. But it wasn't the silence on the dunes.

"I miss you," he said. "I miss our house, my studio, making a fire in my stove to start the day."

"That's very touching," she said, "but how can you come home? We're no longer together."

"We're still married," he said.

"On paper. But were we ever married, I mean really married?"

The Maverick Art Colony was easier; moving to it was built on dreams. "I did terrible things to our marriage," Jacob said. "I want to be with you to make up for it, to work in my studio fulltime, to live with you, Hedwig, not to run off every Sunday—"

"—always to a New York girlfriend," she put in. "And how long would it take before another pretty woman caught your eye?"

"I've turned a new leaf."

"Perhaps, but a book has many pages," she said. "There's nothing you can say or do—"

"When the war is over we can go to Germany and visit your family," he said.

"How often can you do this to me, Jacob?"

"I love you, Hedwig, I've always loved you."

"I've stopped loving you," she said.

447

Beginning to slur, "Grant me one more spring!"

He didn't hear the click of a phone. He heard a scream though clenched teeth.

"Hedwig?"

Was she there? *"Hedwig, speak to me!"*

She was gone. Over the wire Jacob heard the sound of silence, of nothingness. From a shelf he pulled the most difficult book in the English language to read and read three pages, stopping at a pair of short sentences. Saying them aloud in the emptiness of his room: "Life is a wake. Livit or krikit."

Chapter Fifty-Three

At Monday dinner in Willard Hall with seven students in jackets and ties at his table, the assistant dorm master and English teacher Geoffrey Hanselman said to the Darden boy that he'd just finished his father's novel, *The Cardinal*. Good story, well told, easy to see why people were taking to it. But, Mr. Hanselman went on, he believed the author overwrote, and it marred an otherwise excellent novel, in his opinion.

The other boys at the table were looking back and forth between Billy and Mr. Hanselman. One of them was John Spencer, whom Billy had met his first day at Stover.

"In what way does he overwrite?" Billy said.

"Too rich, too many figures of speech. A poetic style is fine but your father lays it on." Mr. Hanselman was a narrow-faced man in his early thirties whose wife, Astrid, in her slinky skirts and loose blouses, was a favorite topic among the boys. "Jacob Darden has a strong sense of narrative," he went on. "That the young priest has a Jewish father and an Irish Catholic mother adds tension at the outset. How will this end up? The interrelationship of faiths makes for a powerful theme."

"I'll tell him what you said," Billy responded.

"Astrid is also liking it."

"So your father is a writer," John Spencer said across the table to Billy.

"Yes, he is."

Carl Lennox, a puffy-limbed kid on scholarship whose tie was usually on crooked, put dishes on a wagon and came back with apple cobbler. No one said anything else and finally Mr. Hanselman laid down his fork, used his napkin. Today was a study day and finals were tomorrow and Thursday, December 21st. That will be the last day of school. He wished everyone "smooth sailing" on their finals, then excused himself and left the dining hall.

Everyone was fairly "studied out" after a day devoted to formal studying, and, with his classmates, Billy drifted into the Willard Hall recreation lounge. Boys were sitting around, playing ping pong, shooting pool. Ever since he'd shot pool with his father in the NYAC, he'd taken to the game and was improving; now he waited his turn to play with a boy name Danny Silver, a light-hearted kid with an even slighter build than he had; they also looked like each other, kids said. Three boys were standing nearby kind of observing, talking among themselves. One of them, Grover D. Blake III, had a father and grandfather who had gone to Stover. One of the other boys, Bo Linden, was the best football player in the class and would likely make the varsity team, maybe even next year if he continued to grow. The other boy was John Spencer.

Finally the table was relinquished. Billy and Danny, against another team, in 8 Ball. On the fifth round, Billy had an easy shot at the 4 ball. The 7 ball at the end of the table required greater skill; then he'd come back for the 4. He looked for the chalk, spotted it, applied it to the tip of his cue. But when he went to take aim—the 7 ball was gone.

"OK, who took it?"

No one said anything and Billy went up to the Blake, Linden, Spencer group. "Who took the 7?"

"No idea," Grover Blake said.

"Bullshit, put it back," Billy said.

"Get lost, Hopalong," Bo Linden said.

"Put the 7 ball back!"

"Make me."

"Billy, forget these jerks," Danny Silver said.

"Birds of a feather," John Spencer sneered.

Billy didn't pick up the significance of the comment except that it was mean. He and Danny walked away. They lived on different floors and Billy went up another flight. His roommate, Ken Winter, was at his desk when he went in.

"Hey, Billy," he said. "I just thought of something. The sac fly."

The last thing Billy wanted was to have Ken expounding on a dice game he was inventing called BATTER UP! "What about it?"

"I've added it to the possibilities."

The game, as Billy understood it, was already overloaded, and way too complicated. Too many variables existed. To get a batter to either ground out, fly out, strike out, walk, hit a single, double, triple or homerun (and now a sacrifice fly), then having a runner attempting to steal second base or third or even home with the possibility of getting thrown out—it took a great amount of dice rolling. In Billy's opinion, BATTER UP! was a lost cause, physically and academically dead. No one was ever going to play his roommate's game, but Ken kept working on it, figuring the possibilities, the averages. His grades were terrible. Chances were Ken Winter would flunk out of Stover...

Billy took off his jacket, hung it over the back of his chair, then lay down on his bed, confused, terribly upset. Those boys had made a fool of him just now. He remembered how Mr. Osterhoudt had defined Champ. Too much pony for Donny. Was Phipps Academy in Stover, Massachusetts, too much school for Billy Darden?

Ken stayed at his desk, shaking dice, making notes. Kid had baseball on the brain. His father, a Stover grad and captain of the school nine, went to Yale and was a college all-star catcher. Now it was Kenny's day to prove himself on the diamond. It was said, by kids who'd seen him play at Stover summer school, that he might make the jayvee team his senior year. Billy had never seen Kenny hit, field or throw—baseball was a spring sport—but he'd heard him talk baseball from day one here in Room 317, referring time and time again to his father, star of the Yale nine.

Then, just as Billy was thinking of a fifteen-minute nap before starting a major cramming session, Ken was at it again. "What got me going on the sac fly," he said, "was the one my father hit against

451

Harvard his junior year. Yale's first-baseman Butch Supple tagged at the catch and scored the winning run. My father hit .389 that year with thirteen homers. Butch would've got next year's captaincy but my dad's sac fly sewed it up for him."

"How do you remember all these stats, Ken?"

"Don't know, they're just lodged in my head. I can give you the whole lineup on my father's team that year. Leading off, the second-base man, Al Romano—"

"Forget it for now," Billy said. "I want to grab ten minutes before hitting the books."

"OK."

"How about you?" he asked his roommate.

"I'm ready, I've done as much as I can."

Billy closed his eyes, recalling how Ken's mother, Evelyn Winter, had visited the school on the first day. She had taken Billy aside here in the room and said how happy she was that Kenny had a good roommate. He doesn't like to study and she was asking Billy to keep after him. His father, she said, was a famous Stover grad and he would be very unhappy if Kenny—

"I'll do what I can, Mrs. Winter."

****

He didn't know who was saying his name, very quietly, almost into his ear, then gently touching his shoulder and saying again, "Billy, wake up."

He opened his eyes, gave his head a shake, looked up into the shadow-framed face of the dorm master, Mr. Dunbar. "Billy, your mother is on the phone. I'll wait for you in the hall."

He swung out his feet, put on slippers and robe, followed Mr. Dunbar down the stairs to the main floor and into his office. The dorm master picked up the phone. "I have your son, Mrs. Darden," he said, and handed the phone over.

"Mom?"

"Hello, Billy. I have some very sad news."

"What is it?" He thought he might be having a bad dream.

"Your father had a terrible accident. He—he fell asleep taking a bath at the Columbia Club."

"Oh my God. How is he?"

She wasn't answering. Billy knew she was struggling to speak, to say what she didn't want to say. Then she said, "He's dead."

"*What?*"

"Your father is dead."

"Mom, I—I don't believe it."

"Neither do I, Billy, but it's so."

He wanted to cry, but something inside him kept him from breaking down. Maybe he wasn't that sad, that stricken. His fantasy—aiming his .22 at his father—flashed on Billy's brain. Head bowed, he sat at Mr. Dunbar's desk, breathing raggedly, gulping air—

"I'm sending Luther to pick you up," his mother said.

The phone was loose in Billy's hand and the dorm master quietly removed it. "I'm terribly sorry, Mrs. Darden," he said. "How may I help?"

****

Rachel and Holly met Billy when he walked into the house that afternoon carrying a suitcase. A glowing fireplace helped dispel the heaviness of the room. They hugged each other but said very little. No one felt like talking. Then Hedi came in and embraced her son, and mother and children sat around like strangers. Billy seemed to think that people in mourning didn't say very much. Words weren't important; thoughts and memories took over. The sparking, settling of the fire made the only sound. Then Hedi said she had something to say.

She sat on the sofa squeezing one of her hands, as if trying to get a numbness out of it. "He called me from the Columbia Club yesterday evening," she said. "In the last month we'd talked a couple of times. He was reaching out, telling me this or that, things that were going on. S&S had published a collection of his poems and he'd just come in from a private reading. 'Rich Men Never Whistle.' But he wasn't happy. Dick Stein had had reservations about his novel-in-progress, *Water of Life*. That was upsetting to Jacob. His relationship with Betty, then with Mia, had failed. He was tired, he said, he was feeling old. He wanted to come home, to work in his studio, to restart his life on Bluestone Road. I heard him, I could feel myself weakening, but I wasn't giving in, going over to him then and there. I'd done it too many times, too many, many times."

Hedi was bowing her head, pressing her lips together as to make them almost disappear. The girls were pressing tissues to their eyes. Billy stared at the flames in the fireplace. "Then your father said, and they were the last words he said to me, 'Grant me one more spring.' I wanted to speak, to say something positive. It was the greatest struggle I've ever had, to answer him...or hang up. I put down the phone. Glad I hadn't succumbed to Jacob, for once in my life had stood up to him. I was no longer 'the German girl.' I was an American woman. Your father wasn't one to give up. How often had he gone to bed beaten by a day's work, a problem he was facing in a book, with a character, in a poem—to wake in the morning and go at it again. I fell asleep knowing we'd have another day, another spring. Early the next morning the phone rang. The manager of the Columbia Club was telling me that steaming water was leaking through the ceiling on the second floor. They'd found Jacob in his bathtub, hot water still running. Police called it an accident. He'd taken a bath and had fallen asleep. He was terribly scalded. Luckily, I suppose you could say, the pills he'd taken had knocked him out."

Then Hedi began to weep, as did Rachel and Holly. Billy stared at the fire.

****

Close to a hundred people were at a Mass in St. Joan of Arc's in Woodstock on a bright, cold day in January. A closed coffin lay on a stand at the foot of the altar. Father Riordan delivered a short, thoughtful eulogy, emphasizing Jacob Darden's novel, *The Cardinal*, and all that it had done to bring a spiritual resurgence of well-being and hope to people of all faiths; and to those of no faith. Jacob Darden's novel, the priest said, was a testament to the unifying powers of religion and art.

Others—Wallis Dupree, Richard Stein, Frank O'Hearn—walked to the altar in turn, stood next to the coffin, and spoke of Jacob Darden.

Silence.

"Say something about your father, Billy," his mother said to him in a subdued tone.

"Mom—"

"Do it," she said, giving his leg a little push.

He went to the coffin, stood by it and faced those who had come to his father's funeral, thinking he had to say something. But what? Then it came to him. He would say what he knew.

"My father didn't like when I said OK," Billy said . "He said it was a commonplace, a lazy habit, and he gave me choices. Such as 'all right,' another was 'I understand.' Then he said he wanted me to never say the expression again, and I said, 'OK.'"

Everyone in the church laughed.

"He gave me a week to memorize the Gettysburg Address," Billy went on, "then to deliver it in his studio, standing up. The delivery was not to his liking. I slurred my words. I should bite off each word like it was piece of celery, he said. He told me about Demosthenes and how he perfected his style of speaking by addressing a raging sea with pebbles in his mouth. I choked just thinking about it. When I was about nine, my father asked Harlan Gray if he could clear a parcel of colony land that touched his land, so Billy and other colony kids could play baseball. The Maverick Art Colony is a hilly, rocky place. Harlan said fine, and me and my father—" Billy paused, glanced at the coffin, "—sorry, Dad, *my father and I* cleared the land. It was all anthills and sumac and pricker bushes and saplings and took most of the summer. When we were done, he painted 'Harlan's Field' on a sign and nailed it to a tree. I remember thinking how nice that was of my father, how thoughtful of him."

Billy went back to his pew. No one spoke in the church for a while. Father Riordan concluded the service with a prayer for Jacob Darden, writer. And everyone filed out.

****

In the house on Bluestone Road some twenty-five people were chatting, walking around looking at photographs of Jacob at different times in his life. No one knew he had served as a gunner's mate in the final days of WWI. A photograph of Jacob as a Columbia undergrad in Spectator, the college paper, as the author of the book-length narrative poem, *Children of Morningside*. A photo of Jacob and Wallis Dupree and Jacob's three children standing next to Wally's plane before he took the kids up for a spin over Putnam County. The author's photo for the dust jacket of his first novel, *If Winter Comes*. A picture of Jacob and Hedi leaving St. Joseph's Church in Malden, Massachusetts, at their wedding, and a picture of them in fanciful clothes at a Maverick Festival in 1928, and one of Jacob and Hedi running out of the ocean in Palm Beach, and a photo of Jacob reading from *Unlocking Finnegans Wake* as a younger man, and a photo of Harlan and Jacob and the sculptor James Flannery standing in front of the Maverick Horse, dated 1925.

Edward Harrigan, the Woodstock writer, made the opening statement in front of the glowing hearth. "Be it known, ladies and gentlemen, that this gathering will be forever known as 'Darden's Wake.'"

Shouts of: "Hear! Hear!"

He then went on to talk about his friend Jacob, citing his work and his career and his life in the Maverick Art Colony. Others spoke. Wes Jamison talked about Jacob's dedication. Whatever he did in the early days to provide a living for Hedi and their children—editing, journalism, the essay—he always came back to the novel he'd started during his first days in the Maverick, called, at the time, *The Red Hat*. It became *The Cardinal*. Jacob Darden exemplified the expression "Life is Short, Art is Long." Rachel said directing her father's play "The King's Pork Chops" gave her confidence in herself as a young woman, and she would always be grateful to him for believing in her. Holly said her father's love of the arts, all the arts, pointed her in the direction she wanted to follow in her life. Nick Bonino, the violist, said that Jacob had the ability to inspire. To inspire others is one of God's great gifts. Since he had retired from the Pittsburgh Symphony, he'd taken to giving lessons; but he was also writing. Jacob had urged him to take up the pen and now he was halfway through his first novel. Jacob's brother, Nigel, the youngest sibling, said a few words about living with Jacob in Green Harbor. With his father largely inaccessible, he had taken to look at Jacob, if not as his father, then as a father figure. Nigel saw a life of letters for himself inspired by his brother.

The last to speak was Hedi. She spoke about living with Jacob in the early years, the hardships of a Maverick winter. On occasion—rare occasions, thank goodness—she would awaken on a January morning to find Rachel's diapers starting to freeze; and the joys of those first years as well, the peace, the chirping of birds outside her window. She had recently received a letter from Harlan Gray scribbled in his own hand. Somehow he had gotten word that Jacob had died. It seemed appropriate, she said, to read his letter now.

"Dear Hedi," she read, a sheet of plain white writing paper in her hands, "I have learned today of Jacob's death and am grieved by it. When we met for the first time in the summer of 1925, I had never met anyone so ready, so enthused about coming to the Maverick Art Colony as Jacob Darden. When he arrived with you the next year as his wife, I rejoiced. What additions you both were, and what a fine poet he is. I find myself to this day saying lines from 'Indian Summer.' Having to take care of his growing family, Jacob took a leave of absence but never really left the Maverick. What the Maverick is and what we stand for was part of him. My health and the state of the world permitting, I hope to open Morning Star in late May. What is required to do that is to kick at the door. My love and condolences to you and the children. Harlan."

Everyone sat quietly for a while. Then Hedi thanked her guests for coming. She announced that Hannah Hardenberg was serving a magnificent shepherd's pie in the kitchen, where there was also a jug of wine.

****

It was later now. Guests gone, house quiet, Billy exhausted but unable to sleep, his mind going back to Stover—the confrontation at the pool table, his roommate running on endlessly about his father at Yale, then Mr. Dunbar waking him, and Hedi on the phone telling him the news. Now he heard her talking again, her voice quietly rising. Billy pushed against his eyes, as if to fully come around. then got out of bed and sat at the register in his room.

"What was he taking?"

"Nembutals, but it might've been something else," Hedi said.

Peering down, Billy could see his uncle Nigel's lower legs and feet on a hassock. "Then what you're saying is Jacob got into the

457

bathtub passed out and the water kept running." His uncle had an unsteady waiver in his voice and was talking aggressively, one word jamming into another.

"It's how the police reported it," Hedi said. "But no mention of drugs. When they found him, he was badly scorched."

Billy thought to go back and pull the pillow over his head.

"Jacob has a huge bestseller going," Nigel said. "The difference between depression and elation is a very slim line."

"Nigel, believe what you want," Hedi came back.

"Nathan said Jacob threw mother to the lions."

"You're trying to tell me something," Hedi said.

"My brother's a complicated man and I think many facets in him cracked," Nigel said. "To please his father, he made the young priest's father a Jew. That redaction—the price in the family and close friends was enormous. Not to mention mother almost died. Then the setback on his novel in progress. Stein didn't out-and-out reject it but he damned *Water of Life* with faint praise. Jacob thrived on accolade and anything less was a putdown. My brother lived in a club, is that where he wanted to be? On drugs he lowered himself into the tub, turned on the water, and passed out. An accident? I don't think so."

Billy wanted his mother to set Nigel straight; but she said nothing, and Billy was afraid his uncle's comments on what happened that night would be set in stone. He wanted to yell down at him, at her—and then she was talking

"I remember the fights you and he would have in Green Harbor," she said. "You loved Jacob but were envious of him, of his first novel, *If Winter Comes*. You didn't have it in you, Nigel. You're a young man, you might write a good book yet; but don't boost yourself by saying Jacob killed himself! It was an accident. The night before he died he asked me to give him another chance. He was starting to fade, to slur his words. I was determined not to play the indebted wife, not to say, 'Poor Jacob, come home.' There's a line he liked: 'Home is a place where, when you want to go there, they *have* to let you in.' I went to bed thinking I'd failed as a wife but deep down knew I'd done the right thing. I'd rather live alone than welcome Jacob home on bended knee. That I fell into his arms on the Green Harbor dunes will always be the happiest moment of my life, but not responding to his plea to give him another chance—that's the proudest moment."

Nigel pulled his legs from the hassock, set his glass down with a clunk. "Your rejection of him—things were going badly for Jacob. That specific juncture it tipped the scale. He took his life, I'm convinced of it."

"You're wrong, Nigel," Hedi said. "Speaking of novels-in-progress, Jacob and I were a marriage-in-progress. My rejection of him on the night he died, was an edit. He could handle edits; they were nothing new to him. Drugs killed my husband. As to how or why he became an addict, look to the family, Nigel; if it isn't drugs, it's alcohol. Look to yourself." She paused, then said, "Now excuse me, I'm going to bed."

Chapter Fifty-Four

Billy didn't do very much of anything for the next several days. He walked around outside, went into Champ's stable, wheelbarrowed a half-bale of hay—it looked as if red squirrels had nested in it—over the cliff. He went into the basement. His traps, hanging on a post, got him thinking—season wasn't half over. He carried in logs and set them at the fireplace; picked up mail in the Bluestone Road box and brought it in; watched Holly make fudge, sampled a piece; took walks into the colony and greeted the Maverick Horse and stood at the concert hall and theater, continued past Bird's Eye and Salamander. As he drew near Raccoon his intentions were to knock. He didn't know the writer that well but he'd say hello, ask after the baby, how was the novel coming along? *Roland*—the man's name popped into his head. But the place was deserted. Billy felt disappointed, saddened; he didn't know why. Then he was at the driveway leading to Canal Boat. Stood there a good while looking at the house. Everything was eerily silent. He took Rocky Hill down—ankle-breaking, it could no longer pass as a road—to Bluestone Road, crossed no man's land and walked on the spur past a lifeless Intelligentsia, by Cayuga Quarry and the Rustovskys' stone-sided house.

Hedi greeted him when he walked in with the news that Mr. Dunbar had called. Billy sat down at the kitchen table.

460

"He extended the sympathies of the school," she said. "The Dean of Students, Mr. Frederick, said you'll have to take makeup finals when you get back."

"OK."

"All students are due back on Monday, January 15."

"Mom, I'm not sure I'll be going back," Billy said.

She gave him a slow, a careful look. "What do you see yourself doing?"

"Going to KHS, staying home."

"I was never behind your father's plan to send you away. You're free to do what you want."

****

"Billy, we need a tree," Rachel said.

He went into the woods with an ax and came back with a six-foot white pine, nice shape but very thin in the branch department. Rachel said her brother was clearly a minimalist, which she considered a good trait. Holly's excellent use of tinsel and colorful Christmas balls filled out the tree nicely. Billy brought in wood for the fireplace and made a fire. Later that day Hedi said she had to go to West Hurley for a few last-minute items for Christmas dinner and Billy went along for the ride, with the idea of stopping by to see the Santarelli kids.

"If you see Mrs. Santarelli," Hedi said, "give her my regards."

"I will."

"I'll be about twenty minutes. If you're not here, I'm not waiting."

Billy got out of the car, passed Lane's Garage, more dispirited a place than ever, and came to the front steps of the West Hurley Inn. Through the glass door he saw four or five people at the bar; red and green lights trimmed the shelves. Billy opened the house door on the right and followed a long corridor to the family apartment. When no one answered his knock, he opened the door and went in, just as Mrs. Santarelli was coming over.

"Ah, Billy. How's the boy?"

"Hello, Mrs. Santarelli. I'm fine. How about yourself?"

"Keeping busy, never a day's rest."

"Is Dom around?"

"He's hunting with Vince."

"How about li'l Jill?"

"I'll give her a call. And how is your dear mother?"

"She's doing well. She sends her regards."

"I heard the news of your father. That poor, poor woman, and you and your sisters—we're praying for you."

"Thank you, Mrs. Santarelli."

Billy sat in the parlor on the big sofa. In a short while she brought him a king-sized meatball dipped in sauce, a slice of Italian bread, fork and paper napkin. Now you see the meatball, now you don't. He sat there, licking his lips, waiting for li'l Jill; and Dom stomped in wearing heavy wool pants and a plaid shirt. Suddenly he was fully grown, bulky, face dark from the wind and the cold.

"Billy! Jeez, where yez been hidin' yourself?"

"I've been away at school.

"Like a reform school?"

"It's a boarding school," Billy said

"You mean you live there?"

"Kind of," Billy said.

"Don't sound good to me."

"Get anything today?"

"Two cottontails and a snowshoe," Dom said. "Snowshoe ran and ran, took us most into the next county. Dogs had the trail and stayed on it. Your father died. Sorry about that, Billy. Just after Thanksgiving I got me the finest-looking buck you ever seen, runner-up in the state Big Buck Award. Hanging in the bar. Got your traps out?"

"Not yet."

"Jeez, Billy, time's-a wasting. I picked up three muskrats this morning. Zero weather like this, fur just glistens. Come on, I wanna show yez."

Billy went with Dom into the kitchen, then down a flight of narrow stairs into a large, shadowy basement. Dom flipped a switch. "Over there, against the wall."

They walked across an unfinished floor to a heavy door resting on a pair of sawhorses. Skins, on stretchers, were propped against the wall. "The one there in the middle," Dom said. "Is that a big muskrat or what?"

He picked up the stretcher. The skin, at the bottom, still hadn't completely dried. With his finger he gave it a small twirl, so you could see the fur side of the pelt. "Look at the color, Billy. That's not dark brown, that's black. And the thickness of the fur. Have a feel."

"That's OK," Billy said.

Dom leaned the stretcher back against the wall. "I'm puttin' him in the annual Best Pelt Competition run by Sears. Five-hundred big ones to the winner." He tapped his chest. Then, turning, "Over there, look at that rack."

Antlers, fixed to the far wall, seemed to glow in the gloom of the Santarelli basement.

"Fourteen points," Dom said. "Buck hanging in the bar has fifteen, but for spread—" he held up his arms, hands wide apart, "— that one has it."

Li'l Jill 's voice trickled down to them like a streamlet into a dismal wood. "Billy? Dom?"

They walked across the basement floor. Dom said, "You keeping your father's double?"

"I haven't thought about it."

"Twenty-eight-inch barrels, you're talkin' sixty, seventy yards' reach. Decide to sell, let me know." They came to the stairs. Dom took them first and was gone when Billy got to the top. Li'l Jill was standing there. She had on a plum-colored dress with long sleeves, hair nicely combed, brown eyes shining.

"Billy!" she said.

"Hi, li'l Jill."

"How you've grown!"

"You too." He meant it in a certain way; and then some.

She gave him a long-lasting hug. They went in the parlor and sat on the big sofa. "How was school this year?" Billy asked.

"Mr. Marr's son was killed in the war and he went on early retirement," li'l Jill said. "I saw him once in the post office. He looked like an old man. We have a new teacher straight out of New Paltz Normal. We never had study hall before, now we have it. When school gets out, you go to the lunch room with Miss Kelly."

"What happens then?"

"She walks around and peeks over your shoulder at the book, whichever one you have open. She says something and that's it."

"Is it helpful?"

"I wasn't meant for school, Billy."

"That isn't true."

"It's too hard for me," she said.

"It's hard for me also, li'l Jill."

She lifted her legs onto the sofa, her knees nudging Billy's thigh. "What's your school like?"

"It's big," he said. "The first couple of weeks I was lost."

"It must be a huge building!"

"It's many buildings, many fields. It's called a campus."

"Not a school?"

"A campus and a school."

"Do you like it?"

"I probably won't go back."

"Billy, that's wonderful!"

He thought to change the subject. "How's Frank doing?"

"Right now he's working with Uncle Vince, learning masonry."

Li'l Jill inched closer; as always she had kissing on her mind, and they kissed, but it wasn't an ordinary kiss; it was a most unordinary kiss, surprising Billy. Her lips were parted and the tip of her tongue slid through and began a little game of "touch, you're it" with his tongue. Then she took his hand and placed it on her knee or slightly above it and took her hand away. Whether he was supposed to keep his hand put, he wasn't sure. He had an impulse to let it slide deeper—

"Billy?"

"Yes, li'l Jill."

"Every day you were gone, I missed you."

"So, now I'm back," he said.

"I've been fixing up my room," li'l Jill said. "Pretty pillows and bedspreads. And a yellow carpet."

"It sounds nice."

They kissed again, the new way, and her hand was nudging his to move, to go in; she was starting to make a cooing sound—

"Li'l Jill, I really have to go," he said, the words popping out on their own.

"You just got here."

He got to his feet. "Someone is waiting for me."

"Come back again, Billy."

"I will. Bye for now, li'l Jill."

He ran down the corridor, out to the porch and down the front steps. His mother was driving away, heading up Rt. 28. Billy waved his arms, to no avail. He began walking. A car was coming along and he put out his thumb.

****

The snowless days continued but then he woke up one morning and three to four inches had fallen. Glad to have something to do, Billy shoveled the walk to the spur, did both terraces, made a path to the stable, as if it were still the stable. He poked around in the library, thinking to find a book (of the thousands available) to read, remembering how his father would stand before the shelves, reach out wiggling his fingers, and in seconds pull out the book he was after.

Then Billy thought, how about *The Cardinal?* Everyone else is reading it. Why not the son of the author?

The book, it so happened, lay on a coffee table next to the easy chair. Billy sat down, looked at the inscription to Hedwig, the dedication to his grandparents, then settled back and began. Twenty-five pages later he put it down as if awakening from a strange and intriguing dream. To settle his brain, to bring it back to real time, he pulled on boots and jacket and went into the woods he knew so well. Animal tracks everywhere, rabbit, squirrel, deer. Likely a fox, by the straight line of its track. Billy crossed the stonewall below Mr. Bagovitch's pond, trudged into the cedar-covered field, and walked along the gurgling stream. On any trapline he'd ever run, here was always the main stretch of it. Could the track he was looking at, right now, be that of a mink? Billy studied the markings. A mink had five toes but only four showed (as a rule), and look for "tail drag" in snow, he had read, and reread, in "Fur, Fish, Game." And there it was. A blurring of snow behind the tracks. Billy felt a burst of excitement...

Back home, he went into the basement and took down a trap, loaded it by using his thigh as a base and pressing on the spring, something he'd found difficult to do in years past—he hadn't had the strength in his hand and wrist. Now, it wasn't a problem. He set the jaws, then, doing what trappers knew how to do (Dom had showed him), he pressed the pan with his finger tripping the spring. SNAP! Billy dropped the trap on a workbench, glanced at the others dangling on a nail, and walked out of the basement.

****

He called on li'l Jill again and they danced in the bar where Dom Santarelli's prize-winning buck lorded it over the patrons of the West Hurley Inn. Billy had to admit he was getting pretty good at slow dancing and li'l Jill kept talking about her room, how pretty her new curtains looked. Frank and Gail were dancing along with five or six other couples and, when you looked again, the pilot and her boyfriend were gone, had taken off. Dom was laughing it up with a woman well over twice his age with permed hair drinking rum and Coke. Billy had already had a short beer that Mr. Santarelli had set before the son of the author of *The Cardinal*. Music on the juke, slow-dancing with li'l Jill, her head tilted as for a kiss of the new variety but quick, a touch of open lip, promise of more. They went back to the bar; no way was someone going to come along and take their places, and all other spots were taken. Dom gave a head nod to his father who set a second short beer in front of the Darden boy.

"Thank you, Mr. Santarelli."

"Anytime, Billy."

The juke was spinning tunes and people were laughing, dancing, drinking. Li'l Jill reached under the bar to Billy's thigh. "I'm going upstairs," she said.

"OK."

"Wait a few minutes, then come up."

He looked at her but didn't say anything.

"You know where it is," she said.

"Second floor, third door—"

"Painted a silvery blue."

Li'l Jill gave his leg a squeeze and moved away, vanishing in the smoke. Billy stayed at the bar while the jukebox kept singing, coaxing him closer to the silvery shore of li'l Jill's room. How could he not go? He lifted his eyes as if in response to someone staring. Looking at him over the crowded room with dead, glassy eyes was Dom's trophy buck. Without giving it another thought, he said good night to Mr. Santarelli, went to the exit and down the front steps of the West Hurley Inn.

****

At home he read another forty pages of *The Cardinal,* and while it carried him along, while he found himself caught up in the story and the challenges that Stephen Rossel faced in the Catholic Church, he still wasn't sure about Stover. Life was one challenge after another. Billy wandered around the house, gave the loose trap back to its rusty mates, and took again to walking in the colony. He passed Buford's burned-down shack. The immediate area had a faded police ribbon surrounding it, hanging low, broken in places. There were no reports, as far as Billy knew, of any arrests. The KKK had done its hateful work and had left.

He stepped over the ribbon and went up to the blackened remnants, an ash heap, a few charred timbers, now covered with snow, and stood at the door, now air, remembering how he had gone in. What had possessed Billy, he didn't know. Whoever he might sit with in the future, statesman or philosopher or artist, no one would surpass in importance sitting with Buford that day.

As he was leaving, Billy saw a rickety shed in a grove of scorched pines some twenty yards behind the ashes. Some of it had burned but was still intact. Billy pushed through the snow-covered brush and went up to it and peered into the space, deep in shadow. It was empty; whatever tools Buford had kept here were gone. But then Billy spotted a long thin handle all but obscured by leaves and dirt. He leaned over, reached for it. The dirt was frozen but not solidly and he pulled the handle free; it was Buford's hoe. Holding it to his chest, there in the man's shed, Billy fell to his knees and cried.

****

He hadn't seen Raphael Hagar for months and months, ever since Labor Day, and when Billy knocked on the sculptor's door at Bearcamp, it was to see a friend.

467

Mallet in hand, Raphael came out of his studio in heavy clothes, a leather vest over his shirt, to see who was calling. He looked at Billy as if asking himself who is this boy? Why is he here putting out his hand and smiling? A fire was going in the ground-level hearth and Billy was thinking they might have a Turkish coffee and sit there and talk. In a quiet way he wanted to thank Raphael for helping him manage Champ. Lengthening the stirrups, alone, had made a huge difference, had given Billy confidence. And then the jumps Champ had cleared, twice around the course without an error. A day, a memory, to share with a friend. Clearly the sculptor didn't care or had forgotten. It was all very strange and Billy was saddened. After a few minutes he said "See you, Raph," and walked out.

Billy walked on the spur, looking about, having thoughts. The Maverick Art Colony would never see another spring, Harlan Gray was nearing the end of his life, Billy's father had died, and he, Billy Darden, was no longer a kid with a pony and a dog. Not a little frightened, he walked slowly home, suddenly knowing, then, a part of his life was over.

****

He didn't know if he liked going to the mailbox because his father had liked going to it; you never knew when you'd be getting an acceptance letter or, even better, a check. He walked down the shoveled path, crossed no man's land to the box on Bluestone Road; pulled down the flap, reached in, and took out the mail.

He tossed it onto the kitchen table, skimmed it, then leaned over and gave a light blue envelope a closer look. He picked it up, went to his room. In his window seat he opened the envelope and took out a letter.

> Dear Billy,
>
> Mom told me your father had died. I want to send my feelings of sorrow to you, your sisters and mother. I said prayers last night in the chapel at Maplewood, where I'm now going to school in Salisbury. I was the only person in the chapel and felt very close to you sitting there in the quiet. Even if we no longer know each other when we're older,

we'll always have the summer when we were kids in the Maverick Art Colony. Our secret place in the big pine, the field where we sat in the yellow grass going over lines, the hike up Ohayo and the old trapper's cabin.

But I believe we will know each other. All kinds of people will pass through our lives. Of the boys in the Maverick, there was only you. There is only one Billy Darden.

Mom has had some great parts and will probably get married again. Drop me a note if you feel like it.

Love,

Bzy

He brought the letter to his face and breathed it in.

****

On a blustery January morning, Billy put on everyday clothes and carried his suitcase, stuffed with a Brooks Brothers sports jacket and flannel trousers, downstairs. "Good morning, Mom."

The radio was on and Hedi was listening attentively. Then, turning it off, "Billy, good morning. Germany was driven back in the Battle of the Bulge. They're calling it a pivotal victory for America."

"That's wonderful."

"The war could be over by summer, they're saying." Hedi started stirring eggs in a bowl. "Anything can happen between now and then, but it's good news. How are you feeling?"

"I'm OK."

She brought over a plate of scrambled eggs and home-fried potatoes. "Your father would be very pleased."

Billy was working on his breakfast. "I suppose."

Sitting down at the table, "Wouldn't he be?"

"Yes, but it's not why I'm going back."

"Why are you?"

"Come on, Mom."

"No, tell me," she said. "I want to know. One reason."

"Buford."

"*Buford?*"

"It's what I said."

Early sun, through the kitchen window, shone on Hedi's face.

"These home-fries are really good," Billy said.

"There's more."

"No, I'm fine. Thanks."

He finished eating, rinsed up, sat with Hedi in the living room. A thought went through his mind. What was he doing? Where was he going? They waited. His mother was looking at him. She smiled. Maybe he smiled back, he wasn't sure. A familiar honk came to them from Old Bluestone Road.

"Here's Luther now," Hedi said.

They got up. He put on his overcoat and gave his mother a hug. "I love you, Mom."

"I love you, Billy."

He kissed her face. At the door, he paused. Then, suitcase in hand, Billy went out to the terrace and walked down the stone path to the car.

Anthony Robinson, author of eight novels and a collection of short stories, taught literature and creative writing at SUNY New Paltz for thirty-four years. Now retired, he lives on Huguenot Street in New Paltz with his wife Tatiana.

Made in the USA
Middletown, DE
28 August 2023

37486443R00286